CONFESSION

Breaking Down a Hurricane

Sarah Forester Davis

PO Box 224
Sharon Center, Ohio 44274
SarahForesterDavis@gmail.com

For more about the CONFESSION series, follow Sarah Forester Davis on social media. #BodhiandEva

Cover by Sarah Forester Davis

Paperback ISBN: 979-8-77727-625-4

To every single Bodhi and Eva fan out there. You make my job as their storyteller, so rewarding. This book is absolutely dedicated to each one of you. Thank you for loving them.

CONFESSION FAMILY TREE

Lenora Bishop/ Phoebe Rialson
-Bodhi's mom

Kenneth Rialson & Annie Edwards
-Lenora's parents, Bodhi's grandparents

Calvin Sullivan
-Bodhi's grandpa

Audrey & Brayden Calloway
-Eva's parents

Coop & Beck
-Bodhi's best friends

Owen Edwards
-Annie's cousin, Calvin's friend

Luke Sullivan/ Sully
-Bodhi's dad, Calvin's son

Miles & Rowan Calloway
-Eva's twin brothers

Rebecca Rialson & Chip Channing
-Kenneth's sister & brother-in-law

Luna Morris
-Eva's best friend

Paul Channing
-Rebecca & Chip's son, Lenora's cousin

Henry Channing
-Distant relative of Paul. Boss of Brayden Calloway

Porter Channing
-Son of Henry Channing, ex-boyfriend of Eva

prologue

Do you ever wonder how many people you pass on any given day? Strangers to whom you don't pay any attention? Depending on what your day entails, it could be fifty, maybe even a hundred. People you'll probably never see again, but people who played a minor role in that day of your life. I find myself questioning all the time if I've unintentionally walked past someone on purpose. If that moment in my life happened because it was planned, and I was just oblivious to the fact that person was there for a reason.

Take Eva, for example. The very first day I met her was when she showed up at my house—or was it? We've both lived in Flagler all our lives; what are the odds we've crossed paths before and just didn't know it, but someone else did? If there's anything I've learned these last couple weeks, it's that life isn't as simple as it seems. People suddenly appear in your life for a reason, people suddenly disappear from your life for a reason, and people are suddenly brought back into your life for a reason. You just don't know why. Yet.

Life is like a constant hurricane. The definition of a hurricane is blunt and simple: *A storm with a violent wind.* It's more than that, though. First, you've got the anticipation. The buildup of seeing it form, of watching its path, of wondering where it might shift and how strong it could become. That's life. A spinning circle of eagerness, as you attempt to follow the right direction laid out in front of you. But suddenly, you're being thrown the wrong way and you can only hope you eventually find the strength to move on.

Then there's the projected path. This path leads right to your heart. You build up a wall, trying to keep yourself safe, but at the same time, you're fully immersed in the power of this dynamic storm and you can't turn away.

Landfall. Next comes landfall. You hang on, wondering how you got to this point, why you didn't leave when you had the chance. Why were you stupid enough to believe you could just sit there and watch this storm, without being affected by its brutal force?

The outcome. You survived, but life will never be the same. You will forever be reminded of that hurricane and its power, each and every time you take in a breath of calm air.

That's life.

If you break down a hurricane, there are three parts. The hurricane itself, the eye of the storm, and the devastation it leaves behind. I might only be seventeen, I might not have the wisdom of people decades older than me, but I do know one thing: my life is a hurricane.

There are a few questions I find myself asking, though. First, which part am I? The actual hurricane? The eye? Or the devastation? Second, who has secretly crossed my path without my knowledge, strengthening this storm behind the scenes? And third, what's going to happen when this hurricane eventually evaporates? Will everyone I love still be standing? Will *I* still be standing? Will we all survive?

Life is exactly like a hurricane. A storm with violent winds. But a hurricane is also exactly like life. Fragile, frightening, and within a moment's notice, it can abruptly vanish into thin air, taking your entire soul with it.

chapter one

Bodhi

I hate hospitals. That's not a secret that needs to be kept locked away and hidden from everyone else. In my opinion, my reasons for hating hospitals are pretty validated. I lost Eva for three years after we arrived at a hospital together. My mom was diagnosed with leukemia while in a hospital that very same day. She also died in front of me while I sat in a hospital with her just a few weeks ago. And now I'm running through the doors of yet another hospital, quick on the heels of the paramedics who are rushing Eva into the back of the emergency department.

I don't want to be here. The smell, and the lights, and the memories are already putting me straight into panic mode. I find myself forcing air into my body, reminding myself to take deep breaths, reminding myself not to panic, not to fall apart. I don't want to be here, but there's no other place in the world I would be right now.

Eva's breathing again. Her heart started beating as the ambulance pulled up under the brightly lit awning of the hospital. I heard the paramedics talking amongst each other; she had literally choked on her own vomit. Suffocated because no air could get into her lungs as the vomit collected in the back of her throat, before relentlessly pouring from her mouth. It was the most glorious moment of my life when she started breathing again, but at the same time, the moment I was reassured she had a pulse was also the same exact moment the ambulance doors flung open to whisk her away from me. I jumped out with them, grabbing her hand that was hanging limply off the stretcher.

They're quick, the paramedics. They immediately rattle off medical terms and frightening words so fast to the doctors who meet us in the hall, I don't even have time to fully comprehend what they're saying before they try to take her away from me. I tightly cling to her lifeless hand.

"Bodhi," the one paramedic who spoke to me numerous times tonight urgently says my name. He grabs at my shoulder as I snap my head in his direction. "You can't go back there with her."

"The hell I can't!" I cry out. "I promised her—"

He pulls me closer and quickly whispers in my ear. "Let them save her. Give her a kiss, tell her you'll see her soon, and *let* them save her."

I look up at him, knowing he's right and that I can't stand here and fight them over this. Not when every second matters right now. I swiftly bend down to her unconscious face, placing a kiss on her clammy cheek. "I'm not leaving," I promise her. "I love you. Just remember that while you're back there."

Then she's gone. She disappears with a swarm of doctors through giant, white double doors, leaving me standing there under these bright lights that are making my forehead instantly break out in a cold sweat. I watch through the tiny windows until I can't see her anymore, and then I back up to the wall and close my eyes. My body is swaying with shock and I feel a hand on my shoulder again. I squint to see the one paramedic still standing there. The others have already walked away, and it's just the two of us now.

"Is anyone coming?" he asks me calmly. "Family? Friends?"

"Eventually. I don't have my phone. I'm not sure they know which hospital we're at."

"I'll stay with you until they get here," he announces. "My name is Graham. Graham Walker. Let's go wait in the main lobby. It's where everyone should come in."

I nod my head, letting him guide me through the hallway until we're in a large reception area filled with a crowd of anxious-looking people. They make eye contact with me and then immediately look away. I have Eva's blood all over my shirt. I have the blood she threw up, all over my legs and shoes. Her blood is on Graham too. We both look like we were just involved in some horrific massacre, and Jesus Christ, we both smell horrible.

"You should change," he says to me. "I can get you some scrubs to put on."

"I need to sit for a minute. I feel like I'm going to pass out."

He puts his hand on my back, guiding me over to a group of chairs by the main windows. "You're probably in shock. Just take a few deep breaths for me and try to stay calm. I know it's easier said than done. I'll go get you some water."

I take a seat and put my head in between my legs, trying to steady my rapid breathing.

In and out. In and out.

I feel Graham's hand on my back again. "She's your girlfriend?" he asks me softly. "Eva?"

I nod my head into my legs.

"Want to talk about her? Tell me something about her? How long have you two known each other?"

I look up at him and he hands me a paper cup filled with water. "Since we were twelve."

"That's a long time," he smiles, taking a seat next to me. "How'd you two meet?"

"She came to my house, for photography lessons. My mom, she was a photographer. I knew as soon as Eva walked in my door."

"At twelve? You knew she was the one?"

"At twelve," I repeat. "I lost her for a while. When we were fourteen. We just ... I just got her back." I don't know why I'm telling him all of this. "I can't lose her again."

"She's in good hands," he states. "I know some of the doctors here. I have a really good feeling she's going to be okay."

"Yeah?"

He nods his head. "Want to use my phone? You can call your mom? Your dad?"

I look down at my hands and close my eyes again. "My mom—my mom died of leukemia a few weeks ago, and my dad—my dad was the driver of the pickup truck that Eva was in." I look up at him, even though I don't want to see his reaction. I don't want him to feel bad for me. I hate when people give me that look.

Graham's eyes are huge, and it doesn't look like he's breathing. "Jesus Christ, Bodhi. I'm so sorry. I think we need to get you seen." He starts looking around like a doctor will magically appear to fix

5

everything I just told him. "I can't imagine what's going on in your head right now. I didn't realize that was your dad—"

"It's okay," I reassure him. "We weren't close. My dad—we weren't close at all. Tonight was the first time I've actually met him. It's a long story, and he's an asshole. Eva, she's the only person that matters to me in my life. She's always been the only person that matters ... she's all I have left—I can't lose her."

"You won't, Bodhi," he shakes his head and looks around the room. "Are you on your own? You aren't living by yourself, right? You're not eighteen yet?"

"I live with my friend and his family, and I have my grandpa ... who I also just met. It's so insane, everything, but Eva; if she doesn't—"

Graham's hand grabs my shoulder. "Sometimes we just need to stay positive, even if our mind is telling us to do the complete opposite. Stay positive and do me a favor? Promise me something?"

"What?"

He grins. "When you marry Eva one day, invite me to the wedding. I'll sit in the back and bring an elaborate wedding gift and my own wine if I have to, but I really want to be there to see that."

I manage a small smile. "Sure." I look out the window as I see shadows moving quickly out of the corner of my eye. "They're here," I bluntly state. "My family."

They all come barreling in at the same time. First, Mr. Calloway with all my friends. Coop, Beck, Luna, even goddamn Porter. I stand to meet them, walking the few feet toward them with Graham right behind me. I swear he's holding me up; my legs are wobbling as I try to move. Not even ten seconds later, Mrs. Calloway runs in with Calvin. They both come to a screeching halt when they see me. We just stand there for a moment, staring at each other. I don't know what to say. I'm covered in Eva's blood, so is Graham, and Eva's obviously not with us. I can't imagine what they're all thinking.

The silence increases. Luna raises her hand to her mouth, expecting the worst. She turns and buries her face into Coop's shoulder, softly wailing into his shirt. He hesitantly brings his hand up to her head, awkwardly patting it, no doubt questioning if he's the right person to comfort her. I try to shake my head to clue them in that Eva's not gone, but I can't move anything. It's almost as if my body has turned into a statue, and all I can do is watch as fear and anguish appear in front of me.

"Where is she?!" Mr. Calloway finally shouts. I jump back as he lunges at me, stumbling into Graham.

Mrs. Calloway throws her arm out, blocking her husband. He bounces off of it and grabs at his chest. She doesn't speak to him, not one word, but she *does* speak to me. "Bodhi," she says my name cautiously. She moves toward me and I manage to move a few steps toward her. "Where's Eva?" Her hand comes up to my cheek, her eyes searching mine for some sort of answer.

I point behind me, to where she disappeared from my sight a few minutes ago. "They took her that way," my words quiver as I speak.

"The blood?" she points to my body. A few tears fall from her eyes and she doesn't bother wiping them away.

"She cut her forehead in the truck," I point to my t-shirt, and then I point to my feet. "Internal bleeding, they think? She started throwing up in the ambulance."

Mrs. Calloway raises her hand to her mouth.

"Her heart stopped," my voice cracks, and I hear everyone gasp around me. I feel the room start to spin and I know my body is about to collapse. Mrs. Calloway's arms instantly wrap around my back. She holds me up, keeping me from falling to the ground.

"I've got you," she calmly says. "I've got you, Bodhi."

"Her fucking heart stopped," I whisper into her ear, clutching at the back of her shirt as tight as I can. "And then it started again, right in front of my face. *Please*," I beg her as I start to cry into her hair. "*Please* go find out what the hell is going on."

She nods into my shoulder. "I will, Bodhi. I'll find out right now." She looks up at me and squeezes my shoulders, giving my forehead a few motherly kisses. "Calvin," she calls out to him. "Let Calvin take you to sit down, okay?"

I feel Calvin's hands on my arms, guiding me back to the chairs.

"Bodhi," Graham calls out. "I'm going to get you something to change into, okay? I'll be right back."

"Thanks," I reply. I watch as he joins Eva's parents at the

reception desk. I see him talking to them. I see Mrs. Calloway worriedly glance over at me, and then back to Graham. He pulls out his phone and starts tapping away on it as he stands next to them.

Before I can sit, Calvin's arms are around me. "Son," he says strongly. "It's going to be okay. She's going to be okay."

"Her heart stopped, Calvin. She died in front of me." I push myself back and look down at the blood all over my shoes. "Luke," I suddenly say his name, looking back up at Calvin. "Luke ... he—"

"I know," he quickly wipes his eyes. "I know. We pulled up to the accident right after the ambulance sped away. We know what happened to Luke."

"I'm sorry," I say to him. I throw myself down into a chair and bring my hands to my face. "I'm so sorry, Calvin."

"You have absolutely nothing to be sorry for," Calvin responds, his voice trembling as he speaks. He brings his hand to the back of my neck. "We lost Luke years ago. I'm just happy to see you. I was thinking horrible things, Bodhi. Horrible things about you, horrible things about Eva."

"I can't lose her," I say once again. "I can't lose her for real."

"Don't think like that, Bodhi. Don't think—"

"Wait! Kenneth, Annie, Owen ..." I say their names slowly. "They were there, they arrived on Owen's yacht with Mr. Calloway. Did you know? Did you know they were all alive?"

He takes in a huge gulp of air. "Yes. Yes, I did. But I didn't know they knew Brayden ... Kenneth and Annie, that doesn't make any sense, and I did *not* know your mom was Phoebe." He grabs my chin. "I didn't know, Bodhi, I really didn't. Not until I started putting things together last night. None of this makes any sense. I'll get it all figured out, I promise. We have a lot we need to talk about, when things settle."

I would like to think Calvin wouldn't lie to me right now.

Graham suddenly reappears, handing me some scrubs as he stands in front of me. "You can use the staff locker room over there," he points behind him. "There are showers in there, too. No one will question anything, I told them you'd be in there. I'm going to head out now, is that okay? I can stay if you want me to."

His genuine concern for me makes my eyes fill up with tears.

8

"I'm okay. Thanks for staying with me."

His hand comes up to my shoulder. "Not a problem at all. Remember what you promised me. I want to be there."

"You'll be there."

He squeezes my shoulder and then leaves out the automatic doors. I watch as he leans up against the stone wall outside and puts his head in his hands, breaking down the moment he believes he's away from all our watching eyes. I turn back, giving him the privacy he deserves, and see Eva's parents heading this way. I quickly stand.

"Eva's being prepped for surgery," Mrs. Calloway says immediately. "She's stable. She has internal bleeding, but the surgeon is pretty confident he knows where it's coming from. Her arm is also broken, but that's the least of their worries right now." Her hand comes up to my cheek. "She's breathing on her own, and they'll tell us more once they know more—"

"How the hell did this even *happen*?!" Mr. Calloway cries out.

I look at him out of the corner of my eye and feel hands on my back. Numerous hands that know I'm not going to stay calm anymore. I'm assuming it's Coop and Beck, but I don't turn to look. My heart is pounding in my chest. "*You*," I point to him. "This happened because of *you* and Henry fucking Channing."

Mrs. Calloway steps between her husband and me. She turns to him and says, "If you're staying to be here for Eva, that's fine. But if you think for one minute you're going to sit here and start a shouting match between you and Bodhi, or Calvin ... I'll ask security to escort you out of here. Do you understand that, Brayden? This is *not* happening here."

He sheepishly takes a seat and leans his head against the wall.

Mrs. Calloway continues. "We can head up to the third floor waiting room. That's where Eva will be brought after surgery."

"I'm going to change," I say quietly, pointing to the locker room down the hall. "I can't stay like this."

"We'll help you," Coop says, his hand pushes firmly on my back. "Me and Beck, we'll go with you."

"We'll meet you up there, okay Bodhi?" Mrs. Calloway confirms. "The third floor?"

I nod my head.

9

Luna places her hand on mine, then turns to Coop. "I'll go up with Porter and them," she points to Eva's parents and Calvin. "Get us all some coffee or something." She then leans in and places a kiss on my cheek. "It will be okay," she says, and then she disappears toward the elevators with the others.

I watch as they all walk out of our sight, and then I turn to the guys. "I'm going to throw up," I immediately tell them.

"Let's get you to that locker room first," Beck declares.

They swiftly guide me down the hall. At this point, I almost feel like my body has stopped functioning. My legs are only moving because Coop and Beck are firmly pushing me. The one thing I know for sure, besides the fact I'm definitely going to throw up at any moment, is that I need to be lying by Eva's side. I need to be next to her. I need to hear her heart beating. I need her to know I'm here and that I didn't leave. I just need to be with her.

I fling open a bathroom door and hang my head over the toilet, throwing up until there's nothing left inside of me. I then sit against the wall, putting my head into my knees, realizing just how utterly useless I am right now. I hear a shower turn on and the guys mumbling under their breaths, but I just sit there, staring down at my blood-soaked feet in this sterile bathroom stall that smells like bleach. I close my eyes, but suddenly feel hands on my arms guiding me to stand, and moving my body into the shower area. I feel my clothes slowly being pulled off me. My shoes, my shorts, my shirt, my boxers. It doesn't even phase me that I'm being undressed and am standing here completely naked.

I then feel the hot water beating down on my back as I place my hands on the cold tile. I rest my forehead up against it and look down, seeing white soap bubbles below me turn pink as they mix with the blood that's being washed away from my legs and feet. Eva's blood.

The hot water continues to rain down on me, almost throwing me into a trance. My eyes close as I let myself fall into this worthless state of emptiness. A few minutes pass and I hear the shower turn off. The heat from the water is suddenly replaced with shivering cold air. I can feel my body start to shake, but then a rough towel is suddenly wrapped around my waist. Another one is thrown over my shoulders, and I'm being guided out of the shower and placed firmly on a wooden bench.

I give myself a minute before I finally look up. Coop and Beck are standing there, staring at me, wet splotches all over their shirts and shorts, little drops of water dripping from their heads. It hits me right then, even though I already knew; this was the confirmation I needed.

My two best friends just gave me a goddamn shower.

"Did you guys really just—"

"It's not the first time we've seen you naked, Bodhi," Coop reminds me. "In fact, it's not even the second or third time."

I take a deep breath, trying to calm down my emotions that are getting ready to explode, but it's pointless. I start sobbing and I can't stop. I literally fall apart right there, in the staff locker room of the hospital, with Coop and Beck standing right in front of me. I feel them join me on the bench, and I feel their arms wrap around my shaking, towel-covered body as I uncontrollably cry.

"Let it out, man," Beck quietly says. "For real, just let it all out right here, with us."

I do. I cry about Eva. I cry about seeing my dad for the first *and* the last time tonight. I cry about my mom dying and leaving me with all this shit. I cry about my grandparents magically appearing on High Bridge. I cry about how insane my life is right now. I cry until I don't have any more tears left in my damaged body, and they stay right there, Coop and Beck, right next to me until I'm finally done.

There's silence for a bit before Coop lets out a dramatic sigh. "Well, I think we can officially check off breakdown in a hospital locker room while naked from our best friends bucket list. One and done?"

I let out a little laugh, staring down at my bare legs.

"Let's get you dressed?" Coop suggests.

I manage to throw my boxers back on and pull on the scrubs that Graham had given me. I toss my bloody clothes and shoes into the giant plastic trash bin. Beck leaves for a moment, running out to his truck to grab me an extra pair of shoes. When he returns, the three of us sit back on the bench. I still feel like the world is spinning, but at least I'm not covered in Eva's blood anymore. I

11

guess that's a positive to be thankful for.

I tightly close my eyes, trying to get this feeling to stop.

"You going to be okay?" Beck carefully asks me.

I open my eyes and glance between the two of them, giving them the slightest of nods. "I'm not exactly sure where I'd be right now if you two hadn't been watching out for me these last few years. I think I probably would have died at some point."

"We weren't going to let that happen," Coop tells me. "We made a pact last year, the two of us, over some beers: keep Bodhi alive until he gets his shit together. I think we spit on it and everything."

"Pretty serious."

"We still won't let anything happen," Beck adds. "The pact is good for life. Though you might owe us your firstborn by the time we're adults and can legally fend for ourselves."

"Got it. Firstborn," I repeat, but then my mind goes straight to Eva. "Guys, what if she doesn't—"

"Nope," Coop shakes his head. "Hell no, Bodhi. You know as well as we do, Eva's going to pull through. She's a badass, and once she's back home and you two are making us gag with your public displays of affection, we'll celebrate huge. All of us. Together."

"This is just a little hurdle," Beck agrees with him. "Something to tell the grandkids about when we're old men smoking cigars on the beach, wearing mismatched clothes like Calvin does."

I let out a little laugh.

"You've got this, Bodhi," continues Beck. "So does Eva. You guys don't exist without each other, and you're sitting in front of us right now, which means she's up there being the badass that she is, letting those doctors fix whatever the hell is wrong with her."

"Is this real life?" I then question. "How can any of what's happened these last few days be real? How am I seriously going to live with all this shit?"

"I ask myself that question every goddamn day," Coop grunts.

Beck nudges my shoulder. "All the craziness aside do you love Eva? Like that insane type of love where nothing else matters but her? You're lost without her? Can't function? Can't breathe?"

"Yes, all of that and more."

He nudges my shoulder again. "*That's* fucking real, Bodhi.

That's how you know this is real life. Eva is real life, and anytime you feel like none of this can possibly be real, you'll just have to look at her. She'll make you remember what's real and what matters. And we'll be there too," he points to himself and Coop. "Just in case you need a swift kick in your ass to get you back on track. No one's going to let you fall apart."

Coop lets out a loud sniffle. "Damn, bro. Making me get all emotional over here."

I wipe my eyes with my hands. "I don't deserve you two."

"Shit, Bodhi," Coop laughs. "I'd probably still be eating crayons and crying every day at school if it wasn't for you; and Beck, he'd be a stoner. Probably wouldn't even know what day of the week it is."

Beck rolls his eyes. "Uh huh, that's exactly what I'd be up to."

"You ready?" Coop then asks. "Ready to get up to the third floor in your fancy doctor scrubs and wait for the news that Eva will be okay, so we can put this awful shit behind us?"

For the first time all night, I actually feel a little better—calmer, I guess you can say. Comforted, like there might actually be a future where everything ends up being okay. I'm nothing without Eva; I don't exist without her, I know this. But I'm *also* nothing without Coop and Beck. I wouldn't be here today if it wasn't for them, and I owe them way more than I'll ever be able to give them.

I stand up. "I'm ready. Bros for life?" I hold out my fist.

They both hit it.

"Of course," Beck replies. "Always."

"Hell yeah," Coop smirks. "No one gets to tap out early on this brotherhood. We're like a triangle; one side goes missing, then we're just some confused, pointy letter L ... or a stiff V," he adds, looking deep in thought. He pulls the door open but just stands there. "You know what word has an L and a V in it?" he turns to us and asks. "*Love,*" he smoothly grins, forming a large triangle with his fingers.

I throw my arms around my two best friends and push us out the door. "Bros for life," I say again. "A triangle, always."

13

chapter two

Bodhi

The third floor is definitely quieter than the emergency room waiting area. We see everyone as soon as the elevator door opens. Luna and Porter in one corner, Mrs. Calloway and Calvin in another, Mr. Calloway by himself. They're the only ones sitting in this section, and they all look up at us the moment we come into view. Luna immediately stands, bringing a drink carrier of coffees over.

"The coffee is horrible," she declares, handing me one. "Like liquid tar, but it's going down somehow and magically helping."

I laugh under my breath. "Thanks, Luna." I nod in Porter's direction. "Porter?" I then question. "He looks like absolute shit."

She frowns. "I know all about how he treated Eva this last year. Probably more than you guys. But his house burned down, his dad's the biggest asshole in Flagler, and he believes everything that happened tonight is his fault. I think we need to cut him some slack and not hate him tonight. We can go back to hating him tomorrow."

"We won't hate him tonight. You guys go sit with him, and I'll be right back." I leave her and the guys, and walk over to Mrs. Calloway and Calvin. "Did they say how long it might be?" I ask her. "How long Eva will be in surgery?"

"No, Bodhi, they didn't. Are you doing okay?" she asks, reaching for my hand. "With *everything* that happened tonight?"

"No, but I think I will be. Eventually." I look over to Mr. Calloway, and then back to his wife. "I'll be right back."

I slowly walk over to where he's sitting. He doesn't see me approaching; his head is in his hands and he's staring down at the ground. I tap him on the shoulder to get his attention, and he swiftly looks up at me. I've never been this close to him before. I instantly see Rowan and Miles in his face, they definitely favor him, but I also see Eva a little bit. She looks exactly like her mom, but the more I stare at Mr. Calloway, the more I realize she looks like him, as well.

"Bodhi," he says timidly. He goes to stand but I shake my head. "I don't even know where to—"

"Stop," I quickly say. "Right now is not the time for you to try to explain everything that happened years ago. I just wanted you to get a good look at me, standing here in front of you, because when Eva gets out of here, I'm not leaving her side. You're going to be seeing a lot of me. I know what it's like to lose her, and I'm *not* spending another moment without her."

"I understand," he says. "I understand that—"

"I love your daughter," I go on. "I always have. And maybe at seventeen you think I'm just talking bullshit, that I don't know what I'm saying or what I'm feeling. But I'm standing here, right now, telling you that I'm going to marry her one day, and it's not going to be *my* decision if you're a part of our lives. It will be hers. I hope you realize that. You don't need to worry about me, but you definitely need to worry about her. Whatever you did, whatever you've done, if you want her to forgive you, stop acting like you're the victim."

I walk away. I'm not sure if my words mean anything to Mr. Calloway. I didn't say them to get him to miraculously like me. I said them because I don't want Eva to have to deal with her father being a dickhead once she's home. But as I sit myself down next to Porter, Mr. Calloway gets up and walks over to his wife and Calvin, sitting across from them instead of by himself.

An hour passes. In that hour I sit here, drinking this awful hospital coffee just so I have something to do, staring at the door I know the doctor will magically appear from at some point. After that hour is gone, I get up and start pacing. I can't sit anymore. Luna falls asleep on Coop's shoulder, his arm draped around her back as he falls in and out of sleep himself. Porter stares straight ahead of him, not speaking to anyone, but once in a while, he lets out a dramatic sigh. Beck randomly responds to texts, which reminds me that my phone is still on Porter's boat. Not like I need it. Everyone I know and care about is in this hospital with me right now.

Another hour passes and just as I'm about to completely lose my goddamn mind, a doctor, looking to be about Calvin's age, walks out of the door I've been watching. He looks at all of us eagerly staring at him, and then his eyes go right to Eva's parents.

"Are you the parents of Eva Calloway?" he questions.

They both jump up.

"Let's go into one of the conference rooms," he points past him down the hall.

"No!" I exclaim, rushing over to him. "Please, please just tell me that she's okay. I just need to know."

The doctor takes off his surgical cap. "Are you the boyfriend? Bodhi, is it?"

I nod my head, not understanding how he knows this.

He moves a few steps closer to me. "I'm Dr. Walker, Samuel Walker. My son Graham managed to send me a few urgent texts about you before I went into surgery. She's going to be okay. You stay put and let me go talk to Eva's parents, all right?"

I throw myself down in a chair, relief flooding my body as I wipe at the tears that stream down my face.

"We'll be right back," Mrs. Calloway promises me, and then she and Mr. Calloway disappear with Dr. Walker.

Calvin's hand rubs my back as my friends come over and sit next to us. No one talks. No one knows what to say. We just sit there and wait ... wait for Eva's parents to come back out and tell us what they know. It doesn't take long. I see them walking down the hallway before anyone else does. I jump out of my seat. Mrs. Calloway is nodding her head before she even wraps her arms around me.

"She's going to be okay," she reassures us all. She then wipes at her eyes with her fingers. "He was right on the source of the bleeding. He was able to stop it. He called it seatbelt syndrome. She was extremely lucky the seatbelt didn't damage any internal organs. They did a CAT scan of her lungs, too. They were worried she aspirated when she was throwing up. They're clear, though. They also did one of her head, small concussion. Uh ... what else? That was the biggest—"

"Broken arm," Mr. Calloway says softly. "Her arm is broken. An orthopedic doctor will take a look at it tomorrow."

"Yes," Mrs. Calloway agrees. "He thinks it's a clean break.

Hopefully no surgery. Just a cast. Oh, and her head. Ten stitches up her hairline, but she's going to be okay," she says again. "They're bringing her up in just a little bit. She's in recovery right now. You guys should all go home and rest—"

"I'm not going anywhere!" I make known. I frantically look between Mrs. Calloway and Mr. Calloway. "*Please.* Please don't make me leave. I promised Eva I wouldn't leave her."

Mrs. Calloway moves my curls off my face. "No, Bodhi. Of course not. You can stay with us."

"I don't have anywhere to go," Porter says quietly.

Confused, Mr. Calloway looks over at Porter. "What do you mean?"

I glance between the three adults standing in front of us. They don't know. They haven't been home. They have no idea that Luke burned Porter's house down tonight.

"Porter's house ..." I say slowly. "Luke ... Porter's house was on fire tonight."

All three of them gasp.

"Where's your dad?" Mr. Calloway questions.

"I have no idea," Porter bluntly responds.

I see Mr. Calloway finally take a good look at Porter. "Porter, what the hell happened to your face?"

Porter looks down at his feet and doesn't say anything.

Calvin puts his hand on Porter's back. "You four, you all can come home with me tonight. I have enough rooms. We'll get some sleep and figure out everything in the morning."

"Luna," Coop says hesitantly. "I can take you home—"

"I'll stay with you all," she instantly says. "If that's okay. I mean, it's already so late and I want to see Eva tomorrow with everyone."

You would think Luna had just asked Coop to marry her with how red his face suddenly becomes. "Uh, yeah, sure. That works," he nervously agrees.

"Audrey. My keys," Calvin hands them to her. "In case you need a car. I'll ride with these four. I'll be up in the morning. Anything you need, just let me know. We'll deal with getting the Lexus tomorrow ... and a new phone."

"What happened to the Lexus? And your phone?" Mr. Calloway

asks.

No one answers him.

"*I* don't have my phone," I remind the guys. "I left it on your boat, Porter."

"No worries," Beck says to me. "We'll stop by and grab it on the way to Calvin's. We'll bring it up in the morning."

"My jeep, the keys are on the table in the foyer at Eva's—"

"We'll bring that up tomorrow, too," Coop says. "And some clothes. Don't worry about all the little shit. We'll take care of it."

I pull the two of them in for a hug. "Thank you."

"Triangle, bro," Coop pats me hard on the back. "Triangle."

Everyone leaves shortly after, and I'm alone now with Eva's parents. I've never been alone with just her parents before. The tension between the two of them almost makes me want to run and hide. They don't talk to each other at all. They don't even look at each other. I could *never* imagine being this cold to Eva. Just the thought makes my stomach start to sway.

"I want to hear everything, Bodhi," Mrs. Calloway suddenly says after way too many silent minutes pass by. She's sitting on one side of me. "Not now, but later. I want to hear how this all happened. I want to know *everything*."

"Okay," I quietly respond, though I'm not sure if I'll ever be able to talk out loud about everything that happened tonight.

She turns to her husband, who's on the other side of me. "Did you bring Lenora and Bodhi back to Flagler all those years ago?"

He looks at me first, then to his wife. He nods his head very hesitantly.

"And how long have you known Henry?" she continues.

His face turns an uncomfortable red. "I've known him a while."

She lets out a defeated sigh, and turns her face from his, staring at the elevators instead. Her whole body shifts. Her back is to us like she can't bear to look our way.

"Audrey, I know I kept things—"

She quickly spins around. Her glare forces him to immediately stop talking. I've seen that same glare from Eva before. "Don't even start. You think I want to hear this *now*? While we wait to go see our daughter who just came out of the surgery that saved her life?"

"No, but I need to—"

"You need to stop talking," she says. "Just stop."

Dr. Walker suddenly appears in front of us. I jump up, anxious to get away from whatever is brewing between Eva's parents. "Room 323," he says. "Technically it should just be parents allowed back right now, but I've worked here for forty years and usually get my way. I'll take you all back. They just brought her in."

"Thank you," I say as we follow him through the doors and down the sterile white hall. "Thank you for bending the rules for me."

"You're welcome, Bodhi," he replies. "But you should really thank my son."

Room 323, far away from the nurses' desk, next to a snack area, and across from a wall of windows that overlooks a lit-up pond in the back of the hospital. My eyes immediately go to Eva as I look into her dimly lit room. Her parents walk in before me, going straight to her side. I stand at the door, staring at her as she lies on her hospital bed, not moving. I have to fight back the visions that want to replay in my mind. The visions of her lying in the back of the ambulance without a pulse.

I walk in a bit further.

Dr. Walker puts his hand on my shoulder. "Jackie, she's Eva's nurse for tonight," he points to her. "She's head nurse on this floor and knows *every* nurse that will cross paths with Eva while she's here. Anyone tries to kick you out ... tell them you know Jackie. She's also my wife," he winks.

Jackie smiles warmly at me and then turns to Eva's parents. "Her vitals are wonderful. She'll probably be a little out of it for a while, but give her a few hours and we should see her waking up. She woke up just a bit when we got her in here, but she definitely wants to stay sleeping, which is absolutely fine. Poor girl has been through a lot."

I walk closer to Eva. She has wires everywhere, cords coming out from under the blankets, hooked up to machines that are next to her. There's an IV taped on the hand of her unbroken arm, oxygen flowing through her nose. Her broken arm is secured in a sling, resting on her chest. I stand next to Mrs. Calloway, and the more I stare at Eva, the more it looks like she's just sleeping. Her hair, though, still has blood in it. I don't know why that bothers me so much, like after everything she went through, I just don't want to see any more blood on her. I go to move the stray strands away from her face, but my hand stops halfway.

"You can touch her," Jackie says caringly. "Let her know you're here. Just be careful of her stomach and arm."

My hand goes to her hair, moving it off her forehead near the stitches that closed up the wound that bled all over my shirt. I run my fingers down her warm cheek. Mrs. Calloway gently touches my arm, and then walks over to the other side of the bed, the one her husband is on. She leaves me by myself, and I feel a chair suddenly appear behind me.

"Sit," Dr. Walker says. He pushes my shoulders down forcefully until my body slams into the chair. He then brings the cold metal railing down on the side of the bed. "Sit here and talk to her."

When my mom fell and was lying in my arms in our kitchen a few weeks ago, everything around me suddenly disappeared. It was just the two of us, alone, as she struggled to talk, even though we weren't really alone. This moment, feels exactly like that. No one else matters right this second. I scooch the chair as close as I can to the bed, instantly forgetting there's anyone else in this room besides Eva and me.

I place her hand in mine, lacing my fingers in between hers and away from the IV. I lower my head and put my mouth right to her ear. "Confession," I whisper into it softly. "You have no idea how beautiful you look right now. I think this *might* be the most beautiful you've ever been." I pause, giving myself a moment to swallow down my emotions. "Eva, I'm so sorry I let this happen. I love you so much. You'll never understand how much I love you. Thank you for not leaving me. Thank you for giving us another chance. Thank you for finding a way to come back to me again."

I then gently kiss her lips, and bring my ear right to her chest. I close my eyes, and listen to the steady rhythm of her delicate heart, and to the sound of people silently crying around me while I slowly drift off to sleep.

chapter three

Eva

The beeping. If this goddamn beeping doesn't stop soon, I'm going to lose it. My mind feels so foggy, so out of sorts, but I can definitely hear this beeping and it's driving me insane. I need it to stop, but I can't get my eyes open to see what's causing it. I want to open them, but I feel like I'm trapped behind my eyelids. I'm here and awake in my mind, but not fully awake in the real world, which is actually starting to freak me out.

Focus, Eva. Focus on what you can hear and sense.

The beeping, definitely the beeping. The warmth of someone next to me, and the feeling of hair tickling my cheek each time this person breathes. Someone's fingers are also loosely wrapped around mine. I can feel the pressure of them on my skin. The smell; I smell saltwater and sunscreen, too.

Bodhi. Bodhi's next to me. Time to wake the hell up.

Shit, it *hurts*. The more awake I allow myself to become, the more I realize I'm hurting, everywhere, my stomach especially. It feels like it's been ripped open. I can't possibly be lying here, feeling like this, without my insides pouring from my body. Why don't I hear people panicking? Why am *I* not panicking? Because I'm absolutely certain I must be bleeding to death, wherever I am.

Blood. The ambulance. The taste of blood in my mouth. The accident. *Shit.*

I'm slowly starting to realize that something awful happened in that ambulance. I remember feeling completely helpless, and completely overwhelmed with the realization that I just might be dying right in front of Bodhi. Obviously, I'm still alive, but I need to wake up, no matter how bad it feels. I need to know what I missed while I was trapped in this dark world of nothingness.

I try to wiggle my fingers first. I tell them to move, and they do. I feel Bodhi jump. He grabs onto my hand tighter and lifts his head away from my face. His warmth is gone. I want it back. Why do I feel like I'm suddenly terrified to wake up?

"Eva?" I hear him whisper. My name seems to bounce around the walls of wherever I am. I feel his fingers touch my eyes, then my lips. Instant comfort. "Baby, I'm right here."

I wiggle my fingers a little more. Still trying to get my goddamn eyes to open. I feel his lips brush against mine. That does the trick. My eyes blink a few times, and his blurry face suddenly comes into my view. I am *so* happy to see him. I can feel tears leave my eyes even though I can't get a single word out of my mouth. His fingers slowly collect them as he leans in and kisses my lips again.

"Hey there, baby," he smiles at me. He looks like hell, like he literally crawled his way out of hell to be here. He gently moves the hair from my face as he continues to stare down at me. My forehead, it suddenly feels tight, too tight. I move my eyes up a little, trying to see why it feels so funny. Bodhi's fingers move right to the spot that feels different. "Stitches. Ten of them, but it looks perfect."

"*Bodhi*," I whisper painfully. My voice comes out all scratchy and my throat aches as I speak. It feels like it's been scraped, like there's a fresh wound there that becomes angry every time I swallow or try to talk. I just want to go back to sleep and make all this pain disappear. "My *stomach*."

"You're okay," he reassures me. "You had some bleeding in there ... they had to fix it. The seatbelt—but you're okay, I promise."

I can't stop the tears from falling again. "It hurts," I whimper quietly. "It hurts so bad."

"Oh, Eva." I can see the sadness in his eyes and it makes me feel even worse. "I know. I'm so sorry. I wish I could take away your pain. I absolutely would. I'd take it all." His fingers run under my eyes, collecting the tears I didn't even know were there. "I'm going to wake your mom and dad," he points to them in the corner of the room. My eyes don't want to focus that far away. "We'll make sure you get something to make it go away." His lips carefully come to my forehead.

He walks away and my body starts to panic. I need him by me.

I don't like how I feel when he's not by my side. The beeping that woke me up increases again. The noise, the pain, the feeling of being completely helpless ... I've woken up in the middle of a nightmare.

"She's awake," I hear him whisper.

Suddenly my mom and dad come into view with Bodhi right behind them. The beeping starts to slow down. My mom's fingers caress my face. My dad takes my hand. I almost jerk it away, but I don't have the strength. I don't want to see him right now. They both try to talk to me, but my body desperately wants to go back to sleep. I can't hear what they're saying. I can only see their mouths moving. It's like I'm fading in and out between this world and the world I was trapped in before. Bodhi takes a seat next to me. I try to focus my eyes on his, but I see a door open behind him, distracting me. A nurse walks in and goes right to my side.

"Hello there, gorgeous," she smiles. "Welcome back. I know you're tired, but try to stay with me for a few minutes." She goes over to the machines that light up the dark room, and plays around with the buttons. "On a scale of one to ten, your pain, beautiful, what's your pain level?" she asks me.

"Nine," I croak. My eyes just want to close.

"I'm going to get you something for that right now," she says. "I'm going to put it into your IV right here," she points to it on my hand. "And it's going to make you very sleepy. Sleep is just what you need right now."

I want to sleep, but I want Bodhi to stay. I want him touching me. I need the comfort of his body next to mine. "Bodhi," I mumble.

"I'm right here." I feel his hand on my cheek.

"Lay with me," I demand. I try to grab at his shoulder with my one hand, but completely miss. My hand ends up dropping off the side of the bed and I can't seem to pick it back up.

"I ... I don't know if I can," he hesitantly says, carefully guiding my hand back onto the sheet. I can hear the uncertainty in his voice. That's not what I want to hear. I want to feel warm, and cozy, and safe with him by my side. I can hear the beeping increase again, faster than before.

"*Please*," I beg him, crying as I say it. "*Please* lay with me."

"He will," I hear the nurse say. "Relax, honey. Let me get you

23

situated, moved over a little, and we'll get him next to you, okay?"

I nod my head and close my eyes, but the beeping doesn't decrease, and I can't help the tears that are pouring down my face. I feel like I'm completely breaking down. I need to get out of here. I need this pain to stop. I need all the noise to disappear. I need to feel like everything is going to be okay.

I need Bodhi.

I suddenly feel hands on me, carefully moving my body closer to the side of the bed. Every little movement makes me cry harder, but then I feel him crawling in next to me. I smell him first, then I feel his breath on my cheek. His arm comes up over my neck and he cradles my face with his warm hand. The beeping slows down. I don't even hear it anymore. The tears stop; my body relaxes instantly with him by my side.

"I'm right here," I hear him whisper into my ear. "I won't leave. Ever."

"I know you won't," I whisper in return. Then I fall back to sleep, lost once again in the world of nothingness from which I had just emerged.

chapter four

Eva

I'm not sure how much time has passed. When my eyes open again, there's light in my room that wasn't there before. Bodhi's lying next to me, awake, watching me as I come out of yet another drug-induced slumber. I quickly look around the room, expecting a crowd of people to be staring at me, but we're the only ones in here, from what I can tell.

"Good morning," he whispers, kissing the bridge of my nose.

I feel a little better, not much, but enough that I can at least form coherent sentences. My stomach is churning though, and I think I might throw up. The room is definitely spinning each and every time I close my eyes.

"Is it morning?" I ask him groggily. I really need some water.

"Give or take," he smiles. "Lunch time. Late lunch time. Early dinner time."

"I need water," I moan in desperation.

Bodhi reaches next to him and grabs a massive cup with a thick straw. I take a few sips, but abruptly stop. As much I want to chug it, I feel like it's going to come right back up.

"Bodhi ..." I say slowly, finally getting a good look at him. "Why the hell are you wearing doctor scrubs?"

He places the cup back on the table. "Long story. I have clothes to change into, the guys brought me stuff, but every time I leave your bed, *you* make the monitors go insane."

I smile a little and close my eyes, immediately opening them as the nausea increases. "I need you, Bodhi. Don't leave."

"I'll never leave you," he says back, kissing my cheek.

"Where are my parents?"

"Your mom went home a little while ago to change and take

clothes to your brothers. They're staying with their friends for a couple days. Your dad, he's out in the waiting room with everyone. Dolly brought lunch up and treated the hospital staff, too. It's like a party out there."

"Everyone?" I question him. "Everyone, who?"

"Coop, Beck, Luna, Porter, Calvin. Ma and Pop were up early this morning, so were Luna's parents. They look like they're our age—"

"My dad, he's out there with all of *them*?"

"Yeah. He's actually talking now. He didn't talk all night. I think we scared him at first. No one's been in yet but your parents. They all want to see you. Luna ... she needs to see you. She's really worried and just looks lost."

I let out a dramatic groan. "I'm sure I look amazing."

"I can't even begin to explain how beautiful you look today."

I look down at myself. I'm afraid to lift up the hospital gown that's under these scratchy sheets. My stomach feels almost sunburnt, a constant pain that won't go away. And every time I move even the slightest, the pain shoots throughout my body like flames of a fire.

"Have you looked?" I whisper, pointing to my stomach.

"No, but no matter what it looks like, it doesn't change how I feel about you."

Bodhi's words always make me blush.

"Eva," my name comes out of his mouth so delicately. "I thought I lost you." He buries his head into the dip of my neck.

I need to comfort him, even though I can barely move. "I'm right here—"

"I'm so sorry. Baby, I'm so sorry."

"You have nothing to apologize for," I make sure he knows. I go to touch his face, the single act of reassurance I can share with him right now. "My arm?" There's a black cast on my lower arm.

"You were pretty out of it when they put that on this morning. You might have sworn at the orthopedic doctor a few times. Clean break though, but you'll have to wear it for six weeks."

"Wonderful," I growl.

"Hey," he gives me a small smile. "The fact you're here, right in front of me, and that at some point I'll be able to wrap my arms around you and hold you all night, is *all* that matters."

"How long do I have to stay here?" I whisper to him.

He leans forward, placing a gentle kiss on my lips. "I don't know. But I won't leave you, I promise."

I hear the door to my room open, and glance over to see two nurses walk in, one of them carrying a tray of hospital food, the other looking much too happy for this type of occasion.

"Morning, gorgeous!" says the older one. I vaguely recognize her from last night. "Your mom is waiting outside and will come in here in a few minutes. Do you remember my name?"

"No. I'm sorry. But if you tell it to me now, I think I'll remember. I sort of feel alive again."

"Jackie," she says kindly. "I've been your nurse all night, and my shift officially ended a while ago, but I'm staying for a bit. I want to get you up and moving a little, get some awful, bland food in that stomach, wash you up, get you using the bathroom ..."

I can feel myself turn red.

"Mind if we ask Prince Charming to step out for a little while?" she points to Bodhi. "Give us maybe an hour with just us girls?"

"Prince Charming?" I turn to Bodhi and grin.

He shrugs his shoulders. "I think they like me."

I lean my head into his. "I don't want you to leave," I breathe into his ear. "Just one hour ... you'll be back in one hour?" I already feel anxiety at the thought of being without him in this room.

"On the dot," he promises. "You know I will be." He kisses my cheek and swings his legs out of the bed.

"We'll take good care of her," Jackie assures him. "Go eat something, Bodhi, okay? Refuel?"

He gives me one last look as he lingers by the door. "One hour, I promise." And then he disappears.

Jackie walks over to my bed while the other nurse places the tray of food on the table up against the wall. "I'm Harper," she introduces and smiles. "I've heard a lot about you."

"Harper will be taking over until I come back," Jackie says, taking a seat on the edge of my bed. "How's the pain? Still a nine?"

"Maybe a seven? It's just my stomach," I tell her. "It feels ..."

"Awful?" Jackie finishes for me.

"Yes. And I'm afraid I'm going to throw up."

"Completely expected," she nods. "I'm going to let Harper give you something for the pain and nausea once we get done doing a few things. I don't want you falling asleep on me right now. You've been falling asleep on me every time I think you're waking up."

"How many times have I woken up?" I ask her. I only remember one other time.

"Four, maybe five times. All very short, and man, do you get *angry* when Prince Charming steps away. You've sworn at us quite a few times when we make him leave your bed."

I smile a little. "I'm sorry about that."

"He's absolutely adorable with you," Jackie winks. "I never thought I'd see true love in two teenagers, but ... now I have. And the sooner we get you up and moving, and feeling better, the sooner you'll get out of here. What do you want to do first? Try to eat? Or get your catheter out?"

I gulp and look down at myself. "I have a catheter in?"

"Yes, ma'am. Let's tackle that first. Quick, easy, and on the count of three."

A catheter. A small, hollow tube used to empty bladders when the owner of said bladder cannot do it on their own. I've had one once before, when I had surgery on my leg, but it was out before I even came to from anesthesia. I would be more than okay with never having one again.

"Harper," Jackie says, once I have full control of my bladder. "Pop on out and tell Eva's mom it's safe to come in. Unless you don't want her to come in ...?" she turns to me. "Totally up to you."

"She can come in."

Moments later, my mom walks through the door, wearing black leggings, an oversized t-shirt, and her hair is up in a messy ponytail. She looks beautiful, but so tired and anxious. I know I saw her briefly in the middle of the night, but her presence right now comforts me so much, I fight back more tears. She comes right up to my bed and timidly hugs my upper body.

"Oh Eva, I'm so happy to see you awake. You look so much better than you did throughout the night and this morning."

"I feel a little better. More alert."

"I brought some stuff from home," she then says, holding up a small bag.

"Good!" Jackie exclaims. "I think we need to sit you up a bit and see how that feels," she says to me. "Your stomach, honey ... it's going to be sore. Dr. Walker was able to locate the source of your bleeding before surgery, bless him. He was able to avoid a bigger incision. But let's take a peek at what we've got going on down here."

Jackie grabs the controller attached to the railings and raises my bed up. I know they can hear me wince as my stomach starts to ache with the movements.

"You okay, honey?" Jackie asks.

"Yeah. It just hurts."

"Every day it will feel a little better," Jackie encourages. "I know it doesn't feel like it right now, but trust me. Your body, though—you were in a car accident, and you're going to be sore just from that. Today and tomorrow will probably be the worst. We'll stay on top of your pain meds, but the key is to get up and get moving. The longer you stay in this bed, the longer it's going to take to heal. Definitely don't assume you can run a marathon tomorrow, but slow baby steps around this room and the halls will get you home quicker."

"Got it." I want to get the hell out of here as fast as possible.

Harper grabs a blanket from a dresser and covers my lower half with it while Jackie pulls up my hospital gown. It's stained with blood, and I gasp at what I see. I immediately close my eyes.

"It's not that bad, Eva," my mom says, though her voice cracks a little as she speaks.

"Are we looking at the same thing?!" I exclaim.

"Look here, honey," Jackie calmly tells me. I open my eyes to see where she's pointing. "The bruising you see is all from the seatbelt. That'll go away over time. The incision may look all gruesome right now under those bandages, but it'll heal, too. You'll have a scar, but our scars make us unique, right?"

I raise my eyebrow up at her.

"Food. Let's get food in you," she suggests. "Some extremely nutritious soup, and if you eat that, I'll get you a popsicle as a treat

29

when we're done," she winks.

Eating is torture. I'm definitely not hungry, but I need something in my stomach to mix with all the drugs that have been pumped into my body. I keep telling myself one more bite, but I feel so hungover that each bite has to be forced down. All I want to do is go back to sleep, but Jackie keeps pushing me harder, and I'll be damned if she thinks I'm weak.

"Let's try to walk to the bathroom," she says, finally pushing the tray of food away. "Now that your catheter is out, we need to see if we can tackle this small walk. If not, we'll get you a bedpan to use until you're ready."

A *bedpan*? "I'm not using a goddamn bedpan," I grumble. "Let's do this, and then bring Bodhi back in. I want Bodhi back."

I see she and my mom exchange a motherly look. "Attached at the hip, those two," Jackie says to her. "Alright, Harper here will help get your legs out of bed. And I'm going to support your upper body. Once your feet hit the ground, you might feel dizzy. That's totally normal. We'll make sure you're okay before we start moving. This pillow right here," she hands it to me, "holding it to your stomach might actually help."

"Dizzy, pillow to the stomach, got it." I feel my legs being moved to the side of the bed. *Fuck*, it hurts. My stomach doesn't like this at all. I grab the sheets and close my eyes, trying to use my own willpower to make the pain stop.

"We can try again later," Jackie suggests.

"No!" I growl. "Get me out of this bed. I can handle it."

"Thatta girl," Jackie grins.

I know it's going to hurt, but I know this pain won't last forever. And the sooner I get out of this bed and get to the bathroom, the sooner I can get back in this bed and Bodhi can come in. I know the more I do this, the faster I can get back home and put this horrific experience behind me. So, I do it. I silently cry as I shuffle my way to the bathroom, with three grown women guiding my every step.

My stomach muscles burn with each and every movement. They literally feel like they're on fire, but I do it. I make it to the bathroom. I manage to sit down on the toilet and pee, my mom standing in front of me wiping away my tears, and making sure my

IV cords don't get tangled up with each other. I brush my teeth without looking at myself in the mirror, but when I'm done, I take a deep breath and look up. I can't avoid myself forever. I *don't* manage to keep it together when I see myself for the first time. My forehead is covered in colorful bruises, wrapping around the stitches that disappear into my hairline. My face is pale with dark circles under my eyes, and my hair is matted down with dried blood.

I look over at my mom. "*Please,*" I beg her as I start to cry. "Please at least get the blood out of my hair."

Jackie hears this. "Right away, honey."

My hair gets washed by my two nurses as I sit on a shower chair in the middle of the bathroom, holding the pillow to my stomach the whole time. They use the sink and plastic hospital bins, and very carefully wash away the hard blood, all while avoiding the stitches at the top of my forehead.

"Tomorrow," Jackie caresses my hand. "Tomorrow we'll try an actual shower. Now, let's get you back in bed and get you that popsicle."

It feels good to be back in bed. I'm so goddamn tired, and I just want something to take away this gnawing pain, but I also want Bodhi. I need him. I don't feel calm unless he's next to me.

"Bodhi?" I say his name out loud, reminding everyone in my room that I was promised he'd come back in an hour.

"Right here," I hear him say.

I look over to the door. He's standing in the doorframe, not wearing the hospital scrubs anymore. He's in shorts and a t-shirt, and his curls are like a mop on the top of his head. I love his hair so much. It was literally the first thing I noticed about him when he answered his front door five years ago. They look damp, like he just took a shower and they haven't fully dried yet. He's too far away from me though, and I need him closer.

"You look great, Eva."

I reach my hand out to him and he walks over, climbing in right next to me.

"Here's your treat," Jackie smiles, handing me an orange popsicle I already know I'm not going to eat. "Harper's going to get you some meds. Great job, honey. For real, you did more in this

31

hour than most adults do in three days. I'll see you later tonight, okay? Every few hours, let your nurses help you get up and move a little. Tell Harper if you need anything at all."

"Thanks," I say to her. "I will." I then turn back to Bodhi, handing him the popsicle. "I just peed in front of my mom, and had two strangers wash my hair."

I hear my mom laugh under her breath. "I'm going to go talk to your dad. I'm really proud of you, Eva. I know that wasn't easy."

"Definitely wasn't."

A small smile appears on her tired face. "You have a crowd of people out there. Do you want me to send them home? Tell them to come back tomorrow? They'll all understand."

"No ..." I say slowly. I'm so tired, and I know once the medicine Harper gives me kicks in, I'm going to be out of it for a few hours. "Send them in. But I'm not going to last long."

My mom nods her head and walks out of the room.

"I won't let them stay long," Bodhi promises me, placing a kiss on my cheek. He tosses the popsicle into an empty cup behind him.

"But you stay," I reply, grabbing onto his t-shirt. "Don't leave."

"I'm not going anywhere."

A few minutes later, everyone slowly walks in together in a heap of exhausted looking bodies. Calvin, Porter, Luna, Coop and Beck. They're quiet at first. Their silent presence makes me feel anxious, like I'm an animal behind a cage at the zoo and they're expecting me to do some sort of trick in front of them. Someone needs to talk before this gets any more uncomfortable than it already is.

"Hey," I finally say. "I don't bite."

They all nervously laugh. Luna's the first to walk over to my bed. She places a kiss right on the side of my forehead. "You scared the shit out of me, Eva."

"I think I might have scared the shit out of everyone."

She laughs and grabs onto my fingers that are hanging out of my cast. She brings her mouth to my ear. "You're my only real friend in this crazy screwed up world. No more of this, okay? No more thinking I've lost you."

"No more," I agree.

She continues with, "When you get out of here, I'm holding you

32

to that sleepover and double date."

"Oh yeah?" I grin, my eyes look toward Coop and then back to her. "Double date? Am I sensing a love connection here?"

"Twenty-four hours later, and I haven't kicked him to the curb yet. No promises, but nothing brings people together quicker than a good trauma, right?"

I can't help but laugh. "Glad I could get things moving for you two."

She smiles in return. "I love you, Eva."

"I love you too, Luna."

She backs up and goes to stand by Coop. He looks down at her hand, and slowly brings it into his own. My heart quickly flutters. Am I surprised? No, not at all, and it's by far the best thing I've seen all day.

"So, Eva ..." Coop says. "When you get out of here, you think maybe we don't do shit for the rest of the summer? I don't think anyone will complain if all we do is float around in a pool and eat delicious food cooked by Calvin for the next two months."

"That sounds amazing," I agree, although I truly don't believe it'll ever happen. If there's anything I've learned over these last couple weeks it's that life can never be that simple.

"You make me a list, Eva," Calvin genuinely smiles. "I'll cook whatever you want, all summer long."

"I might hold you to that."

"And if she doesn't," Coop adds, "*we* all will."

Calvin lets out a little laugh, and then moves closer to me as his face becomes more serious. "Eva, I just want to—"

"Don't," I quickly say. "Please." I'm not ready for Calvin to tell me how sorry he is for what happened. I don't know if mentally I can hear that right now. I don't know if I can handle hearing him try to take the blame, when I secretly know I was the one who caused all of this. I was the one who caused the crash. "I know what you want to say, and it's not necessary. None of it was your fault. Please don't apologize. Okay?"

He quickly nods his head.

Harper returns, ready to give me the pain medicine I was promised. "This will make you a little sleepy," she warns me, as she

33

taps the syringe and inserts it into my IV.

"We'll leave," Beck says. "Let you sleep, but heal up quick. Things feel weird without you and Bodhi around. It's too quiet ..."

"Will do," I promise. They all start to head out, including Harper, but Porter lingers. He hasn't said one word since he came into my room. He's looking painfully between me and the door.

"Porter," I say his name softly. "Your house?"

"Gone."

"Your dad?"

"No idea."

I can tell there's more he wants to say. He's not leaving because he wants to talk to me, alone.

Bodhi suddenly gives me a quick kiss on my forehead. "I'm going to walk the guys out. I'll be right back, okay?"

I nod in agreement and he gets up, raising his eyebrow at Porter in warning, yet closing the door behind him and leaving us alone together in my room.

"I'm so fucking sorry, Eva," Porter says right away, walking closer to me. "This is all my fault."

"No, it's not. Your dad, what your dad did—and my dad—you weren't involved with any of that."

"I knew my dad was an asshole. And I didn't do anything about it. For years. I just let him get away with everything."

"Where do you think he is?"

"I don't care. He wasn't in the house though, at least that's what I was told today. He's mysteriously gone missing. Coincidence, right? We're going to eventually find out there's more to this."

"I know. Where are you staying? Friends?"

"Calvin's," he laughs under his breath. "Believe it or not. Calvin said I could stay with him as long as I need to."

"You should. He's a good guy."

"I can tell ... but I think it's time I leave Flagler. I think I've decided to go live with my mom. I actually decided that even before everything that happened last night."

"In Charleston?" I ask him, surprised. "You're going to spend your senior year in Charleston? With the mom who walked out on you and your dad when you were little?"

"That's what I was always told, but I don't think it's what actually happened."

"What do you mean?"

He shrugs his shoulders. "I don't know. I never heard her side of the story because my dad never gave her the chance. It's the right thing to do. I can't stay here after everything he's done—and you—"

"You're leaving because of me?"

"No," he sighs. "But why should I stay? Besides, I have a little brother and a little sister I know nothing about."

Little sister. As soon as these words leave Porter's mouth, my mind jumps back to Luke. Right before I crashed us into the trees, Luke told me Bodhi has a little sister. I completely forgot about it, and I need to tell Bodhi right away. What else from last night have I forgotten?

"Promise me you'll at least stay until I get out of here?"

He looks confused. "After everything I put you through—"

"*Stay.* Until I get out of here."

"I will," he promises, then he slowly takes my hand, afraid to touch me for numerous different reasons. "I really am sorry, Eva. For everything. I'll never forgive myself for it being like this between you and me. It shouldn't be like this, and I know that's all my fault." He then walks out the door without saying anything else.

Bodhi comes back in moments later. The pain medicine is starting to overtake my body and mind, forcing emotions I had swallowed down all day to rapidly reach the surface. I cover my face with my casted arm, as my eyes fill up with regretful tears. Angry at myself for allowing this sudden breakdown. Angry at myself for everything I've done. Angry at myself for allowing Porter Channing to be the match that lit my internal bottle of turmoil on fire.

I know Bodhi is standing at the side of my bed, unsure how to console me at the moment when usually he's an expert at it. He climbs back in and tucks my hair behind my ear, before kissing my forehead. He then slowly pulls my arm away from my face.

I let out one last sob, and then firmly bite down on my lip, forcing this breakdown to an abrupt halt. I turn my face to him. "I love you," is the first thing I say. I need to make sure he knows this.

"I know you do, and I love you," he whispers back.

"But I'm a horrible person—"

"No, you're not. Don't make yourself the bad guy here, babe. He left bruises on you, remember that."

If only he knew this emotional outburst isn't just because of Porter. "I know he did—"

"I told the guys to be nice to him. I know he's having a hard time with all of this."

"Will life ever feel normal?"

"Define normal?"

Sleep is getting ready to take over. I feel myself fading. "Thank you for being the one person I can always trust. For loving me."

"Always, Eva."

"I have to tell you something—something that happened when I was in the pickup truck with Luke—"

"No," he immediately says. "Please, let's not talk about any of that until you're home."

"Just one thing, Bodhi. It's important—"

"It can wait," he interrupts me.

"No, it can't. It can't wait. I need you to know this now, so that you have time to process it, so that when I get home, we can start figuring it out. If you want to figure it out ... but I think you're going to want to. *I* want to figure it out."

"Sounds mysterious," Bodhi grins. "And exactly the opposite of what Coop suggested we do all summer."

I feel my eyes wanting to close. "Floating around in a pool all summer long is fucking boring and you know it."

Bodhi laughs. "Okay, Eva. What's so important you need to tell me right this very second as you're lying in a hospital bed less than twenty-four hours after surgery?"

I lean in and kiss his lips, and then close my eyes and whisper just as I fall back into the world of nothingness, "Bodhi, you have a little sister."

chapter five

Bodhi – four days later

W hen I get home, where will you be every night?" Eva asks, snuggling her head under my neck. "I don't want you sleeping at Coop's or Calvin's. I want you with me."

Eva's been in the hospital for five days now, and today she's finally being discharged. It's been a *long* five days. I can tell she officially has a love-hate relationship with her nurse, Jackie. She's like her own personal hard ass grandma who knows exactly how far to push before Eva ends up swearing at her under her breath. All the tough love has helped, though. Eva can get out of bed by herself. She can use the bathroom by herself. She can even take a shower and get dressed by herself. Everything is done *very* slowly, but it's amazing to see her up and moving around. I've spent all five days here. I haven't left once. I promised Eva I wouldn't leave, so I haven't, but I'm definitely ready to get the hell out of here.

"I haven't crossed that bridge yet with your parents. Or with Ma and Pop, for that matter. You know exactly where I want to be," I say, kissing the top of her head.

"They don't care where you sleep, right? Ma and Pop?"

"Nah. I think they already assume I'll be with you. Have *you* talked to your parents about what will happen when you get home?"

"No. I'm hoping they just assume you'll be with me, too."

The door suddenly flings open, and Jackie appears on the other side with a stack of papers in her hands. "My two favorite lovebirds!" she exclaims. "I'm going to miss seeing your adorable faces every day."

"Aww. Jackie, we'll miss you, too," Eva declares. "But please don't take it personally when I say I hope I never see you in this hospital again."

She laughs. "Not at all. I actually hope to never see any of my patients again, but you two, I'm gonna miss ya something fierce, that's for sure. I'm going to go over all the discharge paperwork with your parents in a few minutes, but I wanted to pop in and go over one quick bit with just the two of you—to save you some embarrassment. I had teenagers once. I know how this works."

"Oh boy. What'd we do, Jackie?" I question her humorously.

"It's not what you did, but what you *won't* be doing," she smirks. "You see that cast on your arm, Eva?"

Eva looks down at it. "Yeah?"

"When that cast comes off, that's when the two of you will know it's okay to have sex again. And don't try to pretend you both are innocent virgins. No need for lies."

I can feel my face instantly turn red.

"That's like five or so *weeks* from now ..." Eva miserably sighs.

"Exactly," Jackie nods her head. "Just because you're feeling a little better, and you'll continue to feel better every day from here on out, does *not* mean your stomach is up for anything more strenuous than walking. Maybe in a few weeks you can get a little cozier than just a kiss on the cheek, but no sex. You need to give yourself six weeks to heal, so five or so weeks from now."

"Got it," I quickly chime in. I can feel the fire on my face. This is worse than getting lectured by Dolly. The subject needs to change right away, before I combust into flames.

"Yeah?" Jackie raises her eyebrow at us. "I don't want to see you two back here, unless you're coming to visit your favorite nurse."

"Got it," Eva groans.

"Good. Now that that's over, I'll go find your parents and let's get you both out of here." She goes to leave the room but suddenly turns back around. "Oh, one more thing ... I would *love* to be invited to your wedding one day, when that happens. Okay?"

I start laughing. "Graham said the same thing."

"Oh yeah?" she smiles. "That boy knows true love when he sees it," she declares, and then she walks out.

"Graham is ...?" Eva questions.

"Graham is the paramedic who saved you, and he's also Jackie and Dr. Walker's son."

"Small world," Eva says, and then she grins. "Bodhi, are you planning our wedding behind my back? I wasn't aware we were getting married anytime soon."

I wrap my arms around her. "One day. One day, for sure."

WE WALK INTO Eva's house with her parents about an hour later. The first people we see are Rowan and Miles. I haven't seen them in a week and I was fully prepared for them to run up to me as soon as we walked in. But instead, they actually run in the opposite direction, hiding behind Calvin as soon as their eyes land on Eva.

"They're scared of me," she mutters.

"Boys," Mr. Calloway calls out to them. His intimidating voice echoes in the kitchen. "You want to come say hi to Eva?"

Neither one of them move or acknowledge him.

I give Eva's hand a kiss and walk over to where they are, squatting down to their level. "Hey. Your mom and dad, they told you that Eva got hurt, right?"

They both nod their heads.

"She was crushed in a truck," Miles whispers.

I can't help but grin at his innocence. "The truck hit a tree, and it hurt her when that happened. But how she looks right now," I point to her, and they both peek around Calvin, "it's not going to be like that forever. Pretty soon she'll look exactly like the old Eva."

They both nod their heads again.

"Do me a favor?" I continue. "Go over there and give her a hug, because she *really* missed you both. But when you do, just hug her legs. Her stomach got hurt and it doesn't feel too good right now."

"Is she going to throw up?" Rowan quickly asks me.

"Is she going to have gross poops?" Miles adds.

I shake my head and try not to laugh. "Definitely not. You just can't touch her stomach right now, okay?"

They slowly move from behind Calvin and over to Eva, who's using the counter to support herself. She needs to get in bed and rest. This is the longest she's been out of bed since the accident.

"Eva ...?" Rowan looks up at her forehead. "Are you going to look like Harry Potter now?"

39

"Harry Potter is much cooler than I am," she tells him.

"Why don't you two go play, and let Eva rest?" Mrs. Calloway suggests. "The more Eva naps, the faster she's going to get better."

"Will you come play with us, Bodhi?" Rowan tugs on my shorts.

I ruffle his hair. "I think my friends are coming over for dinner, the ones who played soccer with you and took you kayaking."

"*Yes!*" Miles says under his breath.

"How about we play with you guys then? I want to help Eva get upstairs and make sure she doesn't need anything."

Rowan nods his head, grabbing Miles' hand as they both run out of the kitchen.

As soon as they're gone, Mr. Calloway asks with a shocked look on his tired face, "Rowan talks to you?"

"Rowan and I are pals," I bluntly confirm to him. "Miles, too."

"Eva," Calvin walks over to her and gently gives her a hug. "It's great to have you back home. I'm going to leave now, give you a chance to rest, but I'll be back over later with dinner for everyone." He gives her a kiss on the top of her head.

"Thanks, Calvin," she smiles, though she suddenly looks sad with his embrace, and I can't figure out why.

It's just the four of us standing in the kitchen now. It's as awkward as hell. For one, Mrs. Calloway and Mr. Calloway still aren't talking to each other. I'm waiting for an explosive fight to happen at some point. I hope Eva and I are not in the same room with them when it finally happens. The awkwardness is increased by the fact that I'm not sure where to go from here. Obviously, I'm going to help Eva get upstairs, and I'm going to lie right next to her as she falls asleep, as we both fall asleep. I've never been this exhausted. But tonight, are they seriously going to kick me out?

"Can we go upstairs?" Eva quietly asks me.

I glance at Mrs. Calloway to make sure this is okay.

She gives me a small nod. "I'm going to send your dad to the pharmacy to pick up your pain meds," she tells Eva. "You're due for another pill in about an hour. Every six hours for the next few days, and at some point, we need to set up an appointment with your regular doctor to get your stitches and staples out. They said in five days from now. I can call tomorrow—"

"I can call," Eva says softly. "I'll call. I need to call anyway ..." She stops mid-sentence and glances between her parents, turning red in the face.

I have no idea what she's talking about, but Mrs. Calloway seems to catch on as she replies with, "Sounds good."

"Do you need help getting upstairs?" her dad asks.

"Bodhi can help," she makes clear, and then she turns to me. "Can we go upstairs now?" she asks again, more forceful this time.

"Absolutely." She puts her good arm around my waist and I help guide her out of the kitchen and up the stairs. As soon as we get to her door, she stops outside of it. "What's wrong?"

"That last time I was in my room, I hid all the stuff we found at your house in a suitcase in my closet. I knew something awful was about to happen. I just had this feeling."

I let go of her waist so I can stand in front of her. She's crying. *Dammit.* I hate it when she cries. I kiss her tears. I kiss her lips. "What can I do, Eva?"

"Just stay with me," she pleads tearfully, grabbing onto my shirt. "Stay with me tonight. Please don't leave me."

"I won't," I promise her. "I'll talk to your mom."

She releases my shirt and makes her way over to her bed, climbing in carefully without my help. She then looks over at me, patting the spot next to her. I walk over, gently wrapping my arms around her body as I get in. She brings her head to my chest, and suddenly it feels like these last five days never happened.

"Hey, Eva?"

"Hmm?" she mutters.

"Downstairs. Your doctor, what was that about?" I curiously ask her.

She snickers a little under her breath, and then bluntly says, "It's been a year since I got my IUD put in. Sexually active girls should get checked out once a year by their doctor. Not that I'll be sexually active anytime soon ..."

"Five weeks will go by fast."

"Fuck no, it won't."

Her boldness makes me smile. "Babe," I look down at her, "everything that's happened to you—do you really think sex is what

41

we should be worried about right now?"

"No, I don't. It's just that this is another thing about my life that I don't have any control over. That's all."

I didn't think about it like that. "I'm sorry. I don't know what else to say. This all just sucks."

She doesn't respond. She just lies on my chest, running her fingers up and down my arm.

"Eva?"

"Bodhi?"

"I'm so happy you're home."

"Me, too," she replies, she then looks up at me. "Now that I'm home, can we please talk about—"

"No," I interrupt her.

I know what she's going to say. She wants to talk about my little sister. When she told me I had a little sister and then immediately fell asleep, I spent hours lying there thinking about what she had said. It was just too much. My mom, dead. My dad, dead. Eva, almost dead. And now, a little sister somewhere out there. When she woke up and wanted to talk about her, I told her not now. That we would discuss this all once she was home and not to mention it to anyone else. She *really* held me to my word.

"Bodhi. You have a little sister somewhere in this world. Don't you want to find her? Be a part of her life?"

"No," I instantly say. "And we are *not* bringing this up to anyone right now."

"I don't believe you. I know you want to find her."

I hate that she knows what I'm actually thinking. "Okay, so maybe I'm a little curious. But I don't know anything about her. Not one thing. What's her name? How old is she? Where does she live?"

"Skyla. She's eight, and she lives not too far from here, whatever that might mean."

I look down at her and raise my eyebrows.

"You said you didn't want to talk about her until I was home," she reminds me.

"Touché. Let's leave it at that for today, though, and we'll revisit this conversation tomorrow, all right?"

"I suppose," she yawns. "What about Owen, and your

grandparents—"

"We are definitely not talking about them right now."

"*Bodhi.* You can't just ignore them—"

"I can, and I will," I firmly tell her.

She stays silent this time. Her fingers even stop running along my arm. *Dammit.* She just got home from the hospital and here I am snapping at her. Since when do I snap at Eva?

"Eva, I'm sorry, but I can't talk to them right now. Not today, not tomorrow, maybe not even next week or a month from now. I need some time, okay? Just some time."

Her fingers start running along my arm again. "What is it that you need time *from?*"

I bring her off my chest. I carefully roll over her, not touching any part of her body. I bring my hands to either side of her head, while my legs straddle hers. I want her to see my face. I want to see her eyes as I tell her this. "Eva Calloway, the moment those three showed up in front of me, you almost died in front of me. Every *single* time I think about them, I think about that moment when I almost lost you. It haunts me, Eva, and I associate them with you almost dying. I need time for those awful memories to fade a little, before I look at the three of them again."

I watch a couple tears fall down her cheeks. "I'm sorry, Bodhi," she whispers.

"You have *nothing* to be sorry about."

"Did you really think I was going to die?"

I'm not sure if she's aware of what happened in that ambulance. We haven't talked about it all yet, and I'm pretty certain no one brought it up the few random times I wasn't in her hospital room with her. There's no time like the present, though, and I don't want this dark cloud she's not aware of hanging over me anymore.

"When you started throwing up all that blood, you passed out beforehand, and then you suffocated on it. Your heart ... it stopped. You didn't have a pulse. You *did* die in front of me."

Her face is shocked. She didn't know this, it's obvious she had no idea. She starts crying harder and tightly closes her eyes.

"No, no, no," I say quickly. "Don't start crying. Stop, Eva. Stop crying. It will hurt your stomach. Stop," I say again. "It wasn't long.

43

Graham, he was quick and I watched you come back—you came back. That's *all* that matters."

Her eyes pop back open and she brings her hand to my hair, pulling me down until my lips almost hit hers. But I hesitate.

"Kiss me, Bodhi," she demands, confused.

"I don't want to hurt you."

Her eyes narrow and her mouth forms a frown. "Last time I checked, my lips weren't broken, and my mouth sure as hell isn't hurt. I want you to kiss me. To *really* kiss me, right now," she demands again. "You aren't going to hurt me."

"No, I won't," I agree, and then I cautiously bring my lips to hers.

This is the first real kiss we've shared since before the accident. I hover over her like my body is lava and if I touch her, I'm going to burn her. I make sure my forehead stays off hers. I make sure my hand stays away from her cast. I make sure the only part of my body that's touching her is my lips. No matter how awkward this might look, this kiss is absolutely glorious. My tongue slowly moves inside her mouth, and she pulls me down harder as our kiss deepens. Her fingers wrap around my hair and she tugs on it. Every part of my body feels chills when she does this.

I reluctantly pull my lips away and stare down at her face.

"See?" she smirks. "Not hurt."

"No, you're perfect, absolutely perfect, and I could just stare at your beautiful face all day."

"My beautiful bruised face and zipper forehead?"

"Those bruises will disappear," I remind her. "And the stitches will come out soon." She looks away from me, and I see her eyes gloss over again. "Eva? What's wrong?"

She turns back, biting her lip before saying, "I'm just sorry for everything I put you through that night."

"Everything you put *me* through?"

"I can't imagine what you were thinking," she whispers. "What you were feeling. Because I know what I would have been thinking and feeling, and I hate knowing you had to go through that."

"It's going to take me a little while to forget about what happened that night. I'm probably never going to be able to forget about it, to be honest. But every time I remember what happened, and every time I look over and see you next to me, I'll be reminded of how lucky I am that I get to continue loving you forever."

A few tears leave her eyes.

"Baby," I kiss her cheeks. "No more crying."

"These aren't sad tears."

I lean in and kiss her beautiful lips again. "What tears are they?"

"Happy ones, relieved ones, in love ones."

"*Those* tears, I'm okay with. You need to rest, Eva. Why don't you take a nap for a little while?"

"And what will you be doing while I do that?"

I move by body back to her side, gently wrapping my arms around her again. "Lying here, watching you sleep in my arms."

She lets out a long sigh. "Bodhi, can you promise me something?"

"Anything, Eva."

She points to us. "Promise me nothing will ever change this. No matter what. I see my mom and dad, and how they act toward each other. It's awful. I can't imagine us treating each other like that. No matter what happens today, tomorrow, fifty years from now, always hold me in your arms and watch me sleep, okay?"

I kiss the side of her head. "Always."

She snuggles into my neck and immediately dozes off. I'm hypnotized as she sleeps on my chest. Listening to her breathe, watching her chest rise up and down, the warmth of her body on mine. There are no words to describe how this feels. How it feels to fall into this trance while she sleeps so peacefully in my arms.

chapter six

Bodhi

Eva suddenly stirs just a short while later. "Bodhi, can you go see if my dad is back with my pain meds?"

"Absolutely." I walk out of her bedroom and make my way to the stairs, immediately hearing voices as I come down the first steps.

"How long is it going to be like this?" I hear Mr. Calloway ask.

"Like what, Brayden?" Mrs. Calloway responds.

"*This,*" he says again. "You hating me, Eva wanting nothing to do with me. Hell, the boys won't even talk to me right now."

"After what you did to Eva, you think she's just going to forget everything? I'm sure as hell not going to forget everything."

"I want to explain, but no one wants to hear what I have to say!" he exclaims. "I brought them back here to fix everything, but Bodhi won't even meet with them—"

"Leave him alone," Mrs. Calloway harshly demands. "He has been through hell."

I sit on the steps and hear Mr. Calloway sigh. "One day, everyone will realize everything I did was to protect him, and to keep Eva safe," he then says.

"Safe from what, Brayden?" growls Mrs. Calloway. "She was lost for three years because of what *you* did to keep her safe!"

"I had to keep them apart—"

"Bullshit!" Mrs. Calloway hisses under her breath.

"Audrey, if Henry knew—"

"Henry!" she cries out. "This is all about him, isn't it?! Where is he, Brayden?! His house burned down, and he abandoned his son! You can't tell me you don't know where the hell he is!"

"I don't."

"Add that to the list of lies you've told me," she spits out.

"I don't, Audrey. For real, I have no idea where Henry is, nor do I care—"

She starts laughing. "You've been his sidekick for over a decade or longer, apparently—and you expect me to believe you suddenly don't care anymore?"

"I never cared," is his answer.

"Oh, but you cared enough to force Eva to date Porter? And you cared enough to take money from Henry all these years?" she questions. "Money that wasn't his? Money he never should have taken from Lenora?"

"Who told you that?" Mr. Calloway asks her quietly.

"Luke told them all!" she cries out. "While he was here, threatening five teenagers, and then kidnapping our daughter and almost killing her! Porter told Calvin. Calvin told me."

I hear a chair being pulled out. "I can explain—"

"How much Brayden? How much did you get from *all* that money Lenora let Henry have? How much money that doesn't belong to us, is in our bank account right now?"

"Not a penny."

"Bullshit!"

"Not a penny, Audrey," he repeats. "I told you, everything I did was to protect them. To protect Bodhi. I wouldn't take money that was theirs, money that was Lenora's and Bodhi's."

"What the hell do you mean by that?!"

"I don't work for Henry," he says quietly. "He doesn't own a company. He has his own investments, and lives off the profits of those and the interest from an inheritance he never should have gotten. He does other stuff, too, stuff that eventually he's going to go to jail for. Stuff that I have *never* been involved in. Henry thinks that I work for him. He thinks I'm his sidekick, like you said, doing all the shit he doesn't want to do himself. But it's not how it seems."

"What about that year?" she harshly responds. "The year Eva and I lived with Calvin and Rose? The year you almost went to jail? Did Henry not swoop in and save the day?"

"No," I hear Mr. Calloway answer. "I can explain that year, everything that happened. I told you that because it was safer than

47

telling you—"

"Safer?!" she exclaims in a loud whisper. "Who do you work for, Brayden?" she bluntly asks. "You have a paycheck that comes in every other week. Where is that money coming from if you don't work for Henry?"

"I can explain, and I will, just let me—"

"Henry *never* gave you money from Lenora's inheritance?" she interrupts him.

I grab onto the railing, waiting to see what he says.

"He did," responds Mr. Calloway. "And every month when that money would appear in my account, I put it right back where it belonged."

"Which was where?"

"Back to them. To Lenora and Bodhi."

I hear myself gasp and I quickly cover my mouth.

"I was never going to take her money for bringing them back," he tells her. "Lenora knew this. I told her this away from Henry the very first chance I could. Henry knew who she was, he knew before we went to the Bahamas. There's so much to that story that hasn't been explained yet. I met Henry months before that trip, and not by chance; it was planned," he rambles. "Lenora set up a bank account, an account she said would be just for Bodhi, for his future. And as soon as Paul Channing died, I started transferring my share over to this account."

"How much did Henry get?" she carefully questions. "How much money did he get that was never supposed to be his?"

"A little over a hundred million."

I hear Mrs. Calloway gasp. "Paul Channing had a hundred million dollars stashed away when he died?!"

"Paul Channing was a Rialson. His mom was Rebecca Rialson, and the Rialson family were the wealthiest people in Florida for probably over a hundred years. It was family money, money passed down generation after generation."

"And Lenora was ...?"

"His cousin. The niece of Rebecca Rialson."

"And Henry fits into this family *how*?"

"Paul's dad. Chip Channing is a distant relative of Henry's. But that's not why Henry got all that money. That's just what he told people. There's so much more to that story and we all need to sit down and talk about it. All of us, together. Audrey," he softly says her name. "Lenora, Phoebe, she was *extremely* wealthy, even without the inheritance. She didn't need it. She hid her wealth from everyone, and she let Henry have the inheritance because she knew that was the only way to keep Bodhi safe from him, from Henry *and* Luke. Me giving the money back to Bodhi was always the plan."

"You and Lenora ..." she hesitantly says. "Were you ...?"

I hold my breath. If he tells her that he and my mom ...

"No!" he immediately responds. "Absolutely not! Why would you even think that? I saw her, yes, but it was nothing like that."

"I saw her, too," Mrs. Calloway confesses in a sharp tone. "I was friends with Lenora for the last five years."

"You and *Lenora*?" he asks, shocked.

"Yes," she replies. "I followed Eva when she was twelve. Lenora was my friend, and she *had* to have known I was married to you, the man who rescued her and the man who was secretly depositing money into her bank account for over a decade."

"Audrey, you might have been friends with Lenora, but you weren't friends with Phoebe. She led two different lives, and we all need to sit down and talk about everything—"

"Do you see what this has done to *us*?" she cries out under her breath. "Keeping all these secrets all these years? Keeping Eva away from Bodhi because you were afraid of what Henry would do?"

"I had to. I had to keep them apart, to keep them both safe from shit neither one of them should have to deal with—"

"And now? Are you going to keep them apart now?" she asks him. "Because it's not going to happen. That boy you rescued fifteen years ago, he's upstairs with our daughter right this very second, and he is the *only* one who's going to be able to help her get through this mess, this mess that could have been avoided. She almost *died*, Brayden. Eva almost died."

"You don't think I realize that?"

"I honestly don't know where to go from here," she says to him. "I know there are a hundred things you're not telling me, and until I know for certain that our daughter is happy and healthy again, I don't give a shit about any of it. But the one thing I'm going to make absolutely clear is that if you say or do anything to upset Eva or Bodhi, our marriage will be over."

"He's a good kid," Mr. Calloway says. "I know that—"

"He's not a kid. And neither is Eva. In ten months, she's legally an adult, and she and Bodhi, they're so madly in love with each other. He's not going anywhere. He's a part of this family, and the sooner you realize that, the sooner you start treating him like he is, the sooner Eva will start talking to you again."

I've heard enough. I quietly tiptoe back up the few stairs I had already walked down, then loudly run down the entire flight, making sure to make as much noise as possible. They're both looking at me as soon I turn into the kitchen.

"Bodhi," Mrs. Calloway instantly says. "Eva okay?"

"She is. She's wondering if her meds have gotten picked up?"

Mr. Calloway stands up from his chair and walks to the counter, grabbing a pill bottle and handing it out to me.

"Thanks," I say to him. I then stand there for a moment, looking between the two of them, nervous as hell.

"Are *you* okay, Bodhi?" Mrs. Calloway asks me carefully.

I nod my head. "I appreciate you both letting me stay with Eva, in the hospital and such, but now that she's back home ... I don't want to overstep, but I definitely don't want to leave her ..."

Mrs. Calloway smiles. "Bodhi, we're not kicking you out."

"Tonight?" I question quickly.

She touches my shoulder. "If she wants you to stay tonight, and *you* want to stay tonight, then you stay tonight. And if she wants you to stay tomorrow night and the night after that, and that's what *you* want, I'm okay with that, too."

I turn to Mr. Calloway. He looks taken aback that I would actually turn to him for his permission. "I'm okay with that as well," he immediately says.

"Thanks," I say to them both. "I think—I think once she's better, I might move in with Calvin for a while."

Mrs. Calloway smiles. "I think that's a wonderful idea, Bodhi."

"I'm going to go give her one of these," I hold up the pills. "Thanks for not kicking me out." I then turn to head out of the kitchen, but I pause. I need to know. It's going to eat away at me until I do. "My trust fund," I say out loud, my back to Mr. Calloway. "I have a *very* large trust fund. How much of that money is from you?" I ask him.

I hear him take in a deep breath. "I—I don't know how much is in there, or if your mom put any extra in there—"

"Just tell me," I interrupt him. "How much did *you* put in there?"

"The last deposit I made a little while ago brought my share to over twenty-eight million."

I hear Mrs. Calloway gasp. Something gets knocked over and loudly clatters on the floor. I hide my own shock by biting down on my tongue. I can taste the metallic blood in my mouth instantly. With interest that has probably accumulated, *all* of the money in my trust fund was money Brayden Calloway gave back to my mom.

I turn to look at him. "I bet you never thought for even a second that this money, these millions you were secretly giving back to my mom all these years, would eventually be used by me and *your* daughter, when we start our lives together, did you?" And then I turn and walk out.

chapter seven

Eva – roughly two weeks later

Things are slowly getting back to normal, as normal as they can. I'm starting not only to look like myself again, but feel like myself again. The bruises have disappeared and my stitches are out of my forehead. That scar is impressively well-hidden. My staples are out of my stomach, too, but *that* scar is a bit more noticeable. I find myself not looking at it whenever I get undressed or shower. A scar on my leg, a scar on my head, and a scar on my stomach. All these battle wounds on my seventeen-year-old body that shouldn't be there.

Bodhi was the one who took me to get my stitches and staples out. He sat in the waiting room while my doctor slowly removed them—my doctor, trying to make small talk at the same time. I was just trying not to pass out as I watched each staple get pulled from my stomach. She then checked to make sure my IUD was still in the right spot, and told me to have a good summer, as if these wounds on my body meant absolutely nothing. I left that appointment in a bad mood, and it took until later that night when I was lying in my bed with Bodhi, before he brought it up.

"Everything okay?" he asked me, running his fingers through my hair. "You've been really quiet today."

I was wearing one of his t-shirts. They're huge on me and fall down right to my mid-thigh whenever I stand up, but it's all I sleep in now. Wearing his t-shirts as I sleep, smelling like him whenever I take them off, it's like my own form of a security blanket.

I slowly pulled his t-shirt up past my thighs, past my panties, and right to above my fresh scar that was still healing. He didn't make a sound. I expected at least a gasp or something, but nothing left his lips even though he was clearly staring at it.

"I feel like a freak," I whispered to him. "And anytime I wear a bikini, or anytime you and I—I'll feel like a freak."

He sat up, bringing his fingers right to my stomach and drawing a circle around my scar. He then bent down and softly kissed the skin right above it. "Every time I see this, I'll be thankful for it, because this scar is the only reason I can do this as often as I want." He then leaned in and gave me a kiss on my lips.

I try to remind myself of what he said, every time I feel like I'm falling into that dark tunnel I had been in before Bodhi came back into my life. I'm trying *really* hard not to let that happen. My body, it's feeling so much better now. Sometimes I have to remind myself to slow down, to rest, not to overdo it. But my mind, it's a constant struggle not to let certain thoughts, certain actions, throw me back into that awful, depressing world I was in before.

I have nightmares about the accident every night. Ever since I weaned myself off the pain meds that would knock me out, I wake up in a cold sweat, clinging to Bodhi as he tries to calm me down. I keep thinking he's going to leave. I'm scared that once I tell him *I* caused the accident, *I* was the reason his dad died, he's not going to look at me the same way anymore. Every night I have nightmares about this, and every night Bodhi reassures me everything is okay, and holds me in his arms until I fall back to sleep.

Currently, I'm in my bedroom by myself. Bodhi went surfing with the guys. He asked me over and over again if I would be okay if he left. I can honestly count on one hand how many times he's left me since I've been back home. I've loved every single second of him being this close, falling asleep with him, and waking up together every day, but I know it can't last forever. We're seventeen, and we still have our senior year of high school coming up soon. We can't keep pretending this is the new normal, when we're both internally aware that it can't be.

I think it's time to wean myself off my constant need to have Bodhi by my side. So, when he briefly mentioned the guys wanted to go surfing today, I literally pushed him out the door. He needs to do normal things with his friends without worrying that I'm going to get upset. Besides, today I'm actually leaving my house for something other than a doctor's visit. Today is Luna's birthday, and

I am *not* missing that.

"Are you sure?" Bodhi asked, lingering by my bedroom door.

I got up off my bed and walked over to him, wrapping my arms around his warm waist and looking up at his concerned eyes. "Things need to get back to how they were before. I'm really starting to feel better, and although I absolutely love having you with me all the time, your friends miss you. You have to come back here and get me later for Luna's dinner, right?"

"Yes," he replied, kissing my forehead.

"Well, then I'll see you in, like, six hours."

"This is the longest we'll be apart since this all happened."

I stood on my tiptoes and kissed his lips. "It's time. Time to put this behind us and be normal again. I want you to go surfing. I want you to go spend the day with Coop and Beck. I'll be fine, trust me."

"Okay. Tonight, after Luna's dinner, we come back here, though? Together?"

I was *not* ready to sleep without Bodhi. My heart started beating madly in my chest. "Do you think it's time we start sleeping on our own again?"

"I want to sleep next to you *every* night, Eva," he immediately replied. "But I also want you to get your normal back ..."

"Let's see how the dinner goes," I smiled at him, and then I leaned up again and gave him another kiss, before pushing him out the door.

I'm now in my closet, trying to find something to wear for Luna's birthday. Coop has planned this amazing dinner right on the beach. Tables, chairs, twinkling lights, and catered food. He's absolutely head over heels in love with Luna. It's adorable, yet so weird to watch. This is obnoxious Coop we're talking about. I didn't think it was possible for him to behave like this. Tonight, I'll also get to meet Kennedy Wallace, Beck's girlfriend. Her family is moving back to Flagler at the end of the month, and she's been staying with friends this last week as her parents pack up their old house.

"Need help?" I hear a voice from my closet door.

I spin around to see my mom standing there, watching me. She comes further in, grabbing a dark green dress I think I only wore once since it came home from a designer shop in Daytona last year.

54

"I like this one," she says, holding it out to me. "It makes your eyes pop."

"This one will do."

She takes a seat right on my closet floor and pats the spot next to her. I carefully sit down and lean my head on her shoulder.

"It's been what ... three weeks or so?" she asks me.

"Three weeks and two days. Not that I'm counting or anything."

She laughs. "You look amazing, but how are you *really* doing, Eva?" she then gently asks.

I wait a moment before responding. "Some days I think I'm okay, some days my mind doesn't want to turn off."

"Do you think maybe talking to someone about everything would help with that?"

I shake my head. "I don't want to talk to anyone. I just want to forget it all."

"I don't think that's possible," she quickly tells me. "As much as you want to just forget it all, you're not going to be able to. You and Bodhi both. What about his grandparents—"

"He doesn't want to talk to them. I tried."

"He will. When he's ready."

"I think he's scared," I say in almost a whisper.

"Scared?"

"Lenora told him they both died, his grandparents. It's just another lie that he's uncovered. I think he's scared to hear what they're going to say."

My mom leans her head back on my closet wall. "He doesn't want Lenora to be anything less than the perfect mom she always was to him."

"Is there more? Do you know more that you haven't told us yet?"

She shakes her head. "I don't. I promise, and if I did, I would tell you both. She never even told me about your dad and the trust fund money—"

"Wait, wait, wait. *What*?!"

Her face turns red. "Bodhi didn't tell you? *Shit.* Don't get mad at Bodhi. I'm sure he just didn't want to upset you right now—"

"Didn't tell me *what*?"

"His trust fund, the money in his trust fund, it was money your dad got from Henry. The inheritance money. Whenever Henry gave him money, he put it right into Bodhi's trust fund account."

I can't believe what I'm hearing. "Dad didn't keep any of it?"

"None of it," she responds. "It's all in Bodhi's trust fund."

"He didn't tell me," I sigh, shocked. "Why didn't he tell me?"

"Honey, he loves you too much to see you upset right now."

"What about you? How do you feel about this? I mean, it's one thing that dad lied to you all this time, but Lenora lied to you, too."

My mom starts twirling the ends of my hair around her fingers. "I knew she had secrets. I knew there were things she didn't feel comfortable telling me. Can I be honest with you?"

"Of course."

"I lost one of my closest friends, and I miss her every day, but I'm starting to realize I didn't even know her."

"Welcome to the club," I grin. "Bodhi ... every time we hear something else—I'm waiting for him to breakdown."

My mom brushes my hair away from my eyes. "You two. It shouldn't be this hard for you two." She kisses my head. "Bodhi stays strong for you. I honestly think you're the only person he cares about right now."

"Yeah, but keeping things from me that are about *him*, he shouldn't do that.

"Then tell him that, Eva. He's not going anywhere. You can tell him how you feel. I'm pretty confident he's sticking around for the long haul."

I smile at the simple thought. "Does it bother you that he's here all the time? That he sleeps in my bed?"

"No," she immediately answers. "I know you both need each other right now, and I care about Bodhi. I care about how he's doing. He needs someone to care about him. Calvin and I are both trying to let him know we're here for him."

"He told me he's thinking about moving in with Calvin."

"I know, he told me that, too. I think living with Calvin for this next year would be the best thing for him to do. But he can also stay here, for as long as you both want him to stay here."

"Thanks."

"Are you and Bodhi—"

"We're not having sex, Mom," I groan. "We can't, at least not now. And we wouldn't be doing that with ..." I point to the hall.

She starts laughing. "That's not what I was going to ask you."

"Oh," I blush. "Well, we aren't, in case you're wondering. Apparently, when this comes off," I knock on my cast, "we can resume all sexual contact."

"Resume ...?" she questions slowly.

I know my face turns red. The last time my mom and I talked about Bodhi, I told her we hadn't had sex yet, which was true then. But now, now it's not true anymore. "Um, we might have—"

She squeezes my shoulder. "No judging. I don't need to hear the details. You aren't a child anymore, and I know he loves you. Just be safe. Now, the question I was *actually* going to ask, after Luna's dinner, are you and Bodhi staying with everyone?"

I look up at her confused. "What do you mean?"

Her cheeks turn pink. "I might have overheard Bodhi talking to Coop yesterday. After the dinner they're all staying the night at Coop's. Something about camping out on his lanai?"

I look down at my hands. "I didn't know about that, either. *God*," I sigh. "Bodhi probably thinks he can't tell me anything or do anything because of me."

"Bodhi wants to be with you, honey. Trust me on that. When he left earlier today, he literally stood in the kitchen arguing out loud, trying to convince himself to leave. I actually shoved him out the door. He doesn't want to be away from you."

"Yeah, but he should be allowed to do things with his friends, even when I can't."

"I was actually going to tell you that you could."

"Yeah?"

"If you're up to it, I'm okay with you staying," she nods her head. "I know Bodhi will bring you back if he thinks you need to come home. I trust him, and I trust you will tell him if something's wrong. I trust you both, and I know you want things to get back to normal."

I abruptly get up, moving further into my closet, unzipping my hard-shell suitcase. They're all in there. Things will never be normal if we keep hiding secrets. I pull them out and hand them to her.

"What's all of this?"

"We found it all the night of the accident, in Lenora's studio. It explains a lot. Secrets about the friend you thought you knew. We were going to give it to you and Calvin that night, all of it. We were done with this shit. But, well ... we never got the chance. So here it all is. I don't want it in here anymore."

My mom takes it all from my hands. "Eva, please talk to me about this stuff. You and Bodhi, please don't think you can't talk to me. No matter what it is, no matter how awful you think it is, I'm on your side, both of yours. The only way we'll get through this is if we stop keeping things from each other."

"I know, Mom. Trust me, whatever I can do to get things back to normal, I will, but I don't think it's that easy. I think Lenora had a lot of secrets that we haven't heard yet, and I think eventually it's all going to come out." I then pick up the green dress from the floor. "I hope you're ready for that, because I don't think Lenora is who we thought she was. I'm going to go take a shower." And then I walk out, leaving her sitting there, staring at everything in her hands.

AT PROMPTLY SIX o'clock, I'm dressed in the green dress. It took me a while to get the zipper up since my stomach muscles ache in protest when I reach my arm around my back. But I managed without any help, after dropping a few angry swear words. It clings to my chest but flows freely on my stomach, which is perfect. I don't like anything touching my stomach right now.

It's the first time in a while I've worn something other than Bodhi's t-shirts or my own loose, comfy clothes. It's the first time in a while I've put on makeup and used a straightener on my hair, too. I'm at the mirror attached to my dresser, pushing earrings in, when I look through the reflection to my door. Bodhi's standing there watching me, wearing a white button up shirt with dark Hawaiian flowers on it, and black shorts. He looks sun-kissed. Surfing all day has given his skin a nice glow. I'm jealous of the freedom he had, but also a bit breathless with how gorgeous he looks.

"Hey," I say to him, not moving from my spot, and not my typical warm greeting that he's used to.

"Hey ..." he says back slowly, moving further into my room, but not over to me quite yet.

I turn to face him, without saying anything. I just stand there, staring at him.

"Eva, I'm starting to think you're mad about something, and I refuse to let you stand there being angry when you look so goddamn beautiful right now. So just tell me."

I don't hesitate. "When were you going to tell me about the trust fund money?"

His face turns red. "Your mom told you?"

"She did, but I really would have liked to of heard it from you."

He runs his fingers through his hair. "It was the day you came home from the hospital. I overheard your parents talking when I went to get your pain pill. I'm sorry. I should have told you, and I was going to, I was just waiting for the right time. I didn't want you to get upset."

I fold my arms over my chest. "There's never going to be a right time when it comes to hearing about the secrets our parents have kept all these years."

He actually looks worried, which breaks my heart a little. "You're right, Eva. I'm sorry."

He starts to move closer to me until I blurt out, "Why didn't you tell me everyone was staying at Coop's later tonight?"

His face turns red again, but then he clears the space between us, bringing his hand up to my cheek. "You're also mad about *that*?"

"Well, yeah?" I angrily reply.

"Do you know how many times I've slept at Coop's house? How many times we've crashed on his lanai after a party? Been there, done it a hundred times. Eva," he brings his hand to my chin and then swiftly pulls me in for a kiss. "I much rather prefer sleeping next to you, here."

I put my hands on his chest, pushing us apart. "My mom said I can stay if we want. I don't want you missing out on these things because of me."

He laughs, which just pisses me off more. "I'm not missing out on anything, babe. Now, if I stayed there without *you*, then I would be missing out on something. You. I'd be missing you. I don't want to stay at Coop's with the rest of them. I want to be with you."

59

"And I want to be with you, but stop keeping things from me. We don't keep things from each other, that's not how we work and we promised each other we wouldn't do that. Do we need to do a blood oath or something?"

"No, we don't." He runs his fingers along the top of my dress. "Are you still mad at me?"

I give him a little shove to his chest. "I have a very hard time being mad at you, but if you want to stay at Coop's—"

His lips find mine and his hand comes up to my back, pulling me into his chest. I wrap my arms around his neck. My body aches to be closer to him. To have him touch me, undress me, and take me over to my bed. I quickly push us apart, because feeling his tongue in my mouth is *not* helping the situation. I take a couple steps back, trying to catch my breath.

"I don't want to stay," he tells me again, moving the few steps closer to me as he glides his finger over my lips. "Not at all, but if *you* want to stay, we can. You just let me know, okay?"

I nod my head.

"And if, at any moment you feel tired tonight, or are hurting, or just want to get the hell out of there—"

"I'll be fine," I tell him, letting out a frustrated groan.

His eyebrow raises. "You had surgery three weeks ago—"

I put my hand over his mouth. "Three weeks and two days ago, and I'll tell you, okay?"

"Eva Calloway," he then mumbles, taking the fingers of my good hand off his mouth, and giving me a little twirl. "You look absolutely stunning." He then pulls me back into his arms and starts spinning us around in a slow circle, as if we're dancing without any music. "Confession," he whispers into my ear. "I love knowing you're mine. Every time I think about how no one else will ever get to see you the way I get to see you, I feel like the luckiest person alive."

I bring my lips to his neck. I know he loves this, when my lips move against the thin layer of skin that rests between his ear and shoulder.

"Eva," he mutters. I tug on his hair, as my lips continue to trail down his neck. "Don't stop, but you have to stop, but goddammit I don't want you to stop."

I bring my mouth to his ear. "Confession. I love being yours, just yours, and I wish you could take this dress off of me—"

His hand comes up to my mouth and he stops moving. "Don't finish that sentence," his eyes grow large. "If you do, I'm going to need to walk away for a few minutes."

I give him a quick kiss and ask, "Should we head out?"

"Yes," he agrees. "Dinner isn't until seven, but we need to stop and get Luna's gift first. It's ready, she called yesterday."

Bodhi and I had custom charm bracelets made for Luna from a local craft shop in downtown Flagler. I remembered when Luna was at my house, getting dressed for her date with Coop, she had seen mine on my dresser and loved them. They were a birthday gift from my parents a couple years ago. Luna's will definitely have more sentimental value than mine do.

After promising my mom that I'd take it extremely slow tonight, and we would call if anything went wrong, we head out and drive straight to downtown Flagler. Bodhi parks by the Flagler History Museum and we cross the street to the craft shop, walking in together. The owner, Kate, is busy helping another customer, so we aimlessly admire the art on the walls in the back of the shop as we wait for her to finish.

"These paintings are beautiful," I declare, staring at a watercolor one of Flagler pier. Each one seems to be by the same artist, as the initials CC are scribbled at the bottom. "Painters don't get enough credit. This probably took months to create."

Bodhi walks ahead of me and stops in front of a display of framed photographs. "Hey, Eva?" he curiously questions, his head is tilted to the side as he stares out in front of him. "Come over here for a minute."

I walk over to where he's standing. "Yeah?"

He points to the wall. "Do those look familiar to you?"

I glance at the photos and I'm shocked at what's staring back at my face. *My* photos. Numerous photos that I took are on this wall. I grab onto Bodhi's arm. "Those are *mine*," I breathlessly announce. I start counting. One, two, three, four ... I stop when I get to ten. Ten of *my* pictures are on the wall, being sold for hundreds of dollars.

Bodhi's arm comes up over my shoulder, as if he knows he needs to support my stunned body right now. "You edited those in my mom's studio, right?"

"I did. I edited *all* of my photos in your mom's studio."

"There has to be an explanation for this," Bodhi declares.

"There you two are!" Kate walks up to us. "Sorry about the wait, we've been really busy today." She sees us staring at the photos. "You like those?"

Bodhi brings his arm off my shoulder and grabs my hand. "We do. Do you know anything about the photographer?"

"It's a sad story. The photographer recently passed away. Cancer. These are the last of her photographs, which is a huge loss for us. Her photos always sold very quickly. I wish we had more."

I feel my body start to sway. "There were more? These aren't the only ones?"

"Gosh no," she answers. "Close to a hundred have passed through our door, for the last three years, I want to say?"

Bodhi's arm wraps around my waist. "Did you ever meet her?" he asks.

"Of course. Spunky gal, red hair, artsy and carefree. She brought these in a few months ago," she points to the wall. "Said it would be the last. I could tell the cancer was getting worse. I went to her memorial after she passed away ..." she drifts off, giving Bodhi a really weird look. "Wait a second. You're her son! You were at the memorial!"

"I am, I was," he nods.

"I'm so sorry about your mom," she then says. "Oh! I have something for you! She told me you'd be in at some point and left it here. I was told to call you if you didn't come in by the end of the summer to get it, but it's not addressed to you. She said you could give it to the owner?"

I can feel my heart rate increase. "Who's it addressed to?"

She smiles, "Follow me." She leads us to a row of filing cabinets, opens up a drawer and takes out an envelope. "Something tells me you're Eva?"

"I am."

"Here you go," she holds it out. "I'll go ahead and get the bracelets ready for you both. They're in the back."

I stand there, staring at this envelope that's in my hands, not wanting to open it, but dying to know what's inside at the same time. "I don't think I can open it," I say to Bodhi.

"You don't have to," he quietly replies. "Not now. You can open it when you're ready."

"Why was she selling my photos, Bodhi?"

"Babe, I have no idea."

"Isn't that illegal?"

He slowly nods his head.

"I don't think I can wait to open it. I need to know what's inside of here."

Bodhi points to the front door. "Why don't you go sit outside and find out, and I'll get the bracelets and meet you out there."

"You don't want to open it with me?"

He leans in and gives me a soft kiss. "You'll tell me what's in there, and hearing it come from you will be better than us both finding out at the same time that my mom was a criminal."

"*Bodhi—*"

He kisses me again. "Go," he nods to the door, and then he walks away toward the register, leaving me standing there.

I head outside and throw myself down on a bench. I know Bodhi's upset. I know this is another secret his mom kept from him, but she kept it from *me,* too. If whatever is in this envelope explains why she was selling my photos without telling me, I need to know. I carefully open it up. The bottom is heavy, like there's something solid in there, but first I pull out the single folded up piece of paper and start reading.

Eva, I know you have a lot of questions. I'm sorry I never got the chance to tell you this face-to-face. At twelve, when I would watch you take your photos and spend countless hours editing them at my house, I knew your talent was endless. I tried to tell you as often as I could, that you were special and that one day your photos would be your ticket out of Flagler. I took you seriously, but I don't think you did. After every edit, when you deemed your photo perfect, I would print it and save it.

I know that you reading this means two things. One, I'm no longer here, and two, you or Bodhi have discovered I've been selling your photographs. I wanted to leave you with the motivation to dream big, to show you that your talent is special, and that other people agree with me. You're going to find your photos everywhere. You've sold hundreds; embrace it and keep at it. Let Kate know you are the photographer. She will continue selling your work, trust me.

There's a key in this envelope. It opens a lock box that's under a loose floorboard in the closet of my studio. Inside, you will find every single penny your photos have brought in. It's all there and accounted for, including the receipts of every purchase. If you don't include the sales of the photos I'm dropping off today, there's at least sixty thousand dollars in this lock box.

You're special, Eva, and I know you might not hear that often enough, but I believe in you. I always have, and if there's ever a moment you doubt yourself, I know Bodhi will be there to remind you.

Always dream big. Always trust each other. And no matter what, always remind yourselves that everything you hear and find out once I'm gone, I did it all for him—and you. Every little thing.

chapter eight

Bodhi

There's sixty thousand dollars for you under a floorboard in my house?" I whisper to Eva.

"That's what your mom said," she answers. "She sold my photos to prove I have talent."

I sit down next to her and put my arm around her back. "She couldn't just tell you she was doing that? Or ask? Jesus Christ."

Eva leans her head on my shoulder. "Kate said it's been three years. I think she probably started selling them after the accident. I wasn't really talking to you guys then."

"Still, Eva, this is ridiculous. I'm sorry. I'm sorry you're involved in all these damn secrets my mom has kept. It's not fair to you—"

"Bodhi!" she forcefully says my name. "Stop apologizing for shit *our* parents have kept from us. Stop apologizing for them."

"I'm just pissed," I grumble. "I'm tired of all of this. I just want to forget about it. I don't give a damn about it anymore, and every time I think that's the last crazy thing I'm going to hear, something else gets uncovered. I just—I just want ..."

"You just want what?"

"I just want you, without worrying that eventually something we hear or find out is going to hurt that."

She lifts her head off my shoulder. "Never, Bodhi. I promise, that will never happen."

I grin and boldly say, "Marry me, Eva. Let's get married." I can see the blood rush to her cheeks and I force myself not to laugh.

"Bodhi Bishop!" she pulls at my shirt. "I am *not* marrying you at seventeen!"

"Would you rather we wait until April? When you turn eighteen?"

"Bodhi, we cannot get married as teenagers! And if you think you're just going to ask me to marry you as we sit here in the middle of downtown Flagler, then you don't know me as well as I thought you did."

"Eva Calloway, I know you *very* well, and I know exactly how I'm going to propose to you, when you're ready. I'm ready right this second, but I'll wait for you to give me the okay."

She leans in closer to me and her breath tickles my mouth as she whispers, "You've already thought about all of this?"

"Confession. I think about proposing to you, and marrying you, every single second I'm with you. I want you to be mine officially. I want to be yours officially."

"Confession," she says. "Until that day, I can still be yours, and you can still be mine. We don't need a marriage certificate to declare that."

"Of course we don't," I reply, and then I carefully place my lips onto hers.

"Bodhi!" I hear someone shout behind me. I quickly pull my lips away and turn to look. Immediately I see Graham Walker, holding the hand of another guy who looks oddly uncomfortable with our presence. "Oh my god, Eva!" Graham cries out.

Eva gives me a confused look. It's obvious she doesn't recognize him.

"It is *so* good to see you both," Graham says as he swiftly approaches.

I stand and take Eva's hand in mine, pulling her up with me. "Eva," I softly say, bringing our hands up together and pointing at Graham. "This is Graham Walker. He's the paramedic who—"

"Saved my life?" she questions.

The guy next to him makes a funny noise. "I've heard all about you two."

Graham's face turns red. "This is my partner, Holden. I might have left the hospital that night and had a bit of a breakdown over a few glasses of wine, telling Holden more than was necessary."

Eva drops my hand and very cautiously gives Graham a hug. "Thanks for what you did. I think I owe you my life?"

"Hearing you talk and seeing you standing is all I need. How are you?" he then asks.

"Good. All thanks to your mother, who kicked my ass in recovery boot camp for five days as my nurse."

Both Graham and Holden start laughing hysterically. "Sounds like Jackie," Holden says, his dark red hair looking unnatural under the sun's rays. "She's a tough one."

"I actually miss her," Eva says to them. "Will you tell her that?"

"I absolutely will," Graham replies. "She talks about you two all the time. Like you're long-lost family members. Bodhi, you never left the hospital, did you?"

I shake my head. "All thanks to you, right?"

His face turns red again. "I might have pulled a few strings. Having your father as chief surgeon and your mother has head nurse helps a little."

"I really appreciate it."

"I know you do, Bodhi. I'm just so happy to see you both. And Eva, you look great. It's only been a few weeks, right?"

"Three weeks and two days," she tells him. "I'm doing pretty well. This is actually my first real time out since everything, just moving a bit slower than normal."

"You both are adorable," Holden suddenly exclaims. "And beautiful, like movie stars. Graham!" he tugs on his sleeve. "Let's take them out to dinner! I want to hear everything about you both. Join us for dinner tonight?"

"We actually have to get to a birthday dinner for our friend," Eva tells them, and then she turns to me. "But maybe another time?"

"Definitely," I agree. "And it would be my treat, for everything you did for Eva—for us—that night."

"Jesus, Bodhi," Graham puts his hand on my shoulder. "You don't have to do that."

"I absolutely do. That night, in the hospital—taking you and your partner out to dinner is the least I can do."

Graham leans in and gives me a hug. "You doing okay?" he asks quietly in my ear.

I turn to Eva and grab her hand, giving it a kiss. "Never better."

The two of us exchange cell numbers and we make plans for dinner sometime in the next couple weeks.

"When Jackie finds out we saw you two, she's going to be *so* jealous," Holden says.

"Don't make Jackie jealous," I laugh. "Tell her we'll make plans to come see her soon."

"She will *love* that. We won't keep you any longer," Graham smiles. "Take it easy, Eva. I have no doubt Bodhi's taking great care of you."

"Oh, he is," she replies, leaning her head up against my shoulder. "It was nice to meet you both. Or again, Graham, I should say."

Eva and I turn and start walking to my jeep. Her hand is in mine and I nervously keep squeezing it. "We don't have to get dinner with them if you don't want to," I finally say.

"I absolutely want to. Why wouldn't I want to?"

I shrug my shoulders. "Just didn't want it to feel weird or—"

"Why would it feel weird?" she stops walking. "He saved my life. Unless there's more about that night you haven't told me yet?"

I tug on her hand a little and she starts walking again.

"Bodhi? What did he do for you in the hospital?"

"He made sure I didn't get kicked out," I reply quickly, opening the passenger door and helping her in. "I don't think I should have been allowed in your room every minute of the day." I close her door before she can respond, and walk around to my own side.

"I think it's more than that," she declares as soon as I'm in my seat. "What aren't you telling me?"

I don't want to keep things from Eva, but I have no desire to think about the events of that night anymore. I start my jeep and turn to her. "When they took you back, the doctors, and I was left there without anyone, he stayed with me until everyone got there. He calmed me down, kept me talking, made sure I was okay before he left, gave me the scrubs to change into."

Eva stares at me for a moment, and then leans in, kissing my lips. "I want you to be able to talk to me about that night, without thinking I can't handle it."

My fingers move her hair behind her ear and I rest my forehead on her shoulder. "It's hard to talk about that night. I don't want you to think about it, and I don't want to think about it, but I'll talk about it, to you. Just you."

She brings my face up to hers, and holds my chin in her fingers. "I can't imagine how hard it was to be on the other end. To see everything. It's going to take us both a while before we can put it all behind us, but we need to be able to talk to each other about it, or we're going to get lost in it all."

"I feel like if I don't talk about it—it will eventually just go away," I confide in her. "But it's not. I think about that night all the time, and the only time I *don't* think about it is when you're in my arms."

"Bodhi," she whispers. "We need to be able to talk to each other about it, or we're both going to go insane."

"We do," I agree. "And we will, because I refuse to allow us to go insane."

She pulls me toward her, crashing her lips onto mine, deepening our kiss in a matter of just seconds. What I would do to climb on top of her, lift up her dress, and have sex with her right here in my jeep. I almost feel feral thinking thoughts like that right now, like I should be embarrassed for letting my mind wander in any type of sexual way after everything she went through. But I miss her. I miss touching her the way I used to, I miss my mouth on her, me ... in her. I miss Eva's unpredictable sexual side that I was just getting used to before that night happened. I also miss the distraction, how sex with Eva makes me forget about everything else going on around me.

I sigh through our kiss, pushing us apart, knowing this is all we're going to do right now. Eva's forehead rests on mine. I bring my fingers to her collarbone, running them along her neck and down to her chest. "Three more weeks," I whisper.

"Two weeks and five days," she whispers back. "I miss you."

I know exactly what she means. "I miss you, too."

She moves her forehead off mine and gives me a small kiss. "Ready to get to dinner?"

"Yes ma'am."

"Hey, Bodhi?"

"Yeah?"

"Graham ...? Was he the one who cut my dress off of me?" she questions. "He saw me like that? So exposed?"

"Uh, yeah?"

"You're telling me pretty much his entire family has seen me naked?"

I start laughing hysterically.

"It's not funny, Bodhi!" she exclaims, hitting me on my shoulder, but she starts laughing too. "I'm glad you find this so hilarious."

"I don't, babe!" I laugh. "I don't. I promise." But I'm still laughing as we pull up to where dinner will be, and she lets me because I think we both need this. We need to be able to think about that night without letting it absolutely destroy us every single time. One day we'll be able to bring it up without immediately falling into a dark tunnel of despair, but until then, we'll just laugh when we can.

chapter nine

Bodhi

va, this is Kennedy," I introduce. "Kennedy, this is Eva."
"I feel like I'm meeting a celebrity!" Kennedy smiles, her dark
brown eyes look up at Eva with amusement. "My heart is
racing in my chest. God, you're really tall."

Eva blushes. Kennedy comes up to her neck. "Definitely not a
celebrity," Eva grins at her. "But it's really nice to meet you, finally."

Kennedy points to Coop and Beck in the distance, as she throws
her dark brown hair off her shoulder. "They talk about you all the
time."

"I'm sure that's annoying as hell," Eva laughs.

"Not at all," Kennedy warmly smiles.

"Eva!" Luna shouts from a bit farther away. She comes running
up to us, but stops dead in her tracks when she remembers she can't
just tackle Eva for a hug. Her arms linger in midair before she brings
them back down to her sides. "Tell me what to do here. I can hug
you, right?" she awkwardly asks. "That won't hurt or anything?"

"First, happy birthday," Eva tells her. "And you can touch me."

Luna blushes a little but then pulls Eva in for a quick hug.

"Happy Birthday, Luna," I say to her.

"Thanks, Bodhi."

"Should we go sit?" I ask Eva. I want to make sure she stays
comfortable tonight, and standing for long periods of time is hard
on her right now.

Eva nods her head and takes my hand, as Kennedy starts
walking right next to her.

"Now, *that's* got to be annoying as hell," she says softly to Eva.

"What's annoying?" I hear Eva ask her.

Kennedy puts her hand on Eva's shoulder as we walk. "Having

to constantly remind people that you aren't made of glass."

Coop's dinner production for Luna's birthday is definitely impressive. Granted, Beck and I helped him plan it all, but I'm a little shocked he actually pulled it off. There's one giant table right in the sand, underneath a large pergola draped with lights. We're on the beach, right behind Dolly's, who's letting us use her electricity to keep the lights running. One of her chefs is also cooking our dinner, and one of her waiters is bringing everything out. I think Coop had to promise he'd work the rest of the summer for free, but he's so infatuated with Luna, he'd probably agree to anything at this point to make her happy. I've never seen Coop like this before, and I have to admit, as weird as it is, I secretly love it.

"Damn, Coop," Eva exclaims, as I pull her chair out and she takes a seat. "This is beautiful, and not anything I ever would have imagined you doing. It's almost as if you're in love or something."

Coop's face turns red and he uncomfortably looks at Luna. "I surprised myself, too, and Luna only turns seventeen once, right?"

Luna blushes a little. "I appreciate you all coming, and for all of this. And you, Eva ... for being here."

I look over at Eva, and I can tell she's frustrated. "Luna, it's your birthday. Of course I'm here. And it's been three weeks. I'm really tired of sitting at home doing nothing."

The waiter appears, bringing out salads for everyone. I watch as Eva takes a few bites, and then just moves things around with her fork. She might be feeling better, but her appetite is nonexistent. It's been a struggle to get food in her. I question if this is because she just isn't feeling like herself yet, or because Eva feels out of control and this is the one thing she *can* control. I'm afraid to ask her.

"I can't believe summer is already halfway over," Beck groans, throwing his arm around Kennedy.

"I'm ready for senior year," Kennedy announces. "Junior year sucked since I was the new girl in Tampa. I missed my boys," she smiles at the guys. "It'll be nice to be back with you all at school."

"Luna and I don't go to your school," Eva says quietly.

"Oh shit!" Kennedy covers her mouth. "That's right. Luna, you're homeschooled?"

She nods her head. "My parents decided early on it would

benefit me greatly to be educated by them, in our house, with the chaos of my five younger siblings who they also somehow manage to homeschool. And with baby number seven coming eventually, lord help us all."

Everyone laughs.

"Senior year should be a breeze for you," Beck says to Luna.

Luna's face turns red.

Eva lets out a little laugh. "Wait," she then says, looking at all of us. "They don't know? Luna, you haven't told them?"

"Nah," she smiles at Eva. "Just never came up."

"Guys, Luna already graduated," Eva tells us all. "Like a year ago. She's super smart, genius level smart, but you're taking this year off to figure out college, right?"

"I need to save up some more money, but that's definitely the plan," Luna responds.

Fuck. I'll pay for Luna's college. I'll pay for everyone's college if that's what they want to do after high school.

"What about you, Eva?" Kennedy asks her. "You go to that private school, right?"

"I do ..." she says slowly. "But with everything that's happened, I don't really have any friends there. Porter was the only one I ever talked to, and it would just be weird to be back there now."

I've known for a few days that Eva's considering asking her parents if she can transfer to my school. I would do anything to have her at school with me for this next year. The thought of not seeing her for seven or so hours, five days a week, or knowing she's with other people—people I don't know or trust—gives me nightmares. But I also want her to make her own decision without my feelings swaying her in any way.

"You should absolutely come to our school," Kennedy smiles. "I mean, no reason to be by yourself this next year, right? And with Porter leaving tomorrow—"

Fuck. I had completely forgotten to tell Eva what Porter told us all a few days ago. This is *not* going to end well. My heart actually stops beating as I wait for Eva to speak.

"Wait," Eva interrupts her. "Porter is leaving tomorrow?" She turns to me. "Tomorrow? Why didn't he tell me? Why didn't you tell me?" She then turns to everyone else. It's obvious by the nervous looks on their faces, they all knew this. "Why do you all know but I don't? Did any of you date Porter for a year? Have any of you known Porter since you were five?"

I put my hand on her shoulder. "I completely forgot to tell you. He didn't want you to get upset—"

She jerks my hand away. She has never jerked my hand away. I hear my friends gasp in shock. I'm in shock. I feel like I have a lump in my throat and I instantly start sweating.

Eva drops her fork loudly on her plate. "Luna," she looks right at her. "I apologize for doing this right now, at your birthday dinner, but I have to. You four," she points to me, Coop, Luna, and Beck. "Not you Kennedy, but you four. It needs to stop. Right now, right this goddamn second. Stop keeping things from me because you think I'm going to get upset. Stop walking around acting like poor Eva's going to shatter and break if you say something that isn't covered in glitter and rainbows. I don't need my friends and my boyfriend to treat me like I'm broken." She's breathing heavy and has tears in her eyes. "Stop being scared of me."

No one says anything. I slowly put my hand back on her shoulder. She looks up at me, so distraught and angry, but so sad at the same time.

"Well, you heard the girl!" Kennedy loudly announces. "She's not glass. Stop treating her like she is, okay everyone?"

Eva gives her a small smile.

There's a chorus of apologies from Coop, Luna, and Beck, but Eva puts her hand up to stop them. "Don't," she says. "You don't have to apologize. I know you were only doing it because you care. Just don't do it anymore."

They nod their heads, just as the waiter reappears to take our salad plates away. I bring my mouth to Eva's ear. I'm afraid she might push me away. I'm not sure how I'd handle it if she did. "I'm sorry, Eva," I whisper. "I should have told you. I forgot. I wasn't keeping it from you, I honestly forgot. I don't think about Porter—"

"I'm not mad at you," she says to her hands in her lap.

"Then *look* at me, Eva," I whisper back firmly. She looks up, her eyes lock on mine. "I'm sorry," I say again, gently kissing her lips.

"Okay? I'm sorry." She nods her head, but I know Eva as well as I know myself. I've disappointed her again, and I feel like an asshole.

The only thing that keeps the rest of dinner from being absolutely perfect is how quiet Eva suddenly is with me. I'm not sure if anyone else notices, but I sure as hell do. She's not like this with the others, just me.

When dinner is officially over and Luna has opened her gifts, everyone walks down to the water. The sun has just set and the colors in the sky are absolutely stunning tonight. Almost as if they're putting on a show just for Luna's birthday. Eva walks down ahead of me, throwing her shoes in the sand and standing in the tide. Everyone walks further down the beach, but she stays right there, staring down at her feet as the small waves crash over them.

I come up behind her, running my fingers along her neck and down her back. "Eva?" She doesn't look up, but she does lean into my hand, so I take that as a good sign.

"This is the first time my feet have touched the ocean in over three weeks," she suddenly says. "The only other time I went that long without dipping my feet in the water was when I broke my leg." She turns her head a little to look at me. "I remember thinking after my leg surgery that it was going to take me months to walk normally again. It did. Months. And I remember thinking the first time I got out of my hospital bed with Jackie that it was going to take me months to walk by myself because everything hurt so bad. I could barely move that day, but it didn't take months. I was determined to get my body to heal faster than the time before."

I turn her around so that I can wrap my arms around her waist. She places her hands on my chest and stares at me. Her insanely gorgeous green eyes are locked directly onto my worried ones.

"I've been broken," she continues. "I've been broken before, and just like last time, I healed. I became unbroken again. I look at my scars every single day to remind me of that—that I was once damaged and now I'm not. That's all they are now, scars to remind me of what happened. Stop thinking I'm still broken, *please*."

I bring my forehead to hers. "Eva, I will. Right now, and every day from here on out. I promise."

"I might move slower, and still have this goddamn cast on," she

75

knocks it against my chest. "But I just want to be treated normally now, especially by you."

I bring her face up to mine and kiss her. "I'm sorry. I didn't even realize I was doing this. I hate it when I disappoint you."

She finally smiles at me. "You didn't, Bodhi. You didn't disappoint me." She points to our friends in the distance. "Just like them, you didn't tell me things because you care about me. You unintentionally thought it's what I needed."

"I thought you were mad at me. That's a fucking awful feeling."

"After everything you've done for me these last three weeks? It's going to take a lot more than that to get me mad at you."

"You jerked my hand away," I remind her.

"Jerking your hand away sounded a lot more mature than throwing my salad plate across the beach."

"I don't think anyone would have blamed you."

"I would have been mad at myself," she responds.

I leave it at that. I can tell she's upset with the whole situation, and I don't want to push it any further. "Tonight, do you really want to go to Coop's and sleep on uncomfortable patio furniture all night?"

"What do you want to do, Bodhi?" she wraps her arms around my neck.

My lips come to her forehead. "I want to see you put on one of my t-shirts, and I want to pull your body into mine as we fall asleep on an actual bed," I reply.

She laughs, and then her eyes light up. "Take me home, Bodhi."

"Back to the Halifax we'll go."

She shakes her head. "No, not my house. Home. Your house, Bodhi. Let's stay the night there. My mom already thinks we're staying at Coop's. Let's just go home," she says, tugging on my shirt. "We can look for that lock box, you can help me get out of this dress, I'll put on one of your t-shirts, and we can sleep on your comfortable bed for once. Can we?"

Just thinking about bringing her to my house makes my entire body start to quiver. It's agony not being able to touch her the way I want to, or kiss her body the way I did before all of this. If Eva and I were spending the night at my house and everything was indeed back to normal, I know exactly what we'd be doing tonight.

"Yes," I immediately reply. "We can absolutely go home, and the fact you call it home makes my entire body shake."

"It is home, Bodhi. It's always felt like home to me."

"You have no idea how much I love that." I then bring my lips to hers, carefully picking her up in the process. Her arms stay around my neck, her hard cast is digging into my shoulder, but her lips on my lips feels incredible. I almost forget that we're on the beach, with our friends and random strangers probably watching all of this. I push my mouth harder against hers. Her teeth lightly bite down on my lip, and my knees almost give out on me.

"Bodhi," she whispers into my mouth. "This is really making me want to back out of our promise to Jackie."

"No, babe," I whisper back, bringing my lips to her neck and gently kissing her skin. "Six weeks. Halfway there."

"Ugh, you two!" I hear Coop shout from a bit further down the beach. "The embarrassing public display of affection is back!"

Eva laughs into my neck. "I think that's our cue to stop."

But I don't put her down just yet. I kiss her neck again and then bury my face into her warm skin. "Pretend they aren't here."

"You two are the cutest," I hear Kennedy declare, much closer now. "You look like you're in a scene right out of a romantic love story movie."

I gently place Eva's feet back on the ground, wrapping my arm around her waist.

Coop laughs at what Kennedy just said. "Can't say I missed the constant kissing and groping—"

"Coop!" Luna whacks him in his arm. "*I* missed it, and I love how comfortable they are with each other and their bodies. It's beautiful to see."

"We need a girl day," Eva suddenly declares. "The three of us," she points to herself, Luna and Kennedy. "I can't drive for another three weeks, and I'm not sure if I can do anything more than sit, but we definitely need a girl day."

"Oh! A spa day!" Kennedy cries out. "Let me plan it! Please?"

"Sure, just tell me when, and I'll be there. And I'll force Luna to come, too," Eva points to her.

Kennedy turns to Luna, who has a pained look on her face. "You don't like spas?"

"Uh, I actually have never—"

"You'll love it!" Kennedy squeals. "I can't wait to plan our day!"

"My treat," I say quickly. "For all three of you, whatever you plan, Kennedy, my treat."

Eva looks up at me, planting a kiss on my cheek.

"Well, damn," Kennedy smirks. "I like this new Bodhi. Don't tempt me."

"Just let me know, and I'll take care of it all," I tell her. "So, tonight—I think Eva and I are going to head home—"

"I turn into a pumpkin at midnight," Eva jokes. "A tired, comatose pumpkin."

Luna leans in and pulls Eva away from my waist for a hug. "Totally understand," she says. "I love you and this was the best birthday ever."

"Even with my outburst?" I hear Eva whisper in her ear.

"Girl, that was much needed," Luna whispers back. "Can't wait for our girl day!" she says loudly. Then she follows in a barely audible mumble into Eva's ear, "Even though I don't *do* spa days ..."

Eva laughs and pulls herself out of the hug. "You'll love it, Luna."

Luna kisses Eva's cheek. "I'm holding you to that."

chapter ten

Bodhi

Eva and I pull up to my house not too much later. I can tell she's tired. This is the longest she's been on her feet since before the accident.

"You doing okay?" I ask her, walking in through my garage door.

We're on the first floor of my house, which consists of a large recreation room that I hardly ever spend time in. When the guys and I were younger, my mom went all out buying every video console available, a pool table, old arcade games. It's a kid's paradise down here. The room is massive, and there's even a wet bar that we definitely snuck alcohol out of the older we got. The guys and I logged a lot of hours and days down here, and now it just sits, unlived in.

"Yep ..." Eva replies slowly, looking up fearfully at the staircase, like there are a hundred steps in front of her. "Just tired and—and a bit achy."

"Shit, babe—"

"I'm fine," she reassures me. "It's just time to lie down."

I take her hand and we walk up the stairs to the main floor. I start to guide her to my bedroom, but she pauses and points to the staircase that leads to my mom's studio. She doesn't move any further.

"I can't believe the last time I was here was when we found all that stuff," she says quietly. "After that night, I'm sure it looks like a disaster in there now."

"I cleaned it all up. The guys and I did, today actually. After surfing, we came back here. I knew at some point you'd want to come back, and I didn't want you to see that room, how we left it that night."

She looks up at me, her eyes are glossing over with tears. "Have I ever told you that I love you?"

"Once or twice."

She leans in and gives me a kiss. "Can we find the lock box and sleep in there tonight?"

"Absolutely." I point down the hall to my bedroom. "Let's change first?"

I can't remember the last time Eva was in my actual bedroom. It was definitely years ago, when we were fourteen and we used to sit on my bed going through pictures.

"Your room looks exactly the same," she laughs. "I have visions of you and me sitting right here," she points to my bed. "Coop over there," she points to the couch. "And Beck sitting up against the couch. They would be arguing about something stupid. And we would be going through pictures or just—just sitting there ..."

"Falling in love without realizing what the hell was happening?" I question, going over to my dresser. I pull out a t-shirt for her.

She gives me a puzzled look. "Yes, exactly that," she answers. "When did your clothes magically reappear back in your house?"

"Today," I reply. "Just a few things. Between your house, Coop's, and here, I figured it would be nice to have a little something everywhere."

"You live like a hobo."

"Wouldn't want it any other way."

She turns her back to me, and points to the zipper of her dress. I slowly bring it down all the way, feeling my stomach do flips as I do. Look away, Bodhi. Just look away. Do *not* watch her get out of her dress. Do *not* look at her as she stands there in just her bra and panties. Don't do it, Bodhi.

But I do. Because I'm fucking stupid, and I miss seeing her like this. Her back is still to me as her dress falls to the ground. She then points to her bra clasp.

"Eva," I groan. "This is torture, babe."

"Just do it. It hurts to twist my arm back there."

I unclasp it and watch as it drops to the floor. She then goes to pull the t-shirt over her head, but I stop her, because I can't help myself. I know we can't do what we both want to do, but I can at least do something, right? Even if it's the most innocent form of what's currently playing out in my mind.

"Just wait a minute," I softly say to her.

I run my fingers up her smooth back, creating a pattern between the small freckles that line her naturally tanned skin. I then bring them to her neck, moving her head and hair a little to the side. My lips go right to the soft spot under her ear, lining it with slow kisses. I bring my lips from her neck down to her bare shoulder, leaving a trail as I go.

"Do you know how beautiful you look standing here like this?" I whisper to her, running my fingers along the tops of her breasts.

Her breath comes out in shallow bursts from her mouth. "Do you know how badly I want you to take me over to your bed?"

"As badly as *I* want to take you over to my bed right now."

She turns her body around. I refuse to look down at her chest. I can't. I'm not that strong. The desire to make love to her right now is slowly taking over every rational thought in my mind. I pull her toward me so her chest gets lost in mine, and then I bring my lips to hers. If this is all we can do right now, I'm going to give it my all.

I feel her hands on my shirt, working at the buttons as she tries to take it off. With my lips still on hers, I help, bringing it off my shoulders and to the floor. Her fingernails attack my skin, digging in as she glides them around my chest. Our kisses are growing in intensity. This is not good, but hell, it feels amazing. We need to stop, but I don't want to stop. She said she was tired, she said she was achy, why am I allowing this to continue? She's not ready for this, and I will not hurt her because I can't control my sexual desires.

Her fingers suddenly appear at the button of my shorts. I grab at them. "No, Eva," I immediately say. "We can't."

She pulls her fingers away from me, and quickly slips them under the top of my shorts and boxers. "Just let me touch you then."

"*Eva*, Jesus. You can't talk like that right now—"

"I want to touch you," she forcefully repeats. "I miss us, Bodhi. You can't tell me you don't miss this."

"I do, babe. I do miss this."

Her soft hand cups right around me, moving ever so slightly

back and forth. The sound that escapes my mouth reminds me of a feral animal you'd find attacking its kill deep in the woods. Starving and wanting more, but knowing it can't vocalize its excitement as it will alert itself to others. I want more of her. I want more than this and I know we can't. I bite down on my tongue, trying to get myself to speak. But the sensation of her smooth hand on me, moving against how hard I am ... I can't even form a coherent thought, let alone tell her to stop.

I feel my eyes roll into the back of my head. "Do you have any idea how amazing this feels?" I finally manage to blurt out.

Her lips find mine, and I feel her smile through our kiss. She then grabs my fingers with her other hand, moving them right to the top of her panties. "No, so show me."

Jesus Christ.

I slip my fingers under, touching her exactly where I know she wants me to touch her. Her forehead pushes against my chest, and her hand that's under my boxers starts to move quicker. I can't believe I'm standing in my bedroom, touching Eva like this, as she jerks me off. Am I dreaming? I'm sure I've had this dream before. *Come back down to reality, Bodhi.* I can feel myself losing control. I can feel her losing control. Lost in the moment, I start to pull her panties down, only to quickly remember we *cannot* do this.

"*Fuck!*" I growl. I want her to finish me, and I want to hear my name come from her mouth as I finish her, but I want more. I don't want just this. I bring both my hands safely to the back of her head, thinking this will be the point we force ourselves to stop. But instead, her hand comes out of my boxers and she swiftly uses all her fingers to unbutton my shorts. I grab at them before she can pull them down, and with my mouth on hers, I whisper, "We can't do this tonight, babe."

I hear her snarl. "But I *want* to. I want you, Bodhi. I want to feel you inside—"

I bring my hand up to her mouth. I step back, staring directly at her frustrated face. "I'm about one minute away from doing exactly that, Eva, and we can't. Your stomach, those muscles, being out tonight, you said you felt achy. My body on top of yours—"

"Then I'll be on top," she interrupts me, stomping her foot.

I literally throw my hands to my head with the image that immediately enters my mind, and then turn around, away from her. "Shit, Eva. Please stop talking like that," I say with my back to her. "I'm not going to risk the chance of hurting you because we can't control our goddamn hormones."

"Is that all you think this is between us?" she asks quietly. "Hormones?"

Now I've pissed her off again. I'm really making an ass out of myself with her today. "That's not what I meant and you know it. Of course this is more than just hormones. Sex with you has never been about giving into my goddamn hormones. Sex with you is fucking beautiful, Eva. I love loving you like that, because I love *you*. But I am not about to let you hurt yourself right now. We can make it another few weeks. Your body needs another few weeks."

I give myself a minute to calm down, waiting for her to say something back.

"You can turn around now," she says bluntly.

"No," I quickly respond. "I can't see you like that right now, all beautiful and naked."

I feel her hand on my shoulder as she roughly spins me around. I close my eyes tight.

"Bodhi," she laughs. "Open your eyes."

I open them slowly to see her standing there, in my t-shirt. "Thank god," I sigh.

She gives me a little shove. "Let's not talk about this, please. It will just piss me off, let's just go upstairs."

I nod my head quickly and reach for her hand, leading her out of my bedroom and to the spiral staircase. "How about we just go to bed?" I suggest as we enter the room. "We can look for the lockbox in the morning?"

She gives me annoyed look, and points straight to the closet.

"It was worth a shot," I grin.

She flings open the door and looks down. "Do we just start tapping the floor? Rip up the floorboards?"

I get on my knees and start knocking on the wooden planks. Nothing happens until I get to the last row, where the entire plank shifts as I tap on it. I dig my fingers underneath the little slits of space, managing to pull it away from the floor. I toss it to the side, and Eva and I both peek into the dark, long hole that is now there. The metal lock box shines right back up at us.

"Well, shit," she mumbles. "There it is."

I reach in and pull it up, handing it out to her. "You really think there's sixty thousand dollars in there?"

"We're about to find out." She walks over and sits on the bed, patting for me to join her. She takes the key she got from the envelope, and slips it through the lock. The lid instantly pops open. She doesn't hesitate, and quickly lifts it up. Inside, sitting in stacks with thick rubber bands holding them together, is more cash than I've ever seen in my entire life.

"*Holy shit*," I mutter. "She wasn't lying."

"Count it," she bluntly says, taking out each stack and dropping it in my lap, while she pulls out the pile of stapled invoices that were underneath the money.

It takes me a little while to get through it all. I place it next to me in stacks of thousands as each bill slides through my fingers. "Sixty-two thousand, three hundred dollars," I finally declare. I'm still looking down at it all when I realize Eva hasn't responded. I look over at her, and she's just sitting there, staring at the mess of papers sprawled across her lap. "What's wrong?"

"Two hundred and seven photos, Bodhi. She sold two hundred and seven of my photos—"

"I'm sorry, Eva. Really, I had no idea—"

"That's not it," she shakes her head. "I'm not mad she sold my photos, seriously it doesn't surprise me. It's where they *went*. Eighty of them were sold to customers that randomly found them in Kate's shop, but the other hundred and twenty some photos— Bodhi, they were sold and shipped out of Flagler to the same two places."

"Which two places?"

"A P.O. box in Turks and Caicos," is the first thing she says, and then she follows directly with, "and a P.O. box in the Bahamas."

"The fucking Bahamas?!" I exclaim.

"There's more," she cringes, reaching down next to her. She holds up two passports.

"What the hell are those, Eva?!"

"One is yours. They were in the bottom of the box—"

"I've *never* been out of the country," I declare. "Well except to go to the Bahamas when I was two, I guess. Is that what it says in there?"

"This one is your mom's," she holds it up. "And this one is yours. Bodhi, you've been to Turks and Caicos six times with your mom. Six times until you were five—"

"No!" I cry out. "No, I have not!" I jump off the bed, the money falling in slow motion to the floor below me. I start pacing the room. "You're trying to tell me my mom took me to Turks and Caicos six times, and *never* told me about it? Never reminded me of our trips? Never showed me any pictures? I don't remember one goddamn moment of any of that!"

Eva stands up, walking over to where I am. She brings my hands into hers and starts rubbing my fingers.

"There's more?" I ask her. I can tell by how worried her eyes are that's there something else. "What is it?"

"Your mom, Bodhi. That trip to the Bahamas with you, that wasn't the last time she was in the Bahamas—"

"*What the—*"

"And Turks and Caicos," she quickly continues. "She was there twice a year, *every* single year, until about six months ago."

85

chapter eleven

Eva

Bodhi's sitting on top of his mom's desk, staring at his hands. He's been sitting there for a while, not talking, not doing anything, just staring down at his lap. I give him some time, but when it's obvious he's not going to speak, I cautiously start to move over to him. He looks up, raising his hands in the air as if to stop me from moving any closer.

"Don't. I just need a few minutes, okay?"

My heart drops. I nod my head and turn, carefully squatting down to pick up all the money off the floor. I need to distract myself. I know Bodhi needs time to process all of this, but I hate the fact he feels like he has to do that alone.

"Eva, don't do that," he sighs, quickly coming to where I am and pulling me up off the ground. "I'll clean it up."

I just stand there, staring at him as he picks up sixty thousand dollars in cash, biting down on my lip as I wait for him to say more. I'm worried about him. I'm pissed at Lenora for so many reasons I can't seem to figure out the one that makes me the angriest. I feel my eyes suddenly fill up with stinging tears. I'm tired, my stomach is sore, I'm sexually frustrated, pissed off, and the boy I'm madly in love with is so overwhelmed with all these secrets right now, he can't even talk to me about them.

Bodhi stands up, placing all the money in the tin box before turning to me. "*Shit*," he mumbles, bringing his fingers to my eyes. "I'm sorry—"

"Stop saying you're sorry!" I cry out, surprising myself with this quick outburst. "You just cleaned up sixty thousand dollars that belongs to *me*, Bodhi! Sixty thousand dollars your mom hid from both of us! This is not normal and you're naïve if you think this is the last secret we're ever going to uncover! Don't shut me out from what's going on in here!" I jam my fingers into his chest. "Because I'm going through the same shit, too!"

Bodhi's hand cups my cheek, as his finger rubs up and down my ear. "Baby, I know you are." He then takes my hand and guides me to the bed, pulling me in with him. I place my head on his chest as he speaks. "It's just a lot. It's a lot to deal with, when I realize my mom led two different lives. It's hard to even think about it, let alone talk about it."

"I know it is," I agree with him. "But we can deal with it together. Neither one of us knows how to deal with shit on our own, in a healthy way, but together ... we can deal with it together without falling apart. I need you to help me get through it, and I need you to let me help you get through it. Let me be there for you, okay?"

"Okay," he says quietly. "You know I'd be a fucking mess without you. I *was* a mess without you."

I give his bare chest a small kiss. "You don't have to be a mess anymore. We don't have to be a mess anymore." I then ask very gently, "What do you think it all means?"

His fingers move under the top of the t-shirt I'm wearing, and run along my collarbone. "That we've discovered yet another secret my mom has kept. A bunch of secrets within a secret."

"I don't care about the pictures—"

"Yes, you do," he interrupts. "You can't tell me you aren't curious where they are? Why they were shipped to two different tropical locations? Why they were shipped to the goddamn Bahamas? Why my mom went to these exact two places repeatedly? What's so special about these places?"

"I *am* curious, but at the same time, what will figuring it all out do? Is it going to change anything? What more do we possibly need to discover? We could leave Flagler the day you turn eighteen and never have to worry about anything ever again—"

"Let's do it. *Please*, Eva. Let's just leave and start over somewhere new. We can go anywhere. Close your eyes and point to somewhere on a goddamn map."

I squeeze my fingers into his side. "We can't do that, Bodhi—"

"Yes, we can."

"Yes, we *could*, but what I meant was that I have no desire to find out anything else that's going to put some huge plot twist on our lives, when we've already had so much thrown at us. Instead of adding it to all the other shit we have to worry about, let's just put it aside and see what happens. I'm sure at some point we'll figure out why your mom took you to Turks and Caicos so many times, and why twice a year she went there herself—"

"Twice a year ..." Bodhi mumbles. "Her photography seminars. Eva, she went to these photography seminars twice a year."

"You didn't go with her?"

"No, I was at Coop's," he laughs. "We looked forward to them. They were around the same time every year. I remember when we were little, we thought it was the coolest thing ever when I would go stay with them for a week."

"Did she ever tell you where they were?"

"No. But she sure as hell never mentioned Turks and Caicos."

"Maybe that's where they were—"

"I doubt it. If she really was at a photography seminar in Turks and Caicos twice a year, why wouldn't she tell me? I'm pretty certain her so called photography seminars never actually existed."

"Are you okay with realizing this?"

I feel his shoulders shrug. "There's nothing I can do about it now. What about you? Finding out she's been selling your photographs for the last three years. Does it upset you?"

"Upset isn't the right word," I make known. "Frustrated maybe? And confused? Having sixty grand sitting in a metal box kind of softens the blow a little ..."

"What are you going to do with it?"

My fingernails glide up and down his arm. "I'm seventeen. I have everything I need right now, what am I supposed to do with it? I think I'll just keep it in there for a while. Let it be our little secret."

"I like having secrets with you. I also like falling asleep with you here, in this house, in this room, in this bed."

"Remember what happened last time we slept in this bed?"

"*Eva.*"

"What? It's a good memory!"

"It's a *very* good memory," he agrees, kissing my forehead.

"Probably my favorite memory ever. I think about that night way more than I should. That night, and the morning you seduced me in your bedroom."

"Your face that morning, I think about *that* all the time."

Bodhi's arms tighten around my body. "You caught me off guard. Confession, that side of you is sexy as hell, babe."

I feel my cheeks blush. "Confession. You're the only one who will *ever* see that side of me."

"And *that* is sexy as hell, too."

I raise my cast up in the air. "I wonder what my arm will look like once this thing comes off."

"Beautiful," he responds. "It will look beautiful, just like the rest of you." I smile into his chest. "Do you remember, Eva?" he then asks me softly. "Do you remember how it broke?"

"I do," I confidently declare.

He seems taken aback by my response. I know subconsciously he's probably been wondering how much I remember about that night. I knew at some point he'd ask. I knew at some point I'd have to explain it all. I just didn't think it would be tonight.

"How ...?"

My fingers search for his hand and I wrap them around it. "Are we going to talk about everything that happened when I was in that pickup truck, right now? Because I will, Bodhi, I'll tell you everything. But I've been dreading this conversation and I'm scared you're going to hate me afterwards."

"Why the hell would I hate you? Why are you thinking that?"

I sit up and he gives me a curious look, trying to pull me back down onto his chest at the same time. I shake my head and raise my cast back up in the air. "How do *you* think it happened?"

He sits up, too. "I figured you might have hit the glove box with it? When you guys were crashing?"

"No, my head hit the glove box as my arm broke. I think my arm breaking actually saved my head from hitting the glove box harder, but I still blacked out."

"Okay ..." he cautiously replies. "So how did it break, then?"

He looks so worried. It hurts my soul to see him looking at me like this. I know what I'm about to say is going to completely shock him, but I say it as fast as I can anyway. "I grabbed the wheel, Bodhi. I grabbed the wheel and turned us into the trees. My arm broke when Luke—when his body flew out of his seat. I knew he didn't have a seatbelt on. I knew what would probably happen to him, but I did it anyway. His body broke my arm because I was holding onto the steering wheel, then my head hit the glove box. The next thing I remember is seeing you."

I stare at him, watching as he tries to comprehend everything I just said. I start crying, very softly. I don't deserve sympathy, but I can't stand thinking I've upset him with my actions. I can't stand thinking I've disappointed him.

"Please say something, Bodhi."

"You caused the crash?"

"I did."

"Why, Eva?"

I start crying harder. "He wasn't going to his boat, Bodhi! I panicked! He was taking me to the airport, stopping somewhere first, he said. We weren't going to High Bridge. I never would have shown up there, and then you would have thought you were too late. I couldn't live with myself knowing how damaged you would've been, thinking you failed me. I grabbed the wheel and crashed us, knowing we would get found somehow. I didn't care *how* we got found. I just knew I couldn't leave Flagler with him—"

"But you could have killed yourself! Eva, you could have died! You almost *did* die!"

"I know!" I quickly nod my head. "I know I could have, and I didn't care! I didn't care if you found me dead! And Luke, I didn't care about him ..." The realization that *I* caused Luke's death has suddenly overpowered me. I don't give a shit about myself, but I caused the death of someone else. I bring my hand up to my mouth and gasp behind it. "I didn't care if what I did killed Luke!" I cry out loud, shocked. "*I* killed him!"

He reaches for me, but I swiftly swing my legs out of the bed, walking backwards until my body hits the wall. I then slouch down onto the ground and bury my head into my knees, covering my ears as I try to block out the noise in my head, my conscience that's screaming horrible things at me. I'm literally falling apart right in front of him, again, like I have before, but this time it's not something Bodhi can fix. I caused his dad's death, and we're both going to have to live with that forever.

I hear him get out of the bed, walking over to where I am on the ground. "Don't!" I yell at him. "Don't touch me, Bodhi!"

"I want to hold you right now. Can I do that please?"

"Why?!" I shout, looking up at him with my tear-stained face. "I killed your dad, Bodhi! I killed Calvin's son! I almost killed myself! And I didn't care! I *still* don't care! I would do it again knowing exactly what would happen to both of us!"

"I'm going to hold you now, okay?" he calmly tells me, not waiting for me to respond. He sits down right in front of me, pulling my body into his.

I cry harder, burying my head into his chest. "Don't tell Calvin, *please* don't tell Calvin!"

"I won't. I promise."

"I killed him, Bodhi. I killed another person—"

"Do you know how much I love you?" he tries to reassure me. "No matter what happened that night, or what you're still thinking—"

"No!" I cry out, pushing my hands against him as I try to back away. "You aren't allowed to love me after what I just told you! That's fucking stupid! Don't be fucking stupid!"

"*Eva!*" he forcefully whispers, pushing his hands firmly onto my back so I can't get out of his grasp. "Eva, look at me! Just *fucking* look at me!"

I slowly lift my head.

He points to his face. "I'm right here. *Right* here. Does it look like I love you any less? I'm so worried about you, and it kills me you've been holding onto this guilt for the last few weeks. My love for you though, that hasn't changed at all. Not one single bit."

"I *killed* him," I say again. "What I did killed him."

He brings his forehead to mine and holds his hand to the back of my head. "What you did is *exactly* what I would have done."

My hands push against him. My eyes frantically search his for the truth. "You would have killed your own dad? Crashed the pickup truck knowing what was going to happen to him?"

91

He nods his head slowly. "Luke, he's not my dad, and what he did to all of us that night—if I could have grabbed his gun and shot him right on your patio as he was taking you away from me, I would have. I would have, Porter would have, Coop and Luna would have. We all had the same thought that night, Eva. All of us. You were just the only one brave enough to execute it."

My head goes back to his chest.

"What do you think would have happened if the two of you did show up at his boat? We were all there. We heard the crash as we were standing by the docks. Beck, he was planning on running Luke over with his truck."

I gasp into his neck.

"Please, babe," he brings my head up. "Please don't let this eat away at you. We were not letting Luke leave with you that night, and if one of us had to kill him to keep the two of you from leaving, we were absolutely ready to do that."

I wipe my eyes with my hand. "I'm so sorry—"

"No. Don't apologize for something I wish I could have fucking done myself."

Bodhi's blunt words, even with how awful they are to hear as they leave his mouth, comfort me. They reassure me, *he* reassures me. His words wrap my entire broken soul up in the love that he constantly throws at me, regardless of anything I've said or done. He has no idea how much he saves me from myself every single second of the day.

"You are the only person in my life I'm always going to fight for, Eva. The only person who will ever own my heart and my soul. What you just told me does not change that at all." He tenderly brings his lips to mine, and then kisses away the tears that are still on my cheeks. "Why can't I fix this?" he then quietly asks, rubbing his thumb along my face. "I'm trying so hard. Why can't I fix you?"

I look away, only to feel his fingers guiding my face back to his. "I'm too broken. I've been broken too long."

"No. I'm not going to let you be broken forever."

I hear my voice quiver as I tell him, "You can't be my band-aid, not when there are so many pieces—"

"I will be right here, by your side, as we put each and every piece back together."

I bite down hard on my lip, hoping the pain will distract me from my emotions.

"Okay?" he questions. "Every single goddamn piece."

"Okay."

"Can we get up off this floor now? I would really like to hold you in my arms, over there," he points behind him.

He slowly stands, not waiting for me to answer, and pulls me up, keeping my hand in his as we walk back over to the bed. He climbs in first, lifting his arms as he waits for me to join him. I snuggle my way onto his chest again, our bodies fitting together like a puzzle. Both of us are our own separate piece, but we aren't whole until we are together, side by side.

"Eva?" his voice rings out into the still room, almost startling me as I'm lost in my own dark thoughts. "Don't ever second guess my love for you. If you think for even a second that something you did will make me not love you anymore, then I've failed you, and I will not fail you."

"I won't, Bodhi," I promise, my fingernails glide across his warm stomach, and I hear as he catches his breath.

"You and me," he goes on, "it's always been you and me. It's always been *you*, and if you ever doubt that, I'm right here to remind you, okay? You don't ever have to doubt that."

I lift my head up to look at him, and he immediately brings his lips to mine. "I never doubted it. I feared it, but I didn't doubt it."

His face falls. "You feared me not loving you?"

I quickly lower my lips to his again. I love his lips on mine. I love how it feels to forget about everything else going on when his lips are moving against my own. I love how everything in my mind immediately disappears when we're this close. These embraces make all the depressing thoughts simply vanish, like they were never there to begin with.

He pulls away. "Eva, nothing will ever change this indescribable amount of love I have for you."

My face is hovering over his, and I can't help but just stare at him, this perfect person that loves me so unconditionally. His dark eyes that see right into my soul, his bright blonde curls that I've

93

loved ever since I was twelve, his perfect lips that always gravitate toward mine. Does love always feel like this? Like the earth literally stops moving when we're together? Or am I just lucky?

"What is it?" he curiously asks.

I bring my lips closer to his. "I love you," I whisper against his mouth. "I'm *in* love with you, and I can't believe I'm lucky enough that I get to feel this way forever."

Bodhi grins as he moves my hair behind my ear. "I love *you*. I've always been in love with you, and *I'm* the lucky one."

My lips teasingly graze his as I mumble, "Please, can it always feel like this?"

"Always, I promise," he leans forward and his smooth lips move over mine one more time, before he brings me back onto his chest. "You need some sleep, okay?"

"Yes, sir." I move my head to the middle of his ribcage, my ear searching for his heartbeat, the beautiful steady rhythm that has lulled me to sleep so peacefully every night these last few weeks. "Confession," I say softly. "You need to talk to your grandparents and Owen. And you need to deal with the fact you have a little sister. Now. No more waiting."

He doesn't respond right away, but then he kisses my forehead and says, "Confession. You're right. It's time, and I will. As long as you're with me when I see them."

"Absolutely, Bodhi. I'll absolutely be there with you."

His lips find my forehead again, and his fingers run along my collarbone. I wonder if he realizes this hypnotic embrace puts me to sleep, and that I eagerly wait for his fingers to appear on this part of my body as we lie in bed every night. While they gently glide around the valley between my neck and my bone, and as my eyes start to slowly close, the feeling of calmness suddenly fills all the empty space in my soul. I'm never calm. I always feel like I'm about to boil over and explode. I don't know why it took me until right this very second, lying in the arms of the person who always makes me feel so safe, to understand this. That sometimes you have to shatter into a million fucking pieces over and over again before you can finally start to feel whole.

chapter twelve

Eva – the next day

Whating are you doing out here?" my mom asks me, walking out from the kitchen and joining me on the patio with a cup of coffee in her hands. "And where's Bodhi?"

"It's Wednesday," I tell her, taking a slow sip of my own coffee. "Produce delivery day at Dolly's. Bodhi missed the last two which is actually a *huge* deal to Coop and Beck, apparently. Like they'll probably still bring it up to him when they're old men, and don't remember their own names. I made him go help."

My mom laughs and takes a seat. "It's weird seeing you without him. It's like you two are just one person."

"I prefer it that way."

"I do, too," she agrees. "It's definitely better than it was ..." She stops mid-sentence.

"I'm out here waiting for Porter, actually," I make known, fully aware that she's thinking about him right now. "He leaves for Charleston today and I'm forcing him to come say goodbye to me."

"Got it. I think that'll be really good for Porter. I never met his mom, but I'm sure she's got to be better than his dad, right?"

"I never met her either. Never even saw a picture. He maybe has mentioned her two or three times the entire time I've known him. All I know is she divorced Mr. Channing when Porter was a toddler, she's remarried to a dentist, lives in Charleston, and Porter has a little brother and a little sister. I don't even know their names."

"Well, let's hope it's more stable over there than *that* ever was," she points to the Halifax.

"Do you regret smacking him across his face?"

"Absolutely not. The Porter I smacked deserved that. The Porter who is showing up here soon deserves a second chance away from all this shit."

"Yeah, he does."

"How was staying at Coop's last night?" she then asks. "Did you feel okay?"

To lie, or not to lie, biggest question of my morning so far. "We actually didn't sleep at Coop's."

She looks at me out of the corner of her eye. "Where did you sleep, then?"

"Bodhi's house."

"All of you?"

I shake my head. "After the dinner, I was tired and kind of sore. Neither one of us wanted to go sleep out on patio furniture, but I also didn't want to come back home. I've been stuck inside this house for weeks now and I just wanted something different. Please don't blame Bodhi. I was the one who asked him to take me there. We literally walked right in and went to sleep. I was tired and—"

"I believe you, Eva," my mom smiles. "I trust you both. I'm trying to be a cool, understanding mom, remember?"

I laugh. "I appreciate it."

She continues, "And had you called me last night and told me what you were doing, I wouldn't have made you come home."

"Yeah?" I raise my eyes at her.

"Yeah. Do me a favor and just tell me these things, okay? I like to know where you *really* are, and not hear about it the next day. Don't start being one of those sneaky teenagers now."

"Got it. I can do that."

"I can't believe you're going to be a senior this year. It's hard to swallow the fact this might be your last year at home."

"Mom?"

"Hmm?"

"I don't think I want to go back to my school this year."

Her eyes get big. "You don't want to go back to *your* school, or you don't want to go back to *any* school?"

I laugh at how worried she looks. "I want to go to school with Bodhi and my friends. I want to go to their school."

"Oh, thank god! I thought you were trying to tell me you wanted to drop out, or be homeschooled. Neither one of those I can mentally handle right now. I'll take care of it. Consider it done."

"For real? Twelve years at a private school and you're totally fine with me leaving for my very last year there?"

She grabs my hand. "Life is way too short to be miserable for a year around stuck up, spoiled teenagers. You want to be with your friends, who are not stuck up and spoiled from what I can tell. I'm totally fine with that. Plus, I really enjoy seeing you happy. If that makes you happy, I'm all for it."

"Dad ...?"

"Dad will be fine with it," she promises.

"Where *is* Dad?" I find myself asking. "I mean, one day he's here, then I don't see him for a couple days."

"That's how it's always been."

I reach down for my coffee. "I know that. I just thought maybe now that Mr. Channing is gone, he'd be around every day."

"I don't ask."

"Well, you should."

She lifts her coffee at me. "I raised you right. I *should* ask. And I will, when I'm not so pissed off."

I clink my coffee cup against hers. "We are *way* too much alike."

She grins. "Well, there's hope that your brothers didn't inherit our stubbornness."

"Miles and Rowan," I suddenly say. "When they start kindergarten in a couple years, don't make them go to a private school. They're so much cooler than that."

She laughs. "I'll talk to your dad. And I can't believe that I'm going to have you graduating this upcoming school year, and your brothers starting kindergarten the next."

"It's like you're starting all over again."

"Exactly. When you have kids one day, I don't recommend a twelve-year age gap between your first and your second."

"Noted."

Porter suddenly appears from the side of the house.

"I'm going to go check on your brothers," my mom says, giving me a wink. "I'm taking them to Tiki Bar in Ormond for lunch. You want me to bring you back anything?"

I shake my head no. "I'm good."

"Make sure you eat something, please." She then disappears back inside as Porter walks onto my patio. His hands are in his pockets, his baseball cap covers most of his face, yet I can tell he looks almost scared to be by me.

"Why does everyone look at me like I'm going to explode? Or rip them to pieces?" I ask him jokingly.

He snickers and takes a seat. "You've always had that effect on people, Eva. You look great, by the way."

I smack his arm. "You would have known this last week, or maybe the week before, if you didn't stop randomly showing up with everyone. Where'd you go, Porter?"

"I was staying with friends," he answers. "Calvin's great and all, but he lives right across from ..." his words taper off.

"I get it," I nod my head. "I haven't been able to walk my dock since I've been home. I don't want to see it, or what's left of it."

"It's a total loss, according to the insurance guys, but they won't say much to me because I'm a minor. I just heard them talking amongst themselves. There's nothing to save—"

"Your dad?" I ask him carefully.

"Still missing. I don't give a shit about him anymore. The amount of stuff I've found out these last few weeks—"

"What have you found out?" I interrupt him.

"*Eva* ... how many times have I told you to stay out of it?"

"*Porter*, you know I won't back down."

He dramatically shakes his head. "There's an investigation going on. The fire, my dad missing, of course there'd be an investigation. The city has taken it upon themselves to get everything cleaned up. I was at the house when they found a fireproof chest in my garage. Drugs, heroin was inside—"

"Your dad was dealing drugs?! Did you know?"

"Fuck no, Eva. I knew my dad was a shady asshole. But did I think he was a drug dealer? Hell no. And if he ever comes back, he'll twist this around. Someone else will take the blame. I know my dad, there's no way he'll go down for what was in that chest."

"I'm so sorry, Porter."

"I'm not. I'm obviously sorry about what happened to you, and I think I'll always feel like I somehow played a part in all of that, but

I'm not sorry for finding all this out about my dad."

"Are you going to be okay?"

He nods his head. "My mom is overly enthused about me living with her. I think she cried for an entire hour when I called her up and asked if I could move in. She might still be crying, actually. My stepdad, he's a goddamn pediatric dentist, and my younger siblings aren't even ten yet. They're like the picture-perfect family, and I'm ready to start over, be a different person where no one knows me or what's happened here."

"I think that's going to be really good. Porter, you aren't your dad—"

"I was turning into him," he interrupts me. "The way I treated you, how I treated other people. I was absolutely turning into him. And when he told me to make Bodhi disappear, like I was some goddamn seventeen-year-old hitman, I knew right then that if I stayed here, I would have ended up doing the exact same shit he's been doing all these years."

"And now you won't."

Porter lets out a deep sigh, yanking his baseball cap off the top of his head. He throws it down on the table.

"University of Florida?" I point.

He lets out a laugh. "My dad gave it to me when I was a kid. It's where he went. It's where he wanted me to go. He has the same hat. Don't know why I'm holding onto it."

"I think you should light it on fire and watch it turn to dust."

He grins, "I think you might be the only person I'll actually miss in this place. I know I screwed up with you, I know I don't deserve you at all, but I can't leave without making sure you know that I really did love you. I still do."

Porter's eyes search mine and I have to look away. He's waiting for me to answer him. I will never love Porter the way he thinks he loves me. He doesn't even know what love actually feels like. It's not what we had. What we had wasn't even a relationship.

I turn back to him and grab his hand. "One day, away from here, you're going to *really* fall in love with someone so perfect for you. She's going to make you forget about us the moment you see her. And it will be then that you realize what love actually feels like."

His face looks disappointed, but he quickly recovers. "If that happens, I'll let you know. You ever going to forgive me for how I treated you? For that day," he looks up at my balcony, "that day in your room?"

"I already forgive you."

He leans back in his chair. His eyes suddenly well up with tears. "I *never* would have done what you thought—"

"I know."

"I didn't realize I was hurting you."

"I know."

He looks away, shaking his head in disgust with himself.

"Porter, I *know*."

"You were the only person in my life that made me happy," he continues. "The only person I looked forward to being around, to seeing every day, but I knew I was losing you. I had known for a while. I was grasping at straws, and then I was just pissed off. And then Bodhi, I shouldn't have done that to him, on the street."

"No, you shouldn't have."

"I had nothing to lose at that point—"

"Me. You lost me at that point," I make clear.

His eyes narrow and he nods his head. "I did. And now ...?"

"Now I forgive you."

"Yeah?"

"Yes," I respond. "Those last couple days, before the accident, and then that night. I forgive you because I saw the old you coming back. The one you were before we started dating."

"I wish we could go back—"

"Life doesn't work that way."

"No, it doesn't." I think he suddenly realizes that no matter what he says, there's no chance of us ever being more than whatever we are right now. "I should probably go. I have a five-hour drive and my mom wants me there before dinner."

I laugh at how domestic that sounds. Nothing about Porter's life has ever been domestic.

He stands up, so I stand, too, and then he very carefully hugs me. "If you and Bodhi are ever in Charleston, let me know. I promise we can have a very normal, boring, no fighting, no screaming, lunch or something."

"Oh, we absolutely will let you know," I assure him.

"And don't take any shit from anyone. Promise me you'll take care of yourself, you'll let Bodhi take care of you. And both of you, try to stay out of fucking trouble, okay?"

I pull myself out of his hug. "I promise."

He leans in just a little, bringing his mouth to my ear. "Ask the questions, Eva. Don't be afraid to find out the truth. There's more to this, to all of this; you know there is, but be safe. My dad, he's out there somewhere, and he's *not* going to be happy when he comes back. Three people, Eva. There are three people you can trust." And then he whispers the very last three people I ever expected to come from his mouth. "Me, Bodhi, and your dad. Got it?"

I nod my head slowly up against his.

"You'll always be the only person who ever makes me happy." And then he gives me a quick kiss on my cheek before turning from me and walking away.

I make myself wait until he disappears completely before I let the tears drop from my eyes. I don't have one single romantic feeling in my body for Porter. I truly don't think I ever did. But I've known Porter for most of my life, and the Porter I knew before we dated wasn't the same ass he was *when* we dated. I know if he had stayed here, in Flagler, we would eventually have been friends somehow, like we were before. I think I'm just sad he's gone, and I'm confused as to why I'm sad, when I'm fully aware of how awful he was to me this last year.

I stare at my dock, the one place I was always able to escape to when my life felt so out of control. My feet start walking toward it, the familiar sense of comfort hits me as soon as I feel the hard wood through my thin flip-flops. I move further down, walking to the very end, watching my feet move the entire time, too nervous to look up to see what might be staring back at me from across the Halifax. The air is calm, the water looks like it's not even moving. I swear, there's not even a bird chirping in the trees.

I close my eyes, take a deep breath, and then look up. Porter's house is gone. The massive mansion that I used to see every single day of my life for the last decade has vanished. All that's left is a charred mess of burnt rubble, surrounded by still construction vehicles that must be there to clear away what's left of that awful night. How is it possible that Mr. Channing doesn't care about this? How is it possible that he could just leave Porter to deal with all the shit that he brought upon himself, and threw Porter right in the middle of?

I lie down in the little shade I can find on my dock, dangling my feet below me as my head rests on the uncomfortable wood, closing my eyes again. I think I know why I'm sad Porter's gone, and it's not because I'm going to miss him. It's because I feel bad for him. It wasn't until a few weeks ago that Porter realized our relationship meant nothing to me. It was at that same time I jumped straight from him to Bodhi. I will always have Bodhi. I will always be able to depend on him and know the love we have is real. What does Porter have? *Who* does Porter have? He has a father who abandoned him, a mother he barely knows, siblings whose names he's never even shared, and most of his belongings he's lost. He has nothing and no one. No one who understands all the shit his dad has put him through. That is why I'm sad. I'm sad because if he had stayed, at least he would have had me.

"EVA!" I HEAR a familiar voice yell my name through my dreams. My body jerks awake with the sudden sensation of movement below me, as my dock bounces up and down. "Owen, I can't tell if she's breathing!"

My eyes pop open with this name, and I see Calvin hovering over me. He moves slightly and the sun glares right into my eyes. I squint and sit up.

"Thank *god*," Calvin sighs with relief. "You're okay."

"Of course I'm okay," I groggily declare. "Why wouldn't I be?"

"Because you were lying there, not moving, with the sun beating down on you in the heat of the day."

"I fell asleep," I tell him. "You guys really need to stop thinking I'm just going to drop dead." I move my sweaty hair off my neck. "Shit, it's fricking hot out here."

"It's ninety-six degrees outside and you're taking a nap on your dock? You need some water," he grabs both my hands and pulls me into a standing position. "Get on board for a minute and let me get you something to drink."

I look past him to the yacht that is swaying on the Halifax. "Is that Owen's?" I question. I didn't see it the night of the accident, but I'm assuming this massive yacht in front of me can only be his.

Owen suddenly appears in my vision. "Long time no see, Eva," he grins.

I stand there and cross my arms over my chest. "Kenneth and Annie on that thing too?" I glare at him. "I'm not getting on his yacht," I turn to Calvin and say.

"Fine. Then I'll walk you back home and into your house and explain to your mother why I'm making sure you drink a glass of water, and why you're probably going to have a sunburn all over your face and chest later today."

"She's not home," I smirk. "She took the boys out to lunch."

"Then I'll wait inside with you until she gets back."

I push past him and step on board Owen's yacht. "Jesus Calvin, I was just tired!" I head inside the cabin, throwing myself down at the table. Calvin walks in with Owen and they both glance over at me, but neither of them say anything. "Water?" I throw my hands up. "That's why I'm here, right?"

Owen grins. "She reminds me of Annie," he says to Calvin. "At that age. She didn't take shit from anyone either."

Calvin hands me a glass of water and I purposely drain it all in one gulp, slamming the cup down on the table. "Don't talk to each other about me as if I'm not here," I say to Owen.

Owen sits down across from me. "Sorry," he sincerely apologizes. "Last time I actually spoke to you, you were five and you dumped a bottle of bubbles on my lap."

My cheeks turn red and Calvin laughs, "I remember that."

I have no desire to sit here and catch up on my past that I don't remember with Owen Edwards. "Is this the yacht you were picking up in the Bahamas when my dad and Mr. Channing brought Bodhi and Lenora back to Flagler?" I blurt out.

Owen's mouth opens a little and he curiously tilts his head to the side. "No. It's actually not."

"This isn't the yacht that you apparently disappeared on? The one Luke told me was somewhere at the bottom of the Atlantic with you still on board?" I continue.

"Is that what he told you?" Calvin quietly asks.

"It is," I confirm.

"Well, he got part of the story right," laughs Owen. "That yacht *is* somewhere at the bottom of the Atlantic, but I'm not on board."

I roll my eyes. "You both need to understand why it's so shocking to see that you're alive and well, especially since you did indeed leave Flagler and never come back."

"There's a reason for that," Owen tells me.

I lean back in my seat. "I'm sure there's a reason for everything. But I'm tired of trying to figure out what all those reasons are. Especially when they involve me, and *especially* when they involve Bodhi."

"Where is Bodhi?" Calvin asks.

"He's with the guys, helping out at Dolly's," I answer. "Where's Kenneth and Annie?"

Calvin points down the Halifax. "Staying in a vacation rental on the Halifax, but they won't be here much longer—"

"Why not?" I question.

"Because they can't stay in Flagler," Owen makes known. "This isn't their life anymore, mine either. Your dad—"

"What does my dad have to do with the three of you?" I angrily ask him.

Owen folds his hands and places them on the table. "He brought us back here to help Bodhi, to explain everything—"

"Eva," Calvin interrupts. "Do you think you could get Bodhi to join us all for dinner tomorrow?"

I start laughing. "I can try, but the chances are pretty slim."

His concerned eyes look right at mine. "I think he should listen to what they have to say. I think you both should."

I narrow my eyes at him, and then I turn to Owen. "I'll get Bodhi to join you all for dinner if you answer a few questions for me, Owen, right now."

He chuckles, "She is *just* like Annie."

"I have no relation to her, correct?" I quickly question. "Because you keep saying I'm like her—"

"You do not," Owen shakes his head. "You just really remind me of her."

"That's a relief. Because that would really complicate things between me and Bodhi."

They both laugh under their breaths, which only annoys me.

"You going to answer my questions?" I raise my eyes at Owen.

"I will."

"Why did you leave Flagler?"

"I had to," he answers. "I knew things about the past, and I didn't agree with things that had happened, and feeling that way was only going to get me in trouble."

"Get you in trouble with who?"

He slowly turns his head to the window and points right at the charred mess that used to be the Channing estate.

I take a much-needed deep breath. "What did my dad do to you?"

His eyes grow large. "What did he *do* to me?"

"Yes," I respond. "I overheard a conversation with my dad and Mr. Channing, the night you disappeared. That day, what did he do to you?"

"He didn't do anything to me—"

"Now you're lying," I harshly exclaim.

"He's not, Eva," Calvin puts his hand on my cast. "He's not lying."

"Then explain to me what happened," I heatedly demand.

"I don't know what you overheard," Owen says, "and I don't know what your dad told Henry Channing, but the only thing I do know, is that I wouldn't be here today if it wasn't for your dad."

"I think you need to elaborate a bit more with that statement," I frown.

Owen's eyes raise. "Your dad, Eva, he didn't *do* anything to me. He found me on my yacht, explained exactly what was going to happen to me, and he got me out of Flagler before Henry Channing could put a bullet in my head. Your dad, he saved my life."

chapter thirteen

Bodhi

Wait a minute, Bodhi. You're trying to tell us that Eva caused the crash? She turned the truck into the trees?" Beck questions, shocked.

We're sitting on the outdoor patio at Dolly's, eating a late lunch after getting all the produce put away.

"She did," I nod my head. "At least that's what she told me."

"*Shit*," Coop sighs. "You hanging in there, bro? That's a lot to deal with."

"I am," I say. "She said she panicked, that he wasn't taking her to the docks, but the airport. She panicked and knew they would get found somehow, so she grabbed the wheel."

Coop shakes his head. "That girl of yours, she needs her own superhero cape to wear around Flagler or something. Does Calvin know this?"

"No!" I loudly exclaim. "I don't think he'd hold it against her, but I promised I wouldn't say anything."

"We won't say anything," Coop points to himself and Beck.

"She thought I was going to hate her because of what happened to Luke."

Beck grunts. "I was going to run the bastard over with my truck."

"We all would have done something," Coop adds. "You tell her that?"

"Of course I did, after I watched her completely fall apart."

Beck spins his straw slowly around in his water glass. "You worried about her? I mean, she's starting to look normal and everything, but is she *really* doing okay?"

I don't answer him. I just stare off at the ocean. This is a loaded question, one I'm not sure how to break down.

"Bodhi?" Beck presses on. "She okay?"

I look back at him. "I'm not sure."

"Yeah?" Coop questions. "She seems okay around us ..."

"That's the thing," I continue. "One minute she's fine, and then the next—the next she isn't, and she's falling apart."

"Bro," Coop points at me. "Don't try to figure this out on your own. If Eva's struggling, maybe she should get some help—"

"You think Eva's going to ask for help?"

"*No*," Coop replies. "But I know of one super fine gentleman caller of hers that might be able to guide her in the right direction."

I give him a grin. "I think her breakdown about what happened that night might have been a turning point. I think she's been holding onto that guilt all this time. She seemed to be okay this morning, now if I could get her to fucking eat something, then I wouldn't be so worried about her."

"Luna's noticed that," Coop tells me. "She also mentioned that Eva might have had an issue with that in the past?"

I nod my head. "Those three years destroyed her. And right now, she's at home, probably saying bye to Porter. He's part of the reason she was such a mess—"

"You jealous, bro?" Coop asks.

"Of goddamn Porter?! Hell no."

He gives me a look.

"I trust her. I don't trust him, but I trust her. I'm just happy he's leaving. Having him around these last few weeks, and actually feeling bad for him, has confused the shit out of me."

"And now the only other person who has seen Eva naked—"

"Coop!" I shout out his name. "Don't even."

He continues. "I'm just saying. Never having to see his face again, knowing his eyes have seen—"

I start throwing my cold fries at him. "Stop. Please, I'm going to throw up. Yes, I'm happy he's leaving because of *that*, but I'm also happy he's leaving because he adds to Eva's unstable mental state."

Beck starts stacking our empty plates. "Just be there for her."

"I am."

"And talk to her," he continues. "I have a feeling she'll listen to

107

you."

Dolly and Beck's grandpa suddenly appear at our table. Dolly's a normal presence at her restaurant, but Gramps likes to work more behind the scenes—and when I say behind the scenes, I mean on his fishing boat letting Dolly have control over everything.

Dolly throws herself down next to me. "How's it going, Bodhi?" she asks. "Eva? Haven't seen her out at all since she's been home."

"I'll bring her in. She's doing good, all that's left is the cast."

"That's great to hear," Gramps responds. "I want to take her fishing. I heard she kicked all your asses?"

"That story is fabricated," Coop groans. "Beginner's luck—"

"You're just embarrassed," I throw another fry at him. "I have no problem admitting she's better at fishing than the three of us."

Coop throws the fry back at me. "I want a rematch."

"I'm out," Beck chimes in. "She'll kick our asses again, and oddly, I'm totally fine with that."

Dolly picks up one of the fries from my basket and takes a bite. "You tell her I'm making her lobster and steak on the house, bring her in for dinner soon. Hey, that kid find you guys?"

"What kid?" Beck asks.

"Scraggly looking fellow," Gramps replies. "Fourteen, maybe fifteen? Desperately needs a haircut?"

We all shake our heads.

Dolly shrugs her shoulders. "Oh, well. He came in and asked if you three were here today."

"He specifically asked for the three of us?" I question, curious.

"Sure did," she replies. "Looked nervous as hell, too. You three better not be getting drugs from him or some shit like that."

Coop smiles sweetly at her and points to the three of us. "Do we look like the type of fine young men who'd be seeking drugs out from some young punk teenager?"

"You really want me to answer that question?" she raises her eyebrow.

I laugh. "Next time you see him, get a name."

"Don't think I'll see him again," she makes known. "He about pissed his pants when I suggested he sit out here and wait for you all." She stands and grabs our plates, tossing them into Gramps' hands. "Stay out of trouble. And bring Eva in for some dinner."

AFTER LUNCH I head back to the Halifax. Eva's house is strangely quiet when I let myself in, so I head right upstairs to her room, knowing that's where she probably is. Her door is wide open and she's sitting on her bed, her eyes staring at the screen of her camera. I gently tap on her door to get her attention.

"Hey there, Bodhi," she smiles.

I can tell she just got out of the shower, and her natural beauty is literally lighting up the empty space circling around her. Her damp hair is hanging in loose waves around the frame of her face, and her skin looks like it's glowing, almost as if she spent the entire day sunbathing, and just put on some sort of silky after-sun lotion. She's wearing a light gray t-shirt dress that comes down right to the middle of her thighs, and it forms a dangerous dip on her chest. I can see her black bra through the thin fabric and I have to force my heartrate to slow down before I even think about walking over to her.

Does she realize how gorgeous she looks right now? Just sitting there with wet hair and no makeup on. My entire body is screaming at me to go over there and kiss her everywhere I possibly can. I desperately want her skin under my lips. I desperately want to feel her body under my own.

I bite down on my tongue and hold up a plastic bag. "I brought you lunch from Dolly's."

"You did? Good. I'm starving."

I walk over and stand next to her bed, placing the bag of food on the nightstand. She puts her camera down and sits up on her knees, wrapping her arms around my neck, placing a small kiss on my lips. Her chest is pressed right up against mine, and I can't help but glance down for just a second. Stupid move, Bodhi. Definitely not extinguishing my desire to rip off her dress and have sex with her, that's for sure.

"How was Dolly's?" she asks, oblivious to the fact that I'm imagining her naked right now.

I bring my eyes back up to hers, and my hands to her arms. God, she smells good. "Same as usual. Coop and Beck argued about useless shit until I threatened to leave, Dolly made us fish tacos—oh, and some weird kid was looking for the guys and me, apparently, but he left before we got done unloading the truck."

She tilts her head and says, "Well, that's different."

"Yeah," I agree, bringing my hand under her hair and to her neck. I start massaging her tight skin with my fingers, while bringing my other hand under her dress and to her warm thigh. I literally can't stop myself from touching her right now. My mouth moves to her ear. "How has your day been?"

"Good …" she slowly replies, biting her lower lip and giving me a curious look. "But this makes it even better."

"That lip, Eva," I growl, staring at how pink it suddenly has become. "When you bite it …"

"I know," she grins at me. "I know exactly what it does to you."

My hand comes out from behind her hair, and I push at her lower back so she moves in closer. "How are you feeling today?" I then ask, my lips leaving a row of kisses on her neck as my free hand goes under her dress and to her other thigh. They're so goddamn smooth and my fingers easily glide over them with little effort on my part.

"I feel … amazing," she breathes into my ear. "This feels … amazing. I really like your hands on my body, in case you didn't know."

"Is anyone home?"

Her hips slowly move closer to mine as she quietly says, "No …"

I bring my eager lips to hers, carefully guiding her body back onto her bed at the same time. I will not have sex with her. *I will not have sex with her.* "Just this," I mumble into her mouth. "We can only do this. Can we just do this without wanting it to be more?"

"No," she groans, her hands slide under my shirt and her fingers push into my stomach. "But we can try." My lips find their way to the dip in her dress. "Just take it off," she demands.

I shake my head with my lips still on her. They push the front of her dress down further so that I can kiss the tops of her breasts that spill out from her bra. "No," I say into her warm skin. "Just this, Eva."

110

"*Just this* sucks," she whimpers, her fingernails now clawing into my back.

I bring my lips to right above hers, and look into her desperate, hungry eyes. "We could do nothing instead."

Her hand comes out from my shirt, and she pulls my head down so that my lips crash onto hers. I squeeze my fingers into the bed, using them to support my body, as my tongue slowly moves inside her warm mouth. I'll stay exactly like this, for as long as my arms let me, while her mouth moves beautifully with mine. Our lips are like magnets, each one its own force that attracts the other. Once they're together, it's almost impossible to break them apart.

I feel her suddenly bite down on my lip, her fingers grazing my chin. I bring my mouth back to her chest, kissing as far down as her dress will allow me to go. I start sucking on the soft skin of her breasts, moving from one to the other. My greedy lips are starved for the taste of her under them, and her moans only urge me on more. I can't help myself. I want her in ways I've never wanted her before, and knowing I can't have her right now only makes me want her more. I suck harder, fully aware I'm leaving marks on her skin, marks only the two of us will know about.

Her fingers roughly pull at my hair and she whines, "*Bodhi.*" Hearing my name leave her mouth in that tone makes me growl into her chest. She tugs harder as my lips continue to move along her breasts, and I suddenly feel her thighs push up against my sides. "Bodhi, touch me. *Please* can you touch me?" she begs.

Holy shit. I'm currently living out one of the many fantasies I've had about Eva over the last three years. I bring my mouth to hers and say, "You don't *ever* have to beg me to do that."

My hand quickly moves under her dress, my fingers slip around the side of her panties, and she gasps as I start moving them against her. The sound of pleasure that escapes her mouth only makes me move faster. It's instant. Like she's been waiting to feel this way forever, and now that she is, she's fully giving in to every sensation that's overtaking her body. I can't even begin to explain how much of a turn on this is. I'm literally getting sexual satisfaction by just listening to the noises that are coming from her mouth.

"Is this okay?" I ask, my lips pressing hard against her neck. I don't want to do anything that will hurt her, but I also have no desire to stop. I've missed touching her like this, hearing her like this. "Are you okay? Your stomach? Should I stop?"

Her fingernails dig into my shoulders and I wince at the sudden pain. "Don't you dare stop."

I grin into her neck as her body arches flawlessly into mine. I know what she's getting ready to do right here on her bed, with only my fingers touching her, and it's as sexy as hell. She's close, I can tell, and I move faster to get her there, because I want to get her there. I have to get her there. I absolutely love making her feel this way. I love knowing only *I* have ever made her feel this way, and I love seeing her come undone as I touch her.

Her fingernails attack my shoulders again, and her legs squeeze hard against my sides, when suddenly her phone chirps from the nightstand. We both freeze. We know what this familiar chirp means. She quickly grabs it, reads the screen, and then throws her head back on the pillow and lets out a loud growl, as she tosses her phone down next to her.

"My mom and brothers just pulled in," she releases an irritated sigh. She then whimpers and pulls the pillow over her face.

Dammit. I slowly remove the pillow and her stunning eyes stare back up at me. I can see myself in the reflection of the light green. "You were close?"

"God, I was."

"I wanted to hear you just as much as you wanted it to happen," I whisper to her. "That was *really* fun though," I then say, kissing her nose.

"It was."

"But I probably shouldn't have my hand under your dress when your mom walks in the door, right?"

She laughs. "No, you probably shouldn't."

I roll off of her, placing my hands in hers and pulling her carefully to a sitting position. I tuck her still damp hair behind her ear, and run my fingers along her cheek. "Confession. When I see you like that, when I *hear* you like that, knowing I'm the reason you feel that damn good, I forget how to even exist."

She places her hand on top of mine that's resting on her cheek.

"Confession. When you make me feel like that, *I* forget how to even exist."

"Eva!" we hear her mom shout from the bottom of the foyer. Her steps can be heard as she walks up the stairs. "You home?!"

Eva grins at me, quickly placing a kiss on my lips before answering. "We're up here!"

Mrs. Calloway appears in the doorframe moments later. "Hi Bodhi," she smiles at me.

"Hi Mrs. Calloway."

"I told you to stop calling me that," she sighs. "I feel old when you call me that."

"What would you like me to call you?"

"Audrey is fine," she replies.

"Can *I* call you Audrey?" Eva smirks.

"Hell no. I didn't go through twenty hours of labor with you for you to call me Audrey," she points at Eva. "You eat lunch?"

Eva nods to the bag of food on her nightstand. "Bodhi brought me lunch."

"Of course he did. Your brothers want to swim. I'll be out by the pool if you guys need anything, okay?"

"Thanks, Mom," Eva responds, as we watch her walk away.

I grab the bag of food and hold it out to Eva, raising my eyebrow up at her as I wait to see if she'll actually take it.

She does. "Thanks for bringing me lunch," she then says, pulling the container out from the bag. She opens the lid, immediately grabbing a hushpuppy and biting into it.

"Anytime," I reply, leaning up against her headboard. "I want to make sure you eat. I've noticed you haven't had an appetite lately."

Her chewing slows down and she looks over at me. "You've noticed that?"

"I notice everything about you."

She pops what's left into her mouth and brushes her hands on her legs. "I'm not doing it on purpose, I promise. It's just, sometimes my mind is so busy thinking about other things, I forget to eat. Or I just don't feel hungry, don't be worried—"

"I *am* worried."

She gives me a little grin, and scooches herself in next to me, placing her head on my shoulder. "I'll try harder. I swear, it's not a problem—"

"Were the last three years a problem?"

She tilts her head up to look at me. "Maybe."

"But right now, it's different than that time?"

"I think I hope it's different."

"It is," I declare. "Because I'm here now, and I won't let it become as bad as it was then."

She lifts her head off my shoulder and wraps her arms around my neck. "You always save me from myself."

I run my thumb over her wet lips. "We save each other, that's what we do."

Her arms tighten, the damn cast digging into my skin as her fingers wrap around my hair. She tugs a little before placing her forehead on mine. "Porter left," she whispers. Not what I thought she was going to say next.

I move her hair off her neck and place my hand right below her ear. I can feel her pulse through my fingers. "Are you okay with that?"

"I am, and you'll never have to compete with Porter—"

"I know, but you're sad he's gone?"

She nods her head against mine. "Yes, and I realized earlier it's because I feel bad he doesn't have anyone. I just feel bad for him."

"I feel bad for him, too."

"Yeah?"

"Yes," I respond. "He'll always be a dickhead to me, and I'll never forgive him for what he did to you ... but that night, maybe then, and these last few weeks, he's become less of a dickhead and more of someone I actually saw trying to be a better person."

"He was. I really think it was all his dad. He grew up living with that man. That's all he ever saw. Porter told me today they found drugs in his house. Heroin."

I'm not surprised that's what he's been involved in. I trace her face with my finger. "I always wondered if that's what Mr. Channing was doing."

"Do you think my dad—"

"Not at all," I immediately interrupt her. "Not at all, Eva. When

114

I overheard your parents talking, the day we came home from the hospital, I heard more than just the trust fund stuff. I don't think your dad ever worked for Mr. Channing. I think he made it seem like he did, but he actually works for someone else."

"Who? Who does he work for? And why didn't you tell me this? I thought we weren't keeping things from each other?"

"That conversation honestly slipped my mind. Those first few days back are all a blur, and the only thing that stuck out from what I overheard was the trust fund part. I don't know who he works for, he didn't say," I continue. "I have a feeling there's a lot your dad has hidden from your mom all this time."

"I knew *that*," she sighs. She moves her hands off my neck and sits down next to me, grabbing another hushpuppy and popping the whole thing into her mouth.

"I almost wonder if your dad has secretly worked *against* Mr. Channing all this time."

I see her swallow hard. "I saw Calvin and Owen today."

I can feel my eyes raise. "Where?"

"On my dock," she answers. "I actually went on his yacht for a minute—"

"You did what?!" I exclaim. I don't trust Owen, not yet at least.

Her face blushes and she quickly blurts out, "I might have fallen asleep on my dock. Calvin thought I was dead—I was overheated and needed some water. He pretty much forced me on the yacht. Don't be mad. I was seriously on it for maybe ten minutes."

"Calvin thought you were dead on your dock?" I'm trying not to laugh at the vison of Calvin panicking.

"It was kind of funny."

"Did Owen say anything?"

"Just that my dad saved his life," she bluntly replies. "The conversation I overheard my dad have with Mr. Channing, my dad apparently snuck Owen out of Flagler that day, before Mr. Channing could do anything to him. He acted like he had gotten rid of Owen, when actually he saved him."

"Have you talked to your dad about any of this?"

"I haven't seen my dad at all today." She reaches into the container and grabs the sandwich, taking a big bite and waving it in front of my face. "You know what this all means, right?"

I watch her for a minute before curiously questioning, "What does it all mean, Eva?"

She takes another bite, and then tosses it into the container. "We have yet another mystery to figure out."

I place the food on the table next to her bed, pushing her down in the process so that I'm hovering over her again. "I am not letting us get dragged into another dangerous mystery, Eva Calloway."

She quickly kisses me while still chewing. "We've already dragged ourselves into it, Bodhi. We just needed time to overcome the shit we both went through a few weeks ago, before we could start digging for more answers."

I groan and forcefully push my lips onto hers. "I'm just going to keep doing this," I kiss her again, "every single time you bring it up."

She pulls my head down and kisses me. "Wrong way to try to get me to stop. I enjoy this very much, Bodhi."

"I thought we decided weeks ago to let your mom and Calvin take over?" I remind her, before I crash my lips back on hers.

She pushes us apart. "We did, and I gave everything in that suitcase to my mom yesterday."

"You did?"

"I did, and maybe as we uncover shit, we can fill them in, my mom and Calvin. You know, keep them in the loop this time? Not deal with everything on our own?"

I narrow my eyes, but then bring my lips back down. I keep them there, longer than the other times, before pulling myself away. "I find it dangerously difficult to say no to you."

"That's really good to know. Oh! One other thing—"

"No!" I groan. "Nothing more!"

"It's a *good* thing," she laughs. "My mom said I can transfer to your school."

My eyes go huge and I instantly smother her face and neck with kisses. "Are you sure that's what you want?"

"After seeing this reaction? Yes."

I stare down at her. "For real, Eva. You aren't doing this because you think it's what I want, are you?"

"It's what *I* want," she answers me truthfully. "I want to see you

116

throughout the day, and Coop, Beck and Kennedy, too. I want you to take me to school in your jeep, hold my hand in the hallways, and bring me home when school is over. Okay?"

"I can do all three of those," I nod my head. "And I'll add a fourth to that list."

"Oh yeah? What'd I forget?"

I kiss her lips once more. "Lots and lots of my lips, on your lips, in between classes."

"That was a given." She pushes me to the side so I fall onto my back, and she rests her head on my chest. My fingers immediately start running through her hair.

"I can't believe you're going to *my* school. I was dreading school this year, but now, now I can't wait to make-out with you at your locker. Or sneak into an empty bathroom with you."

"You're going to get us suspended on the first day."

"Nah, they love me there," I declare. "Oh, Kennedy stopped by Dolly's today as we finished up. She needed me to pay for your spa treatments over the phone for tomorrow."

"Tomorrow?" she questions. "What time?"

"I think she said she was picking you up at ten? Coop said he'd bring Luna by beforehand. Is that okay?"

"Yes, but you and I have plans at six."

"Oh, we do, do we?"

"We're having dinner at Calvin's, with Owen and your grandparents."

I hear myself take in a deep breath. "Eva Calloway, you planned this dinner behind my back?"

"No. When I saw Calvin with Owen today, he mentioned it, and asked me if we'd like to join them. I simply said yes."

"You're lucky you're so beautiful and I love you so goddamn much, and that you just told me you're transferring to my school, so I'm still riding this happy wave of intense overjoyed emotions."

She grins and places a quick kiss on my lips. "You're welcome," is all she says back. Then she snuggles deeper into my chest and slowly dozes off in my arms.

117

chapter fourteen

Bodhi — the next day

What the hell do girls do all day at a spa?" Coop asks seriously.

Kennedy picked Eva and Luna up about an hour ago, and now the guys and I are down at the beach, lying on our surfboards. No one really wants to surf just yet. The flag is red and the waves look ruthless today.

"From what the receptionist told me over the phone when I paid the bill, it's a lot of facials, nail painting, and hair shit," I shrug my shoulders. "With some fancy lunch in between everything."

"You didn't have to pay for all of them," Beck throws out there.

"I wanted to. Eva's been through hell. I wanted Kennedy to do whatever she wanted without having to worry about money."

"Well next time, let us help," Beck says.

I look over at him and Coop. "Guys, I'm never in my entire life going to blow through that money that's in my trust fund. Hell, it will take me years to go through what's in the regular bank account my mom left for me. Please, let me share the wealth with the people who actually matter in my life."

Coop's eyes grow large. "So, what you're telling us is you're gonna be our sugar daddy from now on?"

"If that's what you want to call me. I'm okay with that. How's everything going with Luna?" I then ask. "Are you two officially dating now?"

"Hell if I know," Coop mutters, throwing sand in the air. "Luna does everything so different from most girls. She's not clingy, she doesn't text me a hundred times a day, she doesn't want me hanging out with her parents or joining her family for dinners. Sort of lost on what the hell's going on."

"Have you two had sex?" I blurt out.

"Shit, Bodhi!" Coop exclaims. "I thought we weren't talking about the details of our personal lives and the stuff we do behind closed doors with people we actually care about."

"I think knowing what you two have done might help us figure this out," I tell him. "Beck, wouldn't you agree?"

He points to me and nods. "Yep. Where are we at here, Coop?"

"Almost there, but not quite." He throws himself back on his surfboard. "I don't want to rush into shit with her. I don't know why I don't want to, I just ... don't."

Beck and I exchange a surprised look.

"Do you want to date her?" I quickly ask. "Or is she just another—"

"I want to date her," he interrupts me. "I think."

"Thank *god*. Eva would murder you in your sleep if you hurt Luna," I make known.

"Trust me," Coop sighs. "I'm well aware of Eva's threatened rages when it comes to Luna. I'm actually scared of her. Don't leave me alone with her in a room, please."

"Coop, just ask Luna," Beck suggests. "Ask Luna if she wants to be your girlfriend. If she wants to be exclusive. Ask her what she wants."

"People actually do that type of shit?" Coop questions.

We both laugh. "Yeah," I then say. "It doesn't hurt to ask."

"I'm not good with this," he sighs dramatically. "How do you make it look so goddamn easy with Eva? And you Beck, Kennedy moves away for almost a year, comes back and everything is exactly the way it was before she left."

"Bodhi and Eva are different," Beck says before I can answer. "And Kennedy and me, neither one of us really dated anyone while she was in Tampa, so why wouldn't we just pick back up where we were before?"

"Well, you both fucking suck," Coop declares.

"You and Luna will figure it out," I reassure him.

"Yeah, yeah," he grumbles. "What about you and Eva?" he points to me. "You two back to how it was before? You looked pretty damn cozy during your sexy beach scene a couple days ago. Did you really take her home after that?"

"No. We went back to my house."

Coop starts laughing. "Oh, so that was just code for needing some alone time away from her family?"

"Wasn't like that at all," I make clear.

"*Sure*, Bodhi," Beck snickers.

"She's three weeks and like—four days out of intense surgery on her abdomen, assholes," I hit my hands in the sand. "Do you honestly think we're just banging every chance we get? No sex. Not for another two weeks and three days, that is."

"Got a countdown going?" Coop winks. "A little paper chain hanging from your bedroom door?"

"Six weeks. We were told six weeks."

"Shit man," Beck mumbles. "From seeing how you two were before this all happened, how rough is that?"

"Fucking hell," I sigh. "But so was watching her die in the back of an ambulance."

I catch the guys off guard with how bluntly I just said that. They both have uncomfortable looks on their faces. I lie back on my surfboard, staring up at the insanely blue sky, waiting for one of them to speak.

"Sorry," Beck finally says. "I know that was awful to witness."

"It was."

Coop hits my surfboard. "And I'm sure in two weeks and three days, you both will have the most insanely hot love making session the state of Florida has seen in over a hundred years."

I grin and sit up. "Definitely counting on it."

"You guys were barely together for a week before the accident," Coop continues.

"Yeah? What are you getting at with this?"

"It was just that once, right? The night of the storm? I mean, waiting six weeks for the second time will almost make it feel like the first time again. Extra special."

I stay silent, ignoring Coop's statement while Beck curiously stares me down. "Unless there already *was* a second time," he says.

Coop quickly looks between Beck and me. "Shit, Bodhi!" he then yells. "You telling us in that week span you and Eva ...?" He quickly covers his ears. "No! Never mind! I don't want to hear anything!"

"I wasn't going to say anything," I roll my eyes.

Beck laughs under his breath. "Your silence is enough."

"You two were safe, right?" Coop goes on. "I mean, goddamn, your future children are going to look like they were blessed by fairies and gods during conception, but please don't start early like Luna's parents did."

"Fairies and gods?"

"Shit, both of you are embarrassingly beautiful," he responds. "Your children will come out of the womb with modeling contracts."

"We were safe," I then say. "We've been safe, we'll be safe. Eva's on birth control, does that ease your mind at all, Dad?"

"Little bit. But at the same time, I was thinking it was only once just to find out it's been more. You sleep next to her every night!" he then cries out. "For real, your hands haven't wandered—"

"*Coop*," I warn.

"I'm just saying," he throws his arms in the air, "almost a month of sleeping in the same bed with her. She's obviously feeling better, you can't tell me you aren't taking advantage of the fact that your extremely hot girlfriend is by your side all the time."

I roll my eyes again at Coop and look over at Beck for some reassurance that I'm not the only one who thinks he's once again being overly dramatic.

"Dude," Beck grins. "I'm with Coop on this one."

I shake my head at both of them. "I said we weren't having *sex*, that doesn't mean since she's been feeling better, we haven't—"

"Knew it!" Coop shouts. "I knew there was no way you could resist—"

"It's not just me," I make known. "Trust me. It's very hard to resist her, but Eva ..."

"You trying to tell us she's not as sweet and innocent as she looks?" Beck asks.

I glance at them both and raise my eyebrows. "You trying to tell me you've thought all this time that Eva's sweet and innocent?"

They both laugh.

"I will drown you two in the ocean if you *ever* tell her I said this," I point at them, "but she's got this side to her, this sexual side—"

"Of course she does!" Coop exclaims. "Look at her, bro! She's like the fantasy of every teenage boy on earth! Jesus Christ! I'm never going to be able to look at her the same again!"

Beck throws his body back into the sand and starts hysterically laughing. "You just discovering this now, Bodhi? Or did you discover this before the accident?"

"Definitely before, and definitely now, too," I respond. "She is *very* comfortable exploring—"

"Stop!" Coop shouts. "I can't hear anymore! You two sexual beings make me blush. I feel like even when you're looking at her, I'm interrupting something my juvenile eyes shouldn't be seeing. Remind me not to be around you in two weeks and three days. Everything within a ten-mile radius might implode that night."

"She's transferring to our school. She asked her mom yesterday."

"*Jesus!*" Coop groans. "Now we're going to have to watch you two make out and be all touchy feely in the halls of our school, too?"

"I think it's great," Beck states, sitting back up. "It's going to be different though, but a good different," he quickly throws in there. "Kennedy's going to love it. She thinks Eva's a badass."

"Eva *is* a badass. But can you both do me a favor this school year? Just help me watch out for her. I'm sure between us, and Kennedy, one of us will be in each of her classes. Don't let anyone bother her."

"We've got it covered," Beck tells me. "No one will bother her."

"I've always wanted to be a secret bodyguard for someone," Coop adds. "Put my ninja skills to good use."

"She just doesn't need any shit to happen this school year."

"What if anyone makes a move on her?" Coop then questions. "Eva's a hottie, a new hottie joining our school for our senior year. Hormones are seeping out of oily pores in that building, and you know how some of those guys are. Throw Eva in the lion's den. You want us to kick everyone's ass who attempts to pursue her without the inside knowledge that she's pretty much wed to you already?"

Shit. I didn't even think about other guys hitting on Eva. Coop's right. There are some pretty shady assholes at our school. "I want you to punch them in their face," I answer honestly, scanning the beach as I see a crowd of people jumping in the massive waves.

"Yes, sir," Coop laughs.

"Speaking of shady assholes," I nod my head toward the water. "Is it just me, or does that kid down there keep staring at us?"

The guys both turn to look, which immediately makes the kid spin in the other direction. He trips as his feet get caught in the sand, and he disappears under the incoming wave.

"He's definitely got eyes for us," Coop agrees. "Fucking clumsy as hell, too. Shit! Fourteen, fifteen, in desperate need of a haircut, looks like he's going to piss his pants ..."

"The kid from Dolly's," I confirm.

"Should we go talk to him?" Beck questions. "Find out what he wanted?"

"No," I immediately reply. "He knows where we are. He wants to talk to us, then he can come over here." The kid suddenly emerges from the water, staring at us the whole time.

Coop points at him. "I think we've got an obsessed stalker on our hands."

Beck squints his eyes. "Who's he hanging out with?"

"Stoners," Coop declares. "I've seen them at parties. Think most of them have already graduated. Isn't that Charlotte down there? She still fixated on you, Bodhi?"

I hit him on the arm. "I haven't heard from Charlotte since the end of school last year." Charlotte and I have a small history, one I don't like to think about.

"Good," Coop grunts. "Don't need the drama of Eva meeting Charlotte. Why the hell is that little shit hanging out with those half-baked losers?"

"You want to go ask him?"

"Hell no. I've already got you to worry about. I don't need to add some greasy kid to the list of shit that keeps me up at night."

"I need to surf," I suddenly declare, jumping up and grabbing my board. "I don't care if these waves beat the shit out of us. Enough about obsessed stalkers, enough about my sex life, enough about Eva, enough about other guys hitting on her, and enough about girls from my past. Let's go surf."

chapter fifteen

Bodhi

A few hours later, the guys and I are dragging ourselves in through Eva's garage door. I don't even knock. Mrs. Calloway told me to stop behaving like a stranger about a week or so after Eva came home. No need to knock, ring doorbells, or walk around acting like I was *just* the boyfriend. So, I don't. I'm starting to feel so comfortable in Eva's house, it's a little unnerving. Even being in the same room with her dad doesn't make me feel like I'm going to vomit anymore. Though he isn't around much. I don't ask questions, but I'm definitely curious as to where he disappears to all the time.

"Rough day in the waves?" Mrs. Calloway asks as we walk in through the kitchen. I'm sure we look like shit.

"I feel like they were brutally attacking my body," I admit. "With purpose."

"I think I might have a concussion," Coop adds.

"I'm good," Beck announces, shrugging his shoulders.

Coop whacks his head. "Only cause you sat out the last two hours like a little chicken."

"What's that you're saying?" Beck leans his ear toward Coop, and cups it with his hand. "I'm smarter than you both? Yeah, I agree with that, too."

Coop whacks his head again.

Mrs. Calloway laughs. "Girls beat you back. They're upstairs in Eva's room."

"Thanks," I say, and I push Coop and Beck out of the kitchen.

When we come down the hall upstairs, Eva's door is slightly cracked. I push it open to see all three girls sitting on Eva's bed, clothes and jewelry scattered around them. Eva sees me before

Luna and Kennedy realize we're even there. Her hair looks like black silk as it hangs down around her face, and she looks like she might be glowing.

She smiles and stands from her bed without even saying anything, walking right to where I am. The guys walk further into her room, leaving me standing there in the doorframe. I pull her waist into mine the moment she gets close enough. Just touching her after five or six hours apart sends chills down my spine.

"You look absolutely beautiful," I whisper in her ear, before giving her a quick kiss. I run my fingers through her soft hair. "How was your day?"

"Best spa day *ever*!" Kennedy says for her.

Eva smiles and then looks at Luna. "Even Luna enjoyed herself."

"I actually did," Luna nods her head in agreement. "I'm shocked and think my parents might believe I've joined a cult. You both have created a monster and I might have to feed this new side of me at least once a month in order to keep it happy."

"We can totally arrange that," Kennedy declares, clapping her hands with excitement.

Eva turns back to me. "It was really great. Much needed and much appreciated. Thank you." She kisses me, and then pulls me by my shirt over to her bed.

"What's all this?" I point to the mess of clothes and jewelry.

"We're helping Eva decide what to wear to dinner with your grandparents tonight," Kennedy answers.

"Dinner with your *grandparents*?" Beck loudly questions.

Coop hits my arm. "Dude, you don't fill us in on this type of shit anymore?"

I sit down on Eva's bed, scooching over and pulling her into my side. "I was told about this dinner yesterday by my very beautiful and caring girlfriend, who I love so very much."

Everyone laughs.

"Doesn't sound like you're too excited about it," Beck points out.

"Excited isn't a word I would use to describe how I feel toward it. *But*, it's time to at least see them. Maybe get a few answers about things that don't make any fucking sense."

Coop starts shaking his head. "I don't see this ending well."

"I think that's the motto for everything that's happened this summer," I agree with him.

Eva brings my hand into hers and starts rubbing my fingers. "I think in order for Bodhi and me to put that night behind us, we need to sit face-to-face with his grandparents and Owen, and let them tell us what they know. There's a lot of stuff we found in Lenora's studio that night, and it would just be nice to hear their side of everything."

"I think you're absolutely right," Luna nods her head.

"*And* ..." Eva continues, "once we find closure in that, we can deal with the other little things that don't make any sense, and then the bigger question."

"Which is?" Beck raises his eyebrow.

Eva looks up at me again and nods toward everyone. I let out a loud sigh and say, "Where my little sister is."

The expected gasps echo in the room.

"What the hell, Bodhi!" Coop shouts. "You have a fucking little sister?"

"I do. Apparently."

"He does," Eva tells them all. "Luke—he told me, when I was in his pickup truck. Before, well—you know."

"Do you know anything about her?" Beck asks me.

"She's eight," I answer him. "She lives somewhere not too far from here, and her name is Skyla."

"Skyla?" Beck questions. "Shit, Bodhi! That was the name of the boat that was docked that night!"

I can't deny the shocked look that's probably on my face right now. "Totally didn't make that connection. Is it still there?"

"Disappeared a few days after everything."

"Where the hell did it go?"

"*Bodhi* ..." Coop slowly drags out my name. "Please don't try to tell us we're about to go down another rabbit hole. The last one, it didn't end very well."

"We aren't," I say. "But to be honest, I feel like we never crawled out of the last one. We're still in it, it's just a different tunnel now."

"Screw this!" Coop declares. "What happened to floating around in a pool and getting fat off of Calvin's cooking?"

Eva lets out a little laugh, but then gets serious. "Coop, Luna ..."

she says softly. "I never heard. How did you get to my house that night? Was it with Luke? Was he following you guys?"

Luna and Coop exchange a look. "He must have been," Luna then replies. "After dinner at Oceanside, we walked across the street to the beach. When we went to the parking lot a little bit later, he was right next to Coop's car. He forced us to his truck which was parked in the back, then took us right to your house."

"Where did he park?" Eva quickly asks. "When you got here. Where did he park his truck?"

"Right outside your gates," Luna continues. "They were open. We walked right down your driveway and to your backyard."

I can feel Eva's breathing increase through her back that's resting against my arm. "What's wrong?" I ask her. "What connection did you just make in that mind of yours?"

She looks me right in my eyes. "That's *not* where his truck was when he and I left."

"What the hell does that mean?!" Coop exclaims.

"Think about it, guys. How could one person go from following my mom to the movies, slashing her tires, stealing her phone, then to following you two to Oceanside," she points to Coop and Luna. "Then back to my house, all while burning Porter's house down across the Halifax at the same time?"

We all exchange worried looks.

Eva continues. "His goddamn truck was parked in the woods across the street. You tell me how he managed to move his truck, while also threatening half of us in my backyard with a gun?"

"He said he didn't light the match," Luna says softly. "I remember him saying that, about Porter's house."

"No, no, no!" Coop covers his ears with his hands. "You trying to tell us someone was helping Luke?"

Eva nods her head. "He told me he has friends everywhere. He asked me how I thought he got his truck."

"Who?!" Beck practically shouts. "Who in the hell was helping him, here in Flagler?"

"I don't know," Eva quietly says. "I think we just need to keep it in the back of our minds, that we weren't the only people in Flagler he knew."

127

"Wow!" Kennedy's voice rings out. "Beck told me you all dabbled in some twilight zone shit this summer, but this is pretty insane."

I lean back up against Eva's headboard, pulling her with me and into my arms. "I've had enough of this twilight zone shit," I finally say. "And I don't think searching for more answers is going to benefit anyone in this room right now."

"Finally!" Coop throws his hands up. "Some common sense!"

"*But*," I then say. Coop throws his hands over his face. "If answers magically appear, without us barely lifting a finger, then I think I'd be okay with that."

"I love a good mystery!" Kennedy excitedly declares.

Coop groans. "You weren't smack dab in the middle of the last one."

"I think we need to find out where the boat went," I tell everyone. "Maybe that will point us in the direction of who was helping Luke while he was here."

"*Bodhi*," Coop sighs. "Look at Eva! Look what happened the last time we decided to search for answers!"

"What happened to me," Eva says, "would have happened regardless of what we searched for. He was already here, watching us, just waiting to do something. The outcome might have been a little different, but it was always his plan to use me as collateral."

Coop throws himself back on the bed.

"No one's going to search for anything," I promise him. "It's not like it was before. The only thing that would really be nice to figure out, that I might have to dig around for answers to, is where my little sister is. Which, by the way, no one knows about her. We're keeping this to ourselves until we have more answers."

"Fine, man. Fine," Coop groans. "This is a slow-moving investigation, you got it? We don't do anything crazy, and in between figuring shit out, we float around in a pool and let Calvin feed us delicious food."

"Deal," I agree.

"This one," Kennedy suddenly announces, holding up a dress from Eva's bed. "This is the one to wear tonight, with this," she grabs a necklace. "What do you think, Luna?"

"Love it," she agrees. "And your bracelets," she adds, holding them out. "The dress is perfect. It reminds me of summer sunsets, and it won't show off your boobs too much."

Eva lets out a laugh while Coop and Beck groan.

"What?" Luna turns to the guys. "She's meeting Bodhi's grandparents tonight. She doesn't want to show off too much of those beauties. We can't deny Eva's amazing, voluptuous—"

Coop's hand covers Luna's mouth. "I think on that note, it's time for us to head out."

They all start climbing off the bed.

"Have fun tonight, guys!" Kennedy cheerfully says, walking out the door with everyone following.

"Yes, and stay out of trouble," demands Coop. "Let us know you're alive after dinner, all right?"

"Yes, Dad," I reply.

"Don't think we won't show up here if you don't," Coop threatens.

I salute him with my hand, as he nods his head in approval and walks out the door. Eva instantly snuggles into my side, wrapping her arm around my chest as she fits so perfectly up against my body.

"I like this," she tells me tenderly. "Just us, like this."

"I like this too, babe. Was today too much?"

She brings her eyes to mine. "Not at all. Spa days are always exhausting, but it was a lot of fun. It felt weird to have fun, almost like I forgot how to? Or I shouldn't be for some reason?"

"You need more days like that."

"Oh, I think those type of days are definitely in my future. Kennedy, I have a feeling she's making it a mission this year to be my best friend, and to convert Luna into a full-blooded Halifax girl."

"Kennedy has always been like that. Very social. She's really popular with lots of girls who *think* they're friends with her, but she's always kept to herself, mostly. She just hangs out with us guys."

"I totally get that."

"She told Beck she thinks you're a badass."

Eva lets out a snort under her breath. "I wish I felt like a badass. I love it, though. I never really had friends before—girls that I would

129

consider friends. Luna and Kennedy, they're so different, but the three of us together, it just works." Her fingers start running along my arm. "How was surfing?"

"Good," I answer, and then I start laughing.

"What's so funny?"

"Coop," I respond. "He's totally freaking out because he's not sure how to label Luna and him."

"That's ironic, because Luna told us the same thing. She's not sure what he's waiting for."

"Coop has never had a girlfriend. He's new at this. I think he second guesses every little thing he says and does with her."

Eva leans in and gives me an unexpected kiss on my neck. "Well, I think Luna's just going to ask him, because she's tired of waiting for him to do it. If you haven't noticed, Luna doesn't do things the way typical girls do."

"Totally noticed."

"And Kennedy and Beck," Eva continues. "Kennedy's worried what will happen to them once we all graduate. I just felt bad."

"Why'd you feel bad?"

"Us. As soon as we saw each other again, it was almost instant. We were together, and the future, no matter what we decide we want to do after we graduate, I know we'll be together, right?"

"I'll follow you anywhere, babe," I reassure her.

"It's comforting," she quietly replies, "to know that we don't question our future together. That at seventeen, I've already found the person I know I'll be with forever."

"You *are* my future. You're my past and present, too. You're my everything, and no, we don't have to question our future together."

"I love that."

"Speaking of our future," I go on, "I'm not sure I want to go to college, though. I feel like there's something better I can do with my time, and all that money. I've been blessed for reasons I don't think I'll ever truly know, and I don't want to waste four years of my life when I don't have to. I'm going to figure it out, I will, but if *you* want to go to college, I completely support that."

"I haven't really given it much thought, and I know I should, which scares me. I think last year I was determined to get out of here, to go to college just so I could escape life, but now," she pauses, sitting up completely and staring at me as a small grin forms on her face. "Now I'm completely fine with staying right here with you, forever. Well, not *here*, but like ten miles down the road from here."

"So you'll marry me now?"

She shakes her head and laughs. "No. Ask me again in a few years."

"A few years?!" I exclaim. "We'll be so old by then."

"*Bodhi*," she sighs.

"I'm joking, Eva." I pull her closer to me. "You know, it's okay to take a year off to figure out if you want to go to college."

"I know. I just feel bad that the world is pretty much ours, we can literally do whatever we want, while our friends are worried about things we don't have to worry about."

I slowly bring my lips to hers, kissing her gently while my hand holds onto her chin. "I'm not going to let any of our friends think the world can't be theirs, too."

"I know you won't, and that makes me love you even more." She rests her forehead on mine. "I love how easy it comes for you and me. Knowing that it's always going to be us, no matter what."

"Why do you think that is? Why does it come so easy?"

"That's simple, Bodhi. It's because we're soulmates. Our relationship is etched in stone somewhere, we were always destined to be together. We just had to find each other first, and then find our way back to each other."

I bring my mouth to her ear. "Confession," I whisper to her. "I truly believe we're just one soul that's split into two separate bodies. Neither one of us knows how to live life without the other one. We stumbled around those three years, just waiting, and the moment our souls were reunited, we felt whole again and could actually live. This theory explains why I feel so utterly lost when I'm away from you for even an hour. My soul feels split without you by my side."

Eva's eyes grow large and she brings her hand up to my cheek. "Confession," she quietly says. "I can't top that. That's the most beautiful thing you've ever said to me, Bodhi. It's as if you took those words straight from my heart. I don't know how you do that all the time, take exactly how I feel, and form those feelings into words."

I smile and move her silky hair away from her eyes. "Because how you feel is how I feel."

She pushes me back down onto her pillow, and lays her head under my neck. "You absolutely own my heart, Bodhi Bishop. Nothing will ever change that."

I tap my chest. "Do you hear that? How my heart races madly whenever you're near me? Every single time I'm with you, I have to remind it to slow down. You absolutely own *my* heart, Eva Calloway. You always have, and you always will."

chapter sixteen

Eva

I'm nervous. I typically dive head first into situations without letting anything change the way I think or feel, but tonight I'm nervous. I can tell Bodhi is, too, which doesn't help calm down my own thoughts at all. I shouldn't have agreed to this dinner. I should have let Bodhi decide when we would meet with them, and not drag him into this right now.

I grab his hand as we start walking through the path that will take us to Calvin's house from mine. "I'm sorry I forced you to do this tonight," I quickly say, and then I stop walking. "I can pretend I'm not feeling well or something—"

"Eva, it's okay. I think it's a little too late to back out now. It will be fine, we'll be fine."

"Yeah?"

He leans in and places a quick kiss on my lips. "I forgot to tell you how absolutely gorgeous—"

"*Bodhi*," I sigh. "Compliments aren't going to change the fact we're three minutes away from meeting—"

"You *are* gorgeous. And as long as you're by my side, tonight will be fine."

"I'll make this up to you."

"I'm going to hold you to that."

I stand on my tiptoes, placing my lips on his. "I'm counting on it." Then I take his hand into mine and we continue on the path through the trees.

Moments later, we walk out directly into Calvin's backyard. They're all out there already. Calvin, Owen, Kenneth and Annie. They look deep in conversation, until they hear us approaching, that is. They freeze, staring at us concerningly like we're wild animals getting ready to pounce on their family picnic and drag away the weakest member.

"Well, this is awkward," Bodhi mumbles as we continue moving closer to them.

"I promise, I'm making this up to you."

"Bodhi! Eva!" Calvin announces our arrival.

"Hey Calvin," Bodhi responds.

"Do we need formal introductions?" Calvin continues, nervously looking between everyone.

Bodhi lets out a little laugh. "That's not necessary."

Annie suddenly steps forward from behind the shadows of her husband, her long red hair looking so much like Lenora's, it almost takes my breath away. I've seen her and Kenneth in pictures, but this is the first time I've seen either of them in person. It's a little strange, to be honest, especially since Bodhi and I both thought they had died decades ago.

"Eva," Annie's warm voice says my name. "Phoebe always talked about you—how beautiful you were. She was absolutely right. You don't see beauty like this every day. It's really nice to see you all grown up."

I look over at Bodhi, whose eyes are staring straight in front of him. He's not even blinking. I turn back to Annie. "Thank you," I sincerely respond. "We always called her Lenora," I then say quietly. "And I think I'm speaking for both Bodhi and me when I say, I'm confused as hell by what you just said."

"Why don't we all take a seat?" Calvin suggests. "Let me run inside and grab the salad."

He disappears up the patio steps, leaving us all standing there in silence. I tug a little on Bodhi's hand and guide him toward the table. I'm not about to stand here and see who moves first. He pulls out my chair and leans his head down to mine as I sit.

"Prepare yourself," he whispers into my ear. "I have a feeling we're getting ready to hear a lot of crazy shit." He then sits down next to me and turns his chair toward mine. "You curious as to why my mom was talking about you to her parents, who we thought were dead?"

I bring my mouth to the side of his face just as everyone joins us at the table. "Let them talk. Whatever we hear, it doesn't change you and me. Nothing from the past changes us."

His fingers appear on my chin and he brings my face to his, gradually bringing his lips to mine as if no one else is sitting directly across from us. When he pulls away, he lets out a little sigh before turning his chair in the right direction.

"Remind you of anyone?" I hear Calvin's voice.

Owen lets out a loud laugh. "These two," he points to Kenneth and Annie. "Definitely these two. Remember that hunting trip we all went on our last year of high school?"

Calvin groans. "The one where you almost shot my hand off?"

"I was aiming for that turkey and you got in the way!" Owen laughs.

"How many turkeys *did* you shoot on that trip?" Calvin asks.

"Legally? One per day," he winks.

Calvin turns to Eva and me. "Owen can shoot a turkey from a mile away. So can Kenneth, but *that* trip, he was too busy with Annie."

Annie blushes and Kenneth throws his arm around her shoulder. He's a large man, not heavy, just built big, like he could snap a massive tree branch with two fingers if he wanted to. His thick white hair parts to the side of his face, and you just know by looking at him that he was extremely attractive when he was younger. I find myself glancing between him and Calvin, Bodhi's biological grandpas, seeing him in both of their faces. I look back at Annie and catch her staring at me. She quickly looks away and down at her empty plate.

Calvin starts dishing salad out to everyone. "Bodhi," he smiles up at him. "When you going to move in with me?"

Without missing a beat, Bodhi replies, "I figure Eva and I would skip our senior year of high school, and just move into my house together instead."

Calvin drops the salad tongs and his face turns white. "Did you discuss that with Eva's parents—"

"Relax, Calvin," I laugh, nudging Bodhi in the shoulder. "He's joking. I'm actually transferring to his school for this last year." I then look over at Bodhi. "I guess we're kind of at the point where it's

135

time to start thinking about when you'll move in with Calvin?"

"Yeah?" his eyes narrow as he questions. "Probably would be better to do it before your dad has an embarrassing talk with me."

"I think it might be better for you to do it before we're *told* it's time for it to happen." I rest my head on his shoulder and then say to Calvin, "We're a package deal, though. You ready to see my face in your house all the time?"

"I've already stocked the cabinet with coffee for you. Whenever you're ready, Bodhi, I'm ready for you—and Eva."

"I lived in this house before," Annie suddenly says.

"That's right!" Calvin exclaims. "For a couple months, we were seventeen, right?"

"You lived with Calvin's family?" Bodhi questions her.

"I did. My parents—there were a few months they weren't around. I came here ..."

"That's ironic," I chime in, stabbing some salad with my fork. "I lived here too. Twice actually."

"Aren't you two cousins?" Bodhi points to Annie and Owen. "Why would you live with Calvin's family and not your own?"

Owen lets out a loud laugh. "*I* didn't even live with my own family. Hell, I stayed with Calvin most of the time."

"Did you live with Calvin, too?" Bodhi questions Kenneth.

"Nah, but I sure as hell was over often enough."

Bodhi leans back in his chair, glancing between the four grown adults sitting in front of us. "Alright," he finally sighs. "The elephant in the room is massive, and obviously there's a lot of shit I don't know about my mom, or her family—*you* guys," he waves his hand at them. "So let's just lay it all out. I'll start. Calvin, I didn't know about you until what, a little over a month ago? Kenneth and Annie, my mom told me you both died in a car crash when she was eighteen, but she never told me your names or talked about you. And Owen, Eva and I were both told you were dead at the bottom of the ocean. Would someone like to explain to the two of us why the three of you are back from the grave?"

There are a few murmurs from everyone, but no one really says anything coherent.

"I think what Bodhi's trying to say," I softly speak, "is that neither one of us knows what to think anymore, and every day we're finding out more things that just don't make sense. We found your journal entries, Annie. The ones that explain your parents—"

"She kept those?" Annie questions.

"She hid them in the backs of pictures," Bodhi answers.

Annie turns to Kenneth. "Why would she hide them?"

"I don't know, honey."

I speak up. "Maybe so that Bodhi would eventually find them? Maybe she wanted him to discover her past, to ask questions. She left him so much money, obviously he was going to try to find out where it all came from. Maybe she was hoping after she passed, Bodhi would figure out about you guys. Her birth certificate, her real one, she hid that in the back of a picture that she left for *me*."

"For you?" Annie confirms.

"Yeah," I nod. "And if Bodhi and I weren't together when I found it, I would have gone right to him when I did. I wonder if she put it there to give us a reason to see each other again."

"I definitely think that's something she would have done," Annie smiles.

"She left behind so many planned chances for us to reconnect," I go on. "I know they weren't coincidences."

"She also hid a whole shit load of other things," Bodhi adds. "Including your and Kenneth's death certificates."

"Those were fake," Kenneth declares.

Bodhi laughs sarcastically. "Well, obviously I'm aware of that now."

"Why did she tell Bodhi you guys were dead?" I question.

"Why did she leave the Bahamas?" Bodhi throws out there. "Why did I not know about either of you? Why do I have a passport with stamps from Turks and Caicos when I don't ever remember being there? Why does she have passports filled with stamps from Turks and Caicos *and* the Bahamas, when she never told me she was going to either of these places? And how the fuck was she so goddamn loaded with money but never let on—"

"We're just really confused," I quickly interrupt Bodhi, placing my hand in his and giving it a tight squeeze. "You have to understand that *we* knew Lenora, and you three," I point to Annie,

Kenneth and Owen, "knew Phoebe."

"My mom," Bodhi's voice shakes a little, and I can tell he's trying to regain his composure. "My mom is *not* the person I thought she was." He looks down at my hand in his, and rubs his fingers on my knuckles.

"I'm sorry, Bodhi," Annie quietly says. "I'm so sorry. Everything Phoebe did from the moment you were born was to protect you from a life she didn't want you to know anything about. She should have told you. I'm sorry she's not here anymore to explain—"

"You are," he bluntly responds. "*You* are here. So tell me. And if you aren't planning on doing that, then just let me know now, so Eva and I don't waste another minute stuck in the middle of this bullshit."

"Start at the beginning," Calvin turns to Annie and immediately says. "When we were teenagers."

Her face softens. "You read some of my journal entries, so you know what our parents did?"

"Drug dealers, money launderers?" Bodhi answers. "Well-respected jobs in society?"

"It was much worse than that," Kenneth makes known. "When we discovered what our parents were doing, it was as if they didn't even bother keeping it a secret anymore. Imagine waking up and having someone sitting at the kitchen table with your mom, eating her homemade pancakes, complimenting her on how fluffy they are, while a gun sits next to his plate. A loaded gun that he would gladly use on her, if your father didn't show proof in five minutes that the millions that were dropped off a few days before were safely dispersed in their proper locations."

"Or coming home after school," Annie sighs, "to some hallucinating druggy sitting on your steps, completely out of his mind and demanding you hook him up or he will ..." she pauses, obviously fighting back memories that have entered her mind. Kenneth leans over and places a kiss on her head.

"I can't imagine any of that," I gently say.

"Owen?" Bodhi questions. "It was the same for you?"

"It was worse for me," he bluntly answers. "But we don't need to bring up those details."

Bodhi turns to Calvin. "You and Rose, you knew about this?"

"We did."

"We all decided that after high school," Kenneth continues, "we were going to get the hell out of Flagler and never look back, but then my dad died."

"Heart attack?" I ask.

Kenneth lets out a small chuckle. "What do you two think?"

I cautiously look over at Bodhi, who just shrugs his shoulders. I turn back to Kenneth. "I think that's what they wanted you to believe, but I think he was probably murdered."

"You've got yourself a smart girl there, Bodhi," Kenneth grins.

"I'm aware of that," Bodhi says back. "Why would your dad dying put a halt to your plans of getting out of Flagler, though?"

"My dad had a lot of money that wasn't his, tied up in businesses that were in his name," Kenneth responds. "I couldn't leave until I knew for sure my mom and sister weren't going to get tied up in any of this. It took some time for things to get sorted out."

"Was there drug money?" Bodhi then asks. "Did you leave Flagler and head to the Bahamas with drug money?"

Kenneth takes Annie's hand into his own. "My family was extremely wealthy," he says. "Going back a hundred years, I would say. Did I know where all that money came from? No. I figured it out eventually, that my family always had ties with the local drug dealers in Florida. We had numerous bank accounts with millions in each one. Family money. When I decided I wasn't going to follow in my family's footsteps, I withdrew one of the accounts that had my name on it. My mom didn't even notice until after I was gone."

"There was no drug money?" Bodhi asks again. "You guys didn't take drug money?"

"They did," Owen responds. "*We* did."

"Money your dad brought in?" Bodhi continues.

Owen nods. "My dad was not a good guy for numerous reasons. The last drop off to Kenneth's dad was money *my* dad had brought in. My dad thought that if Kenneth's dad was out of the picture, and that money mysteriously went missing, the blame would be on Kenneth's family. He knew where that money was, *I* knew where that money was. So before he could get it, I did."

139

"Did your dad kill Kenneth's dad?" I ask, shocked.

Owen shrugs his shoulders. "We'll never know. But I was not about to let him get away with this. Kenneth was *always* my family, not my dad."

"So you took the money and did what?" Bodhi swiftly asks.

"I camped out here, at Calvin's house, while the dust was settling, and while we made our plans to get the hell out of here. My dad, he got what was coming to him. The money he insisted he gave to Kenneth's dad was gone, and the blame was now all on him to get it back. When he couldn't, he was taken care of. I was then free to live whatever kind of life *I* wanted. I left Flagler with these fools, but was able to come back without worrying anything would happen to me—until Henry Channing, that is."

Bodhi waves his hand in front of him as his frustrated eyes look at mine. "*This* is my family."

I turn back to the grown adults watching us. "You not only had the money from the bank account, but you also left Flagler with millions of dollars in drug money that you pretty much stole straight from a drug cartel?!" I ask in disbelief.

"You call it drug cartel," Owen smirks, "but we called it family."

"And no one knew?" I ask, appalled. "No one suspected that the children of the drug dealers and money launderers snuck away with all this money?"

"We didn't stay long enough to find out," Annie replies. "And besides, this was pocket change to them. They got their revenge and moved on."

"Calvin," Bodhi suddenly turns to him. "Your family had *nothing* to do with this? Any of this?"

"No, son."

"But you and Rose went with them?" Bodhi asks. "You all went to the Bahamas together?"

"We did."

"Your parents? Rose's parents?" Bodhi throws his hands in the air. "Did they know where you were? Where everyone was?"

"They did," Calvin sighs. "Rose and I, our parents knew everything. They knew what was going on, how Annie, Kenneth and Owen needed to get out of Flagler, what was going on with their families—"

"And they just let you leave?" Bodhi raises his eyebrow in question.

"They helped us. We had a plan. A strong, solid plan for our future, and yes, they just let us leave. My parents took on the responsibility of all my friends. They treated them like their own kids. They wanted to help, and they did. They also came to visit numerous times. They kept our secret, and so did Kenneth's sister."

Bodhi leans forward into the table. "And no one *ever* found you two?" he asks Annie and Kenneth.

"No one ever found us," Kenneth responds.

Bodhi sits back in his chair, picks up his fork, and starts eating his salad. Everyone follows, doing the same, and the sudden sound of loud chewing makes me want to crawl out of my own skin. I force a couple bites down myself, and watch as Bodhi tosses his fork angrily onto his plate.

"My mom," he suddenly says. "Why did she leave the Bahamas when she was eighteen?"

"Time for some spaghetti!" Calvin announces, pushing himself back from the table. He disappears inside the house so quickly, it's almost as if he wants nothing to do with this conversation anymore.

"Before we talk about that," Annie calmly says, "I think you both need to hear what we did when we got to the Bahamas. What we did with the money we left Flagler with—"

"Restaurants?" I guess. "You guys opened restaurants? We saw some pictures."

"That was part of it," she smiles. "We also bought a few vacant homes on the beach. We lived in them while we renovated, that's where a majority of the money went. In the Bahamas, people don't ask questions. You pay with cash, they thank you. They work hard, and they appreciate your business. These homes, they became vacation homes that we'd profit from all year long. Back in the seventies and eighties it wasn't as easy as it is now, listing rentals online and stuff. We needed an easier way to meet vacationers without getting too involved, so we purchased a restaurant and a coffee shop."

"Who worked in them?" I ask.

141

Calvin pops out from the patio door, carrying a giant bowl of spaghetti. He doesn't say anything at all as he starts scooping it into our bowls.

"Calvin," Kenneth laughs as he says his name. "Eva wants to know who worked in our restaurant and coffee shop in the Bahamas?"

Calvin beams and looks right at me. "Rose and I did," he answers. "Rose was in the coffee shop, and I was in the restaurant. How do you think I learned how to cook so damn well?"

Kenneth, Annie and Owen all laugh with what he says.

"We both also spread the word on the vacation home rentals to any and all tourists," Calvin makes known.

"And Kenneth and I continued to invest money in more homes," Annie chimes in. "By the late eighties we had over twenty houses in the Bahamas."

"Calvin," Bodhi turns to him. "You and Rose left though, right? When Luke was little?"

He nods his head. "Luke was born a couple years after Phoebe was. They knew each other as little kids, toddlers really. I think we were there a good ten years when Rose and I got the itch to leave. We were never planning on staying there forever. It was beautiful, and we were all very successful there, but Rose and I always wanted to travel and see the world. So we took all the money we saved, and left when Luke was around three. If I recall, Owen started his own adventures around that time, too."

Owen nods his head. "I sailed up and down the coast."

"Luke never saw my mom again?" Bodhi questions him. "You and Rose never went back? He never saw her again until she showed up there on her own?"

"Life got in the way," Calvin says to Bodhi. "We never went back. We traveled all over the world, and then as Luke got older and everything started happening with him, our only goal was to try to get him help."

"But my mom told him her *real* name!" Bodhi exclaims. "You can't tell me he didn't know this was the same Phoebe Rialson from his childhood!"

"He was three when we left," Calvin tells us again. "Any memory he might have had of her was no longer a memory as an adult. The last time he saw her, he was three. Do you remember anything from when you were three?"

"No," Bodhi grumbles.

"You and Rose never talked about your life in the Bahamas as Luke grew up?" I ask. "Never mentioned Kenneth and Annie? Phoebe?"

Calvin sadly shakes his head. "Maybe at first, but as the years went by, no. We decided not to tell him about our past here in Flagler, because he was struggling with drug addiction. Telling him about the Rialson family, and Annie and Owen's family, would just add fuel to the fire."

"But Luke showed up in the Bahamas, right? At some point? Did you not run into him?" I question Annie and Kenneth. "I mean, the Bahamas isn't that big. Would you not have recognized him?"

"People change," Annie answers. "The Luke we last saw at three was not the same Luke we eventually saw decades later. We didn't make the connection, not for a while, actually." She pushes her hair off her neck and leans forward a little, like she doesn't want anyone else to hear what she's about to say. "We lost touch with Calvin and Owen. It shouldn't have happened, but it did. No pictures, no letters, no emails, social media didn't exist. And by the time Luke showed up in the Bahamas, we weren't even there anymore."

"Where the hell were you?!" Bodhi boldly asks.

"Bodhi!" Calvin loudly says his name with disappointment.

Annie holds her hand up to Calvin. "It's okay, Calvin."

"Where *were* you?" Bodhi stresses, looking between Annie and Kenneth.

Annie takes a deep breath. "Turks and Caicos. We live in Turks and Caicos now."

chapter seventeen

Bodhi

O f *course* you do," I grind my teeth as I say. "Do *not* lie to me, how many times did you see me when I was little?"

"Five?" Kenneth answers right away. "Six. Six times."

"And my mom?"

"Twice a year? For a long time," he responds.

"Why did she stop bringing me to visit?" I manage to ask. I'm struggling to even get simple words out of my mouth at this point.

"She stopped because she didn't want you to remember us," Annie's voice barely whispers.

"*Why*?" I loudly question.

"Because she didn't want you talking about us here," Annie responds. "She didn't want anyone to know who she was."

"*Why*?!"

"Because of us," Kenneth points to he and Annie. "Because of our families, our past. She didn't want anyone here to know she was our child, that you were our grandson. It's still going on here, the drugs, the people. Maybe it's not obvious, but trust me, it's still going on."

Eva's fingers press down hard on my hand. "Why the hell would she come back here, then?" she asks. "Why would she leave the Bahamas and come here, just to have to live this secret life away from her family?"

"Because she fell in love," Annie sighs.

"*Excuse* me?!" My bowl of spaghetti clatters against the table as I almost knock it over with my fist. "With who?!"

"Declan Ryder," Annie and Kenneth both say at the same time.

My eyes dart between the two of them. "I feel like I've been dropped onto some alternate universe here. I've never heard of this person, *ever*."

"You wouldn't have," Annie agrees. "He died a long time ago."

I need a break. I look down at my bowl, at the untouched spaghetti. I take a massive bite, just giving myself something to do, and some time to calm my nerves down. I know they're watching me, waiting for me to ask more questions, but I can't. One, this spaghetti is the best goddamn spaghetti I might have ever eaten in my life, and two, I'm not sure if I want to hear anything else.

Eva's hand appears on my leg under the table. "Who was Declan Ryder?"

Annie slowly places her fork down against her bowl. "Declan and his family were tourists. They started coming to the Bahamas when Phoebe was around eight. They stayed in one of our vacation homes, and booked the same one twice a year, for a decade at least. Declan was Phoebe's age, and he had twin sisters who were a couple years younger than them, Olivia and Sienna."

"The home they would rent was just a few doors down from our own house," Kenneth adds. "So naturally, Phoebe would spend time with Declan and his sisters whenever they were vacationing. They usually rented it for a month in the summer, and a couple weeks over the holidays."

"Eventually, Phoebe and Declan became more than just friends," smiles Annie. "I would say it was when they were sixteen? By the time they were seventeen, we knew it was more, that it wasn't just going to go away when he and his family would leave."

"By eighteen," Kenneth continues, "Annie and I were ready to let Phoebe decide what *she* wanted to do with her life. We couldn't force her to stay with us, when it was so obvious she didn't want to. We didn't want our past to ruin her future."

"You let her go?" I quietly ask.

"It wasn't that easy," Annie sighs. "We couldn't just shove her into the real world without taking cautionary steps. She knew everything, we never hid anything from her, but we had spent all those years in the Bahamas. Phoebe didn't know life away from there."

"Declan's family was from South Carolina, so our names meant nothing to them," Kenneth adds. "But when Phoebe decided she wanted to leave and go be with him, we had to tell them about our past, because she wasn't leaving home to go to South Carolina."

"Declan was going to school to be a marine biologist," Annie explains. "He got a job at Marineland, not too far from here, and got accepted into Flagler College."

"Of course," I shake my head. "Because why can't anything ever be easy?"

Annie gives me a half smile. "We decided the best thing to do would be to change her name so that in Flagler, no one would think twice when talking to a Lenora Bishop. She and I had fun with that one, creating a name with all the letters of her real name."

"How creative of you," I mutter. "Eva figured it out, by the way."

Annie's mouth drops. "You figured it out?" she asks Eva. "How?"

Eva's cheeks are bright red. "Uh, I had a notebook ... I wrote down everyone's names, trying to make sense of a few things. I noticed how similar Phoebe and Lenora's full names looked, and I just started matching the letters to one another. I don't think I would have made the connection had I not written down their names on the same piece of paper. It was just luck."

"Nothing is just luck," Owen replies. "You're very intuitive."

Annie keeps going. "Kenneth and I also decided to leave the Bahamas at this point. We wanted Phoebe to have her life, her *own* life. We wanted to give her the chance to be happy and to be in love without worrying her past would get traced back to us, and then discovered in Flagler. We made up a story for her to tell strangers, how her parents died in a car crash. We also made fake death certificates. We sold the restaurant, the coffee shop, and all but five of the vacation homes. We had a pretty solid savings from all the time we spent in the Bahamas, but the profits of the houses we sold, we gave to Phoebe."

"You did all of that, just to give her a chance to be happy? To be in love?" I ask, shocked.

Annie points to Eva. "Your mom did the same for you; just let me finish explaining, okay? Phoebe headed to Flagler, and we left for Turks and Caicos," she continues. "We followed the same path we took in the Bahamas. Vacation homes, a cute coffee shop. We love our life there, and as soon as we're certain that you understand everything, we're going to head back."

"We can't stay in Flagler," Kenneth agrees. "It's too hard to be here, and to not feel worried all the time."

"I understand that," I agree. "But what happened between my mom and Declan?"

"Declan's family accepted our past," Annie tells us. "And we trusted they would keep it a secret. Phoebe's new life as Lenora with Declan was beautiful. At first, she lived with Kenneth's sister Rebecca, then she and Declan lived together near his campus, and eventually she bought the house you grew up in—"

"That wasn't your house?" I question Annie. "I was always told that was your house when you were a kid."

She laughs. "No, that was my *dream* house when I was a kid. I used to tell Phoebe about it all the time. How I would imagine raising a family in that house, a family so different than the family I grew up in ... the yellow house across from the beach. When she got to Flagler, she knew exactly which house I had been talking about, and when it was put up for sale, she bought it that day. She said since I couldn't raise a family in that house, she would."

I look over at Eva. Her face looks pained, and she places her head on my shoulder.

"Your mom and Declan never got married," Kenneth makes known. "They said there was no need to, but Phoebe wanted kids, man did she want a house filled with kids."

"They tried," Annie announces. "Your mom had some problems, though. She couldn't *stay* pregnant. She had so many miscarriages—it was horrible. And then, then the accident happened."

"Declan?" I guess.

Annie nods her head. "He was on a motorcycle, there was a truck, he had no chance."

Eva covers her mouth. "That's so awful!" she cries out as tears drop instantly down her cheeks.

"It was," replies Kenneth. "Phoebe sort of fell apart after that. We tried to get her to come to Turks and Caicos, to come live with us, but she refused. She wanted to stay in Flagler with her memories of Declan."

"I came here," Annie makes known. "We hibernated in the yellow beach house for a good month, just the two of us, before I finally saw her starting to come back to life. My journal entries and anything else from our past that you found, that's when I brought it all here. I thought maybe if she could see that no matter how painful life is, you can still find a way to be happy again. I hoped it would help, and it did. She decided she was going to stay in Flagler, got a job at Funky Pelican just to keep herself busy, so I went back home to Kenneth. Declan's sister Olivia was now living in Flagler, too—"

"What about the other sister?" Eva questions. "Sienna?"

"Moved to California," Annie replies. "Last I heard she was a hippy, traveling around in a beat-up van, didn't keep in touch with the family at all. But Olivia, she helped Phoebe a lot. I want to say a good six months passed, then Phoebe decided she needed some closure. She wanted to go back to where it all started, where she and Declan met—"

"The Bahamas," I sigh, as I lean back in my chair and wrap my arm around Eva's shoulder. "She went to the Bahamas, and she met Luke."

"She did," Annie confirms. "When she found out she was pregnant, she didn't think you'd make it, Bodhi. She had no hope. In fact, she had no hope until the moment you were born. That very second you were put in her arms, she knew her purpose in life."

"Why didn't she leave Flagler at this point?" I question. "Why stay here, away from you guys?"

"She created a life here," Annie answers. "She had friends, a job, a house she had envisioned raising her kids in. She had Olivia, too."

"Olivia was the only one in Flagler who knew who Phoebe—Lenora—really was," Kenneth carefully says. "My sister and her husband had both already passed away and my nephew, Paul, was too sick to even care at this point. But Olivia made the mistake of trusting her husband—"

"Who was her husband?" Eva cuts him off.

I hear Calvin make a little noise under his breath. This sudden sound causes both Eva and me to glance his way. He looks worried, and avoids both our stares, but we watch as he jerks his head slightly towards the Halifax.

Eva looks behind her and then lets out a loud gasp. "No!" she cries out. "No! You are not going to say what I think you're going to say!" She frantically looks at me, her eyes filling up with tears. "Henry Channing, Bodhi."

I whip my head back to Kenneth and Annie. "Olivia was married to Henry *fucking* Channing?!"

They both silently nod their heads.

"Does that mean Olivia is Porter's mom?!" Eva's voice quivers as she asks. "I never met her!"

"She is," Annie responds. "She trusted Henry, at first. She told him so much, so many things that Phoebe had told her. She left out the fact that Phoebe was already extremely wealthy, but the conversation did come up at some point, that once our nephew Paul died, Phoebe was set to inherit millions of dollars. It was in his will, that Phoebe would get it all."

"Henry made the connection," Calvin tells us. "The connection that he was also related to Paul Channing—"

"And he wanted that money," Kenneth finishes. "He was going to do anything to get that money."

"Did he know that Lenora was going to the Bahamas?" Eva quietly asks. "When she was taking Bodhi to meet Luke. Did Olivia tell him that?"

"She did," Annie replies.

"This is all her fault?" I question.

Annie quickly shakes her head. "No. Olivia started overhearing things, a plan that Henry had created to ensure he would get that money. A plan that involved Phoebe and *you*, Bodhi."

"Stop!" Eva quickly says. "Please don't say out loud that Henry Channing was going to make sure they never made it back to Flagler?"

"Whatever he was planning," Kenneth swiftly adds, "Olivia told Phoebe. She told her everything. She also told her that if Henry found out that they knew any of this, they *both* would be in trouble."

"What did she do?" Eva asks. "Lenora? What did she do?"

"She told *us*," Kenneth points to he and Annie. "And we got involved."

"How could you do anything?" I ask them. "Weren't you in Turks and Caicos?"

"We were," Annie nods her head. "And we knew we had about two months or so before Phoebe was set to travel to the Bahamas. We had two months to figure something out. We knew Henry was planning on heading there the same time as you and your mom. And she was insistent that she still go. Olivia was scared to death of Henry at this point, scared for you and Phoebe, scared for herself and Porter, too. Phoebe was so worried something would happen to them."

"Wait a second ..." I pause for a minute, narrowing my eyes. "Porter and me ...?"

"I believe you two spent a lot of time together as babies," Annie answers.

Eva makes a funny noise. "Is it too early to get drunk?" I hear her whisper under her breath. She leans her head on my shoulder again. "Okay, so how did this all go down? I'm very curious as to why Henry Channing didn't go through with his plan."

"We had someone on the inside, someone who was close to Henry," Kenneth explains. "We met this person and his family in Turks and Caicos. They were tourists, vacationing for a couple weeks in one of our rentals. He would come in to our coffee shop every morning, and would use the quiet to make phone calls. I overheard him mention Flagler a few times. I also overheard an argument he had with someone I could only assume was his boss."

"Kenneth took a chance," Annie then says. "He sat down with him and they got to talking. Kenneth found out this person was indeed from Flagler. He just lost his job, had a family to support, a new house they were building, and was going to have to tell his wife that he would no longer have any income coming in. Kenneth offered him a choice. He knew of Henry Channing. He knew of him from home. Kenneth told him about our daughter, what Henry was planning on doing to her and our grandson, how we needed someone to help us, without Henry knowing."

"He needed a job," Kenneth continues. "A way to support his family, and if he was going to help *our* family, we would always make sure he was able to care for his own."

My head is spinning. My mind is shouting out warnings at me so forcefully, my entire body actually hurts. I turn to Eva, wondering if she's feeling the same way. She's staring intensely at Annie and Kenneth, her eyes looking so fierce it's almost as if they have the ability to kill whoever is in front of her.

"We offered him eight of our vacation homes," Kenneth keeps going. "Completely his, to make a profit on week after week. We would take care of them, keep up with any work they needed, get them rented out, and he would collect the rent from each one. It was a foolproof way to never have to worry about money again, as long as he could be our eyes on Henry Channing."

Eva stands up. Her entire body is shaking, her chair falls to the ground with a loud clatter as she pushes it behind her. She places her hands on the table and leans forward. "*Who was this man?*" she boldly asks.

"*Eva,*" Calvin's concerned voice rings out her name.

She whips her head in his direction and shoots him a death glare. He doesn't say anything else. She turns back to Annie and Kenneth. "Who the *hell* was this man?" she asks again.

"Me," someone says from behind us. We all turn in the direction of the voice, and there stands Mr. Calloway. "It was me, Eva."

Fuck.

chapter eighteen

Bodhi

Y ou!?" she cries out. She goes to move toward him but I grab at her hand, forcing her to stop and stay by my side. The death grip she has on me instantly causes my fingers to go numb.

"Yes," he says quickly. "I knew I could gain Henry's trust. We had mutual friends—I knew that once I was back home, I could figure out a way to get him to confide in me, by pretending to be on his side, and he did. I knew all about his plan, what he wanted to happen in the Bahamas, and we," he points to Annie, Kenneth, and Owen, "we had our own plan."

"But that all changed when we met Sully," Owen declares. "Everything changed."

"We had to think fast," Mr. Calloway says. "We thought maybe your biological father could actually help us with our plan," he says to me. "But we knew almost instantly that wasn't going to happen, that he was even worse than Henry. Annie and Kenneth were waiting for her, for you and her, Bodhi, on the opposite side of the island. They were going to take you guys to Turks and Caicos, get you away from Henry and Flagler forever, but Sully wouldn't let you out of his sight. The fishing trip was our attempt to get you both out of there, but goddammit if that bastard didn't have you and your mom being watched by some lowlife junkies the entire time—we couldn't risk it."

"We didn't know what to do," Owen then says. "And the worst thing that could possibly happen did."

"Sully told Henry about you and your mom," Mr. Calloway loudly sighs. "How he wasn't going to let you guys leave, how he was going to fight your mom for custody. Henry didn't know Sully was your dad, until Sully told him on that fishing trip. And if we couldn't get you and your mom out of the Bahamas the way we had hoped, we knew we could get Henry to agree to getting you both back to Flagler, if the money was thrown on the table."

"We convinced Henry," Owen goes on. "It was so easy to convince that bastard, and as soon as he was on board, we were able to get you both out of Sully's grasp long enough for Brayden to get you safely to where Kenneth and Annie were."

"He didn't know," Mr. Calloway says. "Henry didn't know you both stayed with them for a few days."

"We almost convinced Phoebe to leave with us," Annie says. "Almost. But she was so worried about Olivia and Porter. So worried what would happen to them, what would happen to Brayden, and Owen, if Henry found out. A few days later, you both left with Brayden and Henry for Flagler."

Mr. Calloway walks a few steps closer to us. "Henry made it clear to Phoebe that she could not leave Flagler until the inheritance was in his hands, or he would let Sully know where you both were. I think we all held our breath until Paul died—"

"But she took me to visit them!" I point to Kenneth and Annie. "Why didn't we just stay?"

"She was allowed to go visit with you, but I had to go, too," Mr. Calloway tells me. "And if I didn't bring you back, Henry threatened—he was going to ..."

"He knew how to find Audrey and Eva," Annie says quietly.

I hit my fist hard on the table. "Why didn't she just tell him she had money?! Why didn't she just give him the millions she probably had sitting in her goddamn bank account?!"

"She couldn't," Owen's voice responds. "Henry, he couldn't know how wealthy she really was. He would find a way to take it all."

"She even had Paul change the will," Annie makes known. "It wasn't good enough for Henry though."

"So she stayed in Flagler," Mr. Calloway continues. "I stayed by Henry's side, being the eyes and ears of everything he did, and you both created a life here," he says to me. "Then Paul died and we thought everything would finally be done and over with, but it was the opposite. Henry was panicked at the thought of his money getting taken away from him now. Of me talking, or Owen, or

Phoebe, so he built his house across the Halifax from us."

I suddenly feel Eva's hand slip out of mine. She moves closer to her dad, walking slowly to him as she folds her arms across her chest. "What happened to Porter's mom?"

"Olivia and Henry divorced shortly after we got back from the Bahamas," he calmly says.

"What happened to Porter?" she questions next, moving a few steps closer.

"He went with his mom at first, but when Henry built his house, Porter came to live with him," Mr. Calloway replies, though his face looks twisted with pain at the memory.

"Were you friends with Lenora?"

He shakes his head. "I checked in with her often, and traveled with her to visit her parents, but we were not friends."

"You knew? Did you know I was at her house for two years?"

He doesn't move. He stares at his daughter as she continues to walk closer to him, but then he shakes his head. "I did *not* know. I had a few suspicions, but Lenora was extremely secretive. She was very good at hiding things, and I didn't know for certain until that day in the hospital."

Eva stops walking. She's less than ten feet away from him now. "Henry made Lenora stay in Flagler all this time? You couldn't convince him—"

"He did convince him," Annie quickly says. Eva spins to face her. "Your father *did* convince Henry to let them leave."

Eva turns back to her dad. "Why didn't she?"

"You," Annie loudly says. "Because of you, Eva."

Eva doesn't turn to look at her. "Me?" she questions her dad.

"I didn't know then," he says to her, "but when I was finally able to convince Henry it was okay for them to leave Flagler, it was around the same time Bodhi and you met."

I look at Annie and raise my eyebrow. "She saw something," she then says. "Something between you two, that same something she had with Declan. She stayed because of that. She stayed so that you wouldn't have to leave Eva. Even after she got sick, she stayed, for you two."

Eva gives me a brief smile, and then moves right up to her dad.

"You and Henry—"

"I despise him. I've hated him from the moment I met him."

"The inheritance money that Henry gave you?"

"All in Bodhi's trust fund," he answers. "Every penny. I was never going to take any of it."

"Keeping Bodhi and me apart?" she asks with a cracked voice.

"To keep him safe from Henry. To keep *you* safe from Henry. If he knew you both were friends, that you both were *more* than friends. I couldn't sit around and wait to see what he would try to do."

"Porter?" she says through tears. "Making me date Porter?"

Mr. Calloway stumbles for his words with this question before he finally answers. "To keep Porter in our house and safe from Henry. I knew what was going on over there. I didn't want him—I tried to keep him away from his dad—"

"But by doing that, you threw *me* into his house—"

"He would never do anything to Porter in front of you. He would never do anything to *you*, in front of Porter ..."

"Do you even *hear* yourself?" she sadly asks. "He would never do anything to *me* in front of Porter? Was I just some sort of bargaining chip to you?"

"You weren't Eva," he immediately responds.

"Bullshit!" she shakes her head. "It's all bullshit!" She goes to walk back to me, but stops in front of Kenneth and Annie. "What about them?!" she points and yells at her dad. "You work for *them*?!"

He nods in agreement.

"You've worked for them since I was a baby?"

He nods his head again.

"Have they met me before?"

"Once," he quickly answers. "In Turks and Caicos, when I first met them."

"And Bodhi?" she questions so quietly I barely hear my name leave her mouth. "Did Bodhi and I meet before we were twelve?"

His nervous eyes quickly find mine, and then he looks back to Eva and slowly nods his head. "Just a couple times when you were little."

"I've known Bodhi ... forever?" She doesn't wait for him to answer. She turns to me. I can't tell if this news is making her happy, or extremely pissed off. Before I can figure it out, she quickly spins back to her dad, walking closer to him again. "Mom?"

He shakes his head. "She knew nothing. She knows nothing. Not yet. I'm going to tell her."

Eva takes a deep breath and looks down at her feet. I cautiously stand up. Her body language has me worried. She hears me and looks back over to where I am. I reach my hand out to her, trying to get her to come to me, but she shakes her head and turns back to her dad. "You've led this secret life for the last fifteen years to protect Lenora and Bodhi?"

"Yes."

"You didn't tell me any of this, because you were also trying to protect me?"

"Yes, Eva."

"You were trying to protect Porter all this time, too?"

"I was," is his answer. "I didn't realize what was going on between you two, how bad it was—"

"I *told* you," she angrily states. "I tried to tell you."

"I know you did. I'm so sorry, Eva."

Her feet shuffle. Her arms become unfolded. Any typical person who doesn't know Eva that well would probably think at this point she's going to hug her dad, thank him for everything he's done. But I know Eva. I know her better than I even know myself, so I'm fully aware this isn't what she's about to do. I move as quietly as I can to her so she doesn't hear me coming, hoping I can somehow diffuse whatever it is that's about to happen.

"Did you ever think for even a fucking second," her voice suddenly booms into the humid evening as she glares at her dad, "that maybe if you had told me all of this when I was fourteen, that maybe if you and Lenora had told Bodhi this when *he* was fourteen, we could have figured out a way to be together while we *both* stayed safe from Henry Channing? Maybe then I wouldn't have spent three years hating you. Maybe then I wouldn't have spent three years of my life wishing I was dead—"

"Eva—" he goes to say.

156

"Stop talking!" she demands. "Do you have any idea how many times I thought about killing myself? How many times I wished I was just gone, rather than deal with the fact that my *father* took away the only person in my life who mattered to me, or that no one seemed to care what was happening? You fucked up my mind, it's *still* fucked up. You might have thought you were doing the right thing all this time, but by having all these secrets, all these lies, you absolutely destroyed me!"

"I was just trying to keep you both—"

"No!" she shouts at him.

I jump as I stand there, and almost reach out for her, but I'm scared to death of what her reaction would be if anyone tried to touch her right now.

"No!" she repeats. "You are *not* allowed to act like the hero, not when you made me feel so worthless, not when *you* were the reason my life suddenly felt like it wasn't worth living anymore! All you had to do was tell me!" she cries out. I try to pull her into my body now, but she struggles against me, drawing blood as her fingernails attack my arm. "Why couldn't you just tell me all of this!" she sobs. "Did you not see how I was slowly dying inside every day?! All you had to do was tell me! But you didn't, and I will never forgive you for that! In fact, I *fucking* hate you!"

She forcefully pushes herself away from me. I try to grab her arm but she's too quick, and all I can do is stand there in a panicked shock, watching her hand move swiftly through the air, as she heatedly slaps her dad right across his face.

chapter nineteen

Bodhi

Eva takes off running down the path, disappearing through the trees before I even have a chance to process what just happened in front of me.

"Damn!" Owen exclaims in amusement. "Annie, she is *so* much like you."

I quickly look at them all, and then to Mr. Calloway, who's rubbing his red cheek. He silently turns to follow Eva, but I grab his arm. "Don't," is all I say at first. I move in front of him, trying to block him from going any further. "Don't go after her. *Please.*"

"She's my daughter," he bluntly states.

It takes everything out of me to not roll my eyes at him. "I know this," I calmly reply. "But she is extremely pissed off, and you running after her is not going to magically help what's going on inside of her head right now. Please don't make it worse."

"What do you suggest I do then?" he asks, exhausted.

"You stay here and let me go. Or at least give me a few minutes alone with her before you make your way back home."

He looks toward the path and then back to me. "Go," he nods. "But I'm right behind you."

I don't hesitate. I run after her, feeling as if my heart has completely stopped pumping blood throughout my body. "Eva!" I shout when I see her in the distance. "Eva, stop!"

Her pace slows down and I watch as she covers her mouth with her hand. She abruptly turns and falls to her knees at the side of the path, throwing up into the Florida jungle. I rush over, holding her hair back as it tries to sway into the vomit coming from her mouth.

"It's okay," I tell her over and over again. "Your stomach. Eva, try to relax. Don't hurt your stomach."

She clutches the wood with her hands and heaves one last time. She then wipes her lips with the side of her arm and hesitantly looks up at me. I've never seen her so broken. I'm actually taken aback with the utter sadness I see on her face. I release her hair, and it falls down in sweaty piles on her shoulders. Her eyes are wet with tears, mascara has left a smokey ring around her eyelashes, her cheeks are red and blotchy. She looks like hell.

"I feel like I'm always falling apart," she whispers. "No matter what, I'm always one second away from completely falling apart."

I sit down in front of her, putting my legs on either side of hers. I reach for her hands and rub them with my fingers. "I'm never going to let you fall apart, Eva. I'm always going to be here to keep that from happening."

"But when you weren't here," tears drop from her eyes. "When you weren't here, I was so close to—to just ending—"

"I know you were," I stop her from saying anything else. I don't want to hear the words come from her mouth again, the words that will confirm how close Eva was to ending her own life. "I'm not enough to fix you," I say slowly. "I thought maybe I could be—"

"You are!" she confirms, fear all over her face.

I give her a reassuring smile, and move her hair off her forehead. "Baby, I'm not giving up. I'm never going to leave you," I make sure she knows. "Never. I will crawl through hell and back for you, but I can't fix those awful thoughts you had—"

"If he just would have told me everything!" she cries out. "I wouldn't have *had* those awful thoughts! I don't want to have those awful thoughts—"

"Do you still have them?" I worriedly ask her.

"No, I don't. But moments like this, moments like this remind me of them, and it scares me. I don't want to feel like that again, because of him. I don't want to feel so lost, and sometimes I still do. Why do I feel like I'm dragging you down with me?"

I can't help the confused look that appears on my face. She looks down at her feet, away from my eyes. "Eva, you're not dragging me down with you—"

"I am!" she looks back up. "Every time I fall apart, you're there picking up all the pieces!"

159

"That doesn't mean you're dragging me down," I bluntly tell her. "That's love, Eva. Do you not realize that? You do the same for me, when I've fallen apart, you're the one who puts me back together." I place one hand on my chest, and my other on hers. "Love," I repeat. "It's love."

"I'm a mess," she whispers. "A fucking mess. No matter what I do, I'm always going to be ... *this*," she waves her hands at herself.

"That's okay, though, because I love *this*," I wave my hands at her. "Mess, no mess, calm, blowing up, sleeping in my arms, crying in my arms. I love all of it. I will always love all of it."

Tears fall down her cheeks and she throws herself into my arms.

"I'm a mess, too, Eva," I whisper into her hair. "You're not alone. I definitely prefer being a mess together over being a mess by myself."

"I do, too," she softly says into my chest.

"I love you so much, but I'm scared that loving you isn't going to be the fix to everything that happened in the past." She tries to pull back a little, but I squeeze my arms around her. "I'm not going anywhere," I tell her again. "But I can't sit here and wait to see if how you're feeling gets worse. *Please*, Eva. Can we try to find someone who can help you—*us*—help *us*, deal with all this shit?"

She tries to pull away again, and I let her. Tears are falling down her face. "You think I need help?"

"I think we both do," I honestly tell her, and then I wipe her tears with my thumbs. "And I think I love you too much to lie to you, and tell you that everything is fine. I'm not going to lose you because I'm too scared to be honest with you."

"I want you to be honest with me. Always."

"Our parents have really screwed with our minds."

She lets out a grunt under her breath.

"But I refuse to allow that to screw up this," I point to us. "Let's stop pretending everything is okay, and that we can handle this on our own, and just admit that it's not, and that we can't."

Her eyes stare into mine, blinking back tears. She lets out a loud sigh and quietly says, "Okay."

"Okay?" I cautiously question.

"Okay," she repeats again.

I give her forehead a kiss, and then stand, taking her hands into mine and pulling her up off the ground.

"I hit my dad," she suddenly mumbles.

"I saw that," I give her a smirk. "It was pretty impressive."

She shakes her head. "I feel so ... I'm just so—"

"Fucking angry?" I guess.

"Yes!" she cries out. "I'm so fucking angry! About everything! All of it! My dad—Henry Channing, and all of them!" she points toward Calvin's. "Aren't you?"

"Yes."

She takes a deep breath and looks away from me, putting her hand up to her face as she hides behind it and starts crying harder. I gently tug her hand away and pull her into my arms again. I'm not sure what to say or do right now to make any of this better. I know she's going through a lot, and hearing what her dad has been doing all this time has ruined her probably beyond repair. I'm just as upset as she is. In fact, I'm so pissed off about all of this, I just want to disappear with her for a few days. Leave all these adults and their secrets behind while we calm down together, alone. But I know one of us has to stay calm and rational; we're no good together if we're both falling apart.

"Baby," I whisper into her hair. "Tell me what to do. What do you need me to do?"

She looks up at me, and then her eyes drift down the path. I follow her stare and see Mr. Calloway standing further down. "Take me away from here," she then says to me, reading my own thoughts. "I can't stay here tonight, with him. I can't talk to him right now," she declares, grabbing my hand and pulling me toward her house. "He's going to want to talk to me, and I can't, not tonight. Your house, can we stay the night there?"

She's dragging me along, quickly approaching her patio. "Let me talk to your mom," I say to her. "You go pack a bag, and let *me* talk to her, okay? Don't get upset with her, she doesn't know any of this. She doesn't deserve to have you angry at her."

She nods her head and pulls the door open. Mrs. Calloway is standing at the kitchen counter, scooping ice cream into bowls. Eva and I both freeze at the sight of her.

161

"How was ..." her face suddenly gets confused as she looks up at us, "dinner? Eva? What's wrong? You look—what happened?"

Eva looks over at me and then to her dad, who has cautiously walked inside the house. "Ask Dad," is all she says, and then she walks out of the kitchen and to the stairs.

"Brayden?" Mrs. Calloway anxiously says his name. "What the hell did you do?"

"I didn't—"

"He didn't do anything," I quickly interrupt. "He explained a lot," I tell her. "Eva, she's not in a good place right now—she's really not in a good place. Neither one of us are, actually," I ramble. "We learned a lot tonight—too much, it's too much to try and process so quickly, and I can't even start to make sense of it all right now."

Mrs. Calloway walks around the counter and over to me. "Talk to me," she says, putting her hands on my shoulders. "I'm on your side, Bodhi. You can talk to me—"

"I know," I nod my head. "I know I can, and I will. But Eva, she's a ticking time bomb right now, and I'm trying to stay calm for her. I have to stay calm for her—"

"Why Bodhi? Why do you have stay calm for her?" Mrs. Calloway nervously questions.

I look quickly at Mr. Calloway, and then back to her before throwing my hand up to my head. I'm trying so hard to not lose it in front of Eva's parents. "Do you remember when I told you I would tell you if Eva wasn't okay?" I ask her. "That morning, at Calvin's?"

"I do remember," she nods her head.

"She's not okay," I make known. "Neither one of us are. We need to fix that, okay?"

At first she looks alarmed, but she quickly regains her composure. "Okay, Bodhi. I'll help you both fix that, I promise. First thing tomorrow I'll make some phone calls."

"Good," I reply. "Thank you. But Eva, if she stays here tonight, it's not going to end well—it's not going to help. She's very confused, she's hurt. Can I take her to my house—"

"You want to spend the night at your house tonight?" Mrs. Calloway questions, her eyes raising. "You and her? What *happened*?"

162

"We need to talk," Mr. Calloway's voice echoes in the kitchen. "Let's get Eva to just sit down—"

"With all due respect, Mr. Calloway," I boldly cut him off. "You don't know your daughter like I do. That is *not* a good idea." I then look right at Mrs. Calloway. "Audrey," I say, using her name for the first time ever, in hopes that what I'm about to say will make a bigger impact now. "If you force her to sit down and talk tonight, everything you and Eva have worked so hard to fix is going to blow up in your face. Please, I don't want that to happen. Don't do this, not tonight. Just give her some time to calm down. Both of us. Don't make us talk about this right now. *Please.*"

Her hands squeeze my shoulders, and then she pulls me in for a hug. Her arms tighten around my back as she says, "Both of you, come back in the morning, okay? And then we can talk? About everything. And call me, if anything—if she—if you think—"

"I will," I nod my head into her shoulder and pull away. "I know I can call you if I need to." My eyes go to Eva, who's standing in the archway to the kitchen, a bag draped over her shoulder. I turn back to Mrs. Calloway, and then to Mr. Calloway. "You need to tell her everything you told us tonight," I say to him, pointing to his wife. "Everything. Because Eva and I are *not* going to do that for you. We are seventeen, you are a grown man. I think it's time for you to stop acting like a coward." I look back to Mrs. Calloway. "We'll see you tomorrow," I tell her, and then I walk over to Eva, take her hand in mine, and lead her out of her house and away from her silent parents.

chapter twenty

Bodhi

A re you hungry?" I ask. We're on my balcony, listening to the waves crash onto the shore. When we got here, she insisted she change out of her vomit-stained dress. She's now wearing one of my old t-shirts, with a pair of leggings she had thrown into her bag from home. Her hair is pulled up in a messy yet perfect ponytail, and there are loose strands that fall down around her face. Dare I say, she looks more beautiful than she did an hour ago?

"I am," she says, which surprises me. "But I don't want you to get up to find us food. I just want to stay like this for a while." She's lying across my lap, and her arms suddenly tighten on my chest like I'm actually going to tell her to get up.

"I have an idea," I announce, moving her body just a little so she can see my face. "Can we stay like this for maybe an hour, then can I persuade you to get up?"

She laughs, "Sure." Her body relaxes into mine again, her head snuggles right under my neck. I pull out my phone without her noticing, and text both Coop and Beck. I have a plan to turn this night around, and if anyone can pull it off behind the scenes as I sit here with Eva, it's Coop and Beck.

An hour later, I place a kiss on her forehead. I almost want to tell the guys to just forget about it, because there's no better feeling than having Eva's warm body snuggled up against mine. But I know they dropped everything to make this happen. "Time to get up," I reluctantly declare.

She groans and stands. "What are we doing?"

"Follow me." I take her hand in mine, leading her through my house and grabbing a few blankets from the hall closet. We then head out my front door.

"We're going to the beach?" she gives me a puzzled look.

"Maybe," I reply. The sun is getting ready to set. The sky looks like it's been painted with a color palette of nothing but pastels, and the ocean water is a murky blue. We cross A1A and walk up the few wooden steps that will take us to the beach. They're all there waiting for us on the other side of the wooden path.

"Heard dinner didn't go as well as expected!" Luna shouts out to Eva. "Even though I'm sure you looked drop dead gorgeous!"

Eva freezes slightly in her steps when she sees the four of them standing there. "You asked them to meet us here?"

"I did. Thought we could use a distraction, and some food."

"We brought Dolly's!" Kennedy yells out, waving a few bags in the air.

"Is that okay?" I quickly ask her.

She stops walking, and plants a huge kiss right on my lips, cradling my chin in her fingers.

"None of that tonight!" Coop loudly groans.

"It's perfect, Bodhi," she then smiles. "You are perfect," she says, then she kisses me again.

"Ugh! If this is a preview of the night, I'm out of here!" Coop hollers at us.

"Come *on* guys!" Beck whines. "I'm starving!"

Eva laughs through our kiss and then quietly says into my ear, "Now I have *two* things to make up to you."

Before I can respond, Luna comes up to us and grabs Eva's hand, pulling her away from me. "Girl, no more fancy grandparent dinners," I hear her saying. "Totally overrated."

"This is for you, ma'am," Coop then says, handing Eva a tall insulated cup with a lid. "And you, Bodhi," he hands me one, too.

I toss the blankets to the sand and raise my eyebrow up at him, shaking the cup a little as I hear ice clattering on the inside. I see more cups sitting in a cooler bag. "What's in all of these?" I ask.

"Chilled white wine," Kennedy lets out a laugh.

"White wine?" I question Coop.

"Fuck, Bodhi!" he exclaims. "You threw this on me with only an hour to spare. All Ma had at home was leftover bottles of white wine from her last book club party. I had to sneak it out in these bastards.

165

Take it or leave it, bro."

I put my hand on his shoulder. "It will do, Coop. We'll be sophisticated tonight."

"I did *my* job," Beck makes known. "A variety of delicious dinners cooked by Dolly herself and sprinkled with extra love."

"You're a suck up," Coop growls. "And you had the easy job."

"Dolly made fried flounder just for you," Beck swings the bag in front of Coop's face.

Coop snatches it. "Dolly has always loved me more than you, bro. I hope you realize that."

"*Boys*," Kennedy moans. "If you two don't shut the hell up, I'm going to snatch all the food. Then us girls will go eat it by ourselves."

"We'll take the sophisticated chilled white wine, too," Eva adds.

"Lay these blankets out and let's eat!" Luna orders us guys.

I go to grab a blanket, but Eva's arms suddenly wrap around my waist. I hear Coop groan under his breath. Eva gives me a small kiss on my lips. "You might possibly be the best boyfriend ever."

"I figured we could use a night off. A night to just be seventeen and not worry about all the shit we've had to worry about lately."

She grins a little and tugs on my shirt. "You planning on getting drunk with me tonight?"

I shake my head. "I don't think there's enough wine in that cooler for us to get drunk, but I'm definitely counting on a nice buzz at some point."

Her mouth hovers over my ear. "Good, because I don't want our first time getting drunk together to happen until *after* this thing comes off," she whispers, hitting my chest with her cast.

My eyes raise, and I bring her face closer to mine. "Oh yeah?"

She pushes her body into me, her chest pressing hard on my own, as she swings her arms around my neck. "Yes, Bodhi," her words float across my mouth. "Because that would make for one very fun night," she teases, quickly placing her lips on mine again. "And I refuse to let our six-week promise get in the way of what could possibly be a very epic experience."

I bury my head into her warm neck, the very same spot I love to move my lips against. "You're my most favorite person ever."

"You're mine, too," she says back, then she's being pulled away.

"Let the girl eat!" Luna cries out, guiding Eva to the blankets. "You have a whole lifetime of romantic embraces ahead of you, but right now it's time for food!"

Eva's laughing as Luna drags her away to sit. I place myself down next to her and start to open one of the containers of food when Kennedy suddenly raises her cup of wine in the air.

"I think we need a toast!" she declares. "A toast to a shitty dinner with the grandparents!"

Everyone scrambles to find their cup and raise it.

"Here's to a much better night with friends," Kennedy goes on. "Cheers to *our* family!"

We all clink our cups together and take a sip. I gag and try to force it down. It might possibly be the sweetest form of alcohol I've ever had in my entire life.

"I think I just drank liquid candy," Beck starts coughing.

Luna puts her hand on Coop's arm. "Who knew being sophisticated meant getting diabetes with one sip of wine?"

"You assholes want to keep going?" Coop narrows his eyes at all of us. "I'll drink it all myself—"

"And then we'll be dragging your naked ass home at some point," I say to him. "No thank you."

Eva takes another sip of hers. "I like it. It tastes like Sweetarts."

Coop raises his cup at her. "See, Eva likes it. Keep complaining, and Eva and I will be the only ones having a good time tonight."

I laugh at him. "No complaints, Coop. A few sips in and our tastebuds will be numb anyway."

"Ha. Ha. Ha," he says with a stone-cold face. "All right you two," he points to Eva and me. "You going to leave us all in the dark on what went down at Calvin's tonight?"

Eva's stabbing a crab cake with her fork when she looks up. "Feel free," she shrugs her shoulders at me. "No reason to keep secrets from our friends. I hate secrets," she grumbles, placing a bite in her mouth. "Secrets are fucking stupid."

Luna's on the other side of Eva, and she places a kiss on her head. "I agree. Secrets *are* fucking stupid."

Eva leans into Luna and picks up her cup. "I'm just going to sit here and eat until I'm actually full for once, and drink until my cup

167

is empty." She takes a big sip and then raises it in my direction. "Have at it, Bodhi."

I tell them pretty much everything. I leave out how Eva threw up off the path, and the conversation she and I had together, but I do end by telling them how she smacked her dad across his face.

"You hit your dad?" Beck quietly confirms.

Eva's now leaning against Luna. Luna's arms are protectively around Eva's body. "I did," she answers. "I shouldn't have—but I was pissed—"

"No judgement," Beck quickly interrupts.

"You guys just lived like ten seasons of a daytime soap opera in one night," Kennedy shakes her head.

Luna places her hand on the top of Eva's arm. "Do you think your dad is actually telling your mom all of this?"

Eva looks directly at me. "I don't have a lot of faith in my dad."

"If he doesn't," I say right to Eva, "if he doesn't tell her all of this tonight, I'm not taking you back home tomorrow—"

"Woah, Bodhi," Coop whistles. "Don't piss off Eva's parents—"

"I'm not *going* home," Eva chimes in, taking a big sip from her cup. She then leans back into Luna and closes her eyes. "Unless my mom knows everything," she then says. "I am *not* going to do my dad's dirty work for him." She opens her eyes again and lets out a frustrated sigh. "He kept over fifteen years of secrets from my mom, and told Bodhi and me about them before he even *thought* about telling her. How is any of that okay?"

"It's not, Eva," Luna says to her, giving her body a squeeze. "None of that is okay."

Eva sits up, draining what's left in her cup and then tossing it into the sand. "I feel like I'm being torn in two. Part of me is so appreciative for what he did for Lenora and Bodhi, and part of me wants to just absolutely scream at him until I can't scream anymore, because I'm so pissed off at every little thing he's kept from me." Her eyes find mine and she blinks back tears. "I wasted three years of my life, scared to death to even think about you, let alone talk to you again. And you guys," she turns to Coop and Beck. "I missed the hell out of you guys, too. It felt like I lost my brothers. The only good thing that came out of those three years was Luna."

Luna's arm wraps around Eva's chest, pulling her back and closer to her. "I will always be thankful for that day you showed up at Hidden Treasure, being the hot mess that you were."

Eva briefly smiles. "Me, too. I honestly don't know what I would have done without our weekly lunches. I think they might have saved me?" she looks up at Luna. "Saved me from—from doing something stupid."

The guys both give me a worried look.

"Well," Eva continues, "now that you all know everything, let's not talk about it anymore tonight, okay?"

"Agreed," I nod. "I'm extremely tired of the past ruining the present."

Eva glances at me. "We need to stop letting that happen. Because I really, really like the present."

It could be the wine, it could be the moment, it could be all the shit we went through tonight, or it could be the simple fact that I'm just absolutely in love with Eva. But I want her in my arms, *right* now. She's a mere few feet away from me, but it's not enough. I have this unexplainable need to be touching her. I use my finger to call her over, and then open my arms, inviting her into them. She gives me a huge grin, and scoots herself in my direction. I pull her into my chest, placing a kiss on her neck.

"I really like the present, too," I whisper in her ear.

"You *guys*," Kennedy sighs, "are just the cutest. *This* Bodhi ..." she points to me, "I'm just so happy to see you like this. This is not the same Bodhi I left last year. This Bodhi is *so* much better," she wipes at her eyes.

"Kennedy," Beck's looking at her funny. "Are you crying?"

"*No!*" she cries out, but then she puts her head into her hand and lets out a loud sob. "He's just *so* in love and *so* happy even after everything that's gone on! It's just so beautiful!"

Beck pulls Kennedy into his arms. "You'll have to excuse Kennedy," he starts to laugh. "She gets very theatrical when any form of alcohol hits her bloodstream."

She pinches him on his shoulder, "I am *not* theatrical!"

Eva starts laughing. "Kennedy, I love you. I've only known you maybe a week? But I love you. And of course, I love Luna, too. She

169

kept me sane when my life was falling apart—"

"You kept me sane!" Luna exclaims. "You were my one and only friend outside of my parents' hippy, love everyone and everything bubble I've grown up in! And then Kennedy came along and we couldn't *be* any more different, but I think I love you, too!"

Coop grabs Luna's hand and tugs her closer to him. "Bodhi, Beck," he shakes his head. "I think the wine has hit the girls."

"Has the wine hit you?" I quietly ask Eva.

She shakes her head into my chest, but quickly stops. "Maybe a little," she then looks up at me, her green eyes only growing in intensity as the sky becomes darker. I could stare into her eyes every single second of the rest of my life, and never fully grasp the exact color staring back at me. She runs her fingers along my cheek. "You're staring at me."

I slowly blink, breaking my trance. I don't say anything to her, we don't need words. We've always had this connection, the connection where I can just look at her and immediately know what she's thinking or feeling. Her fingers move to my lips, and then my chin, where she quickly guides my mouth to hers before resting her head under my neck.

"Eva," Beck says her name, fully breaking my trance even more. "Are you coming to your very first back-to-school dinner with us in a few weeks?"

"Maybe?" she replies. "If I knew what that was?"

"Invitations usually show up at the beginning of August," I tell her. "Our school does a back-to-school dinner at the end of the summer, for all current students. Sort of their way of saying welcome back, we know school sucks, here's some good food to soften the blow."

"Sounds intriguing," she says. "Is it just for students? Luna?"

"Can't go," Luna shakes her head. "And I am absolutely, totally okay with that."

Coop gives her forehead a kiss. "But Luna will be joining us for the party at Hayes' after the dinner."

"Yes I will," she agrees robotically.

"Who's Hayes?" Eva questions.

"Maxwell Hayes," I grumble. "Only the most privileged, taking over my daddy's company when I graduate, asshole in our school."

"He sounds wonderful," Eva lets out a laugh.

"Oh, you'll love him," Beck tells her.

"He's not *that* bad," Kennedy adds. "I mean, he does throw some pretty amazing parties."

"Yes, that is true," I nod my head. "And with all of us being seniors this year, I can only imagine how insane this one will be."

"When is it?" Eva asks.

"According to Hayes' massive text message to every student in a twenty-mile radius of us, it's like three weekends away," Coop answers. "Don't ask me how he knows this already."

"The weekend I get my cast off," Eva looks up at me.

"More reason to celebrate!" Kennedy excitedly says.

"That's it, right?" Luna questions Eva. "After that, you're allowed to be young, wild and carefree again?"

"So they say."

"Well I know where we *won't* be crashing that night," Coop jokingly mumbles under his breath.

I shoot him a look. "Last year, you barely made it back to my house," I remind him. "Beck and I almost left your ass there."

"Yeah, yeah," he waves his hand at me. "Those times are over."

"Sure. Sure they are. Open invitation for whoever wants to stay at my house that night. Because I sure as hell won't be staying at Hayes' house, and I refuse to let Eva get trapped there either."

"He's that bad?" she asks me.

"The only thing good about Hayes," I answer her, "is the fact that he has parents who don't give a shit what he does, and there's an unlimited supply of alcohol that he never has to sneak out of his house because his parents always look the other way."

"So what you're telling me," Eva smiles sweetly, "is that I should be friends with him to score free booze?"

Coop and Beck both start laughing. "Hayes hates Bodhi almost as much as Bodhi hates him," Beck then says.

"Why is that?" she asks.

"I'll take this one," Coop points at Beck. He then turns to Eva, "Your man there, if you haven't noticed, he's rather attractive in a dreamy sort of way. Much more attractive than Hayes will ever be, and this has always pissed Hayes off."

"You're making me blush, Coop."

"This guy sounds like a dick," Eva bluntly replies. "And maybe it's not that he finds you more attractive than him," she turns to me and says. "But maybe that he *himself* finds you attractive and he's not sure how to process those big feelings."

Our laughter echoes around the beach.

"Your girl might be onto something," Coop waves his cup at me.

"Hayes really isn't my type," I grin. "But everyone is welcome to stay at my house after his party, unless you all are intimidated by my attractiveness as well?"

"Bodhi, I've known you too long to be intimidated by you," Coop laughs. "Speaking of your house, what's your plan for the school year? Ma and Pop are cool with anything, but are you moving in with Eva for good or something?"

I shake my head and look down at Eva. "I think soon, really soon, I'm going to move in with Calvin."

"We figured that's what your plan would be," Beck says.

"Yeah, but I feel like even with saying that, it won't be permanent," I tell them. "Between his house, you guys," I point to Coop and Beck, "my house, and Eva's ..."

"You'll really be living like a hobo," Eva declares.

"Bodhi's always lived like a hobo," Beck says. "He's just added a few more options on his list now."

"What about after high school?" Kennedy asks.

I look over in the direction of my house. "Probably move into my house?"

"Let's not talk about the future," Eva suddenly says. "The future seems scary, but the present is perfect. *This* present is perfect." She lets out a loud yawn, and pushes her head into my chest.

"You're tired. Let's call it a night," I announce. "Get this mess cleaned up and crash at my house."

"Ah, memories," Coop nostalgically sighs. "Beck, I get the couch, you get the floor."

"I think those days are behind us," I laugh.

We clean up our dinner and fold up the blankets, walking to the steps that will take us to A1A, when I realize there's someone standing on the other side of the path. His back is to us, but I recognize the hair almost immediately. This is the kid from the beach a couple days ago, the kid who might have been from Dolly's. He doesn't see us coming, but our buzzed selves are noisier than normal, and as we walk up the steps he turns to the noise.

"*Shit*," he mumbles under his breath. He looks both ways on the sidewalk, almost darting down the street, but we unintentionally circle him.

"Hey!" Coop points. "You're the dude! The kid!"

The kid waves his hand up for a second, and then quickly puts it back down. He's shifty, like he wants to get the hell away from us but he's too scared to make a sudden move.

"Were you looking for us a few days ago at Dolly's?" I ask him.

He shakes his head. "Me? No. Nope. Not me."

"Hmm," Beck places his finger on his chin. "I don't think I believe you."

"Don't lie," Coop exclaims. "We saw you on the beach, too. Why the hell you hanging out with those losers?"

The kid laughs. "Family. Those losers are family."

"Damn, bro. I'm sorry," Coop grumbles.

"Don't be ..." the kid says slowly, and then he completely freezes. Eva has appeared from my side, and he looks absolutely petrified with her presence.

"Do I know you?" Eva tilts her head and asks him.

The kid looks down at her cast. "No. No you don't."

"I do," Eva nods her head. "I recognize you, but I don't know where I've seen you."

"What's your name?" Kennedy questions him.

He stays staring at Eva as he says, "Ethan. It's Ethan."

"Ethan," I say his name loudly. "How do you know Eva?"

He looks at me, and then very quickly back to her. "I know Porter," he quietly answers.

Eva lets out a little laugh under her breath. "*I* know Porter," she says to him. "And I don't know you, so ..."

"I know *of* Porter," he changes his answer. "My family is friends with his family ..."

"Well that's unfortunate," Eva replies.

"You're scared," Luna's comforting voice rings out. She walks a few steps closer to him, and puts her hand on his shoulder. "We're good people. Why are you scared of us?"

"I'm not—it's just—I was—"

"Hey," Eva stands in front of him. "It's okay. Don't be nervous." He nods his head and looks away from her for a minute.

"How old are you?" she asks him.

"Fourteen."

"What are you doing out here, on the street, by yourself?" she raises her eyes.

He looks down A1A. "Waiting for my friend to pick me up. I was at another friend's house but they left. They were being assholes ..."

"Sounds like you need some new friends," Beck calmly states.

"Yeah," his eyes move down the street.

"You want to come wait with us?" Eva delicately asks. She points across the street in the general vicinity of my house, and I watch as his eyes go directly to it. He obviously knows where I live.

"No, that's okay," Ethan says. "He should be here any minute."

"I do know you, right?" Eva gets closer to him. She's right in front of his face, her eyes are scanning every feature on him, as if she's hoping something will jog her memory.

He doesn't back up, but instead, holds her stare. "Maybe."

I watch as his eyes raise to the scar on her forehead, hidden in her hair and only obvious to those who know her. Her finger glides across it, and she gives him a curious look. I go to move toward them because I've had enough of this kid's bullshit, but Eva holds her hand out, stopping me. Ethan watches this, smirking like he enjoyed it, and then his face goes back to Eva.

Her fingers push the hair out of his eyes. "I don't like games, Ethan. And I feel like you're playing a game with me right now. I know you, tell me how."

His eyes move to the street as headlights suddenly appear from the dark road. He takes a quick step back from her. "I can't."

"Why did you come to Dolly's?" I hastily ask. "Why were you looking for us?"

Ethan steps further back as the car approaches. "I wanted to make sure Eva was okay."

174

"Why?" Eva swiftly asks him. "Why do you care about me?"

The car pulls up to the curb. The driver doesn't even acknowledge us. Ethan quickly opens up the back door and stands up against it for a split second. He looks at us all, then straight to Eva and says with a smile, "I told you they were coming. I'm glad they found you." And then he gets in, slams the door closed, and the car starts speeding down the street.

Eva lets out a loud gasp. She drops the blanket she's holding, then takes off running down the middle of the road after the car.

It takes my body a full second or two before I take off after her. "Eva, stop!" I scream out. I can hear everyone running behind me. "What the hell is going on?!" I shout to her.

"Eva!" Luna starts yelling. "Stop running! Goddammit you're going to hurt yourself!"

"Listen to Luna!" I cry out. "Fuck, Eva! You're running down the middle of the goddamn street! Don't fucking hurt yourself!"

Her pace slows down just a little, but enough that I can catch up to her as the car disappears from our view. My hands grab at her shoulders and I force her to stop, pulling her to the sidewalk. She spins around, clutching her stomach. She's crying, she's gasping for air, she starts hyperventilating.

"She's having a panic attack!" Luna cries out. "Breathe Eva!"

Her face buries into my chest, and I hold her there as she sobs into my shirt. I look up at everyone, clearly alarmed as I have no fucking idea what just happened.

"Are you hurt?" is what I ask when her crying slows down.

She shakes her head hard into my ribcage.

"Eva," I whisper into her ear. "Baby, what *is* it?" Her fingers claw at my shirt, her nails dig into my skin, and she raises her face from my chest. Her eyes are filled with tears and she struggles to take a deep breath. Then she says the very last thing I expected.

"He was there, after the accident. When I was in the truck. Ethan—I remember him now, he told me you guys were coming and to hang on. He found me before you did, Bodhi. Ethan was there, and then I blacked out. When my eyes opened, he was gone and you were in his place."

chapter twenty-one

Eva – two weeks later

O ne week," I say, shoving my fork down my cast to attack the itch I have on my arm. "One more week and this bastard comes off."

Luna lets out a laugh. "I'm sure you can't wait."

"I just want it off," I complain. "It's heavy, and hot, and I just want to be ordained healed finally."

"How *are* you feeling?" Luna hesitantly asks me.

She and I are at Funky Pelican, sitting outside on the patio that overlooks the ocean. The guys are below us surfing, but it was too hot to bake in the sun, and my cast isn't waterproof. I didn't want to be the reason their surfing day was cut short, so Luna and I left them to grab some appetizers and drinks in the shade.

"How do I look?" I question her, giving her a side smirk as I do.

Luna frowns at me. "Ridiculously beautiful, but that's not what I'm asking you."

I pop an onion string into my mouth. "I'm fine, I feel fine, I'm just ... fine."

"You want to know what I think?" Luna waves her fork at me. "I think you're lying. You barely eat, you barely sleep—"

"I *can't* sleep," I interrupt her. "Not since Bodhi moved into Calvin's. I can't sleep without him—"

"Your mom told you he could move back in," she reminds me.

"No, I don't want him to move back in."

Luna gives me a frustrated look. "Now you're *really* lying."

"Bodhi needs his space—"

"The hell with that," Luna growls at me. She points to Bodhi in the water. "He'd marry you tonight if you gave him the okay."

"He *has* asked a few times," I grin. "What I meant, was normal seventeen-year-olds that date don't sleep in the same bed together every night—"

"Since when do you care about being normal?"

"I don't. I just—I think ... I don't know what I think."

"Uh huh. *I* think you have a lot going on in that mind of yours, and you aren't as healed as you think you are."

I pop another onion string into my mouth. "*I* think you might be right."

"I also think I'm spending the night tonight," she announces. "I'm not Bodhi, but we can watch stupid girl movies and braid each other's hair or some shit like that."

I raise my eyes at her and try not to laugh.

"Eat a ton of candy until we make ourselves sick?"

"I think your perception on sleepovers is a little outdated."

She looks deep in thought. "Sit out on your balcony with some stolen happy smokes, and flash the guys below as they try to sneak into your room?"

"Much better."

"How are things going with your dad?"

My dad moved out. After that night, the dinner with Bodhi's grandparents, he did indeed talk to my mom. He told her everything, everything he had told us, and probably more that we didn't stick around to hear. She asked him to leave—not permanently, they both informed me, but until things calm down at least. Fifteen years of lies and secrets doesn't exactly help a marriage thrive. I know my mom still loves my dad, but I also know my mom is extremely hurt and pissed off at my dad. Kind of feels like we're the same person right now.

"Sunday dinner. We're supposed to have dinner with him every Sunday, his request," I tell Luna. "I saw him then. It was awkward. He tried to make small talk with Bodhi and me. You know Bodhi, he tries to keep the peace mainly for my benefit, I think. Neither one of us have really talked to him about everything—"

"You should. Why are you letting this fester?"

"Because I'm pissed and I don't trust myself to stay calm."

"I don't think it can get any worse than you hitting him across the face, right?"

177

"Probably not."

"How's therapy going?" she carefully asks.

Thanks to the quick actions of my mom, Bodhi and I now see a therapist twice a week. It's weird. We both go together, walk into side-by-side doors at the same time, walk out of our doors an hour later, and then drive home as if that hour never happened. Dare I say that talking to a complete stranger about how out of control I always feel has helped a little? I mean, it's barely been a week, so I won't hold my breath that I'll be completely cured of my depressive thoughts anytime soon, but I'm oddly encouraged at the same time.

"Not bad," I tell Luna. "Not as bad as I thought it would be."

"I'm really glad you're giving it a try. I mean, I could always sit and listen, too—"

"I know," I smile. "And you did, you have, you are." I quickly glance down at my buzzing phone. "Porter," I say under my breath.

"Porter?"

"Yeah," I sigh. "He likes to check in. I think he's bored. After hearing about his family, his dead uncle he never knew, Sienna, his aunt that ran away and was never heard of again ... I have a hard time not feeling bad for him."

"You talk to him a lot?"

"No. Not at all. I let his calls go to voicemail, and then just text him back at some point. Don't tell Bodhi. I've never seen a jealous Bodhi, but I have no desire to."

She gives me a grin. "Annie and Kenneth leave?"

I nod my head. "With Owen, but Owen said he'd be back. It was emotional," I tell her, slowly watching the ice cubes bounce around in my glass as I stir them with my straw. "Before they left, Bodhi asked if they even cared that Lenora got sick. Apparently, they were here a handful of times, always sneaking around while Bodhi was at school. But I guess when Lenora knew she wasn't going to get better, she went to see them one last time and told them not to come back. When they said goodbye to Bodhi, you could tell they want to be in his life but just don't know how."

"Does Bodhi want them to?"

"I think so? We haven't really talked about it. Everything is so unsettled with them. There's so much I know Bodhi wants to ask, but he shuts down whenever I try to bring it up. And now they're gone, but they want to keep in touch. He went from having no family to having three grandparents who all want a relationship with him. He's confused."

Luna's lips form a thin line. "Coop's worried about him."

I raise my eyes and then slyly ask, "How *is* Coop?"

Luna's cheeks turn red, and I swear her ice blue eyes actually glimmer in the sun as she narrows them at me. "Changing the subject, I see?"

I shrug my shoulders. "You owe me details, because I'm almost certain I know what happened after you two left Calvin's last night."

"How are you almost certain?" she laughs at me.

"It's a best friend thing. I was picking up on some pretty cozy vibes, and when Coop mentioned his parents weren't home—"

"It happened."

"Knew it! That's all you're going to give me? Come *on*, Luna."

"It was amazing," she tells me. "Definitely something I wouldn't mind doing again."

I start laughing. "Coop is so different with you. You're the very first girl he's ever dated."

"I sort of like having that title," she smiles. "*So* ... you and Bodhi? One week from today and you're open for business again?"

"Ugh," I throw my head down on the table.

"*Ugh*?" she repeats, shocked. "You telling me you aren't counting down the minutes at this point?"

"I am, but at the same time, the day this damn cast comes off is the same day as the dinner at our school, the same day as the party we're all going to. At this point," I bend my head down closer to her and whisper, "having sex for the first time in six weeks almost feels like some sort of appointment now. Something that's been scheduled on the calendar and circled a hundred times."

Luna lowers her head to mine, "Then don't have sex that day, Eva. It's not as if there's going to be a parade in your honor and some sort of celebratory dinner afterwards to congratulate you two. Do it when the time is right, not just because you *think* you have to."

I sit fully up, popping a few more onion strings into my mouth. "You're like my very own voice of reason."

She lifts her glass up to me. "It's a best friend thing."

I laugh, glancing down to the beach to see the guys lying on their surfboards in the sand. "I think they're done," I point down to them.

Luna waves to our waitress. "Can we get the bill?" she asks.

"Already taken care of ladies," our waitress says, grabbing our empty plates.

"By who?" I curiously question.

"Some kid, actually. Handed me a stack of cash and said to pay for you two."

I push my chair back and stand, frantically looking around the patio for Ethan. He mysteriously disappeared after that night on A1A. We've all been looking for him with absolutely no luck. It's as if he was just a figment of our imaginations.

"What did he look like?" Luna calmly asks.

"Uh, shaggy hair, nervous? Maybe fifteen?"

"*Ethan!*" I shout his name in annoyance, walking to the end of the patio.

"He's not here, honey!" the waitress calls after me. "He left on his skateboard after paying."

"Dammit!" I exclaim.

"Sorry," Luna apologizes for me. "We've just been looking for this kid for the last couple weeks or so. He's hard to find."

"He's in here a lot, actually," our waitress tells us. "At least once or twice a week. Usually by himself, sometimes with some pretty interesting looking people. He's never paid for anyone before, but I'll let him know you all are looking for him if I see him again."

"Thanks," Luna replies.

"Not a problem," she says back, leaving us as she walks away with our dirty dishes.

"This kid," I shake my head in frustration.

"Do you think he realizes you remember him?"

"Yes," I instantly answer. "And I think the fact that he knows I remember who he is scares the shit out of him."

"I CAN'T SAY I've ever been to Tortugas," I announce. I'm sitting in Bodhi's jeep as we drive down A1A. Tonight we're meeting Graham and Holden for dinner.

"The guys and I have been a couple times," he says back. "Pretty good food." He brings his hand under my hair and to my neck, without even looking at me. His warm fingers push into my skin. "It amazes me how dark your hair is, but at the same time, when the sun hits it, I see red?"

"My grandma has red hair," I tell him. "My mom's mom. Sometimes I see the red too."

"Between your hair and your eyes ..." he quickly looks over at me and smiles. "You're absolutely mesmerizing, babe."

No matter how often Bodhi showers me in compliments, I still find myself blushing with his words. "Thank you."

"I really can't take you to get your cast off tomorrow?" he groans. "Or pick you up for the dinner?"

I shake my head. "Nope. My mom is taking me, and Luna and Kennedy are coming over after. It's a complete girl day. You need to spend the day doing boy things, and after we drop Luna off at home, Kennedy and I will meet you guys at school."

"Boy things?" he gives me a funny look.

"You know, surfing, hours of video games, playing in the dirt."

"Is that what you think we do?" he laughs. "Play in the dirt?"

"I don't question what you boys do together. All I know is that you are not to step foot in my house at all tomorrow, and I will see you at the dinner."

He stops at a red light and looks over at me, narrowing his eyes a little. "You're being awfully mysterious."

I quickly lean in and place a kiss on his lips. "I'm getting my cast off tomorrow, which is a huge deal to me, for more reasons than one. It literally signifies the end of that awful night. I won't be reminded of it every single second of the day now, besides when I see my scar."

"Yeah, but—"

"And *you* won't be reminded of it every single second of the day now, too. I want to celebrate that by getting all dressed up and having you wait all day to see me cast-free. Does that make sense?"

The light turns green and Bodhi slowly moves forward. "It makes perfect sense, babe. And I already can't wait to see you. Is your mom okay with you staying at my house with everyone tomorrow night?"

"She is. She was very much appreciative that I was upfront with her and didn't lie about anything," I tell him as he turns into Tortugas. "Though I'm sure at some point tomorrow she'll throw safe sex into our conversation."

"Ah!" Bodhi cringes. "No! I don't want to hear that!" I laugh and go to open my door, when Bodhi suddenly grabs my shoulder. "Hey," he softly says. I turn to face him, and his fingers run along my hairline. "Tomorrow, we both know what tomorrow means, too."

I feel my cheeks heat up. "Yeah ..."

"And although I'm extremely excited we can start exploring that part of our relationship again, I don't want you to feel like we have to rush—"

I stop him mid-sentence with my lips. "You sound like you did about seven weeks ago."

"I just want you to know that tomorrow doesn't mean we—"

"I know," I nod my head in agreement. "I know it doesn't. I think the best plan is to not have a plan. You and me, we'll know. We'll know when we're ready, we don't have to plan anything. Tomorrow just means we no longer have to wait, right?"

"Exactly."

"And this isn't like it was seven weeks ago," I remind him. "We aren't rushing into anything." I scoot a little closer. "We already know what it feels like to have our bodies so close to each other, to be connected in that perfect way, riding out that amazing high together. And I'm *very* much looking forward to sharing that experience with you again. Repeatedly. When the time is right." I then give him a very heated kiss.

"God, *Eva*," he moans, sighing into my lips. "You have no idea what just your words do to my body."

I bite down on my lip, and very casually run my fingers along the middle of his shorts. It's very obvious what my words did to his body. "I think I know." Then I turn and hop out of his jeep, leaving him sitting there.

"Bodhi! Eva!" Graham exclaims a few moments later. He and

Holden are sitting outside on the front patio of Tortugas.

"Look at them," Holden points to us. "Movie stars. Why didn't I look like that when I was in high school?"

Bodhi and I both laugh as we take a seat across from them.

"Did you guys know each other in high school?" I ask.

"Oh hell no," Holden replies. "Graham was a baby when I was in high school."

"I was not," Graham rolls his eyes.

"Let's just say," Holden continues, "I'm pushing forty, while Graham isn't even thirty."

"How'd you two meet, then?" Bodhi questions.

Graham and Holden share an uncomfortable glance. "A few years ago," Holden then says, "I was shot in the line of duty—"

"You're a police officer?" I interrupt.

"Detective. Graham was the first to arrive on scene, and then his dad worked some magic—"

"Looks like we have something in common," I laugh.

"The Walkers are an amazing family," Holden agrees.

"Speaking of amazing," Graham chimes in, "Eva, you look like nothing even happened to you."

"Except for this thing," I clunk my cast on the table. "Coming off tomorrow."

"And you're feeling good?" asks Graham.

I look to Bodhi. "Yeah?" I say with uncertainty. "Physically, I have to remind myself of what happened because I feel so normal."

"But mentally," Bodhi adds, "there's just a lot she's had to deal with this summer."

"Both of us," I include. "A lot both of us have had to deal with."

Graham lets out a sigh. "Holden and I are both firm believers in getting as much help for your mental health as possible."

"We are," Bodhi tells him. "We're getting help."

The waiter comes and brings us menus, leaving us in our own thoughts for a few minutes. After our orders are placed, Bodhi leans back in his chair and rests his hand on top of mine under the table. "So you're a detective?" he asks Holden.

Holden is mid drink, and you can see him swallow hard. "I am. Not too much goes on here in Flagler, but I've had my fair share of interesting cases around the local areas."

"Tell us more about yourselves!" Graham suddenly says. "You met when you were twelve?"

"We did. Bodhi's mom was a photographer and I showed up for lessons at his house. Didn't really leave for two years," I smile at the memory. "But then there was an accident. I broke my leg. We were sort of forced to stay apart for a while after that."

"Why?" Holden asks. "Sounds intriguing."

"Family stuff," I shrug.

"What brought you back together?" he inquires. "Sorry for being so blunt. Your story is just very interesting."

"My mom," Bodhi replies. "My mom did, her death did."

"I'm sorry to hear about your mom," Holden then says to Bodhi. "And you lost your dad the night of the accident that Eva was involved in? He was in the truck?"

Bodhi looks between Graham and Holden, and folds his arms over his chest. "Are you investigating me?"

Graham chokes on his drink and starts shaking his head while coughing. Holden hits him hard on his back and exclaims, "Oh my god! Not at all, Bodhi! Graham told me about you and Eva when he got home that night. Your story just really stuck with me."

"Holden is just a super curious person!" Graham manages to say. "*Holden*," he then dramatically sighs. "Stop questioning them."

"It's okay," I reassure. "There's just a lot to it all, to everything that's happened. Bodhi's dad—"

"He wasn't my dad," Bodhi tells them.

I nod my head in agreement. "He was never part of Bodhi's life. That night, it was the first time Bodhi really met him."

"If you don't mind me asking," Holden softly speaks, "how did you end up in the truck with him, Eva?"

My heart fires away in my chest. I'm always nervous to have these questions get asked, but I'm more nervous right now because I'm going to lie my ass off in front of the guy who saved me, and his detective boyfriend. "He wanted to talk about Bodhi. I was trying to convince him to be part of Bodhi's life. I willingly left with him."

"He was an asshole," Bodhi blurts out. "She never should have gone with him. I shouldn't have let her go."

"Don't hold onto the past," Graham says, raising his glass a little to Bodhi. "It will eat away at you."

"Don't I know it," Bodhi mumbles.

Holden gives Bodhi a sympathetic stare. "Your dad—"

"Luke," Bodhi interrupts. "Not my dad."

Holden nods his head. "Luke. Luke Sullivan? Right?"

I lean forward. "You *are* investigating him, aren't you?"

Holden quickly shakes his head while Graham stares him down. "I'm not." He looks over to Graham. "I'm not," he repeats. "I just heard a lot through the grapevine after the incident—"

"You never told me that!" Graham hisses under his breath.

"There was nothing to tell," Holden says to him. He turns his attention back to us. "There was no investigation on the accident. It was just an accident. You willingly left with Luke, he lost control of the truck and ran off the road. But did you know he was under the influence of a lot of narcotics when you got in the truck with him?"

"We're leaving," Bodhi says, grabbing my hand and tugging on it as he goes to stand.

"Don't leave!" Graham cries out. "Holden, stop this! Not every person we meet needs to be interrogated by you! These kids have been through hell! I'll ask *you* to leave before Bodhi and Eva do. Please sit," he begs Bodhi.

Bodhi slowly sits back down.

"I'm sorry," Holden apologizes. "My job. I have a hard time turning the detective in me off. I really am sorry. I was just curious on what happened that night, leading up to the accident."

"We're trying to put that night behind us," I say to him. "Bringing it up repeatedly doesn't help anything."

"I understand that," he nods his head. "I'm really sorry."

"Jesus, Holden," Graham hits his shoulder. "I'm just going to start leaving you at home if you can't behave."

Holden lets out a little laugh. I look over at Bodhi. I can tell by the look on his face that he's furious and this conversation is *not* over. I slowly run my fingers along his leg to get his attention. He jumps a little, breaking his trance on Holden.

"You're not investigating us, or Luke?" Bodhi questions him.

"I'm not investigating you, Eva, or Luke," Holden replies. "I'm sorry if I came across like I was."

"There was a boat," Bodhi then says. "A boat tied up by High Bridge that night. I think it was Luke's. Do you by any chance know where it went?"

Holden slowly shakes his head. "I never heard about a boat. Why do you think it was Luke's?"

"Just a hunch," Bodhi smoothly replies. "The truck, what ended up happening to it?"

"Junkyard," Holden answers him. "It wasn't registered to anyone, and was totaled. Was it yours?"

"Definitely not. Did they find anything in it?" Bodhi questions.

"Nothing but Luke's wallet."

"Nothing at all?" I confirm. I know for certain there was gun in that truck. He held it against my back the entire time we walked, and he beat it against the window a couple times as he was driving. Where the hell did it go?

"No," he replies. "Not even a scrap of paper or a loose receipt."

I quickly squeeze Bodhi's leg. He taps my fingers in response. He knows something isn't right. "Luke Sullivan," he then lets out a fake laugh. "Man of mystery."

"So I've heard," Holden agrees. "A head scratcher, for sure."

"Was there anything in his wallet?" Bodhi then asks. "Obviously he didn't have any old school pictures of me."

"Like I said before, there's not an investigation on the accident," Holden reminds us. "Maybe some questions ..."

"*But* ..." I stretch out.

"But I know some of the guys are wondering who exactly Luke Sullivan was," Holden responds.

Bodhi grins. "Man of mystery," he repeats again. "I questioned that every day for seventeen years. And then when I finally met him, I realized I wasted seventeen years of my life wondering who he was. Did his wallet give you any answers?"

"No."

Graham hits Holden's shoulder again. "You *saw* his wallet? And you knew all along this was the accident I had told you about? These were the kids? You and I are going to have *quite* the discussion when we get back home."

"Graham. I didn't make the connection until we ran into them a couple weeks ago, and I briefly saw the wallet in the precinct, briefly. He's not listed as your biological father?" he asks Bodhi.

"Wouldn't know. My mom never mentioned him."

"In the system, he has no next of kin," Holden tells us.

"Doesn't surprise me," Bodhi grunts.

"Calvin Sullivan?" Holden carefully says his name.

Bodhi's eyes narrow. "What about him?"

"He didn't want the wallet. I made that phone call."

"Why would he?" I ask. "He and Luke definitely didn't have a relationship."

"That was apparent in my phone call."

"What was in the wallet?" Bodhi curiously questions. "Why would Calvin want it?"

"Not much of anything," Holden leans back and says. "Lots of cash, way too much cash. A driver's license issued in the Bahamas, and a picture. One single picture."

"Of who?" Bodhi questions. "Not me?"

"A girl. A little girl."

I gasp. I can't help myself, and then I quickly cover my mouth. Bodhi looks directly at me. His eyes are wide and slightly nervous.

"That means something to you both?" Graham quietly asks. "And Holden, I'm still pissed at you."

"Luke told Eva I have a little sister," Bodhi makes known. "I didn't know about her. I still don't know about her, but I'm guessing that picture is of her? Do you have it?"

Holden shakes his head. "No, I don't."

"Dammit," I groan.

Holden then pulls out his phone from his pocket. "I don't have the picture, but I might have a copy of it saved on my phone."

Graham crosses his arms over his chest and gives Holden a death glare. "Holden, what the—"

"What do you want?" Bodhi's tired voice asks. "I'm so sick of all of this. Every day there's something new. So just tell me, what do you want from us?"

"Nothing. I have the picture because I saw it *after* Graham and I ran into you both. She looks like you, Bodhi. And I thought it might mean something to you. I quickly snapped a picture of it before it got filed away. I don't want anything from either of you, but if you're willing to give me a little help, I'd gladly take it."

"Help with what?" Bodhi carefully asks.

"I'll help you find your little sister. I'll show you this picture, if you can let me know if you come across someone *I'm* looking for."

He then slides his phone across the table, as an image of Skyla appears in front of Bodhi and me. She's *beautiful*, younger than eight in this picture, but absolutely gorgeous. Her giant brown eyes, her blonde ringlets hanging down over her face. She looks so much like Bodhi I can't help but cry. I quickly wipe away my tears and look over at him. I hate how broken he looks. I hate how one single minute can change everything yet again. I know now that he's seen this picture, he's not going to stop until he sees her, face-to-face.

"You can help us find her?" he bluntly asks Holden.

"I can do everything I can. I *will* do everything I can."

Bodhi looks at me. I can literally see everything he's thinking just by staring into his eyes. He wants to know what I think, he wants me to tell him it's okay. That we can agree to this, agree to helping Holden in exchange for finding out whatever we can about his sister. I lean forward and turn my mouth to his ear. "Do it, Bodhi," I whisper into it. "We need to find her."

He nods his head into my cheek, and then turns back to Holden. "Fine. But we're seventeen. What do you expect us to do?"

"Just keep your eyes open. That's all. Because I'm told when he resurfaces, he might come looking for you two."

"Resurfaces?!" I exclaim. "Well, this all makes a little bit more sense now—why you think *we* can help you. Let me guess, you're investigating the disappearance of my most favorite person ever?"

Holden gives me a small grin. "If your most favorite person ever is Henry Channing, then yes, you are correct."

"Fuck this shit," Bodhi mumbles under his breath. "Curious," he then loudly states. "Who told you he might come looking for us?"

"He was very adamant I keep an eye on you both—"

"Who told you?" I hastily ask.

Holden leans forward and takes his phone, placing it back in his pocket before answering, "His son, Porter Channing."

chapter twenty-two

Bodhi — the next day

This detective sounds as shady as fuck," Coop announces. "He for real is bargaining with you and Eva over fucking Henry Channing?"

The guys and I just arrived at the dinner at our school. I told them all about my evening with Eva last night, and how Graham's detective boyfriend is investigating Henry Channing.

"Pretty much," I agree.

"What does he want you guys to do?" Beck rolls his eyes. "Camp out at the rubble that used to be the Channing estate and hope Henry shows up?"

"Nah," I respond. "Apparently, Porter told him that when his dad finally reappears, he might come looking for Eva and me."

Coop and Beck both stop walking.

"Are you for real?!" Coop then exclaims.

I turn around to face them both. "For real, man. We were told to just let him know if we see him."

Coop shakes his head. "Let me get this straight. This detective knows that Henry Channing, the scariest guy in Flagler, might come looking for you and Eva, and told you both to just keep your eyes peeled for him?"

"Sounds like he's really concerned for your well-being," Beck frowns.

I shrug my shoulders. "As long as he holds up his end of the bargain, I don't give a damn if Henry Channing knocks on Eva's front door and invites us over for coffee and cake."

"You think he'll find your little sister?" Beck questions.

"I think he might be the best chance I've got."

We start walking again, heading through the doors of our

school.

"God, I hate this place," Coop grumbles. "Hey, not to change the delightful subject of Henry Channing, but where the hell were you all day?" he questions me. "Luna said the three of us were supposed to have a guy day, and you were MIA."

"With Calvin," I answer. "For most of it. He's insistent I redecorate my room at his house. We spent most of the day looking at paint colors and bedding."

Beck starts laughing. "That sounds …"

"Very domesticated," Coop finishes. "You going for a Spider Man theme?" he grins. "Surfer boy, maybe?" he rustles my hair.

I swat his hand away. "I'm doing this for Calvin," I make known. "I don't think he ever got to do shit like this before."

"A little grandpa and grandson day?" Coop smirks.

"You can say that. I went to my house afterward."

"With Eva?" Beck asks.

"I haven't seen Eva or heard from her since last night."

"Uh oh," Coop whistles. "Trouble in paradise?"

We head through the halls to the courtyard area, where the dinner is always held. "No …" I annoyingly respond. "She warned me. Wanted to make the first time I see her without her cast on special or something."

"You going to attack her the moment you see her?" Coop laughs. "Sneak into a bathroom? Take her to the football field?"

I stop walking as we approach the doors. "Seriously?" I question. "Sex isn't everything, you know."

Coop raises his eyes and pulls the doors open, "But it's something. And you know Eva's going to show up looking as hot as—"

I shove him in his chest before he can finish his thought, and step outside. "Why are we here again?" I sigh, looking around at everyone that's already congregated in the courtyard.

"Because we love school, and as a senior, this is our year to shine," Beck jokingly announces.

"Shine my ass," I mumble. "Let's go find a seat before anyone tries to talk to us."

"The girls here yet?" Beck looks around as we head to an empty

190

table. "Doesn't look like it," he answers himself.

I throw myself down into a chair.

"Not feeling the school spirit tonight, bro?" Coop raises his eyes at me.

"Not even a little."

"Well, you can go ahead and get shitfaced drunk tonight if it makes you feel any better," Coop suggests.

"Not gonna let that happen."

"But this is a Maxwell Hayes party," Beck reminds me. "It's, like, mandatory to get drunk and not remember who you are the next day."

"This is also Eva's first Maxwell Hayes party. And both of us being drunk isn't really an option tonight. Where are they anyway?" I look toward the doors we came out of.

"Yo! Bodhi!" I hear a familiar voice yell my name. I turn my head to see Wesley Choate, a regular at every party I used to attend, walking our way.

"*Great*," I mutter. "Just who I want to see."

"Bodhi!" he shouts my name again as he approaches our table. "Where the *hell* have you been all summer?"

"Around."

"Around?" he repeats. "You were missing from literally every single party, and trust me, it was noticeable."

"Sorry, bro," I say to him. "Just not my thing anymore."

"Not your thing?!" he exclaims. He starts laughing and looks at Coop and Beck. "He's joking, right?"

Just then, Kennedy appears from the doors, minus Eva. She sees us and walks over to where we're sitting, planting a kiss on Beck's cheek and throwing her arms around his neck as she stands behind him. "I am *so* excited to be back!" she declares. "Feels like I never left—"

"Kennedy?" I raise my eyebrow. "Wasn't Luna dropping you and Eva off, *together*? Where is she?"

Kennedy looks around as if just noticing Eva's absence. "Shit! I left her in the bathroom! I had to make a stop in the office to drop off my transcripts from Tampa and she had to pee—I showed her which doors to come out of—"

"Who's Eva?" Wesley questions.

"Eva?" I hear a voice say. I spin my head to see another Flagler party regular, Easton Bradbury, heading to our table. "Isn't she the new girl? I just saw her, smoking hot. Like porn star hot, if you know what I mean."

"Oh *fuck*," Coop mumbles under his breath.

I feel my face instantly turn red. I literally think my body is getting ready to burst into flames I'm so goddamn irritated. I go to stand and feel Coop rise at the same time, almost as if he's afraid I'm going to implode, or beat the shit out of Easton. "Where is she?" I bluntly question, clutching my fists at my side. Coop puts his hand on my shoulder in warning.

Easton points to the doors. "She's in there with Hayes, but don't even bother Bodhi, he's already called dibs—"

I shove him as hard as I can and he yelps in pain.

"I'm sorry!" Kennedy calls out to me as I storm away. "I shouldn't have left her!"

I head right to the doors I came out of moments ago and yank them open, walking further into the halls of my school. I look to the left, where I know the bathrooms are, and see Eva up against a row of lockers, with Hayes standing way too close to her. His back is to me, and he doesn't see that I'm watching him, but Eva does. Her eyes instantly lock on mine and her entire face lights up as she smiles at me. My body immediately calms down in that one simple moment. She raises her hand a little and calls me over with her finger. Hayes is oblivious to any of this, as he's too deep in trying to impress her with whatever ridiculous bullshit he's telling her. I walk right over, grinning at her as I do. She reaches her hand out to me as I get closer, and finally, Hayes notices me approaching.

"Bodhi! Have you met—"

I grab her hand and pull her away from the lockers, and then I back up with my hand still in hers, so I can get a better look at her. She's wearing a black dress, the straps are braided and wrap around her neck, and it sits tight against her chest but flows from her waist down. Her silky black hair is in loose waves, hanging down past her shoulders, and she's wearing a simple dark green headband that only she can pull off. I raise her hand up a little and give her cast free arm a couple kisses, before twirling her in a circle right there in the hall.

I think I've been holding my breath this whole time, as I hear myself loudly exhale before I speak. "Eva Calloway," I then say, pulling her into my arms. "I think my heart has stopped because you're so goddamn gorgeous." I then kiss her, hard, harder than necessary, but my mind refuses to do anything less right now.

After a few moments, she pulls away, staring directly into my eyes as she says softly, "I missed you today." And then she gives me another quick kiss before we turn our attention back to Hayes.

He's standing there, his mouth slightly open. He blinks a few times and then says, "Uh, you guys know each other?"

I can't help but smirk as I say, "Hayes, I see you've met my girlfriend?"

Hayes looks between Eva and me. "Girlfriend?" he repeats. "You?"

I nod my head.

"Well, now I'm really confused," Hayes grins. "Because you don't date, Bodhi."

I see Eva smile a little, and I wrap my arm around her waist. "I didn't date because I was just waiting for Eva."

"I see," Hayes raises his eyebrow.

I wrap my fingers around hers. "You ready to head out there?" I ask, pointing to the doors.

"Absolutely," she nods. "It was nice to meet you, Hayes," she says to him.

We start to walk away when Hayes coolly replies, "Pleasure was all mine, Eva. I look forward to seeing you at school this year."

I do a quick pause, but don't look back. Eva turns and smiles at him, as I pull her down the hall.

"So, *that* was Maxwell Hayes?" she questions me, as I push the doors open.

I don't answer, and instead of heading to our table, I duck behind a row of palm trees keeping us hidden from everyone outside.

"What are we doing?" Eva curiously asks as I pull her with me. I carefully spin her body so that her back rests up against one of the trees. "I just want a minute with you," I try to calmly say. "Alone."

"Are you okay, Bodhi?"

My eyes scan every inch of her flawless body as she stands there and watches, like being with Hayes has left marks on her or something. "You're fucking gorgeous, babe. I feel like I can't breathe," I yank at the collar of my shirt, "seeing him with you. Like, I swear to god if he even thinks about touching you—"

She cuts my words off by placing her lips quickly on my own, clutching onto my shirt at the same time. I can taste her strawberry lip gloss. I can feel her tongue slowly move against mine. She pulls away and her eyes stay on me, searching for any indication that her kiss has cured my childish meltdown.

"I *hate* Maxwell Hayes," I mutter. "I fucking hate him."

"I can tell."

"I don't want him talking to you."

She frowns a little. "You can't keep other guys from talking to me, you know."

"I know. But he's an asshole."

"He may be an asshole," she says, poking me in my chest, "but it's *you* I'm going home with tonight. And every night. There's no need to be territorial. There's no competition, okay? It's you I want."

I lean in, placing my lips on hers again. Her hands come up to the back of my head, leaving them there even after I slowly pull myself away from her. Her sparkling eyes stare into mine. I kiss her eyelids, forcing her to close them and break this trance she suddenly has over me.

"How's your arm?"

"It feels perfect. I feel normal, finally."

"Good. How was your day with the girls?"

She twirls my hair around her finger. "Fun," she replies. "They're fun. And my mom, she hung out with us for a little while, too. Bodhi, it felt like it should have always been like this."

I love that she's finally having a relationship with her mom again. I love that she has friends, when I know she spent so many years alone. I push my fingers into her waist. "It *should* be like this," I reply.

She gives a little tug on my hair. "How was *your* day?"

I run my fingernails up and down her arms. "I spent the entire day with Calvin, redecorating my room, and thinking about when I would see you."

"You were daydreaming about me?"

"I guess you can call it that."

Her eyes light up and she slyly asks, "What were you imagining in your head when you were thinking about me?"

I give her waist a little shake with my hands. "Maybe I was thinking about my lips on yours, my hands on your body ..."

"While you were with Calvin?"

I nod my head.

"Do you want to know what *I* was thinking about when I was with the girls?" she continues.

My heart might skip a couple beats. "Sure."

She leans in a little closer and her mouth hovers over my ear. "How absolutely amazing it feels when your fingers are touching me, right here," she pulls my hand down, and places it under her dress and on top of her panties.

I suddenly forget how to breathe again. My knees also grow weak. I can feel her tongue slowly moving behind my ear. I swallow hard, shaking off the thoughts of taking her to an empty bathroom right this very second. I bring my hand out from under her dress and place it firmly on her back. I'm starting to realize it might not be *me* who gets us in trouble this school year, but Eva.

She moves her mouth away from my ear, and points behind her as she bluntly asks, "Shall we go join everyone now?"

"Jesus Christ, Eva! You think I can just go sit down with all of them after what you just said and did?"

"I think what I just said and did will make this dinner a bit more exciting, because I think you'll be daydreaming about it all evening now."

My finger glides under her lower lip. She purposely bites down on it. "What am I going to do with you?"

"Do you need a detailed list? Or will the Cliff Notes version be okay?"

"You can give me a detailed list later," I tell her, taking her hand into mine. "But let's go sit down before I change my mind and sneak

195

us out of here instead."

"I like that thought," she replies as I lead her to the table. "Sneaking us out of here."

"I know you do, babe."

"There you guys are!" Kennedy calls out when we come into view.

"Goddamn, there's a lot of people here," I hear Eva mumble.

I'm not paying attention to what she just said, though. I'm too busy watching every single person completely stop whatever they're doing as they see Eva, as they see her hand in mine, as they see us together. There are a couple different reasons for this. One, Eva demands attention when she walks into a room, even if she's not purposely doing it. Her beauty stops people dead in their tracks. They can't help but stare at her, and I've yet to figure out how this doesn't bother the shit out of her, because it sure does bother the shit out of me. Another reason? I'm holding her hand. It's clear the two of us are together. This is not normal for me. The simple fact that my fingers are wrapped tightly in between hers probably has everyone here questioning if I switched from alcohol to hardcore drugs this summer. If too much partying has made me forget who I actually am, who I used to be.

I love it.

I love everyone watching this.

I love everyone seeing me with her.

I love that this is their first time seeing Eva Calloway, and they instantly know she's mine.

"Why is everyone staring as us?" she whispers to me.

"Because they've never seen anyone as beautiful as you," I simply reply.

"I'm so sorry I left you in the bathroom!" Kennedy exclaims as we approach the table.

"It's fine," Eva laughs.

"Everything okay?" Coop gives me a concerned look.

"Hayes will live to see another day," I joke.

"I'm sorry, bro," Easton grumbles. "For real. I didn't know."

"Eva this is Easton," I introduce. "Easton this is my *girlfriend*, Eva."

He blushes red as Eva smiles and says, "We met in the hall."

"Yeah." He avoids my stare. "I think I'll go sit over there—"

"You go do that," I frown. Eva looks up and raises her eyes at me as Easton leaves our table.

"I'm Wesley," Wesley waves to Eva. "Where has Bodhi been hiding you all this time? And where did you come from, because I thought I knew every girl in Flagler that Bodhi—"

"I transferred this year," she confidently cuts him off. She then rustles my hair and adds, "And I've known Bodhi since we were twelve."

"Interesting," Wesley slowly says. "Well, I can totally see why Bodhi wouldn't want to share you with the rest of the world."

I hear myself let out a low growl, but Eva quickly squeezes my side. "Oh yeah?" she responds to him. "Why's that?"

His face turns bright red and I hear the guys laugh. "Well, I mean, you're really—"

"I'm going to save you," Beck says to Wesley, standing and patting him hard on his back. "Let's go get some drinks. And don't mess with Eva—"

"She's a badass!" Kennedy calls out to him.

Eva turns and looks at me. "This year is going to be *really* fun."

I pull a chair out for her and kiss the top of her head as she goes to sit. "Yeah, if we can just keep you out of—"

Eva suddenly pushes her chair out and stands, almost knocking me over in the process. "Ethan!" she shouts under her breath, pointing to the doors. We all turn to see Ethan walking out, with Hayes directly behind him, his hand on his shoulder. Eva takes off.

"Goddamn fucking *shit*," I swear under my breath, chasing after her.

"Ethan!" she shouts out his name the closer she gets. He sees her and quickly turns, slamming into Hayes.

Hayes spins him back around. "Yo little Cuz, what the hell?"

"Cuz?" I question.

"Cousin?" Hayes replies. "Ethan is my cousin? Sort of. How do you two know Ethan?"

"I don't know, *Ethan*," Eva harshly states. "How do we know you?"

197

"Not now. Not now. Not now," Ethan quickly whispers under his breath. "*Please.*"

Eva raises her eyes, and folds her arms across her chest.

Hayes starts to laugh. "You piss the new girl off already?"

Ethan shakes his head. "Nope. Nope, I didn't."

I almost feel sorry for the little bastard. He looks like his might start crying.

"What are you doing here, Ethan?" Eva questions him.

Hayes starts laughing. "My Cuz gets to join me for my senior year. We've got a freshman on our hands."

"You go here now?" I ask.

"I do. Knew you went here. Didn't know Eva did."

"I transferred," she announces.

"Wait," Hayes exclaims. "How do you guys know each other again?"

"How are you guys related again?" is Eva's reply.

Hayes' eyes grow big. He's not used to girls talking to him like this. "Our dads are cousins," Hayes tells us. "And you guys ...?"

"Friends," Eva quickly answers. "We're friends. Ethan, can I talk to you for a second?"

Hayes shakes his head. "We need to go sit down. This shitshow is getting ready to start. Ethan needs to make a good first impression."

Ethan gives Eva a sympathetic smile. "I—tonight—what are you doing tonight?"

"Cuz! She's got a boyfriend!" Hayes laughs. "At least wait until he's not around!"

Ethan turns bright red. "That's not—"

"I'll be at a lame ass party at someone named Maxwell's house," Eva bluntly answers. "Probably not worth even going to."

Ethan snickers under his breath. "This lame ass party, find me there." He then walks away, laughing loudly as he does.

Hayes is staring at Eva. "I'm going to like you," he states.

"I'm a very likable person," she smiles.

"I can see that. Bodhi," Hayes turns to me, "where you'd find this one?"

"She found me."

"Well, watch out," he says as he starts to walk away. "Every single straight guy at our school is busy making plans right this second on how to steal her away from you."

"Hayes!" Eva suddenly calls out. He turns to face her. "They can make their plans all they want, but I don't stray."

"We'll see." Then he turns back around and leaves us.

"Yep," Eva blurts out. "Fucking asshole."

"I told you."

An hour later, dinner has been served, our principal has spoken, and a table has been set up where we can go get our schedules.

"Let's wait for the crowd to disappear," Coop suggests. "All those eager fools up there, actually excited to start school."

One of the art teachers is suddenly at our table. I've never spent time in the art wing at our school, art has never really been my thing. I'm assuming she's here to talk to Eva.

"Are you Eva Calloway?" she questions.

Eva nods her head. "I am."

"I'm Bonnie, actually Mrs. Kramer, but my students just call me Bonnie. I'm the photography teacher here—"

"Oh! Hi!" Eva excitedly greets.

"Hi," she smiles. "I got quite the portfolio of yours from your old photography teacher, Mr. Adams?"

"He dropped it off?"

She nods. "Hand delivered. Very sad to see you go, but his loss is my gain. You're very talented. I'm excited to have you in my classes. I believe we'll see a lot of each other this year."

"I look forward to it."

"Nice to see you all," she says to the rest of us, and then she walks away.

"Damn, Eva!" Kennedy exclaims. "Celebrity status and you haven't even started yet!"

"Are you guys in any art classes?" she asks.

"I am!" Kennedy replies. "Not photography, but a few others. All the art classes are in the same wing of the school. It was built a couple years before we started here."

"That's ironic," Eva's eyes narrow. "We had an art wing, too, that was also built a couple years before my freshman year."

"Crazy coincidence?" Beck slowly replies.

Eva nods her head. "So who would you say spends most of their time in the photography room around here?"

My heart drops. Why didn't I think about this earlier? "Maxwell Hayes," I grumble.

"You've got to be kidding me," Eva groans. She pushes her chair back. "I'm going to get some water—"

"I'll go with you—"

She shakes her head, and plants a kiss on my cheek. "I've got it."

I watch as she walks away. I watch as heads turn and people whisper to each other as she passes. I watch as Eva doesn't acknowledge any of them. I then throw my head down on the table.

"Bodhi, she's fine," Coop points to her. "She's more than capable of taking care of herself."

I raise my head. "Do you see what people do when they see her?" I loudly whisper. "The pointing and the staring? The girls and their dirty looks—"

Coop laughs. "How many girls here have friends or cousins or some shit like that, who you've hooked up with in the past?"

I look around. "A few," I angrily reply.

"They're pissed, bro," he points out. "Pissed to see you're with Eva, pissed to see she won your hard-to-get attention."

"I won't let any of the catty girls do anything to her," Kennedy promises. "All those girls think they're friends with me. Once they see I'm friends with Eva, they'll leave her alone."

"I think this was a mistake," I confide in them. "Having Eva come to our school—"

"Why?" Beck rolls his eyes. "Because people are jealous of her? Because people are pissed off at shit you did in the past? Because other guys are going to talk to her?"

I stare Beck down. "Yes. All of those fucking reasons."

Beck lets out a loud laugh. "Dude, you can't spend the rest of your goddamn life keeping Eva in a bubble."

"He's right, Bodhi," Kennedy softly agrees. "I've only known her a few weeks, but I'm well aware she doesn't take shit from anyone. Stop being so worried. Remember what happened the last time you all tried to *protect* Eva from shit you thought would upset her?"

I let out a growl. "Yeah, yeah." I push my chair back and stand. "I'm getting my schedule. I'm getting Eva, and then I'm getting the hell out of here. You guys?"

"Right there with you. Need to pick up Luna, too," Coop reminds me.

"I guess we'll meet up at Hayes' then?"

"You really want to go to his party?" Coop questions as he stands. "I mean, you don't seem to be very fond of him right now."

"No, I don't want to go at all," I make known. "But Ethan will be there, and Eva wants some answers."

Coop bounces on his feet. "Shit's going down tonight! Might have to pre-drink a little to make it through this love fest!"

I hit his chest with my palm and walk away.

I find Eva over by the drinks. She's talking to a few girls I recognize from random classes I've shared with them these past few years. Their faces turn bright red as I approach. I sneak up next to Eva, wrapping my arm around her waist. She smiles and places her hand on mine, but doesn't look up at me.

"We'll see you around," one of the girls says to her.

"Nice to meet you all," Eva warmly responds. She waits until they walk away before turning to me. "So, those three charming peers just informed me that you're going to break my heart."

I raise my eyebrows. "Oh yeah?"

She nods her head. "And you see that boy over there?" she points to the captain of our football team. "He told me he'll be waiting for the day you decide you're done with me."

"Eva ... don't listen—"

"And *that* girl," she nods her head to Easton's younger sister. "Informed me that her cousin cried for days after you made-out with her at a party, and then never returned any of her calls." Eva turns to face me, her hands on her hips.

"Babe," I calmly say.

"Don't babe me right now," she shakes her head. "I just want to get out of here, okay?"

"Okay," I agree. I grab her hand and hope she doesn't shake me away. We stop quickly at the table to get our schedules, and then head to my jeep in complete and utter silence.

chapter twenty-three

Bodhi

I can tell she's pissed. I call tell her mind is in a hundred different places right now. She just stares out the window as we drive, not saying one word. I can't take her to Hayes' house like this. Plus, Hayes was still at school when we walked out. So instead, I drive to my house and pull into the driveway. I place my jeep in park and sit there, turning my body to face her.

"Eva?"

She looks over at me.

"Please talk to me."

She shakes her head and opens the passenger door. I turn my jeep off and press the button to open the garage, watching her walk inside my house alone. Part of me is happy she feels comfortable enough to just let herself in, but part of me is also nervous as hell. I know she's acting like this because she's hurt.

I head inside, walk upstairs, and stand in my family room, trying to figure out where she snuck off to. My heart tells me she's in one of two spots. Either upstairs in my mom's studio, or in my bedroom. I head there first and find her standing at my dresser, looking at a picture of me and the guys. I take a seat on the edge of my bed and just stare at her for a moment before I finally develop the courage to speak.

"Eva," I carefully say. "Talk to me. I know you're upset—"

"I'm not upset," she sighs. "I'm just ... sad?"

"Sad?" I repeat. It's not what I thought she would say.

"Yeah. I thought maybe all the stares tonight were because I'm the new girl, but it's because they all felt bad for me."

"Eva, they don't. You have no idea what happens when you walk in a room. People can't help but stare at you—"

"*Stop.* I've dealt with the looks and the stares for years now. This was different. Those people, those people I'm supposed to go to school with this year, they all felt bad for me because of *you.*"

"Because of *me*?"

"Like you're going to toss me aside when you're done with me."

"Babe," I run my fingers through my hair, shocked at what just came out of her mouth. "Do you *really* think I'm going to do that?"

"No! Of course not! But they don't know what *we* have. They just know what *you've* done. How you've treated every girl you've been with. They all think I'm just another name to add to that list."

"You're not," I firmly declare.

"I *know.* But try explaining that to everyone at our school."

I'm getting angry now. "I don't need to explain anything to them. Those people, are we ever going to see or care about those people after high school? Coop, Beck, Kennedy—those are the only three people out of the hundreds we saw tonight that I give a damn about. Who gives a flying shit what anyone else thinks?"

"I do," she whispers slowly. "Because their very first impression of me was that I'm just another notch on your belt."

Fuck. I should have known this was going to happen.

"How many, Bodhi?" she looks up at me, tears in her eyes. "How many of those girls that I have to see every day now, were you with?"

I can feel my eyes grow large with this simple question. "None of them, Eva."

"*Bodhi.*"

"*None* of them, Eva," I repeat, as I cautiously stand. "I would never be with a girl I had to see every day. It would be a constant reminder that she wasn't you."

"Who were they, then? Who were all these girls?"

I struggle to get the words out fast enough. "Girls from other schools, someone's cousin or some shit like that."

She looks around my room, and then her eyes go straight to my bed. "How many of them did you bring back here?" she then sadly asks. "How many girls have come back to your house with you?"

Now *this* question I'm not afraid to answer. I move closer to her. "One. Just one, Eva. And I'm staring right at her."

Her chin starts to quiver, and she bites down hard on her lip.

203

"Just me? I'm the only girl—"

"You *are* the only girl, Eva. The only memories of that nature I'll ever have in my house, are the ones of you and me. I would never bring another girl here. I never brought another girl here. And it doesn't matter what anyone else thinks about me, about you, or about us. I've loved you since I was twelve, and I'm going to love you forever, no matter what anyone else says." I collect the tears from her cheeks and softly kiss her lips. "I'm sorry that everyone tonight thinks you're just another name to add to an unhealthy list that I'm not proud of. There is no list anymore, Eva. It ended the second you walked down those steps on the beach and into my arms."

She takes in a deep breath and nods her head, quickly wiping the tears that are left in her eyes.

"I'm sorry. Baby, I'm so sorry."

"I know," she throws her head into her hand. "I know you are."

"What can I do to make this right?"

"Nothing. It's the past. You don't need to keep apologizing for shit you did in the past. It's not like you expect me to apologize for having sex with—"

"Do not say his name right now."

She grins a little, just enough that my heart stops racing in fear that my past has found a way to ruin us. "Well, at least none of those girls beat me up on the side of the road tonight, right?"

"The night is still young," I joke. "They won't touch you, Eva," I then seriously say.

"I'm sorry for how I reacted—"

"You have every right to feel that way."

She groans, "I hate feeling like that. Sad. I hate feeling sad."

"It's okay to feel sad," I let her know. "It's also okay to be pissed at me for things I did in the past—"

"I'm not pissed at you."

"But it's okay if you ever feel that way."

"I just hate the way they look at me."

"I don't want anyone looking at you. Especially the guys. They aren't thinking what the girls are thinking. I *know* what they're thinking, and I'll kick all their asses if you want me to."

"You used to look at me like that. Back when we were fourteen, sitting on your bed. I would catch you looking at me all the time."

"Ah! You noticed that? I couldn't help myself. If only fourteen-year-old Bodhi knew that all his lust-worthy glances would eventually pay off. That he'd get the girl he was pining after."

"You were pining after me?" she raises her eyes.

"Oh, hell yes. I wanted you so bad, and then you were gone, and I wanted you even more."

She reaches out for my shirt and pulls it, bringing me closer to her. "If only fourteen-year-old Bodhi would have been brave enough to kiss fourteen-year-old Eva when he had the chance."

"Fourteen-year-old Eva scared the shit out of younger Bodhi," I tell her. "He knew back then she was a force of nature and he'd never find anyone else quite like her. She still is a force of nature." I can't help but bring my fingers to her face, running them along her lips. "A beautiful, disastrous hurricane that can't be tamed."

Eva casually grabs onto my hand, bringing it to her chest. "Would you want her tamed?"

"Never. Because then she wouldn't be the girl I've been madly in love with since I was twelve."

She smiles, pulling at my arm to bring me in even closer. "I wonder what fourteen-year-old Bodhi would have thought, if he knew back then that he was eventually going to have sex, in this very room with the girl sitting next to him on his bed."

"He probably would have asked when that was going to happen," I respond. "Because it hasn't happened yet, in this room."

Eva tugs on my shirt, bringing my lips to hers. She then releases her grasp on me and stands back just a little. I watch as she reaches behind her neck, slowly untying the straps to her dress until it hangs loosely from her chest. "I think the answer to that question would be tonight."

"*Tonight*?" I hear my voice crack. "As in right now? *That* tonight?"

"I have a lot of memories of you and me in this room, good ones, but I think it's time to create a new one. A more mature one. One that I'm sure fourteen-year-old Bodhi dreamt about repeatedly—"

I don't wait to hear anything else. I slam my lips onto hers, pushing her body backwards until she hits my closet door.

"Someone is *really* excited," she laughs into my mouth.

"Someone was caught off guard, and is *very* excited."

"I told you we'd know when the time was right," she reminds me. "I think this is definitely the right time."

"We could just take it slow," I make known, my lips wandering tenderly down her neck.

"That wouldn't be very much fun."

"We could make it fun," I say, my hands teasingly holding onto the straps of her dress.

"No, thank you."

"Are you sure you feel—"

Eva's hands suddenly grab mine. She hastily lowers them off her neck, as I hang on to her straps. She pulls my fingers away which causes her dress to abruptly fall to her feet. She's now left standing there in just her black lace panties. I try to close my mouth, but it's no use.

"I feel fine," she bluntly says. "I don't want to take it slow. Now show me, Bodhi. Show me that I'm the only name on your list now."

I pick my jaw up off the floor. "Yes ma'am."

My lips go to hers, my hands to her own, pushing them hard against my closet door as our mouths move together. She brings my lower lip in between her teeth, and carefully bites down, while lowering our hands and unbuttoning my shirt. My mouth glides to her neck, then to her collarbone, then to her breasts. She gets to the last button on my shirt, pulling it past my shoulders as I shake it off. My mouth stays on her body while her arms wrap around my neck. She leans her head back against the door and lets out a loud moan.

"God, Bodhi, I've missed this." Her voice is like velvet as she purrs these words into the still air of my room. Her lips reach for mine again and her tongue jams inside my mouth. She tries to move us towards the bed, but I push her back against the closet door.

"Not yet."

I'm more than ready to have sex with her, but there's more I want to do with her first. I want to savor every single second of this, every single inch of her. I trail my lips down her body again, all the way down this time, until I find myself on my knees. I get to the scar on her stomach, her perfect pristine scar, and I tenderly kiss it while her fingers dig into my shoulders. I then get to her panties. I don't hesitate one bit. I yank them down to her feet, my lips immediately going to what's hidden behind them. Eva's hands squeeze my shoulders as she loudly gasps. I've never kissed her here before. I've never allowed my tongue to move against this delicate place on her body before. I know she wasn't expecting this.

The entire act, it's fucking beautiful.

It doesn't take her long, moments almost, before my name is freely flying out of her mouth, before she reaches that amazing peak that I've been so desperate lately to hear her reach. When she's done, her entire body suddenly goes limp against the closet door, as her arms hang loosely around my neck. I quickly stand, scooping her up and carrying her over to my bed. She's panting as I lie her down, but she pulls at my shoulders and brings her mouth to mine.

I can tell how out of breath she is through our kiss. I pull away. "I've wanted to do that for a while," I nuzzle my mouth to her ear.

"You have my full permission to do that whenever you want," she softly replies back. Her fingers unbutton my shorts and she slips her hands under my boxers, pushing them both down. "Just be a little careful at first, okay?"

I quickly look into her eyes, and it kills me to see they're full of fear. "We don't have to—"

"No! I want to," she immediately makes known. "I want to. Don't overthink it. Just don't rush."

"Okay. No rushing."

She reaches down, wrapping her fingers around me. She brings her hand right between her legs, right to the entrance of *her*, and then places her thighs around my back, squeezing and giving my body a firm push until I'm surprisingly fully inside of her. I shiver with eagerness, not expecting to enter her so quickly. Now that I have, I can't control how badly I want to repeatedly lunge myself into her until my name is being screamed from her mouth again. I know six weeks isn't that long, but with how desperately I've missed being with her like this, six weeks felt like an eternity.

"*Jesus*," I mutter, as I slowly start to rock against her. I have to remind myself to not just go full force. "You feel amazing."

She grins, dragging her fingernails across my back as her eyes stare into mine.

"Are you okay?" I question.

She nods her head and wraps her legs tighter around me. Her eyes close for a brief moment, as I continue to move against her. I consciously watch the expressions on her face, the way her body moves in the same rhythm as my own. Her lips, how she bites down on her bottom one. Fuck, she's perfect. She's beyond perfect. She's my own personal train wreck of perfection. She's the hurricane that blows through town, leaving a path of destruction on everyone she meets. But instead of running from her, instead of seeking shelter, I walk right into the eye of the storm, because that eye, it's my heart.

She owns it. She will always own it.

Her eyes abruptly open, and the fear that was there moments ago is now gone. Instead, they're filled with lust, and hunger, and confidence, all things I've seen in her eyes before. "I've missed you," she briskly says. "I've missed having you like this. I've missed feeling you like this."

I can only nod my head, because I'm still trying desperately to hold off as long as I can. My body wants to completely lose itself in her right now, in how epically incredible this feels. She pushes her legs harder on my back, so that my arms give out and my chest falls onto hers, closing whatever little space was between us. I bring my hands under her pillow, while her arms wrap around my back, squeezing my body onto hers even more. She's refusing to let any air flow between the two of us.

We are literally just one person right now.

Her mouth is on mine, her hands and legs pushing against my back, keeping me in place as I continue to move my hips into hers. I can feel the sweat forming on her body, on my body. I can feel her start to unravel again as she arches off the bed, slamming herself harder into my chest in the process. I can't tear my eyes away from her. How sexy she looks, how her sweaty hair clings to her forehead, how her eyes seem to change shape as her head rises from the pillow every time I lunge against her.

My name slips from her mouth again, and I feel her fingernails rake across my back. The pain that shoots throughout my skin forces me to move faster. I know she's ready, that there's no need to be cautious anymore, that she's just waiting for me now. But I love watching her come undone. It's like what I would imagine shooting up feels like. Knowing you're about to experience this epic high, but being utterly disappointed at the same time, knowing it will eventually wear off. I want this high to last forever, the high she gives me by being mine and allowing me to love her like this, in this way that I will never love anyone else.

I hold off as long as I can, watching her twist and turn under my body, feeling the sheets become drenched with our sweat, listening to the noises of pleasure that come from her mouth. I'm relishing in my own personal high. *She* is my own personal high. My drug.

When I know she can't last any longer, when *I* can't last any longer, I grab at her hips and raise my body from hers. Cool air finally flows between the two of us, and her hands cling to the sheet, her moans buried in the sounds of the bed hitting the wall and my own noises of satisfaction. With one last push of my hips, everything in my soul finally gets released into her as we both reach that epic high together, and then I crash down onto her chest.

My body is useless at this point, drained, weak, exhausted. And as we lie there not saying one single word, I wonder how the hell I got so lucky. Her fingers gently run through my hair. Her heart beats steadily into my ear. Her breath dances past my face. Her warm skin sticks to mine. How the hell did I get lucky enough to call her my own? To have her confidently say that she's mine, when she could literally have anyone else in this world?

I feel her face turn. Her breath is suddenly warmer on my ear, and then I hear her whisper, "I love being your hurricane."

My lips tenderly kiss her damp chest, and it's at that exact moment I know why I'm so lucky, why I was gifted with the beautiful Eva Calloway. It's because although *she* is the hurricane, I'm always going to be the eye of the storm, and you can't have a hurricane without the eye. We can't live without each other. We can't survive without each other. We would both just completely evaporate and cease to exist. It's how it's always been from the moment we met. It continued to be like that even when we were apart. And it will *always* be like this, no matter what or who gets blown our way.

chapter twenty-four

Eva

He's so heavy against my body, like dead weight that traps you where you are. I don't want him to move, but he has to because I've held off as long as I can, and I can't get any air into my lungs now. "Bodhi," I gently say. "You're crushing me. I can't breathe."

"Ah! Shit!" he rolls his body off mine. "I'm sorry."

I finally take in a deep breath of air, and turn to my side, placing my head on his sweaty chest. We're both so sticky with sweat, it's almost gross. I pull the sheet up and over my body, because although I'm hotter than hell, the cold air is also making me shiver. It's a weird combination.

"You okay?" he nervously looks down at me.

"I am. I'm absolutely okay. I'm ready for round two."

"I'm going to need at least twenty-four hours here." He pushes my hair off my forehead and rests his lips there. "I have an idea, let's skip Hayes' party and just stay in bed all night. Maybe all I need is a few hours, but you'll never know unless we stay here."

I shake my head into his chest. "I promised Luna I'd be there, *and* I need to talk to Ethan. But when we get back, we can stay in your bed all night, as long as we have a repeat of everything that took place just a little bit ago."

"Fourteen-year-old Bodhi would have been really impressed with his future self."

I run my fingers along his arm. "It was amazing. I—I didn't know it could get any better than it already was, and you always make me feel so incredibly ..." I search for the right word. "Free," I finally settle on.

"Free?" he repeats.

"Yes. Free to explore a different side of myself, one I thoroughly enjoy welcoming. And free to let you ..." I bury my face into his chest. "To let you explore my body like that," I mumble into his skin.

"I love exploring your body," he whispers in my ear. "You sure we just can't stay here? Trust me when I say staying here will be much more enjoyable than going to Hayes'."

I raise my face from his chest. "I need to talk to Ethan. I need some answers."

"I know you do."

I push the sheet off so that it just covers my lower half, but then I kick my foot out from under it. "I'm so hot, but so cold!"

"That was a workout. I need water, and food, and a nap."

"No nap," I tell him, sitting up and taking the sheet with me. Bodhi rolls over to his stomach and stretches his arms along the bed. I start to shiver. "I need a hot shower—"

"No!" he moans into the pillow, patting the empty spot next to him, where I just was. "No shower. Stay here with me."

I laugh under my breath. He's completely naked, just lying on his stomach, the sheet only covering a portion of his way too toned butt. He doesn't even care. I grab a t-shirt that I see at the foot of his bed and throw it over my own naked self. I then turn back to him. He's sitting up now, the sheet covering everything below his waist. His eyes wander the entire length of my body.

"How can it be that after everything we just did, you look even sexier just sitting there wearing my t-shirt?" I don't have time to respond, as he pulls me by the shirt back into his arms. He brings his mouth to my ear and calmly whispers, "Marry me, Eva."

I groan. "Not this again. I *cannot* marry you right now. We're seventeen. Is that even legal?"

"You'll marry me one day, why not now?"

"Because. We. Are. *Seventeen*!" I loudly roar. "Ask me again in a few years. Like when we're twenty-one."

He waves his hands at me. "I'll ask you again tomorrow."

I jokingly roll my eyes. "You're insane, and I'm going to take a shower." I go to get up but he pulls the bottom of my shirt so that I fall back down. My head lands on his legs and he quickly wraps his arms around my chest. "Let me up, Bodhi."

He shakes his head.

"*Bodhi*," I dramatically sigh. He slowly bends down and places a small kiss on my lips. "Can I get up *now*?"

He holds up one finger. "I'm not letting you out of my sight tonight."

I frown at him. "I don't need a babysitter."

"I'm not babysitting you."

"You have to trust me."

"I *do* trust you. I *don't* trust anyone else. Just promise me you'll stay by one of us tonight? The guys, Luna and Kennedy ..."

"You know, for someone who used to frequent the party scene of Flagler on a regular basis, you sure do make it seem like we're walking straight into the fiery pits of teenage hell."

He lets out a snicker. "I have you, I have my friends, I don't need to get wasted or high with people I don't care about anymore in order to have fun."

I sit up and carefully place his chin in my fingers. "You don't have to get wasted or high with them, you can get wasted and high with *me*, while they watch."

"Just don't wander tonight, okay? Stay with me? Or one of us?"

"No wandering, got it. Can I go take a shower now?"

He nods to the door. "The bag you gave me last night is in the bathroom upstairs."

I climb out of bed and stand at the side of it, my hands go to my hips. "I was just going to wear this t-shirt. No bra, no panties? Does that not meet your approval?"

He glares at me as a smile forms on his face. "That most definitely meets my approval, but only here, with me. I'm expecting you to walk out of that bathroom in sweatpants and a hoodie."

I give him a salute and head out the bedroom door.

Roughly an hour later, we're driving down A1A in Bodhi's jeep. His hand is resting on my thigh as he drives, my hand is out the open window, catching the salty ocean air in my fingers. I'm not wearing sweatpants. In fact, quite the opposite. Frayed jean shorts, a tank top, my hair pulled up in a ponytail. It's humid tonight. The kind of humidity you can almost imagine cutting with a knife. It's not scorching hot, but the air is thick and it's already causing

Bodhi's hair to become curlier than it normally is. I run my hand through the top, twirling one of his curls around my index finger.

"Your hair gives me warm, tingly feelings."

"I stopped trying to tame it when I was ten. There was no point."

"I love it," I declare as he pulls his jeep down a side street and parks behind a row of other cars. He points behind him to a massive mansion that sits right on the beach. Possibly the only house in all of Flagler that is located right on the ocean.

"We're here."

"Maxwell Hayes lives *there*?" I question in disbelief.

"That he does," Bodhi sighs, leaning his head back on his seat and closing his eyes.

"You really don't want to be here tonight, do you?"

"I don't. I spent the last couple years going to every single party in Flagler, getting wasted and making stupid fucking mistakes. Being here is like pouring salt in the wounds of my past."

I hate that he feels like this. That he can't go to a party without thinking about shit he did before he and I were together. I unbuckle my seatbelt, and then I climb directly onto his lap, straddling it as his eyes grow large.

"*Eva*, what are you doing?"

I place my finger over his mouth. "We find Ethan, we get answers. We find our friends, show our faces, and then we leave, okay? But until then, I'll be your band-aid to those old wounds."

He lowers my finger from his mouth and gives me a long kiss, squeezing my hips in the process. He then opens the door and points to the road. "Shall we?"

I hop off his lap, immediately grabbing his hand as he steps out of his jeep. We cross A1A and walk down a long driveway that wraps its way to the brightly lit mansion that sits close to the sand. I can already hear the crowd of people on the beach. I can already hear the music. I can already smell the faint aroma of weed. I can already tell that Maxwell Hayes doesn't do anything half-ass.

"*Bodhi!*" I hear a chorus of his name as we both come into view. There's a group of guys standing around a bonfire. They all look absolutely drunk off their asses, swaying as they stand there.

"Hey guys," Bodhi says, walking us closer. I recognize two of

213

them from the dinner, Easton and Wesley. "This is my girlfriend, Eva," he introduces me to the others, squeezing my hand so tight, I have to give it a little shake to get him to release his grip and allow proper blood flow.

"Hi," I wave.

"God, Bodhi!" one of the guys cries out. "We heard you went and got a girlfriend. *Damn*, you can't be from Flagler," he says to me.

"I am, the Halifax," I reply.

"How'd you meet Bodhi? I've never seen you around."

"She's known Bodhi since they were twelve," Wesley answers.

I give him a brief smile. "True fact."

"Eva!" I hear my name being shouted from a distance. I turn to see Luna heading our way with Coop. I can feel Bodhi relax a little, seeing the familiar faces of our friends.

Luna squeezes herself in next to me.

"Who the hell is she?" one of the guys points to Luna.

"Fuck, man," Coop gives him a snort. "This is my girlfriend, Luna. Don't be a dick."

"Coop? What the hell!" the guy's eyes bug out. "You got a girlfriend now, too?"

"I know a good thing when I see it," Coop throws his arm around Luna. "Maybe you should get *yourself* a girlfriend. Teach you some fucking manners. Let's go guys," he says to us. "Leave these idiots to drink themselves right into an afterschool special."

Bodhi looks much calmer as we walk away. We head over to a patio draped with hanging lights, and blaring music that thumps directly into my chest. Beck and Kennedy are curled up on a chair, they each have a cup in their hand, and Kennedy jumps up the moment she sees us.

"Girl time!" she instantly shouts, dropping her cup down in Beck's hand and yanking Luna and me away from the guys. "We'll be right back!"

"*Kennedy*," I hear Bodhi's annoyed voice call out.

"Yeah, yeah, yeah," she waves at him. "I won't let anyone run away with her," she declares, pulling Luna and me over to a table away from everyone else, away from the music still ringing in my ears. "First," she says, pouring punch into cups for the three of us.

"Some jungle juice."

"Jungle juice?" I question, stifling a laugh.

She shrugs her shoulders. "A delicious drink, put together by Hayes years ago, that sneaks up on you like a cheetah in the jungle!"

I take a brief sip. "There's alcohol in here?" I question her. It tastes like Kool-Aid.

"Oh yes," she grins. "Lots of it. Now, are we toasting?" she asks, raising her cup in the air.

"Toasting to …?" I narrow my eyes at her.

"Oh, come *on!*" Luna laughs. "Kennedy said you and Bodhi left the school two hours ago. You can't tell us you didn't sneak to his house and have steamy, hot sex. I know how you two were before the accident," she wags her finger at me.

Normally I would burst out laughing at this point, maybe choke a little on this delicious jungle juice I'm currently sipping on. But I don't. I just continue to sip on it while staring at the eager faces of Luna and Kennedy, without saying a single word.

"She's not going to tell us," Kennedy turns to Luna, shocked. "Her two best girlfriends. She's going to leave us in the dark."

"Well, now I'm sad," Luna puckers out her lower lip. "Guess I'll have to drink away my sorrows."

"Enough," I laugh. "You guys are ridiculous. Yes, we went to his house. *Not* to have steamy, hot sex. Get your heads out of the gutter."

Luna smirks, "*But* …?"

I take a big sip from my cup. "*But* maybe it ended up happening anyway."

"Holy shit!" Kennedy cries out. "I knew it! I knew that's why you guys left so suddenly—"

"Actually, we left suddenly because I couldn't take one more person telling me how Bodhi was just using me and would eventually break my heart."

"Yikes," Luna puts her hand on my arm. "For real?"

I nod my head while taking another sip.

"Ignore them," Kennedy tells me. "They're all bitches. Jealous bitches. Every girl in our school has wanted Bodhi for themselves, and he never gave them *any* attention. Well, except me, but not in

215

that way—I was just always with them because of Beck—"

"Kennedy ... I know what you mean."

She lets out a breath of air. "Good! Okay—a toast!" Her cup raises into the night sky. Luna and I follow suit. "To being able to have sex whenever the hell you want again!"

Now I burst out laughing. "Yes, to *that*."

We give ourselves refills and then head back over to the guys. Thankfully, someone was smart enough to turn the music down.

"Ah!" Coop shouts out. "The girls are attacking the jungle juice!" Coop looks like he's already had quite a few himself.

"This stuff's pretty damn good," I admit. I walk over to Bodhi, who's sitting on the edge of a chair, looking like a stiff board. I stand right in front of him. His hands reach for the back of my thighs and he pulls me onto his lap. "Do you want a sip?" I ask him as I settle.

He shakes his head and relaxes into the chair, throwing his arm around my back. "I'm staying completely sober tonight—"

"Boo!" Coop and Beck both shout.

"When did you suddenly become boring?" Coop continues.

"Who else is going to drive all your sorry asses back to my house?!" Bodhi questions. "We are *not* staying here tonight."

"You live, like, five minutes from here," Beck points out. "We can walk if we have to."

"Do you honestly think six drunk teenagers walking down A1A for two miles is a good idea?" Bodhi frowns at them.

"Son of a bitch has a point," Coop nods toward Bodhi.

"Enjoy this random act of kindness," Bodhi waves his hands at them. "Drink up. But if you aren't in my jeep when I'm ready to leave, you get left behind."

"Yes, *Dad*," Coop grins.

I turn my body to face Bodhi better. "Although I thoroughly appreciate the fact you are so concerned with getting us all home safely, I have to say I'm a little disappointed."

"Oh yeah? Why's that?" he questions.

"We've checked a lot of stuff off our girlfriend-boyfriend bucket list, but have yet to drink together at a party."

"It will happen," he promises. "Just not tonight. Don't let that stop you from having fun, okay?"

I lean in, placing a small kiss on his lips while he squeezes my thigh. "I want to have fun with *you*."

Bodhi whispers, "Did we not have fun just a little bit ago?"

I feel my face blush. "Yes, we did."

He softly kisses my neck. "You enjoy your first Hayes party, and I'll enjoy watching you. Then later tonight, we can have fun together again."

"Lovebirds!" Coop shouts to us. "You're embarrassing the rest of us over here!"

"Speak for yourself," Kennedy laughs. "I think it's adorable."

I smile and turn my body to face them better, when I see a familiar head of hair in the distance. "Ethan!" I hiss under my breath, trying to unwrap myself from Bodhi so I can stand.

Bodhi grabs at my arm. "I'm going with you."

I pull him along through the sand, following Ethan until he stops abruptly at a large group of people standing around another bonfire. He doesn't see us, and I'm actually worried he might trip into the flames if we sneak up on him. He's not exactly what I'd call graceful. I purposely walk through the crowd, in his view, so he has time to process the fact I'm coming for him.

"Eva," Bodhi's voice quietly says my name. "I don't like this. I don't trust these people ..."

I ignore him as I'm right on top of Ethan now.

"Hi," Ethan greets me. He's smoking something and the familiar smell of weed enters my nose.

"Are you smoking a joint?" I question in disbelief. I hear a few people around me laugh under their breaths.

"Maybe," he replies.

I rip it from his hand and throw it in the bonfire. "You're fucking fourteen!"

Ethan stares me down. "And you're not my mom."

"You must be Eva," I hear an unfamiliar voice say. I turn my head to see a girl standing behind me. Long skirt, halter top, her boobs literally falling out. She's the only girl in this crowd of high teenage boys. "Bodhi," she nods her head at him.

"Charlotte," he nods back. "Charlotte is Hayes' older sister," he then says to me.

217

My eyes go back to her as she smirks, "Maxwell has told me a lot about you."

I laugh under my breath. "In the three or four hours that he's known me, he's already told you about me?"

She slowly nods her head. I've never been intimidated by other girls before. Usually it's the opposite, me reassuring girls my age that I'm nothing special, but Charlotte carries herself like one bad move and she's going to rip your head right off. I refuse to let her think I'm scared in her presence.

"Glad I made a good first impression," I calmly state.

She lets out a snicker. "He said you were witty. You want one?" she holds out a joint to me.

"I'll pass, but thanks."

"You don't smoke?" she questions.

"I do. I have. There's just no need tonight."

"Bodhi?" she holds it out to him.

He shakes his head.

"Well, shit. You two are no fun."

"I actually just need to talk to Ethan," I point to him.

She raises her eyes. "What do you want with my baby cousin?"

"Unfinished business."

"Just need to ask him a few questions," Bodhi chimes in, throwing his arm around Ethan.

"Ethan?" Charlotte questions him.

Ethan grins. "Back down Charlotte, they're not going to murder me."

She waves her hands at us, "Have at it."

I grab Ethan's arm and start to pull him away.

"Bodhi!" Charlotte exclaims suddenly. The three of us turn back to her. "I owe you, so take this news as us being even now. Maxwell, he's very infatuated with her," she points to me. "And you know he always gets what he wants."

I hear Bodhi take in a deep breath. "Thanks for the heads up," he manages to say through clenched teeth.

He tugs on my arm to get me to move, but I firmly keep my feet in the sand. "You'll probably see Maxwell before me," I say to Charlotte. "Can you give him a message?"

She laughs. "I have a feeling this is going to be good."

"Tell him Eva said to go fuck himself."

I then turn and walk away, leaving Bodhi and Ethan standing there, and the crowd of guys going absolutely insane with what just flew out of my mouth. I quickly hear feet behind me, and then a hand tries to slip into mine. I shake it off and keep walking. Why do I feel like I'm getting ready to lose it? I get myself further down the beach, as far away from the crowd of assholes as possible, before I stop. Bodhi and Ethan are right behind me. My eyes dart between the two of them, waiting for one of them to speak.

"I can't believe you just said that!" Ethan busts out laughing. He throws himself down in the sand.

"Your cousin is an asshole," I reply.

"Which *one*?" he chuckles.

"Both of them. And you," I shove Bodhi in the chest. "She *owes* you? Care to explain that one?"

He gives me a disappointed look. "The end of school last year, here, on the beach, some drunk guys were messing with her. I might have punched a few of them."

"That was you?!" Ethan exclaims. "I heard about that!"

Bodhi gives a little bow. "Does that clear it up?" he then questions me, raising his eyebrow.

I'm such an ass. Bodhi doesn't deserve my out-of-control attitude. *Fix* this Eva. "I'm sorry," I quickly say to him. "I'm exploding at the wrong person. I'm just—I'm sorry."

He pulls at my hand. "You don't have to apologize."

"Has anyone ever told you that you guys make people gag?" Ethan blurts out.

"As of matter of fact, yes. Coop has. Now talk, Ethan. I've got much better things to do with my time than sit here with you."

Ethan grabs his heart. "Warm and fuzzy feelings. You have such a way with words."

"*Ethan*," I warn. "I know you were there the night of my accident. I remember you."

"I was wondering if you did," he looks up at me, his entire demeanor has suddenly changed.

"What were you doing there?"

219

"I can't tell you that."

"Ethan! What the hell can you tell me then?!"

"That I'm sorry," he whispers. He looks down at his feet, avoiding any eye contact.

Why do I suddenly feel bad for him? I can't handle all these extreme emotions. I look over at Bodhi, wondering what to say or do next. He nods toward Ethan, and I gently place myself down in the sand next to him. He looks up at me, and straight to the scar on my forehead.

"I thought you were dead," he quietly announces. "All that blood, and the way you were just lying there. I mean, I knew *he* was dead, but you—I had to shout your name a few times before you opened your eyes."

I place my hand on his shoulder. "I'm sorry you saw that."

"I can't *unsee* it," he sadly declares. "Every fucking night ..."

Bodhi sits down next to him on the other side. "Bro, I understand. I see it every night, too. But Ethan, I *heard* the crash. I was at the docks when it happened, and I was there within a minute or two. How did *you* get there before me?"

"I was on my bike," he immediately responds. "I was right there when it happened. I saw it all, how he flew through the—I saw the whole thing. I think I even screamed."

Something doesn't make sense. "Why were you right there, on High Bridge, on your bike?"

He twirls his fingers in the sand. "I was at the docks first. When I saw Porter's boat flying down the Halifax, I left."

"It was like nine at night," Bodhi points out. "What the hell were you doing at the docks by yourself at nine at night?"

He stares out into the ocean. "Maybe I wasn't by myself."

I let out a loud sigh. "Ethan, I understand you might be stuck in a position where you don't feel comfortable telling us everything you know. But shit doesn't make sense—"

"I was at the docks, I saw the boat coming, I left on my bike without your friend in the truck seeing me, and saw the crash as I was riding down High Bridge—"

"You told me they were coming," I remind him. "You knew they were coming for me, my friends, Bodhi. How did you know that's why they were there?"

"He told us—"

"Who told you?" I question.

Ethan throws himself back in the sand. "I'd rather not say."

"Ethan!" I yell. "This is bullshit—"

"Everyone works for him," he suddenly mumbles. "Do you not realize that? Half of Flagler works for him. *My* family works for him. Doesn't your *dad* work for him?" he sits up and points at me.

"Are you talking about Henry Channing?" I ask, shocked.

Ethan's eyes grow large and he waves his hands in the air.

"Are you trying to tell us," Bodhi says, "that Henry Channing knew we were on our way to try to save Eva?"

Ethan doesn't answer, but he does say, "He's a powerful man."

I shake my head. "His house was burning down, he sure as hell wasn't on my patio with all of us, how the hell did he know they all left on Porter's boat to try to find *me*?"

"I don't know, Eva," Ethan responds sarcastically. "It's almost as if he might have overheard everything you guys had said that night."

"What the *fuck*," Bodhi mumbles.

"That's not possible," I nervously reply. "He wasn't there—"

"You don't have to be present to overhear conversations," Ethan makes known.

I let his words settle for a moment. "Henry Channing overheard everything that happened on my patio that night?"

Ethan nods his head.

"Porter?" I spit out his name. "Did Porter have anything to do with this?"

Ethan lets out a snicker. "That dumbass is as clueless as a pile of dog shit."

Bodhi laughs under his breath.

"And telling us *how* he overheard everything would ...?"

"Not be a good idea."

"I'll figure it out—"

"I know you will."

I lean my head on Ethan's shoulder, which catches him by surprise. "Ethan," I then calmly say his name. "Were you at the docks by chance, or were you there for a reason that night?"

"I was there for a reason," he instantly replies.

I carefully reach my arm behind Ethan, to find Bodhi. Ethan doesn't notice my little movement. He doesn't notice that I give Bodhi's arm a squeeze before I say out loud, "Luke said we were stopping somewhere first. We were making a pit stop before he got me out of Flagler. By any chance was that pit stop to see you?"

"Maybe," Ethan says in a whisper, and then I hear him start to cry. My heart breaks for this kid, this kid I barely know, who has been thrown into this nightmare whether by his own doing, or by the hands of someone else. My nightmare. He's been thrown into *my* nightmare.

He wipes at his eyes. "Maybe I was with someone he was going to meet. Maybe I found out you were with him, maybe I knew what road he was on, maybe I thought I could save you."

"You were on High Bridge, on your bike, trying to save Eva?" Bodhi questions.

Ethan nods. "I was too late. I turned the corner and saw the crash happen. I saw it all. I tried—I was going to ride out in front of the truck—make him stop, give Eva a chance to get away—"

"Why?" I ask him. "Why risk your own life to try to save mine?"

He looks down the beach, to the crowd of people we left just a little bit ago. "Because I'm tired of the bad guys always winning." He then suddenly stands, shakes the sand off his shorts and says, "I'm sorry I was too late. That you had to go through all of that— that I couldn't save you."

"You did save me," I declare. "You told me to hang on, that they were coming. You gave me hope."

He gives me a small smile, and then turns toward the bonfire and starts walking away.

I have one more question though. "Ethan! What'd you do with the gun?"

He freezes. I see his back rise as he takes a deep breath. He doesn't turn around, but he does point straight out to the ocean. Then he continues down the beach, back to the crowd of people who probably don't give a damn about him.

chapter twenty-five

Bodhi

How'd you know he took the gun?" I ask Eva as we head back to our friends.

"I just did," she says. "There's more. There's got to be more. He's scared. Did you see how scared he was, talking about this?"

"I did. I think he's protecting his family—"

"Hayes?" she questions. "*His* family?"

I shake my head. "Hayes is a fucking asshole, and Charlotte isn't too far behind, but I don't think they're involved with Henry Channing. Then again, I feel like nothing is ever as it seems."

"So his parents, then?" Eva goes on. "Maybe the other side of his family? Hayes said their dads are cousins. What about his mom? Do we know who she is?"

"I don't even know Ethan's last name, to be honest."

"Looks like I'll be digging around for some info tonight."

I groan. "No digging around. Let's just let answers appear—"

"That never happens, Bodhi," she snorts. "But it's nice that you're so optimistic."

We're getting close to where we left our friends. "Don't let this ruin your night, okay? Or everything that we've managed to put behind us."

She stops by the table of jungle juice. "Henry Channing somehow overheard everything that happened on my patio that night. Luke was taking me to the docks where Ethan was with someone he's too nervous to mention. And the gun that Luke waved around in front of our faces is now at the bottom of the ocean somewhere, because a fourteen-year-old kid got rid of it."

She stands there with a frustrated look on her face.

"It's a lot," I agree. "A lot of shit on top of all the other shit."

"Did you see anyone that night? At the docks?"

"No. I wasn't really looking, though. All I saw was Beck, and what I later found out was Luke's boat. There were no other cars, no other people, just us."

"Someone else was there," she points out, pouring jungle juice in a cup. "Someone else was there the same time you were, waiting for Luke. And whoever this person is, they probably got rid of his boat after the accident."

"They probably did."

She starts drinking, looking deep in thought. "Whoever Ethan is protecting probably knows where Henry is. And if we can find out where Henry is, maybe we'll have a better chance of finding your little sister. Leverage," she then says. "We don't tell Holden anything we found out tonight, until he finds out more information about Skyla—"

I chuckle, and move closer to her. "Do you hear yourself? Maybe you should work for Holden, or open your own private investigating firm after high school."

"You'd like that, wouldn't you? Me, in tight business suits with a low bun on my head every day, bright red lipstick ..."

"Actually, I prefer you in just my t-shirt—"

She kisses me, her hand cradling my neck. I can taste the alcohol on her breath, and it makes me crave her even more than I normally do. She tastes good, she smells good, her warm hand feels good on my neck. Even with what we just did a couple hours ago, it's not enough. I'm ready to take her home and do it all over again.

"I prefer being in just your t-shirt, too," she says, pulling her lips from mine.

I point toward the road. "We can leave."

I can see the sudden excitement in her eyes, but then she shakes her head. "Not yet." Then she drags me back over to our friends.

"How'd it go?" Coop asks the moment we come into view.

"Oh, you know ..." Eva throws herself down on Luna's lap. "Secrets, mysteries, no real answers, more shit to solve."

"So exactly like the entire summer has been?" Beck questions.

"Exactly," I answer.

"Give us the short version," Luna then says.

"Short version?" Eva narrows her eyes. "Henry Channing heard everything that happened on my patio that night. Ethan was at the docks with someone he won't mention by name, waiting for Luke. When he found out *I* was with Luke, he left on High Bridge on his bike to come save me, apparently. And he threw the gun Luke had into the ocean."

"*That's* the short version?" Kennedy gasps. "What the hell is the long version?"

"More details," I reply. "And Eva told Charlotte to tell Hayes to go fuck himself."

Coop chokes on his drink, literally spraying it all over the ground as he coughs. "You did that?" he asks, pointing at Eva.

She raises her drink, "Sure did."

"Girl, can I be *you* when I grow up?" Coop laughs.

Kennedy abruptly stands, pulling Eva off Luna's lap. "I am going to *love* having you at school this year. Alright girls, time to mingle with the bitches," she announces, pulling Luna up next. "We're going to show *both* your faces to the crowds of future homewreckers and trophy wives, so that every other social gathering we attend this year, no one questions who you are, who you're dating, and who you are friends with."

"Kennedy," I shake my head.

"No!" she raises her hand at me. "I've waited three years to have girlfriends I actually like. You are *not* going to deny me the privilege of parading them around their first school party side-by-side with me. Got it?"

I look at Beck and he just shakes his head. "Don't deny her the privilege, man," he repeats.

She then turns to Coop. "Do you have a problem with this?"

"Not at all, Kennedy," he smiles. "Just throw my name in there when you introduce her, okay? Give me some props for the beautiful lady. Let everyone know she's taken by the one and only Coop."

"Not a problem," she agrees. "Girls, say goodbye to your boys, we'll be back in a bit."

Eva leans down, placing a quick kiss on my lips. "Don't worry about me, I'm in good hands."

"You hear that, Bodhi?" Kennedy remarks. "She's in good hands. No worrying. Talk boy talk or something, let's go ladies! Drink refills first!"

We watch them walk away, and then Beck casually says, "You realize they're going to come back totally wasted, right?"

"Oh yes," Coop agrees. "And that will be our cue to leave. A wasted Eva actually sounds like something straight out of my nightmares. You ever see her drunk? She gonna start a riot? Beat the shit out of anyone who's ever wronged us? Hold up. You sure you want us coming home with you two?" Coop gives me a funny look as he continues. "I mean, we all know what today marks."

I lean back in my chair. "You have a really strange obsession with talking about my sex life."

"Just keeping it real, bro. Don't want to block any action happening between you and the lady tonight."

I roll my eyes. "You don't need to worry about that."

"*Okay*, Bodhi," Coop continues. "But at least put some background noise on the speakers, or wait until the rest of us have passed out—"

Beck's laughter interrupts him. "Fuck, Coop. Unless Bodhi's going for round two tonight, we're in the clear from accidentally interrupting the two of them."

"Round two?!" Coop blurts out under his breath. "You and Eva? *Already*? Goddamn, Bodhi. I can't keep up with this shit. Good for you guys—jumping right back into it—"

"Stop," I shake my head. "Just stop."

"I'm being supportive!" he cries out. "I mean, you gonna talk to Calvin about this shit? Or maybe Pop can pull out a banana and a condom—"

"I'm well aware of how to put a condom on—"

"Ah! Scary image in my head!" Coop throws his hand over his eyes. "I know you're insanely knowledgeable about sex! All I'm saying is that we should be comfortable enough to talk about this type of shit with each other. You both," he points to Beck and me, "live with old people! I'm your only good option here if you need advice or someone to relate to!"

Beck and I both start laughing. "Beck," I turn to him. "You have

226

any questions about sex with Kennedy?"

"Nah," he shakes his head. "I mean, we've been doing it together since we were sixteen. Pretty sure we're at that comfortable spot now where we really don't question much anymore. What about you and Eva?"

"She's like every fantasy I've ever had, rolled into one beautiful human being," I proudly announce. "I might need some advice on how to keep up with her, but I'll let you both know if that becomes an issue. Coop," I raise my eyebrow. "Luna giving you any problems? Something keeping you up at night that you want to share with your boys?"

Coop looks between the two of us and squints his eyes. "You know what, fuck you two. I was being serious here. Thought we could open up a little with each other. You both are parentless and I was just trying to let you know I'm here for you—"

"Dude," I shake my head. "Luna has changed you. For the better. You're right, you two are my family. You're the ones I'd come to whenever I need sex advice. Does that make you feel better?"

"It does, bro, because you bastards are the ones I come to for everything."

Beck stands. "Do we need a group hug now?"

"Nah, man," Coop shakes his head.

"Fist bump?" I question.

"Sure, bro," Coop nods.

We fist bump, then I pat Coop on the head. "Bros for life, the three of us, always."

He forms a triangle with his fingers. "Well, no shit," he then smirks. "We know way too much about each other to not follow through until the end."

"True," Beck agrees. "Some of our secrets have to go to the grave with us."

"I'll drink to that," Coop laughs. "In fact, I need another drink."

"Same here," Beck nods. "Bodhi, you sure—"

"Nah," I wave my hands at them. "Not tonight." I suddenly see Charlotte wandering down the beach alone. "I'll meet you guys back here in a second," I tell them, then I walk down to the water.

Charlotte stops moving as I get closer, spinning around and

227

folding her arms over her chest when she sees me. "Bodhi," her lips turn up in annoyance. "Where's the prom queen?"

"Eva's not a prom queen. She's actually a lot like you."

"Oh yeah?"

"Unpredictable. Hayes, what's he want with her?"

"I figured that's why you followed me. Why do you care? She's just another girl. You don't exactly date, right? At least that's the impression I always got around you—"

"Eva's different."

"Why?"

"She just is—"

"You're in love with her?"

"I've always been in love with her."

Even in the moonlight, I can see Charlotte's face turn red. "Well damn, Bodhi. Here I thought you were a perpetual one-night stand type of guy."

I sit down in the sand. "I did some pretty fucking stupid things this last year."

Charlotte sits down next to me. "We having a heart-to-heart, Bishop?"

"No. It's just, Eva. She's not like the other girls. Hayes—"

"I'll tell him to leave her alone."

"He's not going to listen to you."

"No, but at least I'll sleep better at night knowing I tried."

I laugh. "Your brother is—"

"An entitled dick," she cuts me off. "He thinks everything should be handed to him as soon as he snaps his fingers."

"So I've noticed."

"Eva ..." she goes on. "Is she the reason you never gave anyone at school a chance? I mean, I threw myself at you hundreds of times—"

"She is," I quickly interrupt. "About that night—"

"I was drunk. I didn't mean to kiss you after you beat the shit out of those guys."

I know she's lying. "You didn't mean to?"

"Well, maybe I meant to, but I was hoping you'd forget."

"I didn't forget. I thought about calling you, but the next

morning, that's when my mom took a turn. She ended up in the hospital and never came back home."

"Jesus, Bodhi. I'm sorry."

"Yeah, this summer hasn't exactly been a summer of memories."

"What were you planning on saying, if you had called me?"

This isn't what she wants to hear, but I need to say it anyway. "That I would never be able to be what you wanted me to be."

"Ah. It was going to be *that* type of phone call."

"Wasn't going to leave you hanging in suspense after your *accidental* kiss."

She starts laughing. "Never could figure out why I'd see you making out with girls from other schools, but not anyone from ours. Figured I'd give you the chance to see what you were missing, but apparently Eva is what was missing?"

"She was. I've spent the last three years just waiting for her—"

"She played hard to get?"

"Not like that at all. It's a long story with so much bullshit, but I can't screw this up. I won't screw this up with her. I almost lost her this summer. I watched her die in front of me, and I'll beat the shit out of Hayes if he tries anything."

Charlotte's eyes look concerned. "She died?"

"She did," I confirm. "Right in front of me, and I swear to god if he puts a finger on her, I'll snap it off."

Charlotte snickers under her breath. "I'll give him the message. That one, and Eva's go fuck himself."

"She's not as tough as she acts ..."

"I beg to differ. She *did* come back from the dead and everything, right?"

"Yeah, she did."

"Then give the girl some credit. I'll do my best with Hayes—"

"Where is he?" I look toward their house. "I haven't seen him."

"Probably getting high somewhere, or deflowering some freshman."

I raise my nose in disgust. "He's such a—"

"Dick," she cuts me off again.

I stand, brushing the sand off my shorts. "You getting the hell out of Flagler? Please tell me you're going to college or something?"

She nods. "Soon. Virginia, much to the disappointment of Daddy, who would rather I stay here."

"Cut the future trophy wife chains as soon as possible," I joke.

She shakes her head. "I will *not* end up like that."

"Never thought you would. Take care of yourself, Charlotte."

"Will do, Bodhi," she says back. I start walking away. "Hey, Bishop!" she calls out. I spin back around. Her face looks different, softer, like she's let her guard down suddenly. "Do me a favor, keep an eye on Ethan this year, okay? He could use the guidance of someone who's not such a ..."

"Dick?"

She grins. "Exactly."

"Will do, Charlotte," I reply, then I head back to the guys.

It's a good hour before the girls wander back over to us. We see them walking arm in arm through a crowd of people, laughing about something they find absolutely hilarious. The alcohol that I assume is floating through Eva's veins has given her face a flushed look. Her hair is now down, blowing slowly behind her with the breeze the ocean is humoring us with tonight. It's wavy, something I notice happens in the humid air. She's in the middle, her arms locked within Luna's and Kennedy's. I can't help but glance between the three of them, as they're each beautiful in their own unique way. The guys and I, we're definitely the luckiest seventeen-year-old sons of bitches in Flagler, that's for sure.

"We're back!" Kennedy announces their arrival. "Miss us?"

"Absolutely," Beck answers, pulling her onto his lap.

Luna stands in front of Coop. "Well, thanks to Kennedy, every single person at your school now knows you're dating me. And they were all extremely surprised. One guy even fell over. He could have just been extremely wasted, though."

Coop tugs on the fray of Luna's jean shorts until she falls down next to him. "Good," he replies. "Job well done, Kennedy."

She raises her cup at him. "And Eva," Kennedy starts laughing. Luna abruptly joins her.

Eva walks closer to me, smirking.

"What's so funny?" I ask her.

"Nothing!" Kennedy and Luna both shout.

"We're allowed to have secrets," Eva states. "Right, girls?"

"Shit," Coop grumbles. "You start a riot, Eva?"

"Not exactly," she grins, then she throws herself down onto my legs. "But I can officially out drink a few of the dumbasses that go to our school."

"I don't know how she's standing, to be honest," Luna admits.

"Practice," Eva replies, she then turns to me. "Take me home?" Her eyes are actually sparkling in the moonlight.

"Yes, ma'am." I turn to everyone else. "We ready to get the hell out of here? Continue the festivities at my house?"

"Will you be continuing the festivities with us, sir?" Coop questions me.

I look back to Eva; her eyes grow large with excitement. "Sure. I might have found a few bottles of vodka in a cabinet recently."

"You've been holding out on us!" Beck exclaims.

"Just saving them for the right time."

Eva stands, placing her hand in mine as she pulls me up.

"Look at us," Coop loudly hoots as we start walking. "Leaving a party before eleven, no one throwing up in the sand, no one skinny dipping, no fights—"

"Dare I say we're maturing?" I laugh.

We start heading up the driveway when Hayes suddenly appears from his garage. He's alone, but looks absolutely stoned out of his mind. Just the smell coming off of him is enough to get the six of us high.

"Jesus *Christ*," Eva chokes, waving her hand in front of her nose. "You smell like shit," she says to him.

He grins, and then asks, "Where the hell are *you* going?"

"*We* are going home," she replies.

"All of you?"

"That's what I meant when I said *we*," she sarcastically replies.

He points to me and the guys. "You three never leave my parties this early."

"Times have changed," I calmly state, wrapping my arm around Eva's waist.

"Thanks for having us," Kennedy sweetly smiles. "We'll see you at school—"

"Charlotte gave me your message," he frowns at Eva, completely ignoring Kennedy. "Couldn't say it to my face?" he then laughs. "Where are your manners?"

Eva leans her head on my shoulder. "I've never been known for my pristine manners or desire to be dominated by the opposite sex."

Hayes lets out a chuckle and then looks at me. "She seems fun."

I give Eva's waist a squeeze. "You have no idea."

The door leading into his house suddenly flings open. A few guys stumble out, with Ethan trailing behind, looking ghostly white and tripping as he tries to walk down the two steps. He falls to the ground, and laughter erupts from the idiots standing around him. No one helps, they just stand there, finding this whole scene hilarious. Eva immediately moves over to him, forcefully pushing the drunk guys out of the way as she does.

"Are you guys fucking stupid?!" she cries out. She squats down to where Ethan is. He's laughing at himself on the ground, and tries to stand back up but falls down each time. Eva helps him to his feet and firmly holds him up.

"*You,*" Ethan points to her as this one word slurs out of his mouth. "You are *very* pretty."

The group of guys laugh at him. Eva shoves the loudest one and he falls back into a tool bench.

"You shouldn't be by me!" Ethan suddenly blurts out to her. "People will see!"

"People already see," Eva states. "And who gives a damn?"

Ethan stares at her funny, and then he raises his finger, rubbing it over the scar that leads into her hair. The guys around them start silently laughing, but Eva doesn't acknowledge anyone. Instead, she slowly moves Ethan's finger off her head, holding onto it until he pulls it from her grasp.

"I'm sorry," we hear him whisper.

This kid, he's really hitting my emotions tonight. I know he's not apologizing for touching her. He's apologizing once again for what happened to her, because he feels responsible.

"You don't need to apologize anymore," Eva gives him a small smile.

His eyes grow large and his hand goes to his mouth. "I'm gonna puke!" he frantically mumbles behind it.

She pulls on his other arm until they're both safely out of the garage. "You three!" she yells at me and the guys. "Help him!"

I give the guys a push toward Ethan. "Goddammit!" Coop shouts. "I thought we were getting out of here vomit-free tonight!"

We guide Ethan to the sand, where he starts forcefully throwing up. It's intense, his whole body is shaking each time he leans forward. Suddenly, over the sound of vomit hitting the ground, I hear Eva shouting behind us.

"What the hell is wrong with you assholes?!"

"Dude," Coop shakes his head, looking up at me. He pats Ethan hard on the back as he heaves again. "She's gonna start a fucking riot!" he mumbles under his breath. "Scary Eva has come out! Do something!"

"We've got this," Beck calmly states, nodding toward Eva.

I leave them, rushing back to the driveway where I see Luna and Kennedy holding Eva back, as she's right in front of Hayes. They both turn to me with a look of desperation on their concerned faces.

"He's fucking fourteen!" she shouts at him. "Fourteen, you asshole!"

"And *we* are seventeen. He can handle himself," Hayes bluntly replies.

Eva shoves him in the chest. I grab her by the waist, pulling her back with Luna and Kennedy's help.

"He's your goddamn cousin!" she continues. "He probably has alcohol poisoning! Do you know he could die from that?! What's wrong with you?!"

Hayes looks over in the direction of Ethan, who's still throwing up in the sand. "Looks like he's getting most of it out of his system."

Eva lets out a growl and lunges towards Hayes. For someone who barely weighs one hundred pounds, she's a lot stronger than she looks. Luna, Kennedy, and I, don't move quick enough, and Eva smacks Hayes hard across the face. There are shocked gasps from the group of guys watching this play out, including one from me.

"Goddamn, Eva," Kennedy whispers. "You *are* a badass."

Hayes is standing there, not moving, just staring at Eva as she glares at him.

"Time to go," I say, scooping Eva up and throwing her over my shoulder like a sack of potatoes. She doesn't resist. "Coop! Beck!" I shout, turning toward them. "We're leaving!"

"What do we do with him?!" Coop exclaims, pointing at Ethan. "Bring him with us!"

"You fucking serious?!" Beck questions.

"Yes!" I cry out. "He's better with us than with these assholes!"

Coop and Beck throw Ethan's arms over their shoulders and start walking toward us.

"Just one night," Coop moans. "I thought we were gonna get away with one night of being normal!"

"Look at you guys," Hayes laughs loudly. "The Bodhi who would drink himself into a coma and make out with some random no-name girl is now being the responsible *dad* of the group."

"It's better than living like you the rest of my life," I quickly say back. "I found my reason to grow up." I spin around so Eva's facing him, and then quickly spin back. "I hope eventually you find yours."

"It won't last," Hayes smirks. "You're Bodhi Bishop. That," he points between Eva and me, "won't last."

"It *will* last," I confirm, squeezing Eva's body tighter. "I'll bet my life on that." And then I turn, and start walking up the driveway.

"Hayes!" Eva suddenly cries out. I feel her hands leave my back, and I grab onto her body a little harder than I mean to.

"She's giving him the finger!" Coop mumbles under his breath. "Bodhi, she's giving him the finger! Don't do it, Eva. Don't do it."

But then we all hear her confidentially shout to Hayes, "Go fuck yourself!"

"She did it," Coop sighs, heaving Ethan up a little higher. "She fucking did it. I'm done. I'm done with this shit. We stay home every night now. Play board games. Take up knitting. That's right you guys, we are going to start knitting goddamn sweaters in the dead of the Florida summer!"

Ethan stops walking and we all freeze, thinking he's going to throw up again, but instead he starts hysterically laughing, literally doubling over into the cement. "You guys are great!" he wheezes.

Beck pulls him up and gives him a push to get him moving

again. "Love us in the morning, when you aren't one small heave away from throwing up on my shoes."

My jeep comes into view, and I place Eva down on the sidewalk. She stares me dead in the face, and then a little smile appears. "That was *so* much fun."

"Eva," Luna shakes her head. "I can't—I just—shit. I have no words."

"You," I point to Eva, "up front. You five," I start to do the math in my head. I definitely don't have enough seats in my jeep. "Goddammit! I don't know! Just get in the back!"

"You want the five of us to all get in the back?" Beck confirms.

I'm seriously getting ready to lose it. "I don't give a shit where anyone sits! Five of you are semi drunk, one of you is totally drunk and throwing up everywhere, and my girlfriend just smacked Maxwell Hayes across the face at his own house! I do *not* want to be here anymore! I don't think any of us should be here anymore, and I'm leaving in one minute! Get in the goddamn jeep! *Now!*"

Coop salutes me. "Yes sir. Get in the jeep fellow comrades, before we're left to fend for ourselves in this warzone of teenage hell."

I walk to the passenger side and open the door, waving my hand for Eva to get in. She plops herself down and I reach over her, buckling her seatbelt. She starts laughing at me and quickly grabs my chin, planting a kiss on my lips.

"I like seeing you pissed," she then says. "It's hot."

"I'm not pissed."

"You're still hot."

I let out a sigh, placing a kiss on her forehead, and then I close her door. I get in my seat and start the jeep. Everyone is still piling in, fighting on where to sit. I start counting down like an irritated dad. "Ten, nine, eight, seven, six, five, four, three, two, one."

Everyone is in and the doors slam shut. I then make a quick tire screeching turn down A1A. Me and Eva in the front, Luna and Kennedy on Coop's and Beck's laps in the back, and Ethan hanging his head out the open window screaming into the night, "I love these people!"

235

chapter twenty-six

Eva

Bodhi's arms are tightly holding my body. One under me, one on top. I have to delicately peel the top one off in order to not wake him. I then slowly scoot my way to the end of the bed and climb out. He's still asleep and lets out a little snore. It's five in the morning and we've only been asleep for a few hours, but I want to check on Ethan. I tiptoe down the spiral staircase and see him still sound asleep on the couch, a small garbage can next to him on the floor, the wet washcloth I placed on his forehead last night, thrown onto his chest.

He's cute while he sleeps, much cuter than he was as he threw up for almost an hour straight after we got back here. He finally passed out sitting on the couch with his head resting on the garbage can. I watched Bodhi gently lie him back, as careful and smoothly as possible, then the six of us sat there for a couple hours, making sure he wasn't going to throw up in his sleep. I heard Bodhi get up a few times in the middle of the night to check on him, each time climbing back into bed and pulling me into his arms before whispering, "He's fine," into my ear. It made me love him even more than I already do. Sometimes I feel like Bodhi is too good for me.

Coop and Luna are in Bodhi's room. Thankfully before we left for Hayes', we changed the sheets we sweated through earlier. Beck and Kennedy are in the guest bedroom. I don't hear a sound coming from either one. I head to the kitchen in just Bodhi's t-shirt and start some coffee, then stand out on the balcony as I wait for it to be done. It's still dark, but I can see the sun starting to make its grand appearance over the horizon, and I can't drag myself away from it, even after I hear the coffee maker buzz that it's ready.

I'm still standing there, staring out at the water, when I hear someone moving around in the kitchen, mugs quietly clanking. I don't turn to look. I know who it is. I hear the mugs being placed on the small table on the balcony, and then I feel his arms around my waist. I smile and lean into him, knowing his lips will find their way to my neck, and they do.

"I hate waking up without you next to me," he softly says into my ear. "But then I smelled the coffee, and knew where you were."

I wrap my hands around his arms. "I wanted to check on Ethan."

"He'll be fine," Bodhi assures me. "Might have a wicked hangover all day, but he'll survive."

I turn to face him, searching his eyes for any hint of him being mad at me. We never got to talk about my outburst with Hayes, and I know it pissed him off.

He gives me a small smile and tucks my hair behind my ear. "I'm not mad, babe. I know that's what you're thinking."

I nod a little and look away, suddenly embarrassed over how I behaved last night.

He pulls on my hand, "Come sit with me."

He guides me over to one of the lounge chairs where a blanket is waiting, one he must have brought out with the coffees. He sits down first and I climb onto his lap as he throws the blanket over the two of us. I snuggle my way onto his chest, grateful for the warmth of his body and the blanket, as the ocean breeze is actually cool in the morning. And grateful for him, for Bodhi.

"I shouldn't have hit Hayes," I mumble under my breath.

He hands me my coffee. "Probably not, but he deserved it."

I take a big sip. "My therapist is going to be pissed, and I don't want you to think I go around just hitting people all the time—"

He starts laughing. "I don't. But maybe we should try to use our words from now on when we're angry, and not our hands."

"I can try. But no promises."

"That's all I ask."

We sit there in silence. Words aren't always necessary between Bodhi and me. Besides, watching the sun rise over the ocean is an event in itself, one that can't be explained with words.

"It's so beautiful. All the different colors. It's just ... beautiful."

"It is. When my mom would have really bad nights, when her

nurses would struggle to get her pain under control, I would sleep out here. I've watched the sun come up so many times."

I turn a little to look at him. I hate knowing how sad these last few years have been for him. I hate that I wasn't there to help him get through it. "I should have been there."

He places a gentle kiss on my lips. "You're here now. And walking out here and seeing you standing at my balcony wearing my t-shirt makes up for every sunrise I've seen by myself. In fact, it was more beautiful than any sunrise I've ever seen."

"Bodhi Bishop, your words make me swoon."

"*Yes*," he smirks. "Mission accomplished."

I give him a long kiss and then sit up, resting my forehead on his. "I miss her. I miss the possibility of talking to her again, knowing that chance is there. I miss having that chance. Even after everything—everything we're finding out, I would do anything to see her again."

"You and me both. I miss having a mom, having a parent in this world. It's a weird feeling, being parentless. The more time goes by, the more I realize being on your own isn't as cool as it sounds."

"I know it's not the same, but you have more parents than anyone I know. This whole list of adults who would step up at any moment to be there for you."

"I do," he agrees. "And I have you. I think she knew—my mom. Did I ever tell you what she said to me that day? The day she fell in the kitchen?"

I shake my head and hold my breath.

"That I needed to get you back. That we needed each other. She made me promise I would try."

My eyes grow big and I bite down on my lip.

Bodhi's eyes go straight to my mouth as he says, "I think she knew her death would bring us back together."

"Wherever she is, she's definitely loving this." I bring my lips to his again, deepening our kiss as I wrap my arms around his neck. "Please tell me it's always going to be like this—this magnetic force between you and me."

"It will *always* be like this," he promises. "You're stuck with me for life. I'd marry you—"

I quickly kiss him to get him to stop talking. He's laughing as I pull away. "No marriage proposals today."

He nods slowly, and then runs his finger down the side of my face and to my collarbone. His dark brown eyes then stare into mine. "Do you remember our first confession?"

I give myself a minute, running through those years in my head. Then it's as if a lightbulb suddenly goes off. "I absolutely do," I grin. I sit up a little straighter. "I had just shown up at your house. You were in the driveway. It was maybe a couple months after I started coming over. You smelled awful, and I told you that you smelled like rotten eggs—"

Bodhi lets out a loud laugh. "Smoke bombs. The guys and I had been setting off smoke bombs."

"That's what you told me. Then you pulled me into your garage and said—"

"Confession, I think I found a picture of my dad."

"And I said—"

"Confession, I thought you didn't have a dad."

"Yes," I laugh. "Exactly, and after that, every few days you'd throw another one my way."

"Do you remember our last one? Before the accident?"

I smile with the memory. "You told me you thought I was your soulmate."

"I knew from the moment you walked in my door."

"Oh yeah?"

"Oh yeah. It was instant," he admits. "And I wasn't sure how to act around you at first—"

"I think you figured it out," I grin.

"That I have. Confession," he then says, wrapping his arms around my back. "Eva Calloway, I love you, and I wish there was another way to tell you that, something more meaningful, a bigger word. Because every day I fall in love with you even more than the day before, and I'm not sure how that's even possible. The love I feel for you already takes up every cell in my body. Sometimes I find myself just staring at you, wondering how our paths even crossed to begin with. I just hope you always know how much I love you."

I stare at him for a moment, gathering my thoughts and trying to think of what to say back. He's so good with saying what he's feeling that sometimes I'm speechless after he talks. I run my finger over his perfect mouth, thankful for his ability to create such beautiful words. "Confession. I can't express out loud how I feel— so perfectly like you do, but I love *you* Bodhi. It's the type of love that will never leave, the kind you read about in fairy tales, the kind other people can only dream to find. And you don't have to search for a bigger word," I tell him, rubbing my finger along the stubble I see on his chin. "The way you are with me, the way you treat me, the way you make me feel, *you* are my bigger word."

His arms tighten on my back, pulling me in closer. "You're actually pretty good at expressing how you feel," he replies, then his lips are on mine. His hands come up and under my t-shirt, his fingers trailing along my bare back and giving my body goosebumps. We stay like that for a while, wrapped up in each other's arms, as our mouths move against each other, the blanket shielding us from the outside world.

I pull away first, a little out of breath, but with no desire to deny my body what it really wants right now. I give him a look, running my fingers on the elastic of his gym shorts.

"We can't do this right here," he grins.

I slip my fingers under the elastic a little. "We *could.*"

"Eva," my name is moaned under his breath, and he nods toward A1A. "I love this about you, but I refuse to let every car passing on A1A see us out here—"

"We're under a blanket," I remind him.

He then nods toward the balcony doors. "And if our friends wander out? Or Ethan?"

My face turns red at the simple thought, and I bring my fingers out from his shorts. "Yeah, that would scar me for life." He laughs and squeezes his hands on my backside. I lean in and give him a soft kiss before saying, "Another time, then."

His eyes look amused, and his hands wander out of my shirt. He wraps his arms around my neck. "Eva?"

"Hmm?"

"Move in with me."

My jaw drops and he gives a little laugh at my shocked face.

"Now? At Calvin's?" I raise my eyes in question.

He shakes his head, smiling as he says, "No, not Calvin's. The house is legally mine in March, but I think I'll stay with Calvin until after graduation. After graduation ...? If you won't marry me, then after graduation? Unless college happens? Even if college happens, move in with me, wherever we end up." His face is starting to turn red. "I'm rambling now. Baby, I just want to wake up with you every morning lying in my arms. I want to end our day together by kissing you goodnight *every* night, and holding you until we both fall asleep. I want *this* to be every day. I selfishly don't want to wait any longer. I lost you for three years, I watched you die, I know how quickly life can change. I want to be with you every second that I can." He stops talking and watches my face for a reaction. "You think I'm crazy, don't you?"

I slowly shake my head. "Not at all."

"No?"

"No, Bodhi Bishop." I reach behind me, unwrapping his arms from around my neck. I hold his hands in mine as I say, "I'll move in with you after graduation. Here, or wherever we end up."

His eyes grow large. "You will?"

"Of course. This magnetic force between you and me isn't going anywhere. Plus, rumor has it, you find me rather attractive and I'm pretty sure I find you rather attractive—"

He stops my words with his lips, his hands cradling my face. "Wherever we end up?" he seriously asks.

"Wherever we end up. I'm yours."

He rubs his thumb under my chin and gives my forehead a kiss, bringing me down onto his chest. His fingers move along my collarbone, throwing me into an instant trance, his heart thudding peacefully in my ear. "Eva?" he suddenly whispers, jolting me out of the light sleep I didn't realize I had fallen into.

"Hmm?"

"You're going to marry me before we're twenty-one," he confidentially declares.

I smile into his chest. I know he's right. *He* knows he's right. I purposely wait a few moments before responding though, and then I kiss his warm skin and admit, "Yes, I probably am."

chapter twenty-seven

Eva

Look at them," I hear a voice say. "They are *so* cute."

I slowly open my eyes, the intense morning sun making it difficult at first to keep them fully open. I feel Bodhi stretch underneath me and he lets out a long yawn. Kennedy and Beck are standing on the balcony.

"What time is it?" he asks them.

"A little after nine," Beck responds.

"Ethan?" I point inside.

"Sleeping like a baby," Kennedy remarks. "Little dude's going to have a killer hangover today."

I sit up a little, pushing the blanket off my body as I'm roasting under the sudden heat. "We should probably stir him and try to get some water in his system."

Coop and Luna wander out, both with coffees. I silently reach for Coop's. Luna takes it from him, handing it to me.

"What the hell?" Coop mutters.

Bodhi laughs. "Glad to see you with clothes on," he says to Coop.

Luna's face turns red.

"Not like that!" Bodhi exclaims. "Coop is notorious for walking around my house with just a blanket tied around his waist. Since we started puberty, pretty much."

Coop throws himself down in a chair. "We'd stumble our asses back here so many nights, I'm lucky if I remembered your garage door code, let alone my boxers."

"Why would your boxers be off, may I ask?" Luna questions.

Beck and Bodhi both start laughing.

"Shit, Luna," he blushes. "I'd get up to pee, and just forget what the hell I was doing."

"And you'd wake up naked ... where?" she continues.

"Usually on the couch in Bodhi's room," Beck answers her.

She takes a sip of her coffee. "Well, isn't that cute," she then replies. "If you're comfortable enough to lay naked on the couch in Bodhi's room, while I'm assuming he and Beck are sleeping in there as well, have at it boys."

Coop's nose turns up. "When you say it like that. Shit guys!" he yells at Bodhi and Beck. "What happened to secrets going to the grave with us?!"

We're all laughing when we hear Ethan start to stir inside.

"The bear has awoken," Coop mumbles. "Who's going to sacrifice themselves to see if hibernation has done him some good?"

"I will," I announce, peeling myself out of Bodhi's lap, and tossing the blanket to an empty chair. I forget I'm just in his t-shirt, until I stand up. I look down at myself; the shirt is resting on my upper thighs. I look back up at everyone else and shrug my shoulders. "It's like a dress, right?"

Ethan's sitting up on the couch, rubbing his hands on his head and making some ill-fated noises under his breath. He looks up when he hears Bodhi and me coming. His hair is flying in ten different directions, and his body looks like he's swaying. "Your house?" he points at Bodhi.

"Yeah, bro," Bodhi replies.

"You live here by yourself?"

Bodhi shakes his head. "I'm living with my grandpa for a while."

"Got it. This is just your love shack for now." He throws himself back on the couch, but then quickly sits up, looking paler than he was one second ago. "Room is definitely spinning."

"Why'd you drink so much last night?" I ask him.

"Because everyone else was. And they kept handing me more."

"Very logical reason there," I nod my head.

"Don't jump off bridges just because everyone else is," Bodhi throws out there.

Ethan gives us a thumbs up. "You both are going to make killer parents one day."

"You're a smart ass," I declare, throwing myself down next to him. His eyes grow large and I grab a blanket, covering my naked legs as I lie against a pillow on the opposite side. "Trust me when I say, drinking yourself to death isn't very much fun the next day."

"Noted," Ethan nods, leaning up against the back of the couch. "Thanks for this," he waves his hands in front of him. "Hey! Did you really smack Hayes across the face last night or was I dreaming everything I overheard?"

"Not a dream," Bodhi confirms. "You were too preoccupied throwing up repeatedly in the sand to see the actual event."

"Jesus, Eva ..." Ethan sighs. "I don't think anyone has ever smacked Hayes across the face before, except for maybe Charlotte."

"He deserved it."

"I'm sure he did. Speaking of Hayes," Ethan smiles sweetly. "Can one of you maybe drive me back over there? I could walk, but no promises that I won't pass out cold in the street and get ran over by some old dude on a golf cart—"

"I can take you," Bodhi talks over him.

"I'm coming, too," I stand up. "Just let me change—"

"Going back to the scene of the crime?" Ethan raises his eyebrow. "Badass is right. Hope you're locked and loaded. Hayes takes revenge seriously."

"I can handle him. Give me five minutes."

I quickly throw on some shorts and a tank-top, pull my tangled hair up into a messy bun, and run a toothbrush over my teeth. I head back downstairs, picking up on the conversation happening in the kitchen before anyone sees me.

"You're letting her go back there?!" Coop grumbles. "Did you check her pockets for knives?!"

"Coop!" Bodhi exclaims. "Are you kidding me?"

"Eva's not a delinquent," Luna punches him in his shoulder.

"I might be if you guys keep talking about me like I am."

Coop sheepishly looks my way. "Just be careful, Eva. You're too important in this inner circle of love we have going on over here. You fall, we all fall with you."

"Oh, I'm definitely taking you all down with me when I start my rebellion."

"Wouldn't expect any less," Coop sighs.

I walk over to him, placing a kiss on his forehead. "Thanks for caring. I'm actually going over there so I can apologize. Maybe clear the air a little bit—"

Ethan's laughter from the couch interrupts me. "You're going to apologize to Hayes?"

"Was thinking about it."

He looks at the six of us standing in the kitchen. "Not to be blunt, but Hayes isn't going to want your apology. What he wants is to get into those tight shorts you're wearing—"

"Dude!" Bodhi cries out.

"Jesus, bro," Beck frowns. "Your welcome here has expired."

"Yes, it has," Bodhi agrees. "Let's go, Ethan."

"Bring us back some Swillerbees?" Kennedy sweetly asks from the counter.

"I like the way your girl thinks," Coop nods to Beck, he then points to Bodhi. "Your kids are hungry."

Ethan starts laughing again. "You guys are like some weird, fucked up, blended family."

"We prefer just family," Kennedy cringes.

"You've got the mom and dad," he looks over at Bodhi and me, "who act normal on the outside, but are riddled with secrets and bang like rabbits because I mean, look at the two of them—"

"Ethan!" I shout in disbelief.

"Then you've got these two kids," he continues, staring at Coop and Luna, "smoke a lot of weed and would be satisfied living in a tent on the beach for the rest of their lives, or on some huge ass sailboat, going from port to port. And then the scholars," he points to Beck and Kennedy. "The smart ones, who will probably have six figure jobs one day even though they don't need them, because together you're all the richest fucked up, blended family in Flagler. But you keep it all hidden because it's safer that way." He stands and stretches, running his hands through his messy hair, letting out a disgusting burp at the same time. "How close am I to being right?"

No one says anything at first, and then Coop blurts out, "Where the fuck did you come from?"

"Flagler Beach, baby. Conceived, born and raised."

"Go get in the jeep," Bodhi frustratingly demands. "Before I make you walk back to Hayes' and run your ass over myself."

245

"Yes, Dad," he smirks.

It's a quiet drive back down A1A. Ethan's head hangs out the window like a dog enjoying the breeze.

"You want to head back to your house in a little bit?" Bodhi quietly asks me.

I shrug my shoulders. "My mom and the boys are gone until this evening, and my dad— there's no real reason to go home if no one's going to be there."

He gives my hand a kiss. "Then we stay at my house until we're forced to go back to the Halifax tonight."

"Love shack," Ethan coughs under his breath.

By the time we get to Hayes', Ethan's windblown hair is literally standing straight up. Bodhi pulls down the driveway, and we immediately see Charlotte sitting on the back of a boat that's hitched to a pickup truck. Bodhi puts the jeep in park and Charlotte jumps down, walking over to us.

"Didn't expect to see you two back here," she raises her eyes. "Ethan?" she then questions as he steps out of the back. "You were with them last night?"

"I'm their new foster kid."

Bodhi and I get out of the jeep. "He threw up most of the night," I say. "Thanks to your brother not giving two shits about him."

"Ah, I see your love for Hayes has only dramatically increased in the last ten hours," Charlotte laughs. "Tell me, Eva. The rumors that spread like wildfire last night—did you really smack my brother across his face?"

"I did."

She moves closer to me. "I'm actually a little sad our paths didn't cross sooner. Hayes has finally met his match." She then turns to Ethan. "Go take a shower, you smell like shit. Then we'll take the boat back to your house."

He salutes Charlotte. "Thanks for the fun pow-wow last night, Mom and Dad," he says to Bodhi and me. He starts to walk toward the garage door, when Hayes appears from the back of the house.

"Cuz!" he cries out, raising his hands in the air. "You're alive! Looking like death, but nothing a morning beer won't cure."

"I'll pass," Ethan shakes his head, looking as though he might throw up at just the thought.

"Suit yourself," Hayes shrugs. He walks closer to Bodhi and me. "Eva," he frowns. "You here for the other cheek?"

"Well that all depends, are you going to piss me off this morning?"

Bodhi wraps his arm around my shoulders. "Just dropping Ethan off and heading out."

"Stay," Hayes points behind him to the boat. "We're cruising to Ponce Inlet, going to do some fishing, get lunch at Off the Hook ..." His invitation actually sounds sincere until he continues with, "Eva, I'm sure Charlotte has a bikini that will fit you." He then waves his hands over his chest.

"You're such a dick, Hayes!" Charlotte shouts.

"We're leaving," Bodhi states, trying to move our bodies toward the jeep.

"And to think I was actually going to apologize for hitting you last night," I sigh, keeping my feet firmly on the ground. "But now, hitting you again actually sounds more logical."

Hayes lets out a laugh. "Calm down, girly. I was just joking. Be on your merry way, don't want to make you late for whatever you two fun kids have planned for the day."

I bring my hand up to Bodhi's that's resting on my shoulder. "I can assure you what we have planned is much more enjoyable than what you have planned."

I hear Charlotte and Ethan both laugh under their breaths.

"Bye, Charlotte," I wave. "Ethan, stay away from the alcohol."

"Yes, Mom," he nods. "Thanks for the warm hospitality."

Bodhi and I turn to the jeep as we hear Hayes say behind us, "Aww, Granger, you have such good manners!"

We both stop dead in our tracks.

"Bodhi, did he say Granger?" I whisper to him.

"He did."

"Granger," I repeat. "My neighbors across the street—"

"Frank," Bodhi groans. "Frank Granger."

"Frank Granger is my neighbor."

"What?!" Bodhi cries out in a hush. "The asshole that works at Tacklebox is your neighbor?!"

"He lives across the street from me, his mom is Sharon Granger."

"Everything okay over there?" Hayes calls out.

Bodhi and I spin around. Ethan's face is ghost white. He knows we heard Hayes. He knows we're on the brink of figuring something huge out.

"Ethan," I calmly say. "Your last name is Granger?"

He slowly nods his head.

"Who are Sharon and Frank Granger to you?" I ask him.

I see him gulp. "Sharon Granger is my dad's cousin, the other side of his family. She never married. Frank is her illegitimate son, my second cousin, just like them," he points to Hayes and Charlotte, who are staring at Bodhi and me. They don't notice Ethan giving us a little shake of his head as he mouths, "*Please.*"

I nod my head in agreement and instantly he looks relieved. "Small world, Ethan," I then smile at him. "Sharon and Frank live directly across the street from me."

"Small world indeed," he replies.

"Frank, he works at Tacklebox, right?" I continue. "The bait shop *right* on High Bridge?"

Ethan smirks. "That he does."

"Frank can also hook you up with any drug of choice," Hayes adds. "But don't tell him I told you that. The Granger family *owns* Tacklebox by the way, perfect place to pick up anything you might need for a good time. And doesn't your Aunt Sharon's family install pretty much every single security system around Flagler?"

I know my eyes grow huge. Bodhi's hand wanders down my back and he firmly loops his fingers in the hooks of my jean shorts. "You don't say?" he slowly responds. "Eva's family had one put in this summer. Wonder if your family were the ones who put it in?"

Ethan looks straight at me as he answers, "I would say the odds are rather high."

"Shit," Hayes laughs. "Sharon Granger's family is scary as hell. I'm glad I'm not blood related to that side of the genetic pool. No offensive, Cuz. I wouldn't be surprised if they have half of Flagler bugged by now."

"Bugged?" I repeat.

"Oh yeah," Hayes continues. "Watching people, listening to conversations. With all the security systems they put in every week."

I grab onto Bodhi's arm. "If—if they were to bug someone's backyard, I wonder how many cameras they'd have to hide to pick up everything that happens out there?"

"What the fuck, Eva?" Hayes gives me a curious look. "You got some sort of secret espionage job on the side?"

"Three," Ethan states. "I think three would get the job done."

"We're going to go now," Bodhi declares, tugging on my shorts. I give his arm a tight squeeze.

"Hey, Ethan? Your parents—what do *your* parents do?"

He doesn't answer me right away. He knows once he tells me this, there's no turning back. He knows if he doesn't answer me, Hayes or Charlotte will. He knows there's no way around this question. He swallows hard. "My mom spends most of her day avoiding the fact she's actually a mother, yet as long as she stays drunk, she's the perfect trophy wife to my dad, who is a pilot and flies his own planes in and out of Flagler airport."

I try hard to stifle my gasp, to keep myself standing upright.

"I'm going to go take that shower now," Ethan quietly says, walking away and leaving us standing there.

Bodhi keeps his fingers on my belt loop, but I suddenly feel his other arm wrap around my waist. He gives my body a firm tug toward him. "Have a good day, you guys," he quickly says. He pulls me to the jeep, avoiding the curious stares from Hayes and Charlotte.

I climb into my seat and Bodhi slams the door closed, swiftly walking to his side. We peel out of the driveway and are down A1A before I can form any words. "Bodhi," I gulp. "You know what this all means, right?"

"I do, babe. Ethan Granger's entire family are the ones that were helping Luke. Your security system probably feeds right into their fucking house. Cameras, there has to be cameras in your backyard that go straight to them. This is bullshit!" He hits his steering wheel and looks over at me, bringing his hand up to my neck. "They work for Henry Channing, babe. They all do. And Ethan's dad, he was the one who was going to fly you and Luke out of Flagler that night.

249

chapter twenty-eight

Bodhi

Y ou guys really need to think this through," Beck demands as we drive toward the Halifax. "If someone placed cameras in Eva's backyard to spy on you two, what do you think's going to happen when you find them? You wave hello and say thanks for spying on us? They'll know, and then what?"

I look through my rearview mirror. "We should just let them continue spying on us?" I question. "This is how Henry Channing heard everything that happened that night!"

Beck is shaking his head. "No, Bodhi. You just need to figure out a way to do this, without putting us all in the line of fire."

"How many are back there?" Luna quietly asks.

"Three," Eva replies. "Ethan pretty much told us there were three."

"You trust the little bastard?" Coop asks. "Bro was puking all night into a bathroom garbage can, and has Maxwell Hayes and Frank Granger as his relatives. You really think he's not just being a fourteen-year-old asshole who's trying to impress you both?"

"If by impress you mean turn ghost white and piss his pants as soon as we started to ask questions," Eva sighs. "Then sure, he was trying to impress the hell out of us."

"I feel sorry for him," Kennedy's soft voice rings out. "He's pretty much on his own and dependent on his shitty second cousins to take care of him. Do you think he'll tell you anything else?"

"Ethan doesn't really tell us anything," Eva makes known. "He answers our questions in his own twisted way without actually answering our questions."

Coop points ahead of us to Tacklebox. "Why not just start there? See if Frank's around?"

That's actually not a bad idea. I quickly swerve my jeep down the gravel road, causing everyone in the backseat to fly to one side.

"A little warning would be nice!" Coop shouts out. "I think I just whiplashed back two years of my life!"

"Uh, Coop ... your hand," Kennedy is trying not to laugh.

"Shit!" hollers Coop. "Now I just got to second base with Kennedy due to your lack of driving skills—"

"You know," I loudly say, dramatically putting my jeep in park. "Eva and I can just do this on our own."

"The hell you will!" Coop exclaims. "You two aren't doing shit on your own. You both are like those stupid beautiful kids in a horror movie, who run straight to the guy with the chainsaw, while your way smarter friends have a perfectly good hiding spot that you completely ignore! And you know who ends up getting cut into little tiny pieces and eaten? Your friends, trying to save your asses. Then you both live happily ever after, driving away into the mountains, and a few years later we see you popping out some adorable chubby cheeked kids that you end up naming after the friends who sacrificed their goddamn lives for you. We do this together, so I can keep you both away from the guy with the chainsaw. Let's go, shitheads," he demands, throwing open the door. "I'm starving, and after this, you both are treating us all to an elaborate lunch someplace fancy, because *someone* didn't bring home Swillerbees like they promised they would."

Coop climbs out, standing at the side of the jeep while the rest of us just sit there.

"He gets really hangry," Luna stifles a laugh. "How the hell have you guys put up with this all these years?"

"We ignore him," I reply.

"But that just angers the beast," Beck chimes in. "So occasionally we throw pretzels or goldfish crackers at him."

"Like a circus animal," I add.

"So, I should just always carry a purse filled with toddler snacks?" Luna confirms.

"Precisely," I nod. "Let's go guys."

When we walk into Tacklebox, Frank is at the counter, scrolling through his phone. He doesn't even look up to see who's walked in.

251

Employee of the year for sure.

"Wait!" Eva whispers loudly, turning her back to Frank and facing the five of us. "What the hell are we going to say to him? We can't exactly ask him any specific questions!"

"Frank's not the sharpest crayon in the batch," Beck whispers back. "He'll probably confess to anything without even realizing he's doing it."

"*Guys,*" Kennedy hisses. "He's staring at us!"

Eva swiftly turns, and Frank goes from looking extremely annoyed, to looking extremely distraught. He falls off his chair, catching himself on the counter and knocking over a tin cup of pens and loose change.

"Shit, Frank," Coop laughs. "Hitting the bottle early today?"

Frank gives him the finger as he scrambles to catch the pens before they roll off the counter. Eva leads the way over, catching a few of them and dropping them back in the cup. "Hey, Frank," she smiles. "Definitely been a while."

"I see you around all the time," is what he instantly says.

Coop lets out a snort. "That's fucking creepy, bro."

I step around Coop and stand next to Eva. "Question for you," I say to Frank. "There was a boat tied up out there back in June, named Skyla, do you know where it went?"

He quickly shakes his head. "I don't know what boat you're talking about."

"Frank, my man," Coop sighs. "You work here almost every day, and never noticed a boat tied up at the docks?"

He shakes his head again.

"That's okay you guys," Eva grins. "I guess we can just ask the police to check the cameras outside—"

"Wait! Just let me think for a minute!" Frank stammers. "A boat? Back in June? Named Skyla?"

"Yes, Frank," I confirm. "Was probably tied up there for a week at least. Just wondering where it might have disappeared to."

"It was towed away," he suddenly replies. "I remember now. The owner, he never came to get it. We couldn't keep it here any longer. I was here when it was picked up—"

"Who picked it up?" Beck asks.

"A towing company."

"Did they have a *name*?" Beck presses further.

"Uh, no?" Frank's face turns red. "I mean, they probably did. But I don't remember."

"Of course you don't," I grumble. "But someone definitely came and took it away?"

Frank slowly nods his head. I stare at him for a moment, and then leap over the counter.

"Bodhi!" Eva shockingly cries out. "What are you doing?!"

I find the picture of Calvin and Owen that I saw last time I was in here, and pull it off the wall. I wave it in front of Frank's startled face. "In June, when you told me I look like him, you weren't talking about anyone in this picture, were you?"

As red as Frank's face was just a second ago, it's now pale and sickly looking. "No," he simply says.

I hop back over the counter, taking the picture with me. "I didn't think so. We're out of here."

I grab Eva's hand and start making my way to the door. "Bodhi!" Frank calls out my name. I freeze and don't turn around, but that doesn't stop Frank from giving me a warning. "Whatever it is you guys are trying to do ... don't."

I flip him off and head out the door.

"That was entertaining!" Kennedy announces as we climb back in my jeep. "Where to now?"

I throw my head onto my steering wheel and say, "We feed the beast—"

"Hey!" Coop grumbles. "That's not very nice—"

"Then we go to my house," Eva finishes.

I look up at her and raise my eyebrow.

"We won't do anything dangerous," she replies. "Well, nothing *too* dangerous."

"Define *too* dangerous please?" Coop questions.

Eva turns around in her seat to face him. "Shh!" she replies. "If you're a good boy and do as I say, I'll make sure you get a cookie after you eat your lunch."

Two hours later, after an elaborate Italian meal at Romero's, Coops choice, we're driving back to the Halifax when Eva suddenly jumps in her seat.

"What's wrong?" I ask her.

"My phone is buzzing like crazy," she replies, reaching under her to grab it from her back pocket. She looks at the screen and then back to me. "My alarm system is suddenly offline."

"What do you mean it's suddenly offline?" I question.

"Jesus!" Coop cries out. "Here we go, you're driving us right to the guy with the chainsaw!"

Eva swiftly turns around. "You know what, Coop? I thought if we fed you, you'd stop being such a whiny bitch."

Everyone laughs under their breaths.

Coop points to her. "I put up with this shit when we were kids. You always picking on me—"

"*Me* picking on *you*?" she questions, shocked. "Coop! You whine worse than my little brothers! And they're four! I just don't take your shit—"

"Not taking sides," Beck grins, "but Eva's right."

"How the hell is *that* not taking sides?!" Coop exclaims. "Fine, everyone pick on Coop—"

"I love you," Eva smiles at him. "But you're annoying the shit out of me right now."

"I love you, too, which is why I'm gonna let your negative comment pass," Coop stares at her. "And because, to be honest, I'm scared to death to piss you off. And I'm scared to piss Luna off, too. You ladies together give me nightmares."

Luna throws Eva the peace sign and says, "I got your back, babe."

Eva returns the peace sign, and then turns back to me. "I can't get any of our cameras to pull up anything."

"Do you think someone's at your house?" I nervously ask her. "Screwing around with them?"

"Ethan," she says under her breath. "I bet it's Ethan."

Moments later we're pulling down her driveway. "Backyard?" I quickly question.

"Backyard," she agrees.

We quickly pile out, running along the side of her house. As soon as we turn the corner, Ethan, carrying a skateboard, runs right into Coop, knocking him to the ground in slow motion.

"*Son of a bitch!*" Coop shouts, grabbing his nose as blood instantly pours down his face. "Why is it always me?!"

Eva grabs his arm and yanks him up off the grass. "It's *not* always you! I'm the one who fucking died, remember?!" She then punches Ethan in his chest. "What the hell are you doing here?!"

"Jesus, Mom ..." Ethan sighs, rubbing his ribs. "Here I thought I was your favorite."

"Ethan!" she shouts. "I'm about one second away from beating the shit out of you—"

"God, the violence," he replies. "Surprised you haven't been reported to CPS yet—"

I yank the top of his hair. "Tell us what the hell you're doing here, before I *let* her beat the shit out of you."

He releases an angry snarl and drops his skateboard, reaching into his pocket with one hand, and gently taking Eva's hand with the other. He then turns her hand around and slowly drops three little plastic squares into it.

"*Ethan*," Eva softly sighs.

"I knew you'd try to find them," he calmly responds.

"What are those?" Kennedy asks.

"Cameras," Ethan answers. "You both have to stop—"

"How did you know where they were?" I interrupt him.

He looks down at his feet. "I didn't. But I've seen some videos this summer. I had a general idea of where they'd be."

Eva grabs his chin and raises his face. "You did this, for me?"

"It needed to be done," he responds. "And if you tried yourself, you were only going to make this worse. They won't be able to watch your camera feeds anymore either—"

Eva pulls him in for a hug. "You shouldn't have done that. I mean, I'm thankful and all, but Ethan, don't get in trouble for us. How the hell did you know what you were doing?"

"I've seen a few things over the last couple years," he smirks.

Coop groans. "Can we take this adorable family reunion inside?" he nasally asks, pinching his nose. "I would love to get the blood out of my mouth."

"Yes," Eva announces, pointing back to the front of her house.

"Everyone inside, you too, Ethan," she pushes him.

Ethan's face turns red. "Uh, I don't think—"

"Just listen to her, bro!" Coop shouts, flailing his body around. "You're not going to win!"

A couple minutes later, Eva's at her kitchen sink, wetting paper towels. She walks over to Coop who's at her counter, and gently wipes the blood off his chin. She then holds a dry paper towel under his nose. "Pinch it and look down," she tells him.

"I knew you loved me," Coop beams.

"Of course I love you," she pats his head. "I also would love to avoid a trail of blood all over my house."

Ethan throws himself down at her kitchen table. "If I get caught here, I'm pretty much dead. I like tulips, just make sure there's tulips at my funeral."

"Tulips?" Coop repeats. "I struck you more as a thorny rose type of guy."

"Who's going to find out you're in my house?" Eva asks.

Ethan points to everyone in front of him.

"You think one of *us* is going to blow your cover?" I ask.

Eva sits down next to him. "Ethan, can you just be honest with us? No more going in ten different directions when we ask you a question?"

"We aren't going to turn you in," Luna states. "I mean, we have a lot of shit we could go straight to the police for, and we haven't yet."

"We like to work alone," Eva adds. "Even if that—"

"Ends up getting you killed?" Ethan's eyes narrow at her.

I sit down next to Eva and lean into the table. "Ethan, the six of us, we aren't your enemies. If anything, we're the ones you should trust. Do you know I have a little sister? I've never met her, never even knew about her until Luke told Eva that night. I would love to meet her, and the *only* way that might happen, is if we figure out where Henry Channing is—"

"What the hell does Henry Channing have to do with your little sister?" Ethan curiously asks.

"Nothing really," I tell him. "Except the one person who can help me find her is currently trying to find Henry Channing."

"You're being blackmailed?" Ethan laughs under his breath.

"*No*," I sigh.

"*Yes*," Ethan sighs back. "You are."

"Dude's right," Coop says from the counter, pointing at Ethan as two rolled up pieces of paper towel hang out of his nostrils. "Your detective buddy is blackmailing you both—"

"Detective?!" Ethan shouts, jumping up from his seat. "You're working with a detective?!"

"No!" Eva exclaims. "No! We aren't! He came to us, cornered us pretty much. He's investigating Henry Channing, but no one can find him. He thinks when Henry finally shows up, he's going to come after Bodhi and me—"

"Do you hear yourself?" Ethan softly questions as he sits back down. "Come on woman. You know this is fucking screwed up."

"Finally!" Coop throws his hand up. "Someone joining our group with some goddamn common sense!"

"Ethan," Kennedy walks over, placing her hands on his shoulders as she firmly massages them. "Do *you* know where Henry Channing is?"

"No," he immediately replies.

"Does someone in your family know where Henry Channing is?" I then ask him.

"Maybe?"

"Stop with the bullshit," Eva bluntly demands. "Just be honest."

He lets out a frustrated groan. "Yes, someone in my family probably knows where Henry Channing is."

"Why are you protecting this person?" I ask him. "The entire police department in Flagler is looking for Henry."

Ethan glances between the six of us, and suddenly I'm reminded that even though he's just three years younger than me, he's a kid, and he looks scared to death. He points between us all again. "You guys have each other. Just in the brief time I've spent with you, it's so easy to see that your fucked up, blended family unit is strong. Do you know who I have? I have Frank Granger, and Maxwell Hayes, and a mom who doesn't even know what day of the week it is anymore. But I do have one person, just one person who is always on my side—"

"Your dad?" I carefully ask.

He nods. "My dad. If my dad disappears, that's it for me. I end up like Frank, or worse, living with Hayes and having him as my role model. Obviously last night proved that's really not in my best interest—"

"You have us," Eva softly says.

"I just met you guys."

"But you have us," she repeats. "You've sort of grown on us—"

"Like a thorn in my foot," Coop mumbles.

"Ethan, you risked your life that night to try to save Eva," I include. "And that act alone makes you a permanent member of our fucked up, blended family."

"You're just saying that—"

"No, we aren't," Eva responds. "I promise, Ethan. I promise we won't let anything happen to you."

"And my dad?"

"We'll do our best," she says. "But you know he's working with some pretty—"

"Fucked up people," Ethan sighs. "I know, trust me, I know." There's a long pause, but then Ethan finally grins and says, "Fine, I'll join your band of misfit renegades, but only if you adopt me if shit hits the fan, and give me a share of the millions you all are secretly sitting on."

"Deal," I instantly reply.

Ethan's eyes grow large. "So you aren't denying the fact—"

"All I'm saying is deal," I repeat. "You can interpret that any way you'd like. I'm taking a page from the book of Ethan, and answering your question by not answering your question."

He laughs. "All right then. It will be a pleasure doing business with you all."

"The gun, Ethan," Eva suddenly blurts out. "Was it by any chance your dad's?"

He nods. "It was. He gave it to Henry, and Henry gave it to Luke—"

"Wait! Hold up!" I cry out. "Henry gave the gun to *Luke*?"

"Yes ...?" he slowly answers.

"Henry actually handed the gun to Luke?" Eva asks.

Ethan looks between Eva and me. "What am I missing here?"

"Were Henry and Luke working *together*, Ethan?" I hurriedly ask.

Ethan's eyes dart back and forth. "You guys being serious? Sometimes it's hard to tell—"

"Yes!" we both cry out.

He leans back in his seat. "Wow. Okay, I thought you guys knew this already. Here goes nothing. From what I've heard, seen, gathered—"

"Ethan!" Eva shouts in exasperation.

"Okay, okay," he throws his hands up to his hair. "Luke came to Flagler on his own, but shit didn't go his way, so he showed up at Henry's the evening before the accident. My dad was there, I was there—"

"Was Porter there?" Eva quickly asks.

Ethan shakes his head.

"He was with us," I tell her. "Porter was with us, remember? After you talked to Luke and left with Porter, I bet Luke went right to Henry's."

"And then when Porter showed up after he left your house, I bet that's when he had the fight with his dad." She turns to Ethan. "What happened at Henry's house? Did he know Luke was coming over?"

"Hell no," Ethan loudly replies. "Shocked the shit out of him, actually."

"So what happened?" I ask.

"Long story or short story?" Ethan asks.

"Short."

He doesn't pause. "Luke went nuts, screaming about a ton of shit. I hid on the stairs. I've seen a lot of psychos, but this guy definitely took the lead. Henry was quiet at first, but I think once he realized Luke was after his money, things took a turn. Henry said they could split it, all the money, as long as Luke found those letters and shit that apparently your mom had," he points to me. "They both thought you were hiding it all. My dad, he had given Henry a gun a few days back, Henry gave the gun to Luke. I think the plan was to just scare you guys? Scare you into giving him the proof? And

259

once Luke had done that, he was supposed to meet my dad and Henry at Flagler airport, where they would leave for the Bahamas."

"Henry was leaving?" I ask. "He was leaving Flagler with Luke?"

Ethan nods his head. "That was the plan. To take all the proof, leave for the Bahamas, and never look back."

"I don't buy it," Eva briskly responds. "I mean, I believe you, but I don't think Henry was ever going to give Luke any of that money. He's all talk. And what about Porter? He was just going to completely abandon Porter?"

"What if he gave Porter the option to go with him?" I ask Eva. "What if that was part of the fight? I mean, can you imagine how pissed off Henry Channing would have been if his own son said he wasn't going with him?"

"I guess I can ask Porter?" she grimaces.

"Your dad?" I then ask Ethan. "What was he getting from this?"

Ethan shrugs his shoulders. "He always gets something—being Henry's personal pilot. He's compensated generously for his service and his silence."

"If Henry was planning on giving Luke half of his inheritance, why would he tell Porter to get rid of Bodhi?" Eva asks out loud. "Right after making this deal with Luke? It doesn't make sense. It's like he had two different plans going. One to get Luke off his back, and then the real one. I bet his plan was to actually have Luke get the proof from us, and then once he had it in his hands, he was going to get rid of Luke. With Luke gone, and with you gone," she points to me, "the money would always be his."

"Yeah," I agree. "You're probably right. But there's still *you*, Eva. You could still talk and ruin everything."

She shakes her head. "Henry still believed at this point that he controlled my dad. He might still think that. I bet he thought he'd be able to convince my dad to keep me from saying anything."

"Neither plan worked out, though," Coop suddenly declares. "Luke thought the proof burned down with Henry's house, which should have been the end to all of this, right? If Luke was getting the proof to give to Henry, so that the inheritance always stayed with him, wouldn't the proof burning down be a good thing for those two bastards? No proof, no reason to think the money would get taken. Then Henry gives Luke his share, and they fly off into the sunset together holding hands?"

"You're right," I sigh. "Luke and Henry, they both were just playing each other. Luke was never going to give the proof to Henry; he wanted it for himself, like he told us. And Henry was never going to share his inheritance with Luke."

"Ethan, you said Henry heard everything on the patio that night?" Eva questions.

He nods his head. "I did, too. Bits and pieces, minding my own business at Tacklebox—"

"You were *all* at Tacklebox?" I ask him.

"No. Just Frank and me. Henry and my dad were at the airport, but I know they were listening, too."

I look over at Eva. "I wonder if Henry knew at this point what Luke was doing, that his plan blew up in his face?"

Ethan grunts. "He did. I heard the conversation. He knew Luke had you, he knew Bodhi had a trust fund. Luke was picking up shit from Frank, then you two were heading to the airport. But they weren't there. Henry told my dad to leave, and then he disappeared. He wanted Luke to think they left without him, but really my dad was the only one on the plane."

"We were going to the docks, right?" Eva softly asks. "His stop to grab something, was at the docks?"

Ethan nods. "Frank—Frank had drugs for him."

"And then we were going to the airport, where the plane was already gone?"

"Yes," Ethan quietly confirms.

Eva abruptly stands and goes into her kitchen. She rests her hands on her sink and leans into it, staring down as if she's getting ready to get sick. "I don't know why it didn't register when you mentioned it last night. But what happened in the truck, it didn't need to happen. The docks, the empty airport ... two different chances. I didn't think I had a choice—"

"You didn't know, Eva," Luna says. She walks up to her and puts her hand on her back. "You didn't know that's where you were going, or that the plane was already gone."

"You wouldn't have made it there, anyway," Ethan suddenly

reminds her. "Even if you hadn't crashed. I was on the road, heading your way, remember?"

Eva nods a little. "You heard all this, and you left Frank at Tacklebox to try to save me?"

"I did," Ethan sighs. "I had to try. I had to give you a chance. Then when I saw everything, I saw the accident, and I saw Luke, I took the gun. It was my dad's and I knew this would somehow get pinned on him. That Henry would find a way to make this all my dad's fault. I made sure you were okay, I knew they were coming for you, and then I took the gun and got the hell out of there before you all saw me."

Eva walks closer to him. "Thank you," she says. "Thank you for trying to do something good when you were stuck in the middle of all this horrible shit."

"The fire," Luna swiftly says. "And your mom, Eva? Luke was obviously following Coop and me, so who followed your mom?"

"Frank," Ethan replies. "Frank was. I was with him—I didn't know until it was too late. I swear I didn't know what he was doing."

"What about the truck?" Eva asks Ethan. "Did Frank move the truck when it was parked outside my house?"

Ethan looks down at the table and slowly nods.

Eva continues, "So if you were with Frank, Luke was after Coop and Luna, your dad—"

"Was at the airport, and then flying the empty plane."

"Then who started the fire at Henry Channing's house?" Eva curiously asks him.

Ethan's mouth forms a sly smile. "Think about it. His plan was to escape to the Bahamas and never look back. So the best way to escape would be to hope people think you're dead, right? Clean slate, everyone thinks you're gone? No one looks for you? Obviously, you let someone else tell people close to you that *they* did it, someone who doesn't care about consequences, so no one would even think for a second *you* did it—"

"Just say it, Ethan," I interrupt. "Who started the fire?"

He lets out a small laugh. "You already know the answer to that question. Henry Channing, of course. Luke planned it, but Henry Channing started the fire at his house."

chapter twenty-nine

Eva – about a week later

offee," Bodhi says, placing a cup on the table. "And your avocado toast," he continues, putting my plate down.

"What'd you get?" I ask him, taking a sip from my steaming cup as I eye my toast with anticipation.

"Breakfast wrap, and of course, coffee."

It's early, and we're at SunBros Café, a local spot here in Flagler that has the most delicious breakfast options. It also has amazing coffee that gives me the exact caffeine fix I need to get my day started. Bodhi has been a regular for a while, and I'm happy to say the owners now know me on a first name basis, too.

Bodhi and I start school on Monday, and this last week we've been two ships aimlessly passing each other most of the day and night. He's been squeezing in as many surf lessons as possible before summer break in Flagler is officially over. As for me, Kennedy's been keeping Luna and me occupied with back-to-school shopping, spa days, and last-minute social gatherings that are apparently imperative for a good start to the school year. Even though Luna is already done with school, Kennedy insists she come along, which is great for me because Luna always says exactly what I'm thinking. Tonight, we're all heading to our high school for the first home football game, another must in the mind of Kennedy, but Bodhi and I are making an effort to spend the day together first.

"I feel like I haven't seen you in a month," Bodhi says, biting into his breakfast wrap.

"You saw me last night."

"An hour, after I finally pry you out of Kennedy's grasp just long enough to kiss you goodnight before heading to Calvin's with the guys, doesn't count."

"Well, you have me all day today. We just need to be back at my house by six because everyone's coming over before the football game."

"Yeah, that's what the guys said, too."

"What do you want to do all day?"

"Stare at you."

"That's boring," I proclaim.

"Eva!" the owner of SunBros greets me as he walks by our table.

"Hi, Travis," I smile.

"Your dad just placed a huge to-go order," he tells me. "Twenty minutes ago. He should be in any second."

"Nice. Thanks for the warning," I mumble as he walks away.

"When's the last time you saw him?" Bodhi asks me.

"The last time *you* did."

"Eva, I think maybe we should—"

My raised hand stops him mid-sentence. "Please let's not start the day off like this. We've barely spent two hours alone together in almost a week. And we start school on Monday. Can we not do this right now? Ruin our day?"

He nods his head. "No ruining our day."

Just then my phone starts ringing. I look down to see who's calling. "Porter!"

"Talk about ruining our day."

I give Bodhi a look. "I texted him a hundred times since our little conversation with Ethan, and he's finally calling me back."

"You texted him a hundred times?"

I give him another look.

"Answer it."

I hit accept. "Hey, Porter."

"Eva!" his familiar voice responds. "Can't say I wasn't a little surprised to see all your text messages. Football practice has taken over my life, though. Sorry about not getting back to you sooner."

"Sounds like you're picking up where you left off in Flagler."

"Pretty much. You with Bodhi?"

"I am. I actually have a question for you."

"Oh yeah? Figured you had a reason for all the texts."

My heart drops. Why does my heart drop?

"Should I be scared?" Porter continues.

"Probably," I admit. "First, your dad—"

"Nothing," he interrupts. "I haven't heard a single whisper."

"Are you worried?"

"No," he immediately replies. "He's around. Trust me, he knows exactly what he's doing."

I pause, trying to gather my thoughts.

"Was that your question?" he suddenly asks.

"No. That night, Porter. The night you had that fight with your dad, did he ask you to leave Flagler with him?"

I can hear Porter loudly breathing into the phone. "He did. How'd you know that?"

"It's a long story. The Bahamas? Did he say he was going there?"

"*Eva*," Porter's voice comes out like a warning. "What part of stay out of trouble don't you understand?"

"Did you tell Holden that?" I ask him.

"Holden?" he questions.

"The detective that met with you."

"Oh, you mean the quack that blows up my phone twenty times a day with questions? The dude with the red hair? He's even got my mom involved now. He calls her more than he calls me. No, I didn't tell him—"

"Maybe you should have."

"My dad is all talk and you know this," Porter points out. "Every week or so he would tell me different places we could move to. That night it was the Bahamas, the week before it was Aruba. It doesn't mean anything."

I can tell he's getting pissed.

"Eva, just stay out of it. Please."

"Fine," I agree. "But for someone who wants me to stay out of it, you sure threw that demand out the window when you told me not to be afraid to ask questions."

I hear Porter sigh. "Can I talk to Bodhi for a minute?"

"What?!" I shockingly ask.

"Can I talk to Bodhi for a minute?" he repeats.

I hand the phone out to Bodhi. "He wants to talk to you."

Bodhi slowly puts down his breakfast wrap and takes my phone.

"Porter, hi," he bluntly says. I watch Bodhi's facial expressions as he listens to Porter on the other end. He laughs moments later as he says into the phone, "Yeah, she definitely is."

"I'm definitely what?" I whisper in annoyance.

Bodhi smiles at me but doesn't answer my question. "I will," he says to Porter. "We will—you too." He then hits end and hands me back my phone.

"What was that?!"

"Porter said bye, and for us to come to Charleston. Hey, do you think he knows about his missing aunt? Sienna? He ever mention her to you?"

I let out a growl. "Fine, don't tell me. You and Porter can just run off together."

Bodhi starts laughing under his breath, and then sits back in his seat, folding his arms and waiting for me to calm down. "Who's ruining our day now?"

I look down at my avocado toast, which is only growing soggy the longer it sits on my plate. I stab it forcefully with my fork repeatedly. "Fine. I'm done."

"Good," Bodhi grins, and then his mouth forms a frown. "Don't look now," he nods to the door. "But your dad just walked in and you won't believe who's with him."

I don't turn around. I have no desire to turn around. "You going to tell me or do I have to start guessing?"

"They're heading this way."

"Eva, Bodhi," my dad greets us. I look up to see Holden standing right next to him.

"Holden?!" I question. "What the—"

"I'm using your dad for a little case I'm working on," Holden uncomfortably says.

My dad looks between us all, confused. "How do you guys know each other?"

"Holden is dating Graham," Bodhi answers. "The paramedic who saved Eva that night?"

My dad looks curiously at Holden. "You don't say," is what finally rolls out of his mouth. "Weeks into this case? I guess that conversation would have eventually come up at some point, right?"

"Absolutely," Holden agrees, his face now as red as his hair.

"You two have big plans today?" my dad asks us.

"I'm stealing Eva away from our friends," Bodhi tells him. "Then we're going to our school's football game."

"You're going to a football game?" my dad humorously questions me.

"Sort of being forced."

He gives me a sly smile. "Well, have fun. We're just picking up breakfast for the police station."

"Why?" I question. "Why are you going to the police station with Holden?"

"Your dad is helping us with something," Holden immediately replies. "It's just a little get together."

I give my dad a look. "Interesting."

He winks at me, and then asks, "Dinner on Sunday? At home?"

"We'll be there."

He gives my head a little tap, and then walks to the register.

Holden lingers behind. "Your dad's a good guy. Helpful."

"Uh huh. Any news on Bodhi's sister?"

"Yes, actually, I've got a few leads."

Bodhi chokes on his breakfast wrap. "Were you planning on telling me this at some point?"

"Was waiting to see if they pan out. I'll be in touch, okay?" He gives us an odd look, and disappears around the corner. I glance down at my toast, which suddenly doesn't seem appealing anymore.

"Obviously your dad's helping him find Henry," Bodhi's quiet voice says. I don't respond. "Eva?" I look up and he reaches over the table, rubbing my fingers with his. "Don't let this ruin our day."

I nod my head and give him a little smile, but I know he can read right through my fake demeanor.

"I know what we're doing today," he suddenly declares.

"Oh yeah?"

"Yep," he releases my hand and pulls out his phone. "I just need to make a little phone call to get my plan rolling—"

"Bodhi, you don't need to do anything special—"

"Eat your toast," he points to it, pushing himself back from the table. "I'll be right back."

chapter thirty

Eva

An hour later, we're pulling into Ma and Pop's boat rental store in Ponce Inlet.

"Bodhi, you did *not* have to rent a boat for us—"

"I didn't rent it," he lets me know, parking the jeep. "Ma and Pop love me." He jumps out, and before I can even unbuckle my seatbelt, he's at my side opening the door. "Your carriage awaits."

I grab my bag and hop down. "Should I change into my suit?"

He points to the bathrooms across from the boats. "Absolutely. I'll meet you at the end of the dock when you're done."

I quickly change, throwing shorts on over my bikini bottoms, thoroughly impressed with how determined Bodhi is to make this day special. When I'm done, I walk out and see him talking to Ma and Pop at the end of the dock. I pick up on their conversation the closer I get.

"Did you see them today?" I hear him asking.

"Oh yes," Ma responds. "All over. Stay on the Halifax, head toward Piddler Island."

"Watch out for the sandbars," Pop includes. "Saw a few boats stuck last week."

"Got it," Bodhi replies, noticing my arrival. "Ready to go, babe?"

I nod my head.

"You two have fun!" Ma smiles, and then she throws her arms around me, squeezing me tight before pulling out of this quick hug, and grabbing my hands. "Never thought I'd see the day that Coop brings an actual gem home. I hear you're the one who introduced him to Luna?"

I let out a little laugh. "Coop pretty much lost all verbal skills the day he met Luna."

"She's exactly what that boy needs!" Pop chimes in. "Have her back by four, alright?" he then says, throwing Bodhi the keys.

"Yes, sir," Bodhi nods, then he grabs my hand and starts walking me toward what looks like a brand-new Hurricane deck boat.

"Ma and Pop are just letting you take this out all day?"

He steps over the side. "Like I said before, they love me. They also trust me a lot more than they trust Coop."

"You know, we could have just taken my boat out—"

"Not today," he grins, starting up the engine. "There's a reason we're here at this specific spot. Untie us?"

I swiftly release the ropes, jumping over the side as the boat starts to drift away.

"Take a seat," Bodhi points to the sundeck. "Take a nap. I'll let you know when we're there."

I give him a curious look.

"Just trust me, okay?"

I walk over to him, placing a small kiss on his lips. "I trust you completely," I say, then I walk over to the sundeck and do as he asked. I close my eyes, enjoying the breeze blowing as we gain speed once we're out of the wake zone. It's not long, maybe ten minutes, when I feel the boat start to slow down.

"Close your eyes," I hear Bodhi request.

"My eyes *are* closed."

"Well don't open them, okay?"

"Bodhi—"

"Please. Just don't open them."

"Okay." I hear the engine turn off. I hear Bodhi drop the anchor, and then I sense him standing in front of me. His hands are suddenly in mine, pulling me up. My body is guided into his, my back is against his chest, his hand is covering my eyes. I feel him move me to the side of the boat.

"Ready?" he asks.

"Not exactly sure what I'm ready for, but yes?"

He lets out a little laugh, and then his hand comes down. "Open your eyes."

I do, and it's bright at first. I blink a couple times as I let my eyes adjust, and then I focus directly on the movement I see in the water.

Swimming next to our boat, gliding so effortlessly, are at least ten massive sea turtles. I gasp, throwing my hand over my mouth. The last time I'd been here and saw these beautiful creatures, I was with Bodhi and Lenora, and broke my leg. I haven't been back since. I didn't want to see them and be reminded of everything I lost that day. But now I'm here, watching them as they swim gracefully through the crystal-clear water, and the only thought running through my mind is about the one person I thought I had lost.

Him. Bodhi. I turn to face him, no words leaving my mouth. He stands there, knowing he's outdone himself with this simple yet astonishing act.

"I thought maybe you needed to see them again," he softly says, his fingers moving my hair behind my ear. "With me, with you and me, together. A new memory to take away the old one."

I wrap my arms around his neck. "I can't believe this was even a thought in your head."

"You, Eva. Making you happy is always a thought in my head."

I press my lips to his, keeping them there as long as possible while his hands wander up my back. "I'm never going to forget this," I whisper to him.

"Good," he says in return, tugging slightly on the strings to my bikini top. He then pulls his t-shirt off. "Want to go swimming with them?"

"For real? We can do that?"

He shrugs his shoulders. "Why not? Boat's anchored, we can swim over to the island, and if we happen to pass some sea turtles along the way—"

I'm already stripping out of my shorts, not wanting to miss this opportunity. Bodhi hooks the boat key to his swim trunks, and lowers the small ladder into the water. He climbs down first, wading for a couple seconds before reaching for me.

"Feels like bath water," he declares.

I take his hand and lower myself in. It's almost too warm, and it's deep, deep enough that I have to doggy paddle to keep myself from going completely under. Bodhi's able to just barely touch the bottom.

"We can swim over to the shallow waters," he points to Piddler

Island.

I suddenly feel something brush against my back. "Ahh!" I let out a yelp, spinning around just in time to see a sea turtle float by. I find myself backing up right into Bodhi. "Jesus! They're so much bigger when they're right next to you!"

I feel his arms wrap around my waist. "They're beautiful," he says. "The way they just glide through the water."

I turn my body around so I can face him. He tugs on my waist so that our noses are practically touching. "I feel like this is a dream," I tell him, looking over his shoulder as I see another one head our way. There are more swimming at our sides. "They're surrounding us."

"Let them. They won't hurt us."

My legs are growing tired and I gently wrap them around Bodhi's waist. My hands move to his neck and he leans in, his lips brushing gently against mine while his hands cradle my head.

"Stay with me tonight," his words float past my mouth.

I pull myself back a little. "I'm not sure if Calvin would approve of that."

"Not at Calvin's. On the beach, my house."

"Just us?"

"Just us."

I run my fingers through the bottom of his hair. "And what exactly should I tell my mom?"

"That we're all crashing at my house after the football game. You won't be lying. We'll just forget to invite everyone else."

"I like the way you think."

"I like having you to myself. Even if it's just for a night."

"After this," I wave my hand at a sea turtle swimming by, "you definitely can have me all to yourself tonight."

"I didn't do this to get you to stay with me tonight. I did it because I really enjoy seeing you happy."

"You always make me happy, Bodhi."

His lips taste salty as they press against mine. I squeeze my hands tighter around his neck as the current tries to break us apart. He starts walking slowly, while our lips are still together, his sturdy arms holding me up as he trudges through the sand. I feel my body

271

gradually coming out of the warm water, but I don't open my eyes. I don't want anything to end this perfect embrace, this incredible feeling that has taken over my body. He slowly places me down on the shore, the water crashing like a pattern on my legs over and over again, as his lips move with my own. I crave for more, and I let him know what I want by slowly pushing his hips into mine. There's no denying that he's craving more, too.

A few moments pass when I hear him growl. His lips suddenly pull away. I can see myself in the reflection of his dark eyes. He gradually points to other boats sailing by in the distance. "I refuse to share you with everybody that has the honor of passing by us."

"Where's your sense of adventure?"

"I'm not sharing that side of you with anyone else. I refuse. I claim it all for myself. That side of you is mine."

As dominant as he suddenly sounds, I secretly love it. I love that he feels like there's a certain side of me that he owns, because he's right. That side of me *is* his. I take my thumb, rubbing it under his pouty lower lip that was just moments ago smoothly gliding over my own. "That side of me *is* yours."

He responds by placing a gentle kiss on my forehead, and then lying down next to me in the sand. His fingers weave in between mine, and we stay like that in silence, as the sea turtles swim in the water in front of us, and until the heat forces us to finally move.

"Ready to do a little boating before we head back?" he asks, pointing to the boat rocking with the subtle waves. "Head down the Halifax for a bit?"

"Absolutely," I agree, turning a little to look at the island we had just inhabited for the last hour or so. "Do you notice all the sea turtles keep swimming straight to that inlet over there?" I point. "Do you think that's where they lay their eggs?"

"Only one way to find out," Bodhi grins.

We start walking, staying in the wet sand as we don't have any shoes on, until we get to where the inlet forms. It doesn't look deep. I can see the bottom through the ice blue water. But it's wide, and it disappears into the massive trees that overtake this small island.

"I bet when it rains, the water level floods this inlet," Bodhi says as he steps down into it. "The chance of rain is maybe five percent today. Want to risk it to see what we find?"

I look back to the boat that's just a speck in my sight now. "Will it be okay just sitting there?"

Bodhi nods. "I've got the keys," he taps his pocket.

"Let's do it."

The water in the inlet is even warmer than the water we were swimming in earlier. Bodhi takes my hand as we both slowly walk further in, disappearing from the Halifax and any sign of civilization.

"This is creepy," I declare moments later. "If the sea turtles use this area as a nesting ground, they sure did pick a horror story type of home."

"Want to head back?" he points behind us.

"Not yet."

We walk a little bit more, when the inlet suddenly splits into two different directions. "Right or left?" Bodhi questions.

I look both ways. The right seems to thin out, but eventually opens back up into the Halifax. The left goes deeper into the unknown. I squint, trying to see if there's anything worthwhile down there, or if we should just go right and head back out. I quickly see something glimmering further down, on the bank of the inlet, but almost hidden from anyone that would simply be strolling along on some ill-fated adventure like us.

"Bodhi, do you see that?" I question him.

He looks to where my finger is pointing. "Looks like a boat?"

I start pulling him along. "What if someone got stuck back here? What if someone's hurt?"

"Or what if they want some privacy and they're doing exactly what you and I almost did an hour ago?"

I shake my head. "There's been no rain. How would they have gotten the boat down here? It's too shallow."

"True," Bodhi agrees. We start walking further. "Let's not pounce on it though, okay? Approach it slowly? Because someone might be living on that thing, and maybe they don't want to be bothered."

The water suddenly starts to get deeper. What was floating against my knees is now slowly creeping its way up my stomach.

273

We're close now, and almost right on top of the boat, when Bodhi suddenly freezes. He tugs hard on my hand as I try to continue walking. I turn my head to look at him. He's not moving, just staring at the boat for some ungodly reason. My feet are sinking into the soft sand, and I'm having a hard time keeping myself from just completely collapsing into the water.

"Eva, look," he points.

I turn back to the boat and immediately see what has caused him to become frozen in this nightmarish inlet. Skyla. The boat says Skyla. We both just stand there, sinking further into the water until it's almost up to my shoulders.

"Bodhi," I calmly say. "Is it his boat?"

"It's his boat."

"We're sinking Bodhi, we need to move."

He pulls me up by my arms, and we walk the twenty or so steps to the shore. It's covered in twigs and debris, and the boat has obviously been here for a while. It's not anywhere near the water, and is tucked more into the trees than the sand. Bodhi hits the boat with his fist a few times, trying to stir anyone that might be inside. It's silent. The only thing I can hear is the soft ripples of the water, and our own breathing.

"How the fuck did it get here?!" he suddenly cries out, causing me to jump.

"I don't know," I whisper, walking along the sharp twigs and shells to get closer. I grab at the metal railings at the back of the boat, and hoist myself up.

"Eva! What are you doing?"

I turn around to face him, and hold out my hand. "We aren't going to come across your insane dead father's boat that mysteriously disappeared from Flagler after I pretty much died, and *not* check to see what might be inside of it, are we?"

"No," he carefully replies.

"He's not coming back, Bodhi. We both know that. He's not on this boat."

He grabs onto my hand, pulling himself up. "Just stay behind me, okay?"

"Sure thing."

274

There's trash everywhere. Food wrappers, water jugs, a couple lighters, a lone blanket thrown on the seats. "Someone was living on this boat for a while," Bodhi concludes.

"Who?"

"I have no idea."

I start picking through plastic grocery bags on the ground, all filled with trash and a handful of receipts. "Cash," I say moments later. "Everything was paid for with cash. The earliest receipt was a few days after the accident. The last, was just three weeks ago."

Bodhi throws himself down in the captain's seat. "Whoever was on the boat had someone else bring them shit? Because there's no way this boat got here, and then continuously left every few days."

"Right."

Bodhi suddenly stands, yanking open the glove box. He reaches in and pulls out the random objects inside. A few joints, a carton of cigarettes, lots of cash, a couple pictures, and a key on a palm tree keychain. He stares at the first picture for a moment, and then hands it to me, keeping his eyes on mine and ignoring everything else in his hand. I look down, and his bright blonde curls and chubby toddler face stare right back up at me. I flip it over, the words *my son* are scribbled on the back.

The air trying to escape my lungs makes a desperate noise in the back of my throat. "Bodhi, I'm so sorry."

"No! Just because he had a picture of me from when I was two shoved in this box on his boat, it doesn't mean shit!"

"It's okay if it means something to you."

"It doesn't."

"It's okay if tomorrow it does."

His lips start to tremble and he looks away.

"Bodhi," I whisper. "It's okay to suddenly feel something."

He looks back at me, a mix of hate and empathy on his face. "I don't want to feel anything."

I press my forehead against his. "We can't help what we feel, and nothing you might think about this will make me feel any less toward you."

His breath hits me hard on my lips. "He took you away from me. You almost died, and one fucking picture suddenly makes me hate

275

him a fraction of an inch less than I did one minute ago. I hate that."

"And that's okay."

He squeezes the other picture in his hand and quickly brings it under our eyes. "What the hell!?" he shouts out.

The picture is shaking in his hands and I have to grab it to keep it steady. I stare down at it, and almost feel as if the boat has suddenly started to spin. It's Skyla, which isn't that surprising, but it's the exact same picture Holden had showed us on his phone.

"It's the same," I mutter.

He flips it over and an address is scribbled on the back. "Isle of Palms?" he questions. "Where's that?"

"South Carolina."

"Is this where she is?"

"I don't know Bodhi. Maybe? Or maybe this is where she *was*?"

"Why is it the same picture? Why is the picture that was in Luke's wallet now on his boat? This doesn't make any sense!"

"I need to think!" I exclaim. "Holden said the picture was found in Luke's wallet, but there's no way that's true if it's now here on Luke's boat—"

"Unless whoever was on this boat was given it by someone at the police station?"

"Holden, he has to be lying to us."

Bodhi raises the palm tree keychain up in the air. "Do you think this key belongs to the address?"

"Possibly. It doesn't look like a key to a house, though."

He looks at the address on the back of the picture again. "Do you really think she was here?"

"I think Luke knew where she was, or where she had been at least. He told me she wasn't far from here. Isle of Palms is what, five hours away?"

"Don't tell anyone, okay?" he then says. "About any of what we found in that box. I don't know who to trust, Eva. You're the only one I know for certain I can."

"I won't."

"What do we do about the boat?"

I look around at the chaos. It's so obvious someone was living on this thing. It's so obvious someone was helping this person as they hid out on this island. To me, there's only one person that comes to mind.

"We need to figure out who was hiding on this boat," I say.

"How do we do that?"

I start moving around, rummaging through the trash, looking for any clues that would confirm my suspicions. I yank at the blanket, and suddenly a baseball cap falls out from under it. University of Florida.

University of *fucking* Florida.

I pick up the hat. The exact same hat Porter was wearing the day he left for Charleston. "Bodhi. I think it was Henry Channing."

"What?!"

"It was Henry Channing. I know it was. He was hiding here. Probably until things calmed down. This hat, Porter has this hat. His dad has one, too. It was him. It had to have been Henry."

"What do we do? Do we call Holden? Do we tell him we found the boat?"

I flip the hat over in my hands, remembering what Porter had said to me on my patio the last time I saw him. I throw the hat to the ground. "Bodhi, do you trust Holden?"

He looks confused. "I don't know Holden well enough—"

"Bodhi! What is your gut saying? The picture! Not telling us about my dad! Do you trust Holden?"

"No!" he cries out. "No. I think he's got some fucking shady ulterior motive for whatever the hell he's doing to us—"

"We can't call him. We can't tell him this. He wins then. This little bit of information that we give him puts him in the lead." I grab the picture that's still in his hands. "We have *this*. I think this is where your sister was. And if it's not, then it might be a start. Screw Holden—"

"So we do nothing?!"

"No. There is *someone* I think we need to call."

"Who Eva?"

It takes me a second to get the words out of my mouth, because I *never* thought I would ever say this. "My dad, Bodhi. I think we need to call my dad."

chapter thirty-one

Bodhi

How long has it been?" I ask Eva.

She looks down at her phone in her hand. "Over an hour. He should be here soon."

We made it back to Ma and Pop's boat, where Eva immediately called her dad. Her goddamn hands were shaking as she did, and her words all came out in such a fast jumble, she had to repeat herself twice. We're waiting on the boat now. He told her not to leave, that he was on his way and not to call anyone else.

Eva stands from her seat and walks over to the back of the boat, leaning over the railing, looking deep in thought.

"He wasn't with Holden?" I confirm.

She shakes her head. "He specifically said not to call him."

I stand and join her, my hand slowly slipping under the warm hair on her neck. "You suddenly trust your dad now?"

Her head lifts and her exhausted eyes find mine. "No. But I want to believe he's past the point of royally fucking up my life on purpose." She looks back out to the water and suddenly points. "I think that's him."

I glance out at the horizon and see a boat swiftly approaching. The closer it gets, the easier it is to see it definitely is Mr. Calloway, but he's also with someone else.

Eva lets out a laugh. "Owen Edwards," she mutters under her breath. "He's with Owen Edwards."

Sure enough, Owen pulls a boat up right next to ours. We start rocking with the sudden waves and grab onto the sides. Mr. Calloway lowers the anchor in without even acknowledging us, and then climbs over the railing. He balances on the edge of the boat, and makes a leap directly onto ours. Eva backs up into me, throwing me off balance. Both of us stumble into the seats of the boat as her dad approaches. He immediately pulls at both our arms until we're steady on our feet again, and then he shockingly wraps us in a hug.

"What the hell are you two doing chasing after Henry Channing?!" he cries out.

Eva quickly looks at me. I'm too confused to form words right now. "We weren't," she says to her dad's back. "We were out here boating, chasing the sea turtles, and stumbled on the boat—"

He pulls out of his fatherly hug. "You *stumbled* upon Luke Sullivan's missing boat while chasing sea turtles, and just so happened to figure out that Henry Channing had been living on it?"

Well, when he says it out loud, it does sound pretty far-fetched.

Eva reaches over the seat, grabbing the hat she brought back from the boat. "Porter has this hat," she says to her dad, waving it in front of his face. "I know for a fact Henry Channing does, too. I'm sure you recognize it. Coincidence or not, it was on the boat."

"There was food," I include. "Lots of wrappers, receipts, even a blanket. Someone was living on that boat, hiding out on Piddler Island."

"Do you think it was Henry Channing?" Eva carefully asks her dad.

"Of course it was that bastard!" Owen shouts.

Mr. Calloway shakes his head at Owen. "Yes. It was probably him."

"Where is he now?" I ask.

"Out of the country is my guess," he answers, and then he slowly sits down. "He won't stay gone forever, though."

Eva carefully sits next to her dad. "Why? Why would he come back here? He completely abandoned Porter and—and I know what was found in his house, what he's been doing in Flagler. I know more, we know more," she points to me. "If he comes back here, he's going to go straight to jail."

"He should," her dad agrees. "But he's dodged that bullet a hundred times already. If Holden has his way—"

"Why are you working with him?" I question.

"Why are you?" he looks up at me and asks.

"We aren't," Eva quickly answers.

279

Mr. Calloway doesn't break his stare on me. "Holden has asked me to help him find Henry. He thinks if anyone knows his hideouts, it's me. Which is true. I know every single place Henry would sneak off to, except this place," he points to the island. "If he was indeed here, it was just to slip off the radar while he waited to make his escape. I'm going to help him find Henry, so this bullshit can finally come to an end." He pauses for a moment before asking, "You guys?"

"I'm looking for someone," I instantly respond. "Holden said he'd help us find her if we let him know anything we find out about Henry."

"That son of a bitch is blackmailing you both," Mr. Calloway says.

"You sure do know how to pick em, boss!" Owen laughs. "All the bastards flock to you!"

"Owen, now is not the time for comedic responses!" Mr. Calloway shouts to him. He turns back to us. "Holden knows how dangerous Henry Channing is. And he's asked two seventeen-year-old kids to keep an eye out for him. He should be protecting you both—"

"Dad, protecting us from Henry?" Eva curiously asks. "Why do we need to be protected from Henry still? Why did Holden tell us that if Henry comes back, he's going to be looking for us?"

I can tell he doesn't want to answer her. "We aren't little kids anymore," I remind him. "I think we've both been through enough shit this summer that whatever it is, we can handle it."

"I know," he immediately agrees. "I just never thought the time would come that I'd ask you two to help me protect you. I've spent the last fifteen years doing it myself, and I know the way I went about it was all wrong. I know that now. I'm sorry," he says to me. He shifts his body to look at Eva. "I'm sorry, Eva. The guilt I have for what I did to you will be with me forever, and just saying I'm sorry will never be enough."

I watch as the unexpected tears leave her eyes, as they slowly drip down her cheeks, but she never once changes her demeanor as she stares at her dad. In fact, she doesn't say or do anything at all. I'm afraid this conversation is going to ruin her, cause her to shut down and fall apart yet again. I go to move toward her, but Mr. Calloway very carefully holds out his hand, asking me to give him a moment.

"Eva," he says softly. "I am *so* sorry."

She looks out at the water and quickly wipes at her eyes. "I heard you," is all she says.

He lowers the hand he'd been holding out to me, almost as if silently giving me permission to comfort his daughter now. I sit down next to her, kissing the side of her head as I throw my arm around her back. She leans in and the heat radiating from her dark hair hits my chest like I just opened a hot oven.

"Please don't try to find Henry Channing," Mr. Calloway says to us both.

"We won't," she replies. "But what does he want with us?"

"Revenge!" Owen's voice is carried over our way.

Mr. Calloway points at Owen and repeats what he just said. "Revenge. He's lost everything. His money—all his accounts are frozen—his son, his house, his livelihood. He's going to come back at some point because there are people here who are scared of him. People who will give him what he needs to start over somewhere new. And there's me."

"You?" I ask.

"Yes," Mr. Calloway nods. "Me. He might not know that I betrayed him, that I was working for someone else all this time. He might think I've still got his back and that I'm just waiting for him to tell me what to do next. That's the best scenario. The other scenario is that he knows exactly what I've done and he's going to show up and take it out on you two."

I swallow down the lump in my throat. "He knows I have a trust fund."

Mr. Calloway's mouth drops. "How the hell does he know that?!"

"Does it matter?" Eva answers. "He just does."

"Does he know where the money came from?"

We both shake our heads.

"Well, this just adds another reason why he'd come back here."

"What about mom?" Eva blurts out. "And Miles and Rowan?

Are you worried about them?"

"Not as worried as I am about you two," he honestly answers.

"My grandparents?"

I can hear Owen laugh from his boat. "Calvin can take care of himself!"

"Henry wouldn't know where to find Kenneth and Annie," Mr. Calloway then says. "I promise they're safe."

"What do you want us to do?" I ask. "I feel like all summer we've been running from someone, always looking over our shoulder—"

"Don't trust Holden," he firmly says. "Let me deal with him. I think he's a decent guy, but he doesn't care about either of you. You hear anything about Henry, you *see* Henry, you tell me. And just—just don't go looking for trouble."

"Dad," Eva suddenly says. "Do you know Ethan Granger?"

"Ethan Granger?" he repeats. "Mark Granger's son?"

"Is Mark Granger a pilot?" she continues.

"He is."

"Then yes, Mark Granger's son."

"What about him?" he asks.

"Has Mark Granger been in Henry Channing's back pocket all this time?"

Mr. Calloway gives us both a funny look. "No. He's his pilot. He's flown both of us hundreds of times—"

"Maybe he knows where he is," Eva bluntly declares. "Maybe he's mixed up with all this shit. Maybe he was with Henry the night of the accident."

We all hear Owen laughing from his boat again. "Your daughter has mad skills!"

Mr. Calloway rolls his eyes. "You two are friends with Ethan?"

"I wouldn't say friends," I smirk at the thought. "More like he imprinted on us."

"He needs friends like you guys. I'll look into Mark. Thanks for the tip, but stop searching for more."

"What's your plan with the boat?" Eva nods over to the island.

"Search it, see if there's anything we can find, and then do nothing," he surprisingly says. "We leave it there and let someone else find it. I need you two to do me a favor, okay? That boat, you

282

never saw it. You were never on it."

We both nod our heads.

"I want you to sail back to Ponce Inlet, tell the Coopers you had a fantastic day boating, and then go home and go to that football game. We didn't see each other here, okay?"

We both nod again.

Mr. Calloway stands up. He kisses the top of Eva's head. "I'm going to redeem myself if it kills me," he makes known. "Sunday dinner, looking forward to it." And then he climbs onto the railing, reaches out for Owen's hand, and leaves our boat for his.

chapter thirty-two

Bodhi

"M a and Pop let you take out one of their new boats?!" Coop exclaims, shocked. "Did you christen it?"

I smack him upside his head. "There you go again! Your unhealthy obsession with my sex life is becoming ridiculous!"

Beck's laughing from the couch in Eva's family room. "Bodhi, it's a simple question. He's not asking for details on *how* you two christened it."

I grab Rowan's NERF gun from the kitchen table. He just left with his mom and Miles for dinner at Calvin's. I aim it at Beck and shoot off a round. I then grab Miles' gun and shoot off a round at Coop as he tries to hide behind the counter. "We did not christen your parents goddamn boat!"

"Okay! Okay!" he shouts.

I throw the guns on the table. "If Eva's mom asks tomorrow, you all stayed at my house tonight."

Coop pops up from behind the counter and points his finger at me. "Smooth bro, smooth. Using your friends to cover for your asses so you can have a romantic night alone. I get it—"

"I'd do the same for you two."

Beck stands up and walks over to us, placing all the NERF darts I shot at him next to the guns. "We know," he simply says. "We've got you covered. Enjoy your night. No details needed tomorrow. Kennedy!" he then shouts loudly toward the foyer. My ears are ringing. "We're going to miss kickoff!"

Coop snorts. "Since when do we care about fucking football?"

"*We* don't," Beck replies. "Kennedy does. This will get her moving."

"We're coming!" we hear Kennedy yell. "Calm the hell down!"

"See?" Beck points to the foyer.

Moments later, the girls enter the kitchen. They're each wearing tight jean skirts and they each have on an equally tight t-shirt with our school's mascot on it. They also each have their hair pulled up in a high ponytail with a dark green ribbon tied in it, matching their t-shirts, and dark green face paint striped on their cheeks.

The three of us just stand there staring at them, quite possibly with our mouths hanging open.

Coop is the first to speak. "I think I've died and gone to heaven," he mutters under his breath.

Luna wags her finger at him. "This was all Kennedy's doing, and if you tell my parents or show them *any* pictures, I will force you to babysit my youngest two sibs. Alone. For an entire day."

He walks over to her and plants a kiss on her forehead. "Your secret is safe with me, and will stay on replay in my head, forever."

Eva walks over to where I am and painfully mumbles, "*Kennedy*." She then wraps her arms around my neck. "Is this enough school spirit for you?" she asks in my ear.

I gently tap the bookbag hanging on her back, the one I know she packed to stay the night with me tonight. "Your school spirit is making me want to skip the football game and start our night early."

She grins and responds by placing a soft kiss on my lips.

"Let's go, family!" Kennedy demands, grabbing Beck's hand and pulling him toward the front door. "We can't miss kickoff!"

We drive separately to school, and the parking lot is already filled by the time we get there. I lose the others as I swerve the jeep down a dirt path, knowing there's an empty patch of grass hidden next to the dumpster that I can park us at.

"Luna said they found a spot up front and they'll save us some seats," Eva says, reading a text on her phone.

I nod my head, throwing the jeep in park and reaching for Eva's hand before I open my door. I give it a kiss. "Will it offend you if I bring up how goddamn hot you look right now?"

She snickers under her breath. "No, not at all."

"The only thing that's going to keep me from beating the shit out of every guy that looks at you tonight is knowing I get to have you all to myself in roughly three hours." She goes to talk but I place my fingers over her lips. Any words that float out of her mouth right now will have the ability to make me forget why we're even here. I'm suddenly playing out a fantasy in my mind, one of the two of us in my jeep unclothed. I shake it off. "Let's not make Kennedy mad."

We walk through the parking lot and head under the archway of the football field. The crowd is insane. Nothing brings out every single person in Flagler like the first home football game of the season. We don't make it far, not even ten feet inside, when I see the heads turn. Guys I used to not give a damn about, guys I wouldn't even think twice about, I now want to take behind the dumpster I just parked next to and throw my fist at their face. I know why I have this undesirable need to make sure no other guy in Flagler thinks about Eva the way I do. It's not jealousy. It's because she possesses every thought in my mind all day long, and this makes me possessive of *her*.

That's not healthy, is it?

"Eva Calloway!" I suddenly hear her name being called as I try to push us through the crowd.

"Mr. Adams!" she excitedly responds. I look to see an unfamiliar fatherly figure walking toward us, juggling bags of popcorn as kernels fall to the dirt below him.

"I was so sad to hear about you leaving," he says to her. "First Porter, then you. Who's going to be my star student this year?"

Eva lets out a nervous laugh. She puts her hand on my shoulder almost in reassurance. "Bodhi, this is my photography teacher from my old school, Mr. Adams. Mr. Adams, this is Bodhi, my boyfriend."

"Nice to meet you," I casually say.

"You too," he responds.

"Curious," Eva then says to him. "What are you doing here?"

"My daughter. Couldn't convince her to come to the school her dad teaches at. She wanted to be with her friends. She's a freshman this year. Keep an eye on her, okay? You'll probably see her in the photography room. Name is Callie."

"I'll definitely look out for her," Eva smiles.

"Yo Bishop!" I hear my name being shouted. I turn to see Easton walk by. "Your crew is over there," he points to the bleachers.

I nod my head and turn back to Eva.

"Bishop?" Mr. Adams raises his eyes. "Lenora Bishop? Were you related to her?"

I feel myself swallow hard. "Yes, she was my mom."

Mr. Adams eyes grow large and he shoves all the popcorn into the crook of his one arm. He then throws his empty hand out to shake mine. "It's a pleasure to meet you. I owe your mom my entire career. Hell, so does Bonnie, the photography teacher here."

"My mom saved your job?" I ask with uncertainty.

"Sure did," he replies. "She fought to keep the arts in the schools of Flagler. Became part of the board at my school and yours ... then she singlehandedly funded the art wings—"

"Hold on," Eva grabs my upper arm, her fingernails digging into my skin. "Lenora funded the art wings at *both* schools?"

Mr. Adams looks worriedly between the two of us. "I didn't know that wasn't public knowledge."

I let out an angry laugh. "It probably was. Just not to *us*."

He looks uncomfortably toward the bleachers, but then reluctantly meets our gaze again. "Flagler was getting ready to get rid of all the arts. The funds weren't there, and neither was classroom availability. We were busting at the seams at both schools. Your mom stepped in, funded everything, and is the reason I kept my job, and both Flagler schools kept the arts alive."

"That's a lovely story," is the only thing I reply.

Eva glances toward me, frustration written all over her face. I can tell my attitude is pissing her off. "Mr. Adams?" she questions. "Was it Lenora's idea for local artist week all those years ago?"

He nods his head. "It was. When the new art wing was finished, she wanted local artists to come in and introduce themselves. Kind of her own way of showing the board members what they would have lost if the arts weren't around in our community."

I grunt under my breath.

"We never knew that," Eva calmly says, ignoring me. "Thanks for sharing it with us."

"My pleasure." He then gives me a hesitant smile. "I'm sorry for your loss."

"Thanks."

"I expect Bonnie to be singing your praises this year, Eva," he

287

says to her, then he walks toward the bleachers.

Eva very slowly turns to face me. I'm expecting her to confront me on my miserable arrogance, but instead she asks, "This isn't necessarily bad news, right?"

I irritably shake my head in disgust over hearing yet another thing my mom had kept from me. I turn around, heading back to the parking lot. I know Eva will follow me, even though the very last thing I want to do is discuss my mom with her right now.

"Bodhi!" she shouts, heads turning in our direction as we both rush away from the game. I wait until I'm clear from the crowds of people before I turn to face her. She's standing there, her arms folded over her chest, glaring at me with such intensity, I suddenly feel scared in her presence.

Shit.

I point back into the stadium. "You can go watch the football game with them—"

The quick look of repulsion on her face stops my words dead in their tracks. "You think I care about a *fucking* football game?!"

I can feel the heat rise on my face. "No! But I don't want you to miss it because of me!"

"And what will *you* be doing while I sit with our friends watching a football game that I don't give a flying fuck about?!"

Her anger is making it hard to remember simple words. "Waiting in my jeep?"

She stomps her way over to me, shoving me hard in my chest. "You think because we've heard yet another secret your mom has kept from us, that *you* get to go off and be all moody and pissy, and expect me to be peppy and social? Fuck no!" She grabs my hand, pulling me into the parking lot. "Give me your keys!"

"Eva!" her name rushes out of my mouth. "We don't have to leave!"

"We aren't leaving! Just give me your goddamn keys!" I hand them over to her as she continues to pull me toward my jeep. Once there, she opens the back door. "Get in!"

I scooch myself into the back, quite frankly, scared to death of pissing her off any further. I watch as she opens the driver's door, hovering over the wheel for a brief moment as she starts the jeep.

She then gets out, slams the door closed as hard as she can, and climbs in next to me in the back. She makes herself comfortable, leans up against the window, and stares me down.

I nervously look away from her piercing eyes.

"Look at me!"

I bring my anxious face back to hers.

"Stop doing this!" she exclaims. "Stop shutting me out every time we find out something new about your mom! It's never going to stop! She kept secrets from you your entire life, and I'm not going to spend the rest of *my* life getting shut out by *you* repeatedly!"

"I'm not trying to shut you out!" I cry, looking away as I try to regain what little dignity I might have left. "I just don't know how to handle the constant flow of secrets!"

Her fingers force my face back to hers. "This wasn't a bad one."

"Bad? Good? Does it matter?! It's just another thing she never told me!"

Eva nods her head and her face suddenly softens. "I get that. I understand you're pissed off finding this out because she kept it from you. But she's not *here* anymore. Stop letting things she did force you to shut down and put up this instant wall between us."

I can almost see it, this wall she's talking about. It's there, because I let it be there ... again. I gently run my fingers down the length of her cheek. She closes her eyes with my touch. "You're the very last person I would ever purposely do that to. Why do I do it?"

Her eyes open and she frowns. "Because it's how you *always* process overwhelming news. You shut out everyone who loves you. You still do it to Coop and Beck, but you can't do it with me, because I won't let you." She reaches over my arm, grabbing her phone from the center console and madly moving her finger against the screen. Suddenly, music starts playing through the speakers of my jeep. She leans back into her seat and against the window again, patting her lap this time. "Lie back," she says. "Just lie here with your eyes closed for a few minutes."

I give her a curious look.

"Trust me."

I trust her more than anyone else in the world. I lie my head back on her lap and close my eyes. Her fingers immediately start running through my hair, while the raspy voice of Stevie Nicks starts to croon with the instrumental music.

"Stevie Nicks?" I can't help but ask, opening one eye to look up at her.

"Trust me," she says again. "Now close your eyes and stop talking."

I do what she says, letting the music flow in and out of my ears, letting Eva's fingers move gently through my hair, letting my emotions calm their way down. When the song finally ends, a new one picks up right after, but I cautiously open my eyes to see Eva staring back at me.

"Are you better?"

I nod my head and pull her down by her shirt for a backwards kiss. I rub my thumb under her chin until her lips leave mine. "How did you know that would help?" I then ask her, sitting up.

"Because when my world was crumbling down, Luna would make me sit at Hidden Treasure with my eyes closed, listening to Stevie Nicks until I felt better. It always helped for some reason. I thought it was worth a try."

"I'm sorry," I apologize, feeling like an idiot for how I just behaved. "I don't know why I act like that every time I hear something new. You think I'd be used to it by now. There's just so many secrets."

"It's a lot," she agrees. "But you need to let me be there for you, okay? You don't even have to say anything when you're feeling like this, just don't push me away. Let me sit here with you until you're ready to talk, or not talk. Can you just let me love you?"

"Baby, I will."

She gives me a big smile. "Therapy has done me some good. You notice I didn't slap you across your face?"

I let out a huge laugh. "Jesus, you're so goddamn cute."

"Cute?" she turns up her nose. "That's something you say to a five-year-old."

I tug on the ribbon in her hair. "The ribbon, the face paint, the school shirt, this jean skirt I've been dying to slip my hands under all night," I tug on the frays.

"You want to slip your hand under my skirt?"

I nod my head. "I also want to punch in the throat every guy who undressed you with their eyes in that stadium."

Her lips form a thin line. "Don't start this again. Ignore them."

"I did ignore them," I make clear. "I might have had to imagine the two of us having sex probably five or six times in a span of ten minutes to ignore them, but it worked."

"Five or six times?" she grins. "Was it any good?"

"Eva, it's always good."

She scoots closer to me. "It *is* always good."

My fingers run along the paint under her eyes. "If I make out with you right now, will I ruin this?"

She shrugs her shoulders. "I think it's worth the risk."

I bring my hand up to the back of her head and push until her lips hit mine. Her mouth immediately opens, allowing our tongues to brush up against each other. She takes it further, pushing me back against the seat, and straddling her smooth legs over me. Her jean skirt gets pushed up to above her hips with this movement, and she moves my hands below it.

"You said you wanted to slip your hands under my skirt," she reminds me. Her lips start sucking on my neck. "Now's your chance."

My fingers trail her upper thighs as her mouth moves down the paper-thin skin under my jaw. She quickly pulls my shirt off, throwing it behind her, as she starts sucking on the skin that was underneath. I shudder as it's pulled harder in between her lips. It's not painful, but the opposite, actually. It feels amazing. At this point, every part of my body is tingling each time her mouth presses against a new spot. I'm going to have one hell of a bruise trail lining my upper chest that's for sure.

Her lips go back to mine, and the wet marks she left on me suddenly feel chilled with the absence of her mouth. I feel her hands cover where her lips were moments ago, and then she firmly claws her nails down my stomach. She starts rocking slowly, purposely, as she's smirking with what she feels through the fabric beneath her. Her fingers start to teasingly play with the button of my shorts.

I can't take it anymore.

"*Fuck*, Eva," I groan into her mouth. "I want you. We're going home. I have to have you *right* now."

I feel my shorts come undone. "We don't have to go home. Just *have* me right now."

"Here?" I mumble. "What if someone—"

Her hand quickly covers my mouth, then she slowly slips my shorts and boxers down, never once moving her eyes away from mine, even though it's now very evident how badly she's turned me on. "No one will see us. I promise. If you want me right now, then *have* me right now."

To hell with my anxious conscience. I bring my lips to hers and start to lie her back on the seat, but she forcefully pushes her hands against my bare chest and gives her head a little shake.

"Not this time," she murmurs. "This time, it's my turn."

Her hands leave my chest and she stands slightly, slipping off her panties. I watch her, the way her eyes stare at me, the way she eagerly brings her body back onto mine. It's her confidence that's sexy as hell. I know she's never done this before. I know I'm the only one she would ever do this with, because I'm the only one that makes her comfortable enough to bring out this side of her.

Her knees appear next to my hips, her hand disappears below her, and I feel it wrap around how hard I am. She then cautiously guides her body to her hand and lowers herself down. Our moans match each other, and I can't get over how instantly amazing this feels. I can't get over how innocent yet erotic her face looks. I can't get over the fact that Eva's on top of me like this, in my jeep.

"Jesus, Bodhi," she whimpers. "I can feel you ... everywhere. Does—does it feel okay for you?" her voice is uncertain, and her face looks worried.

"Baby," I bring my hand to the back of her head. "It feels fucking incredible."

She starts to rock her body against mine, slowly and carefully at first. I close my eyes, pushing my forehead against hers as she starts to find her rhythm.

"Open your eyes," her breath wraps around my face. I do, and she places her hands on my shoulders. "I want you to watch me."

"*W-what?*" my voice stammers. "You want me to—"

"Watch me," she says again. "I want you to watch me move this

292

way on you. I want you to remember every second of my body on top of yours, what it looked like ... how it felt." Her hips rock harder into mine, and I bite down on my tongue to keep myself from being too loud. "This school year, when other guys look at me, this is what you're going to remember, okay? This exact moment in your jeep. Those other guys can look all they want, but *you* are the only one who gets to see what I look like, while I move this way with you inside me."

"*Jesus Christ!*" the words fly out of my mouth due to an equal mixture of shock from what she just said, and the intense sexual pleasure I'm currently experiencing. I grab her thighs, pushing her faster into me as this forceful need to have us both finish has now taken over. I slam my lips onto hers, burying my internal gratification into our kiss.

"I'm close," she murmurs into my ear. "Watch me."

She throws her head back, her hands squeezing my shoulders as she pushes against my arms. I couldn't stop watching her even if I tried. The way her ponytail swings behind her as she moves, the way her perfect mouth opens slightly each time she thrusts into me, the way her eyes stay on mine, as if daring me to close my own.

"God, you entrance me," I whisper. "You own me, Eva, every bit of me." She bites roughly down on her lip, and my hands purposely push harder against her warm thighs in response. "Baby—"

"I *love* it when you call me *baby*," she growls.

I bury my head into the sweaty crook of her neck, absolutely infatuated with this flawless human being. "I'm yours," I groan into her skin. "I'll always be yours."

No truer statement has ever left my mouth.

"I've always *been* yours," she breathlessly declares back, lifting my head off her neck. Then with one last push of her hips, the air literally stops circulating around us. Our bodies stay tightly wrapped around one another, our heavy breathing overpowers the music rushing through the speakers, as we both reach the height of our passion-filled climax together.

Just one person.

Just one soul.

Just one hurricane, and the eye it possesses.

293

chapter thirty-three

Eva – roughly a month later

I love the month of September. It might be my favorite month, to be honest. It's still hot in Flagler, hot enough we can have beach days and float around our pool, but you can almost sense the change in temperature coming. We might not have seasons, but we do have cooler months for part of the year, and I feel like September is the last month where the heat consistently stays around. After this month, the temperature does a downward spiral, until it starts to pick back up in March and April. I love the heat and I miss it when it's gone.

September came and went. The days passed by like a blowing leaf. It's hard to believe we've already been in school for over a month, and September is almost over. I actually don't mind having a routine again. After the summer I had, knowing what happens for a majority of my day five days a week is actually welcomed. Bodhi picks me up every morning, simply driving from Calvin's driveway to my own. I lucked out and ended up in classes with either him or our friends; every class except for photography, that is. After school, we all meet up with Luna for a bit, and then we usually grab dinner together before heading our own ways. Bodhi and I will go to my house, his house, or Calvin's, and do homework until the night creeps up on us.

It's normal, and I'm strangely okay with that.

Sometimes after Bodhi and I say goodnight, I find him sneaking back into my bed. Lately, we just need that comfort, that reassurance, that calmness we get by sleeping intertwined together. Alone, our minds can't turn off and we struggle to feel at peace. But together, it's an instant sense of serenity.

My phone alarm is what wakes me up this morning. Five thirty on the dot. I place it on my nightstand and feel Bodhi's arms pulling me back onto his chest, where I had slept all night. His eyes are still closed as he kisses the top of my head.

"Let's skip today," he mumbles, his raspy morning voice always makes my heart flutter.

"I can't," I declare. "I have a test in two different classes."

He groans. "Shit, I do too, but they're both early. Let's leave after."

I playfully smack his arm. "Bodhi, we can't just leave school whenever the hell we want."

"Yes, we can," he replies, pulling gently on my hair. "We don't need high school—"

I pinch the skin on his tight stomach. "We are graduating, understand?"

He's quiet for a minute, and then lets out an overly dramatic sigh. "Fine. You win. But I really hate the fact school takes up all my time with you."

"Did you forget we're seventeen? This is exactly what our life is supposed to be like right now."

"Maybe if we were normal."

I look up at him. "We need to pretend we're normal, at least until we graduate."

"If we didn't have to pretend, today we could have woken up on the beach, at my house, hours from now when the sun is actually up. We'd be sleeping in late, because we spent half the night having insanely hot, passionate sex—"

"Bodhi!" I quietly exclaim.

"You'd wake up to me bringing you breakfast in bed," he continues. "We'd sit out on the balcony for a while drinking our coffee, then we'd walk down to the beach and do a little fishing. We'd grab a late lunch at one of our favorite spots. Then we'd take our boat out—"

"*Our* boat? When did we get a boat?"

He covers my mouth with his hand. "We'd bring our dog—"

"We got a dog, too?" I mumble into his palm.

"I bought you a puppy," he simply responds. "A big one. Not one of those little yappy dogs, and we bring him everywhere, like a kid.

We'd take him on our boat and float around the Halifax for a while, plotting out our epic journey we're going to take sailing around the world, so that you can take pictures of every single city and country that your heart desires. Then we'd head back home. I'd make us dinner, because I have all this free time and Calvin has taught me how to cook. Then as we're cleaning up the kitchen, I'd slyly sneak away to the studio and light some candles. I'd persuade you to come upstairs with me, where I'd then spend the rest of the night making you repeatedly scream my—"

"Bodhi!" I jump up, covering his entire face with my hands as my cheeks flame red.

He slowly removes them. "Sounds perfect, right? I love how red you are right now."

I squeeze his hands hard in response.

He shakes my hands off his. "After a day like that, you'd finally agree to marry me."

I roll my eyes and cover his mouth again. "We're *seventeen*," I remind him for the hundredth time, trying to sound firm, but truthfully, his perfect day has just made my entire soul swoon in my body. I gradually remove my hand. "But that day sounds amazing."

He grins. "Just wasting our time sitting in high school."

I stare down at him for a moment, at his beautiful, confident face. "I have to graduate, for my parents. And you need to, for Calvin, okay?"

He leans up on his elbows and nods his head, while bringing his lips to mine. "Sitting in high school will just give me more time to daydream more perfect days like that, so I'll take that as a win."

I push my palms into his warm chest and look toward my balcony doors. "You have ten minutes before you need to climb back down my balcony and sneak your way into your own bedroom." I pull at his arms and lie back down. He now hovers over me. "Do you think we could quietly make some of your daydreams a reality in those ten minutes?"

WELL, I TOTALLY bombed that test," Kennedy sighs as we walk out of our chemistry class.

I try not to laugh at her. "By bomb, do you mean a B instead of an A?"

She groans. "There goes college."

"Kennedy," I struggle to take her seriously. "You'll be fine."

"Thank god it's Friday. Can we get drunk tonight, please?" she begs me as we get to our lockers. "I need to drown my declining grade point average in some hard liquor."

"Did I hear hard liquor?" Coop's voice echoes from behind Kennedy's locker door. She slams it closed and Coop, Bodhi, and Beck stand behind it. "I'm down for that," Coop grins.

Bodhi walks over to my side, placing a kiss on my cheek. Memories of our quick ten minutes in my bed this morning suddenly flood my mind. I lean into his firm shoulder. "Kennedy says she bombed the chemistry test. She needs a night off."

Beck throws his arm around Kennedy. "I highly doubt you pulled off anything less than a B," he says to her. She gives him a small smile, a very fake one in which we're all aware that deep down she's actually worried about this. "Bodhi," Beck looks up at him. "Can you arrange a night of mindless drinking in which no one remembers their name in the morning?"

"Why do *I* have to arrange this?" he asks.

"Bro!" Coop shoves him. "You're the one with the empty house!"

"*Bro*, you don't think at some point all your parents and our parental guardians are going to put a stop to the nights we spend at my empty house?" he bluntly asks us.

"Is this a trick question?" Coop comments. "Are you being serious?"

"Maybe?" Bodhi replies. "What's Luna doing tonight anyway?"

Coop smirks. "Getting mindlessly drunk with all of us at your house."

Just then, Ethan comes barreling down the hallway so fast I find myself questioning if someone's chasing him.

"You guys!" he shouts, pointing to us, not slowing down. "All of you! All five of you! We need to talk! Now! Right now! Not here! Family meeting! Outside! Courtyard! Now!" he demands, running past us and straight out the courtyard doors.

"Well shit, man," Beck stares at where Ethan just abruptly

disappeared. "Dude looks serious."

We all head to the courtyard and find Ethan trying to catch his breath at a picnic table.

"We're missing lunch, little bro," Coop says as we approach him. "This better be more important than the cafeteria food that's calling my name."

"It is," he wheezes. "He's back. He's coming back. Today. Back to Flagler—"

"Henry Channing?!" I say under my breath.

Ethan's head nods so forcefully I swear I hear his bones crack. "I heard my dad this morning before he drove me to school. My phone, it's dead, goddamn charger never fucking works—"

"What did he say?!" Bodhi exclaims.

"I couldn't find you guys this morning!" Ethan goes on, shamelessly pointing at all of us. "You five fucking delinquents don't get to school until the last goddamn warning bell or something?!"

"Ethan!" we all shout.

He waves his hand at us. "My dad flew out this morning. After he dropped me off. I don't know where to, but he had his phone on speaker in his office as he was working out! I mean come *on*, Dad. Does he think I don't listen? Why are parents so stupid! I heard Henry's goddamn voice from my foyer!"

"Focus, Ethan!" I shake his shoulders hard. "Details!"

He throws himself down on the table. "Today, three o'clock. They're arriving," he points in the direction of Flagler airport. "Henry said there'd be a driver waiting at three o'clock."

"Nothing else?" I confirm. "Nothing you're forgetting to tell us? No reason why he's coming back?"

"Is this not enough for you?!" Ethan shoots up from the picnic table. "God, Mom ... I give and I give, and I'm totally missing corndog day in the cafeteria—"

"It's enough, Ethan," I pat him on the head. He throws himself back down. I turn to everyone else. "We need to be at the airport at three o'clock."

"Are you fucking insane?!" Ethan shoots back up.

I push him down and ignore him. "I'm going to text Luna, see if she can get us an outdoor table at High Jackers—"

Ethan jumps off the table now. "You're going to sit at the restaurant attached to the airport and wait for Henry Channing to appear? You do realize this is insane, right? Please, someone," he points at everyone else, "someone tell her how insane this is!"

Coop throws his arm around Ethan. "You're my new favorite."

I raise my eyes at Coop and he slowly removes his arm. "We need to be there," I then say. "We need to see him with our own eyes—"

"And then what, Eva?" Ethan honestly asks. "Then what? You walk out on the runaway and say welcome home?"

"No. Then I call my dad."

"Your dad?!" he shouts. "I thought we didn't like him!"

I look to Bodhi, questioning if now is the time we fill them all in on what happened at the end of the summer. We kept it a secret like my dad asked us to do, but it's been eating away at us and we knew at some point we'd end up telling them everything.

"Why do I feel like there's shit you two haven't told us?" Coop's voice rings out.

Bodhi lets out a loud groan. "At the end of the summer—"

"Hold on!" Coop quickly demands. He grabs Ethan, pulling him over to Beck and Kennedy. The four of them form a line. "Figure we need to show the divide here. Should I get Luna on speaker?" Coop then asks. "You know, so she can hear whatever the hell you two have been keeping from us at the same time we all do?"

"Shit, Coop!" Bodhi rolls his eyes. "Calm the dramatics down, okay?"

Coop throws his hands up. "Dramatics?! We don't keep shit—"

"We found Luke's boat!" I shout over him. "Bodhi and me, the day we took Ma and Pop's boat out. We found it, hidden on some goddamn island."

The silence coming from them makes my ears ring with alarm.

"And you couldn't tell us this?!" Coop suddenly shouts.

"We think Henry Channing was on it for a while," I continue. "That he hid out on it. My dad—my dad is trying to find Henry. I called him and he asked us not to say anything about the boat to anyone—"

"We aren't *anyone*," Kennedy interrupts. "We're your family."

"What she said," Coop points to her.

Ethan starts shaking his head. "Shit. Don't make me choose now who I end up living with, or who gets me at Christmas. I'm already missing corndog day, don't throw this on me, too."

"You could have told us," Beck speaks up.

"Fuck this," Bodhi sighs. "What do you want us to do? The amount of shit we find out every day, we constantly have to watch our backs! Then there's all the secrets we hear about, everything that's been kept from us, yet Eva and I are just supposed to be normal, and walk around like everything is completely fine—"

"Bodhi," I grab his arm. "Calm down—"

"No!" he cries out, and then he points to all our friends. "Don't get pissed off because we didn't tell you we found my fucking dead dad's boat! That same day, we were told Henry Channing will probably show up to get his revenge on Eva's dad, and that *we*," he grabs my body and pulls me into his a little harder than he probably meant to, "are his revenge! If I had my way, I would have gotten all of us the hell out of Flagler—"

"Me too?" Ethan interrupts.

"You too," Bodhi confirms.

"Carry on," Ethan smiles.

"I would have gotten us all the hell out of Flagler weeks ago!" Bodhi continues. "I want us all to get the hell out of Flagler! I can do that. I can support every single one of us for the rest of our goddamn lives—"

"I *knew* it," Ethan mumbles.

"But here we are," Bodhi goes on. "Standing here in high school hell as we discuss what to do when Henry Channing shows up back in Flagler. Fine, get pissed that we didn't tell you Eva's dad is trying to find Henry, and make up for being a goddamn shitty father for fifteen years. Get pissed because we didn't want to drag you all into yet another one of our insane messes. Meanwhile, I'll just sit here and keep dreaming about the day I get us the fuck out of this place so we can all be happy and safe for the rest of our goddamn lives!"

There's a moment when I'm not sure where this is going to go. Coop and Beck are just standing there, eyes wide, staring at Bodhi. But then they both move at the same time, pushing me out of the way and wrapping their own bodies around him.

"We love you, bro," Coop declares. "Triangle. Triangle always."

"Sorry man," Beck pats him repeatedly on the back. "We shouldn't have gotten pissed."

"Shit, that was *intense*," Ethan shakes his head. "For the record, I would have chosen you and Dad," he then points to me.

"Luna said she'll be there at two," Kennedy tells us, staring down at her phone. "And that she'll bring binoculars." She then looks at me. "I understand why you both kept this to yourself, but telling us wouldn't have changed anything. I wasn't around when this all started at the beginning of the summer, but it's pretty obvious everyone needs to know what the hell's going on with you two, because we're *all* one crazy plot twist away from being on the nightly news."

I don't think I've ever heard a blunter remark come out of Kennedy's mouth before. "You're right," I agree. "I think we both forget sometimes that you all are involved in this, too. We shouldn't be keeping shit from you guys."

"We won't," Bodhi chimes in. "Not anymore, okay?"

"Now *that's* what I call a successful family meeting!" Ethan declares. "Missing my favorite Aunt Luna, of course. So you six idiots really going to High Jackers after school?"

"Yes," I announce. "I need to see that it's really him. And I need to see who the hell is picking him up."

"Here's a suggestion," Beck calmly states. "We call the police and tell them Henry Channing is arriving at Flagler airport at three o'clock, and then we go to Bodhi's and drink until tomorrow rolls around, knowing we did our civic duty for the year."

Bodhi puts his hand on Beck's shoulder. "Normally, I would agree with you there. But how do we explain Ethan's dad being the pilot?"

"Jesus!" Ethan cries out. "Don't make me lose my dad on the same day I miss out on corndogs at lunch—"

"Bro!" Coop hollers. "You've still got time to get your damn corndogs!"

"What about this detective guy?" Beck continues. "You trust him enough to call him and tell him what's going on?"

"Hell no," Bodhi replies.

"Pretty sure Holden doesn't give a damn about us," I tell them all. "He's got my dad working for him, trying to find Henry—but my dad doesn't want us telling Holden if we hear anything—"

"How do you guys sleep at night?" Ethan asks. "It must be hard trying to keep track of whose side you're on, who you're trusting that day, which family member you're supposed to hate, which story you're telling your friends—"

"*Ethan*," I sigh his name in warning.

He continues. "Not to mention keeping the secret that you're probably the richest sons of bitches in Flagler—"

Coop gives him a shove. "Go get your corndogs, Ethan!"

"I'm being serious here!" Ethan exclaims. "I don't envy either one of you guys."

"Thank you?" I cautiously reply.

He throws his arms around Bodhi and me. "You're not going to get my dad in trouble, right?" he then asks.

"No, man," Bodhi promises. "If it's really Henry, we'll call Eva's dad. We'll let him handle it—"

"And then we go drink!" Coop declares.

"*We* go drink," Bodhi points to everyone but Ethan. "Ethan goes home."

"What?!" Ethan cries out.

"You're fourteen, Ethan!" I whack him on the head.

"You all are seventeen! Your point is invalid!"

"It's not happening, Ethan," I make known.

"Fine, fine," he grumbles. "But I'm going to High Jackers with you all, and after we confirm it's Henry Channing, you're buying me some food, because I'm starving, and it's your fault I missed—"

"If you say corndog day, I'm going to beat you over the head with my shoe," Coop squints his eyes and mutters.

Ethan pauses briefly. "I'm a growing young man," he declares. "Being the snitch that keeps this family afloat can't rob me of my daily nutritional needs."

AS SOON AS school ends for the day, the six of us make our way to

High Jackers.

"When the hell are you going to buy a vehicle that fits us all?" Ethan cries out from the back of the jeep. "Not that I mind getting to know everyone on a very personal level back here—"

"A Suburban," Coop nods his head. "We need a Suburban. An all-black one with tinted windows. We'll be rolling around Flagler like we're—"

"Part of a drug cartel?" Bodhi chimes in. "Why didn't you guys just drive yourself?"

"Because we're on a secret mission!" Kennedy excitedly announces as she tries to make herself comfortable on Beck's lap. "We can't show up in three different cars when we're on a secret mission. It will blow our cover."

Bodhi looks over at me and rolls his eyes. I give him a reassuring smile, and turn to face the others in the backseat. "I agree we need a bigger vehicle, but stop complaining or you walk your asses to High Jackers."

"Which actually isn't that far," Beck points out as we pull into the parking lot.

Luna is there to greet us, and I immediately pull her in for a hug. I don't let go, even as she starts walking us toward the table she secured. Don't get me wrong, I love being in school with the guys and Kennedy, but Luna just gets me. She calms me. She's the female version of Bodhi.

"Rough day?" she whispers in my ear.

"I wish you were there with us."

"I love you, too," she smiles. "So, Ethan," she pushes him in the arm. "I hear you're the reason we're here?"

"That is correct, Aunt Luna," he grins. "Spied on my dad, overheard his phone conversation, and here we are, ready to lay our eyes on Henry Channing."

She kisses the top of his head. "Well, that deserves a feast," she points to the table, where numerous plates of food sit.

"*Yes!*" he quietly cries out, throwing himself down and immediately diving in.

Luna looks at the rest of us. "Figured I'd treat him the way I treat you, Coop. Food, just feed him to keep him happy."

Coop walks over to her and places a soft kiss on her lips. It makes my heart jump in my chest. "I wish you were at school with all of us," he says to her.

"Wow," Luna smirks. "Really feeling the love today."

"We sort of fall apart when we aren't all together," Kennedy honestly tells her.

"We do," I agree. "I'm starting to think Bodhi has it all right. We just need to leave Flagler. Sail off into the sunset, all six of us."

"Seven of us," Ethan mumbles from the table.

"Seven of us," I can't help but laugh.

Bodhi tugs on my hand and swings it playfully next to him. "I'm ready whenever you all are. Imagine all of us, on some island. Surfing, fishing, boating every day, away from all the shit here ..."

"What about our family?" Luna quietly asks.

Bodhi gives it some thought. "You guys *are* my family, so I guess I'm the only one that question doesn't apply to."

"You'd miss Calvin," I remind him.

"I *would* miss Calvin, but something tells me he'd be fine going with us."

"Plane!" Coop shouts out, pointing to the sky.

We all run over to the chain-linked fence to watch as a plane makes its way to the small runway.

"That's not him," Ethan coolly states. "Relax. I'll let you know when I see him."

"Look what just pulled up," Kennedy whispers, nodding further down the runway. A black Suburban has just arrived. Tinted windows, no way to tell who's inside.

"See!" Coop mutters under his breath. "Look at how fucking cool we'd be. Pimping around town in that monster."

Luna quickly pulls out binoculars from her pocket. "I can't see anything," she says, handing them out to me. "You try."

I push them up against my eyes, and lean into the chain-linked fence, but she wasn't lying. It's impossible to see who's driving the Suburban. "You're right. I can't see—"

"What in the *hell* are you guys doing here?!" a familiar voice roars out behind us. We all spin around and see my dad standing there, looking beyond pissed.

"Shit," Bodhi mumbles under his breath.

"Shit is right!" my dad yells out. "I expected this from you Eva, but Bodhi ... why in the hell are you allowing her to put herself in danger like this?!"

"Don't talk about me like I'm not here," I angrily respond back. "This was my idea, not Bodhi's—"

"Of course it was," my dad says through clenched teeth. "I thought we had an understanding here, the three of us, that you two stop searching for Henry Channing and let me handle it. And you all!" he points to our friends. "You guys have a death wish or something?!"

They awkwardly look away.

"Yo, Mr. Calloway," Ethan says from the table, wiping his greasy hands on a napkin. "She was going to call you. That was the plan, right? If Henry does indeed walk off my dad's plane, Eva was going to call you."

"You were?" my dad asks me.

"I was."

His face calms down. "I can't protect you if you throw yourself right in Henry's path on purpose."

"It's not like we were going to run out to the runway and say hi to him," I sarcastically reply. "I just wanted to see him. I just wanted to know that it's really him, that's he's back. Then I was going to call you. Even though I don't know why ..."

"Why are *you* here?" Bodhi suddenly asks him. "How did you know to come here?"

I put my hands on my hips. "Yeah! How the hell did you know this was happening?"

"Because I took your advice last month and went to Mark Granger."

Ethan chokes on his food. "You—you went to my *dad*?"

"Your dad is a good guy, mixed up with the wrong people—"

"Is this all a setup?!" Ethan then worriedly asks.

My dad quickly shakes his head. "No, not at all. I convinced your dad to call me if he heard from Henry. I got the phone call this morning—"

"My dad is now working for you?" Ethan asks, shocked.

305

"I wouldn't use the word working; helping me is a better term."

Ethan stands from his seat and stares straight at my dad. "What's in it for him?"

I can tell my dad's getting frustrated. "Knowing the day is coming where he won't be associated with Henry Channing anymore. Knowing that I'm not going to do anything about the fact he almost assisted in the kidnapping of my daughter."

Ethan points at my dad. "Smart move there, sir." But then he narrows his eyes. "Something's not clicking. Why aren't the police here? Isn't that your goal? To get Henry behind bars? Why didn't you call them? If my dad is *helping* you, I'm sure you could have convinced the police his innocence in bringing Henry back to Flagler. So that's not it ... why didn't you alert the police department that Henry might be coming back?"

I slowly move behind Ethan, bringing my hands to his shoulders. "Yeah Dad, why didn't you call the police?"

My dad carefully sits himself down in a chair. "You kids need to understand something," he bluntly remarks. "Things in Flagler aren't picture perfect. I've been working alongside Henry for over a decade. There are also numerous people in this town who have worked alongside Henry too—"

"You don't trust the police," Bodhi interrupts him.

"I trust the police ... I don't trust a few people in the department. Henry needs to be turned over to the right people, and I'm not sure who that is right now."

"Do you trust Holden?" I ask him.

"I want to trust Holden," he nods his head. "But something about him keeps nagging at me."

Ethan suddenly moves over to the fence, pointing through the chains at an airplane approaching. "He's here. That's my dad."

We all rush over, staying out of view of the black Suburban that's sitting on the runway.

"What happens when Henry walks off that plane?" Bodhi whispers. "We pretend we didn't see him and act like life is normal?"

"Your life has never been normal," my dad swiftly responds. "You guys are going to stay the hell out of trouble, and let me figure this out. Now, stay down!" he pushes at us just as the plane lands.

We watch as it crawls down the runway, stopping a few hundred feet away from the Suburban. The door on the airplane immediately opens, and Henry fucking Channing steps right out. He's in a baggy sweatshirt, holey jeans, and he looks so disheveled, I'm finding it hard to believe this is the same guy who used to be so put together and seamless every day.

"Son of a bitch needs a haircut," Coop mumbles.

"Maybe that's a disguise?" Beck grunts.

Bodhi laughs under his breath. "He plays the role of a homeless bum really well."

I look further down the runway, to the Suburban, just in time to see the driver open the door and step out. No one else has seen this yet, as they're all too wrapped up with Henry Channing's wild appearance. Seeing the driver takes my breath away, but then again, I totally expected this.

"Uh, Dad," I tug on the sleeve of his shirt. "That nagging feeling you had?" I then point to the Suburban, and everyone turns to watch as Henry Channing approaches, smiles, and shakes hands with the driver.

The beaming red hair is a dead giveaway. Holden. The driver of the Suburban is Holden.

chapter thirty-four

Bodhi — that night

Eva?" I whisper her name into the darkness of my mom's studio. "Are you sleeping?"

She rolls over to face me. "No. I can't sleep."

"We need to leave Flagler," I seriously say. "I've been lying here thinking about it, and it's the only thing we can do. We need to leave. I have more than enough money to keep us afloat until I have access to my trust fund—"

"Bodhi—"

"No Eva! I'm serious! Why are we staying here? So Henry Channing can come after us? So Holden can lead him right to us while pretending to be on our side?"

She doesn't say anything, just stares at me as the moonlight shining in through the windows reflect off her eyes in an eerie way.

"Eva, we can't stay here."

"I can't leave my family, Bodhi. I can't leave my mom, and my brothers—"

"Everyone can go with us."

She shakes her head, and I wait for her to start arguing with me, but instead she starts crying.

"Babe?"

"We *should* leave!" she cries out. "We really should! But what's that going to do? He's here for a reason, and if that reason is *us*, he's always going to find us!"

I pull her closer to me, her tears dripping onto my bare chest. "We'll figure out something," I try to reassure her, completely changing my mind. "We'll stay here and figure out who to trust."

"We can't even trust the police," she mumbles against my skin.

"We can trust your dad, right?"

She lifts her head from my chest, wiping at her eyes as she asks, "Do you know how crazy that sounds? We can trust my *dad*? I've never trusted my dad! I've hated my dad since I was a little kid! All the lies and the secrets, and now I'm supposed to put all my trust in *him*?! The only person I trust is you ... and the four wasted people sleeping downstairs!"

"I trust Calvin, and your mom—"

"So do I! But they've lied to us, too! You tell me one person, besides our friends, who hasn't lied to us or kept shit from us."

"Calvin? I mean, I know he didn't tell me shit about my dad, but he didn't know about anything else."

I can tell she's thinking about what I just said. "You're right. But he also knew about you for years and never did anything about it."

"I'm not holding that against him—"

"Why are we arguing about this!" she sits up and asks.

I lean my back up against the headboard and pull at her hand, but she doesn't move. She just sits there, looking frustrated, and angry, and scared. Exactly how I feel. I pull her hand again, harder, and this time she moves right into my arms. "We aren't arguing," I softly say.

"Do you really trust my mom?"

"I always have."

"And Calvin?"

"I trust him, too."

"My dad? Do you really think we can trust him? Porter told me I could."

"Porter?" I give her a disgusted look. "When did you talk to Porter again?"

She frowns. "This was before he left for Charleston. He told me I could trust my dad, him, and *you*."

"Me? He seriously said that?"

"Yeah, he did."

"Porter Channing is the most bipolar person I've ever met. Did he forget about the time he punched me in my face—"

"I think he realizes you're not his enemy."

"I think he's still madly in love with you."

"I think you need to stop being jealous of someone who isn't even in the same state as us anymore."

Silence. I can hear myself breathing. "I'm not jealous," I finally say. "I just hate that he's still a part of your life. That he's done things with you that only I should have done with you."

"That's called jealousy," she makes clear. "And what I did with Porter is *nothing* compared to what I've done with you. He has never made me feel the way you have. But he's always going to be part of my past, and your past," she pushes me in the chest. "You guys used to run around in diapers together, remember?"

"Don't remind me," I grumble. "You going to tell him that his dad's back?"

She shakes her head. "Why? So he can tell Holden? And then Holden will question how he found out? My dad said not to tell anyone. My dad said he needs to figure out what Holden is doing."

"So you *do* trust your dad?"

She growls into my chest. "I don't know. I want to, but I don't know if I ever really will. There's just too much ..."

Her head pushes into my ribs and I scooch down further onto the bed, keeping her in my arms as I lie my head back on my pillow. I give the side of her head a kiss and say, "I think trusting your dad might be the only thing we can do right now."

I can hear her sigh. "I really hope this doesn't blow up in our faces."

"Sunday dinner, let's see what happens when he shows up for dinner on Sunday. What he figures out before then. And until dinner, we stay just like this. You in my arms, forgetting about all the other shit, lost in our own world."

She leans up and gives my lips a tender kiss. "How'd you know that's my most favorite place to be?"

"WHEN IT GETS cold outside, can we still surf?" Rowan asks me.

I join him at the kitchen table, placing myself down next to Eva. "Of course! I have wetsuits. We can surf all year."

"You have wetsuits that will fit them?" Eva asks.

I nod my head. "I have a collection stored somewhere from when Coop and I were little. Hey!" I turn to Rowan and Miles.

"Don't you guys have a birthday coming up soon?"

They both nod their heads with excitement. "Will you come to Legoland with us?" Miles questions.

Eva lets out a groan. "My mom and dad are taking them to Legoland for the weekend of their birthday." She turns her mouth to my ear. "Trust me when I say, there is nothing for us to do there. Please say no."

I kiss her cheek. "Let me think about it," I say to the boys.

"Think about what?" Mrs. Calloway asks, walking into the kitchen.

"Legoland," Eva grimaces.

"Boys, Bodhi and Eva do not have to go to Legoland with us," she laughs.

Mr. Calloway appears from the foyer. "I think it'd be fun."

"I think you need to look up the definition of fun," Eva snidely remarks.

Mrs. Calloway loudly places a platter of food on the table. "Let's eat," she demands.

Dinner is pretty quiet. The boys talk about all the rides at Legoland, Eva and I briefly talk about school, and her parents just sit there and listen. These Sunday dinners have become a normal part of our week now, but tonight something seems off, and I can't put my finger on what it is. When dinner is over, Mrs. Calloway hands the boys their tablets and tells them she downloaded new games, but they can only play them in their rooms. As they rush away, Eva gives me a worried look.

"Are we in trouble?" she asks her parents.

"No," her mom shakes her head. "Why would you be? It's not like you two have been doing anything wrong, like sneaking into Eva's bedroom every night, right?"

Shit.

"It's not every night," Eva replies in a pissed off tone. "And if you and Calvin knew, why didn't you confront us?"

"We're sorry," I quickly blurt out. "We won't—"

"I don't care that you've been doing that," Mrs. Calloway cuts me off.

"I care," Mr. Calloway adds.

I can't meet his gaze.

"You don't care?" Eva repeats to her mom.

"I *care*," she stresses. "I care enough to know that you don't have nightmares when Bodhi stays over. I care enough to know that when I see you in the kitchen on the mornings after he sneaks back to Calvin's, you look like you actually slept for more than an hour. I care that on those mornings, I also see you eat breakfast. I care enough that I haven't said anything to either of you."

Eva looks down at her hands and mutters, "I have a hard time sleeping by myself."

"We're sorry," I say again. I can feel the heat on my face as I finally look at her parents. "We'll stop. We'll just—"

"Oh, Bodhi," Mrs. Calloway actually laughs as she says my name. "If I had a problem with it, I would have told you two to quit it weeks ago. You are the sole reason my daughter smiles, and if you both need each other so that you can sleep soundly at night, I'm okay with that."

I look straight at Mr. Calloway.

"I'm okay with that, too," he raises his eyes. "But we do have a small problem with the situation."

"What's that?" Eva asks.

Mrs. Calloway points at us. "You two can't be walking between houses in the middle of the night now that Henry Channing is back."

"Dad told you?" Eva asks.

"I'm not keeping secrets from your mom anymore."

Eva grunts. "Took you long enough."

"I thought we weren't keeping secrets from each other anymore either, Eva," Mrs. Calloway says with a tone.

Eva leans her body into the table, a telltale sign she's getting pissed off. "One, Henry Channing literally showed up two days ago. I haven't been home all weekend! I've been hiding at Bodhi's avoiding life because I'm so sick of all of this! And two, what am I supposed to do when I have one parent wanting to know everything, and the other parent telling me not to say anything?!"

"That won't happen anymore," her dad bluntly remarks.

"Oh yeah?" Eva hisses. "Why is that? You finally grow some—"

I slam my hand over Eva's mouth and pull her body into my

312

chest. "Before this escalates into another screaming match, I'll speak for both of us and say that it's very hard to know what the right thing to do is anymore." I cautiously remove my hand. "It's getting a little out of control, trying to respect both of you, when you both want us to do something different."

"There can't be anymore secrets between the four of us," Mrs. Calloway makes clear. "We are done living like that, and we won't be living like that anymore, agreed?"

"Yes," Eva and I reply.

"No more sneaking around," she continues. "Drive over here, Bodhi. Don't be walking through that path in the middle of the night."

"I won't," I instantly agree. "I promise."

"Is there anything you two need to share that we don't already know?" Mr. Calloway questions.

I can feel Eva laugh under her breath. "Do you need specific details on everything Bodhi and I have ever done—"

"No!" her parents shout in unison.

I bury my head into Eva's back. This is turning into one hell of a Sunday dinner.

"Is there anything you two need to share with *us*?" Eva inquires.

"Yes," her dad immediately replies. I lift my head up, knowing my face is still bright red with embarrassment. "We need to talk about that year ... that year I was away? The year you and your mom lived with Calvin again. I don't want you questioning my trust anymore, and we think telling you—"

"When you say *we*, do you mean Mom already knows what you're going to say?"

"I do," Mrs. Calloway nods. "And I don't think it's going to surprise either one of you."

Eva rolls her eyes. "Well, it's nice to know you two are a united front for once."

I squeeze her side. "Will you excuse us for a minute?" I say to her parents, and then I tug Eva up by the hand and pull her into the foyer with me. "Eva!" I cry out her name in desperation. "Your parents just told us they know I've been sneaking into your room at night, and they're cool with it! They're trying to work out their issues by not lying to each other anymore, and you're giving them an attitude. *This* is what we wanted! We wanted reasons to trust them, and they're trying to tell us these reasons, and you're just being cold and sarcastic!"

"Wow," she looks taken aback and leans up against the wall, folding her arms across her chest. "Never thought I'd see the day you side with my parents."

"I'm not siding with them, Eva!" I hurriedly whisper. "I'm giving them a chance!"

She looks around the foyer, her eyes go right to the small table filled with picture frames. She then looks back at me and says, "This spot right here, this is the exact spot my dad told me, just months ago, that I was ruining my life over some fucking teen romance with *you*. But sure, let's give him a chance."

She turns to walk back to her parents, but I grab her arm, swinging her up against the staircase, away from the archway to the kitchen. I then forcefully press my lips against hers, my hands desperately pulling her body into mine. She returns the kiss, her mouth starts to open further, but then her hands push at my chest and she breaks us apart.

"What the hell was that?!" she asks under her breath.

"*That* was a kiss. And I want to be able to kiss you like that every single day for the rest of my life. And if the only way I'm going to be able to do that is to trust your parents right now so that neither one of us ends up in the back of a fucking ambulance again with our hearts not beating, then I'm going to give them a chance to explain themselves, okay?"

I know I've gotten through to her. I can see it in her eyes, but she still leaves me in limbo, waiting a minute to respond. Her finger suddenly runs along my mouth, and then her lips replace her finger. It's small and short, but perfect.

"Okay," she then says. "I'm doing this for *us*, not for him." She then walks back into the kitchen.

Both her parents watch us as we sit back down. They've opened a bottle of wine, which is never a good sign. "Everything okay?" Mrs. Calloway worriedly asks.

"Yep," I reply. "We're good." I throw my arm around Eva's

shoulder, placing my hand in hers under the table. I give it a squeeze and rub my thumb along her fingers, silently reminding her to stay calm.

"That year?" she questions her dad. "The year I don't even really remember?"

"You were four," her dad says. "And Henry Channing's wife disappeared with Porter."

"This is about *Porter*?!" I shout out. So much for staying calm.

"Why does that surprise you?" Eva mutters. "Where'd they go?"

"That was the big question. Henry was livid, no warning at all. I mean, I'm sure she had asked for a divorce, I'm sure Henry refused. One morning he woke up, and Olivia and Porter had disappeared in the middle of the night."

"Good for her," Eva declares. "Can you imagine being married to that piece of shit? What does this have to do with that year, though? What does that have to do with us?"

Mrs. Calloway picks up her wine glass, takes a small sip and then asks, "Bodhi? You knew that your mom was friends with Olivia Channing, right?"

I nod my head.

"Henry immediately put the blame on your mom," Mr. Calloway tells me. "He thought if anybody knew where Olivia and Porter were, she did. He was out of control, demanding she tell him where they were. She insisted she didn't know."

"Did she?" I ask.

"Probably. But she never cracked."

"Obviously, they were found," Eva suddenly says. "Let me guess, she went and stayed with her twin sister in California? Sienna? Who found them?"

"I did," Mr. Calloway confirms. "Not in California. Sienna's been missing for decades. That year that you and your mom lived with Calvin and Rose, I was searching for Olivia and Porter."

Eva leans back into my body. "You're the reason Porter ended up moving in with his dad?"

"I am. After they were found, Henry was going to press charges, kidnapping charges. He was going to send Olivia to jail, and he would have, without a doubt. I convinced him to let her go, but he

315

would only do that if he had full custody of Porter, and if she broke all contact with him."

Eva starts shaking her head. "You took Porter away from his loving, stable mother, and shoved him right into the hands of the scummiest person on Earth? Why would you do that? Why did you even go find them?"

"Henry knows exactly what to do to get what he wants. He knows who to threaten, who to scare. I had four people I was trying to protect, you and your mom, and Bodhi and Lenora. I had to find them to protect you guys."

"Is that why we moved in with Calvin?" Eva asks.

"Your father actually tried to convince me to move back home with my parents, but I stubbornly didn't want to leave Flagler," Mrs. Calloway tells her.

"I didn't want you two staying here alone while I was constantly gone—"

"You jeopardized your marriage and your family, for Henry Channing?" I ask, appalled. "You lied and made it seem like you were possibly heading to jail, and you were on the verge of losing your house, all because Henry Channing controlled you?"

I can see the stress on his face. "I had no choice—"

"You always have a choice," I calmly state. "You just didn't make the right one."

Mr. Calloway picks up his wine glass and waves it in front of me. "And what would you have done in my shoes?"

Without hesitating, I reply, "I would have packed up my family, and my mom and me. I would have left Olivia and Porter alone, and I would have gotten the hell out of Flagler, after telling the police every little thing I could about Henry Channing. I would have never put my marriage and my relationship with my child on the line for that man, even if it ended up killing me. You realize you not only ruined your life by doing this, but also Olivia and Porter's?"

He looks down at the table, ashamed. "I know."

"And what about Eva?" I continue. "Your daughter? You were more worried about keeping Porter safe from his dad than what she was going through? That's why you insisted she be with him, right? You were trying to make up for being the reason why Porter was even *in* that house."

He doesn't say anything.

"And when you realized Eva and I knew each other?" I keep going. "You kept us apart because of Henry. Because you were once again controlled by him and your fear of what he would do? But all you had to do was turn him in, give the police a reason to arrest him. You had those reasons, and you could have done that years ago. Henry's gone, Eva's happy, I'm happy, Porter goes and lives with his mom. I won't even bring up *my* mom and grandparents. But instead, you ruined everyone's lives, as you sat there and just let it all happen."

I can tell Eva's crying, and I bring her hand out from under the table and give it a kiss. "I'm okay," she softly responds. "I'm fine."

I look back at her parents, her mom just sitting there staring down at her wine glass, her dad looking beyond distraught. I'm not finished, though. I need to make myself clear to this man, that he no longer has a say in how Eva lives her life. "My mom, your wife, Eva, me, Olivia, Porter, Kenneth, Annie, Owen, even Calvin. These are all the people whose lives you've screwed over by not doing the right thing. You had so many chances to end this all, and maybe you're trying to make up for that now. But I will *not* let you be the reason Eva cries anymore. I will *not* let you ruin our future together when I know how perfect it can be. So, tell me Mr. Calloway, tell me why I'm sitting here right now, asking myself if I should trust you, when just a few months ago *you* were the reason the girl I love wanted to die?"

A sound leaves Mrs. Calloway's mouth, one I never want to hear again. The wail of a mother who has just grasped how close she was to losing her daughter. "We can't do this anymore!" she cries out. "*You!*" she points to her husband. "You can't do this anymore!"

"I know," he quickly agrees. "I know. It has to end. I'm trying."

"Turn him in!" she shouts. "Tell the police where he is—"

"I don't know where he is—"

"Then *find* him!"

"I will! I'll find out where he is, who's working for him, why he's here, exactly who I can trust—"

"And what are we supposed to do while you do that?" Eva's quiet voice asks.

Mr. Calloway takes a deep breath. "Trust me."

She counters with, "Why should we?"

He looks right at me before answering her. "Because one day you'll leave this house, and you'll marry Bodhi, and I will not let the mistakes I made in the past be the reason I'm not welcomed in the life that you two create together in the future."

Goddamn. The son of bitch actually listened to me in the hospital waiting room.

I can sense Eva's crying again. I can feel it through her back. I can hear it in her voice as she boldly responds with, "Don't make me regret this."

He leans forward, grabbing her hand and giving her a reassuring smile. "You won't regret it, honey. I'll fix this, all of it. I promise."

Eva pulls her hand away from his. "How are you going to fix over a decade of mistakes?"

"I've thought about it," he tells us. "All weekend. How to put an end to this. I met with Holden—"

"What?!" Eva cries out. "But we saw him! We saw him with Henry—"

"He's undercover, Eva," Mr. Calloway calmly states. "Trust me when I say he's doing his job."

"How do you know he's not lying to you?" I ask. "How do we know he's not just telling you that because you caught him with Henry?"

"I don't," he truthfully answers.

Eva throws her hands up in the air.

"Did he tell you where Henry is?" I cautiously ask.

"No."

"Why isn't he arresting him?" I continue.

"Holden's building a case against not just Henry, but numerous other people in Flagler. He's just buying some time, gaining Henry's trust—"

"This is bullshit," Eva says through clenched teeth. She pushes away from me and stands. "Just for the record, this is not me storming off in a fit of rage. This is me, just deciding I don't want to hear anymore. If you think trusting Holden is what we need to do, fine. If you think Bodhi and I should trust you, fine. But I'm done listening to how there is yet someone else pretending to be pals with Henry Channing. Arrest the bastard whenever the time is right, but please, can I just not be involved with the day-to-day life of Henry Channing anymore?"

"Of course, Eva."

"Holden knows where he is?" she asks her dad.

"Yes."

"And you trust Holden?"

"I do. I didn't, but I do now."

Her shoulders shrug. "Then I'm done here."

She walks out of the kitchen, leaving me sitting there with her parents. I go to stand, but Mrs. Calloway shakes her head. "Let me," she says.

Wide-eyed, I lower myself back down into my chair, watching her follow after Eva. I slowly bring my eyes to Mr. Calloway. He's staring at me, almost like he's seeing me for the very first time.

"That picture you and Eva found, of your dad and us, I saved it for you."

"What the hell for?"

"Because I didn't know if you'd ever see him, your dad. I didn't know he was Calvin's son that day. I didn't make the connection until Owen did, so many years later. I took that picture and hid it, because I thought at some point, you deserved to see who he was."

"Do you want me to thank you for that?"

He lets out a chuckle. "No. I don't. You know, on the boat back to Flagler, your mom gave you to me for a few minutes," he then tells me. "She wouldn't let anyone touch you, she was very protective ... scared, I think."

"Why are you telling me this?"

"I watched her with you. How she could always calm you down when you were upset, how she would stare at you while you were sleeping. It was getting late, and she wanted to make you a bed, she asked me to hold you for a moment. You fell asleep on my chest, exactly like Eva always did. It was right then I realized I would do anything for her, for Eva, just like your mom was doing for you. But

I screwed up, Bodhi. All these years of doing the wrong thing—"

"I don't think you ever realized—"

"I never thought of how my choices would eventually hurt my family so badly. Hurt Eva the way they did." He looks down at his wine glass and picks it up, twirling it in his hand so the wine sloshes around on the inside. "I don't expect to ever have a perfect relationship with her. I barely have a year left before she leaves this house, but I'll be damned if I spend that year screwing up her life even more. I need you to do me a favor."

"Me?" I question.

"You."

"Okay. What is it?"

"Holden, he has a plan. And I can't tell you what that is, because it needs to look real. I'm part of it, and I'm trusting him, trusting him that this will work. But there's this little sliver of me that knows you can't ever fully trust someone." He takes a sip of his wine, and then gently places the glass back down on the table. "If it doesn't go the way I hope, I need you to promise me that you'll take care of Eva—"

"What?!" I exclaim under my breath.

"Audrey and the boys, they'll have her parents, and Calvin. But Eva, you're the only one she trusts. The only one she lets love her. Please just promise me that you'll always be there for her—"

"I promise," I nod my head. "I will. I'll take care of her, but there's got to be something else—"

"This is it," he calmly states. "And if this goes the way I hope, Henry Channing will be put away for a very long time."

"And if it doesn't?"

"Then you'll be there, right? For her?"

"I'll be there for *all* of them," I make clear. "Not just Eva."

Mr. Calloway grins as he stands, pushing his chair hard under the table. "You know, I don't have too many accomplishments in my adult life that I'm proud of. Marrying Audrey is one, my kids are another. I always thought that was it. My wife, my kids ... because even without me being the husband and father I should have been, they've turned out pretty damn perfect. But there's actually another thing in my life that I can say I'm proud of. Just one other. You."

I hear myself catch my breath. It's loud, and obnoxious, but he doesn't seem to notice.

"I shouldn't have kept you and Eva apart when I realized how close you two were," he continues. "I'm sorry I couldn't see the bigger picture then. All those years wasted. Losing Eva in the process. But you ... this all started to protect your mom, and you. And had I not done that ... Eva would have never found you. There's a reason why our lives crossed paths, and I really do think it's because you were always supposed to be a part of mine, a part of my family, *in* my family. You," he gives me a small salute with his fingers, "you are the only other thing in my life I'm proud of." And without another word, he turns and walks away.

chapter thirty-five

Eva – about a week later

ow do you make it look so perfect?" Callie asks me, hovering over my computer in the photography room.

"Lots of practice, and a good photography teacher," I laugh, closing out of the editing program I was showing her.

She groans. "I'm not going to tell my dad you said that."

The bell rings, signaling the end of the day. "Why don't we print these off, and over the weekend you can use your dad's programs to try some different filters on them."

She looks up at the clock. "Sure, but I might miss my bus."

"That's okay, Bodhi and I can take you home—"

"Leave it to Eva and Bodhi to be the picture-perfect role models," Hayes chimes in, leaning against my chair. His face is just a couple inches away from my own. "Riding off together on their magical unicorn every day. If I miss *my* bus, can you give me a ride all the way home, too?"

I elbow him in the cheek. "You're vile. And I wouldn't give you a ride home if I was the last person in the world with a car, and the entire school grounds were on fire." I then push my chair out, knocking him back a little as I go to stand. I walk over to the printer, waiting for Callie's pictures to shoot out.

"Admit it, Eva," Hayes continues, swinging his bookbag over his shoulder. "You love me."

"I would love it if you just disappeared."

He starts laughing, lingering in the doorway of the photography room. "Have an amazing weekend, ladies," he bows. "Don't get in too much trouble." He then disappears into the hallway.

I let out a nauseated groan.

"He makes my body cringe," Callie then quietly says.

I look up at her, putting my hand on her arm. "You and me both. Stay away from him."

"Stay away from who?" I hear Bodhi's voice ask as he walks in with Ethan trailing behind.

"Hayes," I reply, grabbing Callie's first photo that comes out of the printer.

Bodhi places a quick kiss on my cheek. "Ah. Yes, definitely stay away from him."

"My cousin is a dumbass," Ethan bluntly says.

"Your cousin?" Callie's face looks alarmed.

Ethan's eyes dart to her, as if he just noticed she was there. "Uh, yeah. My cousin. Hayes. He's my cousin, like once removed or something. And he's a righteous dumbass."

Callie starts laughing, which only makes Ethan's face turn bright red. "You're a freshman, too, right?" she asks. "I think we're in the same history and math classes."

"You don't say?" Bodhi smirks, nudging Ethan in the arm.

Ethan shoves Bodhi in his side. "I think you're right," he nods to Callie.

"We're about done here," I let the boys know. "I told Callie we'd take her home."

Bodhi nudges Ethan in his arm again. "I told Ethan we'd take him home, too."

"I won a bet," Ethan makes known. "With Bodhi. If I got anything higher than a C on my French vocab test, Bodhi said you two would drive me home for a week."

I raise my eyes at him. "What'd you get?"

"B plus, baby!"

I ruffle the top of his way too shaggy hair. "Nice job. Who'd you pay to cheat off of?"

He grabs his chest. "Mom! You're honestly implying that I cheated?! I studied my ass off for an entire night! Alone, in my room, as life went on sadly without me."

"I can help you with French," Callie suddenly says. "I'm actually in honors French. My mom's parents, they're French. I've spent every summer in France since I was a baby. If you need any help, just ask."

"Uh—well, yeah," Ethan stammers. "That'd be great."

Bodhi leans in and whispers in my ear. "Are we playing matchmakers?"

"They're so cute and innocent—"

"I knew I was in love with you at fourteen."

I squeeze his side. "Don't embarrass them!"

We take Callie home first. She lives close to Bodhi, her house being only a few blocks away from his.

"You have the beach as your front yard, too," Bodhi says as we pull into her driveway.

"Best part about living in Flagler," she smiles, opening the door. "Having the beach to go to whenever I want. Thanks for the ride. See you guys on Monday!" She hops out of the jeep, and Ethan slowly lowers his head into his lap as we turn back onto A1A.

"You all right there?" Bodhi asks him.

"I don't know," he honestly answers. "I feel weird on the inside. Like my body is suddenly made out of jello?"

I turn around to face him. "Ethan, I think you like her."

"Nope," he calmly states. "I refuse. Girls are nothing but trouble. I mean, look at Charlotte, and you," he points at me.

Bodhi stifles a laugh as I hit his arm with my phone. "You're both hilarious."

"Actually, can I retract what I just said?" Ethan then questions. "You're more trouble when you're pissed off. Charlotte is nothing but trouble, and you're a delightful young lady that never does anything bad, unless someone wrongs you."

I look at him through the rearview mirror. "I'd stop while you're ahead."

"Noted," he nods. "You guys have any plans this weekend? Shacking up at Bodhi's? Searching for Henry? Risking your life to better Flagler?"

"*Do* we have any plans this weekend?" Bodhi asks me.

"No. Dinner at my house on Sunday ... that's about it."

"Shacking up at Bodhi's it is," Ethan laughs under his breath.

Bodhi shakes his head. "Dude."

"Kool Beenz!" I suddenly shout as I see the sign up ahead. "Can we get some coffee? Ethan, if you stop talking for the rest of the ride home, we'll buy you something."

"For real?"

"Yes, but you have to stay silent the entire ride back, or you forfeit this bet you and Bodhi made."

"Damn. That's going to be hard, but I think if I have my mouth occupied with one of their delicious smoothies, I can make it happen."

Bodhi pulls the jeep around the back. "I don't think even a smoothie will keep you quiet. Duct tape maybe."

We start walking to the entrance. "Hayes duct taped my mouth shut once," Ethan tells us. "Hurt like a bitch when I finally pulled it off. Think I lost a couple layers of skin."

Bodhi pulls the door open, "Hayes just keeps getting better and better."

"Eva!" I hear a familiar voice shout out my name. I walk a little further in, past the shadows that linger around the entrance. There, standing in front of the cash register, are Jackie and Graham Walker. We haven't seen Graham since that horrible dinner, but he and Bodhi text each other frequently. And although we made promises to go see Jackie, life got in the way and we never made it back to the hospital.

"My favorite nurse ever," I smile at her.

"Bodhi! Of course you'd be right behind her," Jackie continues. "Get over here, you two." She pulls at us, wrapping us up in an awkward hug while everyone sitting in Kool Beenz watches.

"Mom, you're embarrassing them," Graham calmly states.

"Embarrassing?" she cries out. "This is nothing. Ask them details about their five days spent with me." She pulls out of the hug and stands there, staring at me. "You, you look amazing."

"All healed," I declare.

"I had no doubt you'd heal up perfectly. Bodhi, you still glued to her side?"

Ethan lets out a grunt. "I can answer that question. Yes."

I give Ethan's shoulder a pinch. "This is—"

"Ethan Granger?" Graham gives him a curious look.

Ethan's face turns red. "Yeah."

"You two know each other?" I question.

Graham gives Ethan a wink. "Doesn't everyone know everyone in Flagler? How do you guys know each other?"

"Long story," I declare.

"Can't shake these two off," Ethan sneers. "They love me."

Graham starts laughing. "You could do worse."

Jackie's eyes light up. "Hey! What are you two doing tomorrow—"

"No!" Graham shakes his head. "Bodhi and Eva do not—"

She steps hard on his foot and he yelps. "We're having our annual cocktail clam bake and I would *love* for you two to stop by. Please tell me you can make it for a little bit?"

I glance over at Bodhi. "Uh, we don't have any plans—"

"We'll stop by," Bodhi replies. "Graham? Text me the details?"

Graham lets out a grunt as he pulls out his phone. "I'm going to apologize in advance—"

"Graham!" Jackie cries out. "Stop acting like you're still in high school and I'm forcing you to invite friends over or something. These two are practically family. I'm inviting them to our clam bake for *me*, not for you."

"Yeah, yeah," he waves her off. "Sending Bodhi the info now."

"Got it," Bodhi waves his vibrating phone in the air. "We'll be there."

"Perfect! I'm so happy we ran into you both. See you tomorrow!"

Graham follows his mom, mouthing, "I'm sorry," as he walks out the door.

"So," Ethan whistles. "Should we order?"

We move to the register. "Can I get an iced coffee with a splash of cream?" I ask.

"Make that two," Bodhi adds. "Ethan?"

"Tough decision here, but I'll go with the sweet sunrise smoothie, please."

Bodhi takes out his card to pay. "You going to tell us how you know Graham?" he asks him.

Ethan shakes his head. "Nope."

"Didn't think so," Bodhi replies.

"You two going to tell me how *you* know Graham?"

I reach for my coffee. "He was the paramedic who showed up

that night. Sort of saved my life. And his mom Jackie, she was my nurse in the hospital. His dad was my surgeon."

"Ah. That makes perfect sense."

"Still not going to tell us how you know him?" I question.

"Nope, but I am going to tell you both that you're as stupid as hell for agreeing to go to their clam bake when you know Holden will be there."

Shit. Didn't really think that one through.

Ethan keeps going, "Does he know that *you* know what he told your dad and what your dad told you?"

"Say that again?" Bodhi looks down at him and asks.

"You two just gonna sit around slugging down gross clams, pretending everything's normal? Good luck. Let's hope this isn't just some mass setup, and you know who shows up with all his Flagler homies." He then reaches over the counter for his smoothie. He takes a huge swig. "Damn that's delicious. I'll text you my address because my vow of silence starts right now." He then points to the door and heads out.

Ethan doesn't make a peep the entire drive to his house. All that's heard from the backseat is the occasional slurp. It's nice, not listening to his sarcastic comments every time Bodhi and I speak, but at the same, I miss them.

"Why are we turning down my street?" I ask Bodhi.

"That's the way the GPS is taking me?"

I turn quickly to look at Ethan. "Do you live on my goddamn street?!"

He shakes his head and remains silent, but he's grinning at the same time.

I turn forward, watching the familiar road pass by.

"Looks like we're turning," Bodhi points ahead. It's literally the only side street on this stretch of road.

"You live down here?" I turn around and ask him.

He shrugs his shoulders.

"You can speak now!" I shout. He shakes his head no. "Jesus Ethan, you could have told us all this time that you live less than a mile from me. I mean, you can walk to my house."

"Or ride a skateboard?" Bodhi mutters under his breath.

327

There's a dirt road up ahead, smack dab in between two massive palm trees. Bodhi turns down it, and we're unexpectedly driving on a tree lined path, going deeper and deeper towards the Halifax. The weeping trees branch over us like an arch. The further we go down, the darker it becomes, giving the false impression that we're driving in the middle of the night.

"Does this road ever end?" Bodhi mumbles.

Suddenly, the trees up ahead become lit with twinkling lights, and you can see that the path takes you directly to a house in the distance. It's beautiful, two stories, white with black trim, massive porch, the Halifax directly in the backyard. It's the perfect farm house smack dab in the jungle of Florida.

Bodhi parks in the driveway and turns to look at Ethan. "This is your house?"

"Yes, it is," he finally speaks. His eyes suddenly wander over to the front porch. "Ah *shit*," he grumbles.

I follow his gaze to see a woman in a skimpy white bikini, wearing thin stiletto heels. She's standing directly in a flowerbed, pruning rosebushes while drinking a beer. Her body sways as she stands there, completely oblivious to the fact we just pulled up.

"Is that your mom?" I carefully ask him.

"If I said no, would you two believe me?"

"Is she okay?"

"All depends on who you ask. I'm going to get out now. Thanks for the ride, and the smoothie. Can you please just drive away and pretend you didn't see this?"

He goes to open the door, but at the same time, his mom sways a little too hard, and trips over a cooler on the ground. She goes head first into the rosebushes, disappearing completely from our view. All three of us swing our doors open at the same time and rush over to where she is, her heels kicking in the air as she tries to regain her balance.

"Mom!" Ethan cries out. "Just stop moving!" He reaches into the bushes, trying to grab at her arm. "Shit!" he yells out in pain. "Goddamn thorns!"

"I'll grab one arm, you grab the other," Bodhi very calmly says, reaching in. He and Ethan give her arms a firm tug and pull her safely back to her feet.

She stands there, covered in little drops of blood all over her almost naked body, rocking on her heels as she looks at the three of us. "Ethan!" her eyes grow large with excitement as she focuses on him. Her sandy brown hair matches his perfectly. "Shouldn't you be at school?"

"It's after four Mom, school's done for the day."

"Friends!" she cries out, grabbing onto Bodhi and me. "You never bring friends over!" Her fingers suddenly squeeze my cheeks. "You're stunning. Are you dating my son?"

"Jesus Christ," Ethan groans.

"I'm Eva, and this is my boyfriend, Bodhi," I point to him. "You've got a few cuts we should get cleaned up. Can I help you do that?"

"God you're so sweet! Ethan never brings anyone here. Come inside! I'll get us some iced tea!" She goes to turn but almost trips again. "Damn heels," she laughs.

I loop my arm around hers, and turn my head to face Bodhi and Ethan. "I've got her—"

"Eva," Ethan looks like he's on the verge of tears. "You don't have to do this."

"I've got her," I say again. "You and Bodhi go clean up your arms."

Ethan's mom leads us in, her thin heels echoing in loud clanks as we walk through their massive ship lapped foyer. "Let's get some drinks!" she announces.

"How about we let Ethan get the drinks, and you and I go wash up a little?" I suggest.

"*Great* idea," she slurs. "My room. Ethan, you know where the kitchen is."

He waves her off, turning in the opposite direction.

"You okay?" Bodhi mouths to me.

I nod my head. "Go take care of Ethan," I quietly say back.

"What's your name again?" Ethan's mom asks, as she drunkenly stumbles us down a hallway. She trips again and knocks a few framed paintings off the wall.

"Eva."

"Eva," she repeats. "That's a *beautiful* name. Here we are!" she pushes her bedroom door open. The cathedral ceiling and floor length windows that cover the entire back wall give off the feeling of being in a church. "My bathroom," she points to a barn door, throwing herself down on her bed.

I nervously slide the door open, and I'm met with the same cathedral ceiling. Instead of floor length windows, skylights take their place and create warm streams of light all over the floor. I quickly rummage through the cabinets, grabbing cotton balls, rubbing alcohol, tweezers, and band-aids. I also pull a bathrobe off a hook next to the shower. I walk back out to see her inspecting the wounds all over her body.

"How the hell did these get here?!" she looks up at me and asks.

"Thorn bush," I reply. "Out front?"

"Oh, yeah," she sighs. "I remember now. I tripped, didn't I?"

I nod my head and dab a little rubbing alcohol on a cotton ball. "I'm going to clean these, okay? It might sting a little."

She winces as I press down on the cuts that grazed her skin, but doesn't say one single word as I remove each thorn still lodged in her body. She looks stone-faced and lost in her own world as I place a few band-aids on the deeper ones. She only moves as I gently wrap her bathrobe over her body when I finish.

She smiles up at me. "I'm glad Ethan has friends like you."

I unbuckle her heels. "He's a good kid—"

"He hates me."

"I don't think that's true," I shake my head, placing her heels in a basket of other shoes.

"Last year ... he found me, right here," she pats her bed. "I was pretty much gone. Mixed alcohol with pills. He called 9-1-1. Watched them bring me back. He's hated me since then."

"The paramedics came?"

She nods, pulling her robe tightly around her body.

Graham.

"I can't seem to stop," she sadly declares, then she lets out a little laugh. "I don't know why I'm boring you with my sappy story—"

"You're not," I smile.

"Well, aren't you the sweetest?" She lies back on one of the ten

330

pillows on her bed. "I think I need to take a nap. Can you turn the lights off?"

I look around her room. "Uh, the lights aren't on? It's the sun coming in through all the windows."

She moans into her pillow. "Damn natural light. Florida sun is worse than California's. Don't know why we live in this hell hole. But I'll stay for them. I won't lose them," she mumbles. "Not like I lost the others ..."

I wait for her to say more, but she doesn't. She has completely passed out. I take the decorative blanket from the end of her bed, cover her up, and then leave to go find Bodhi and Ethan. They're in the kitchen, silent, a bunch of pink stained wet paper towels thrown on the counter. I look up at the wooden beams that line yet again another cathedral ceiling.

"Your house is beautiful," I say to Ethan.

He gives me a small smile, and points to the foyer. "She alive?"

"She's sleeping. You guys good?"

Bodhi reaches for my hand, pulling me closer to him. He gives my temple a slow kiss before saying, "We're good. Couple thorns, but we'll survive."

Ethan brings his forehead to the counter. "I'm sorry you had to see that."

"Don't be," I rest my hand on his back. "Don't ever be ashamed, or afraid to tell us if you need help."

"I don't need help. *She* does."

"Has she gotten help?" Bodhi asks.

Ethan nods into the hard granite. "A few times. Only seems to make a difference for a couple months. She's a lost cause."

"She mentioned last year—"

Ethan's head springs up from the counter.

"That's how you know Graham, right?"

"Yep. Graham to the rescue. Did she mention anything else?" he worriedly asks.

"Just that she doesn't want to lose you ... like she lost the others?"

He rolls his eyes. "Not that ridiculous tale again."

"What did she mean?"

"My mom, she isn't exactly sane. I honestly think the only time she's been sober, was when she was pregnant with me, which she didn't realize until halfway through her pregnancy, and I was born a month early. She rarely leaves the house. She couldn't find her way around Flagler if her life depended on it."

"Your dad must really love her," Bodhi gently says. "If this has been going on for a while."

"He tries. But he's not home much, and doesn't see what I see. When she *is* sober, she paints. She has a studio above the garage. She's actually really good."

"Who are the others?" I ask again.

"Ah, yes. The soap opera tale she likes to tell. When my parents met, it was in California. My mom was out there, living life on the road, constantly high. My dad picked her up hitchhiking, drove from southern California all the way to northern California with her. Fell in love on the road trip, the rest was history. They lived there for a really long time, and then one day they just packed up and moved here."

"That's actually a beautiful love story," I say.

"*Their* story is beautiful," Ethan grunts. "But my mom comes from a bad past. She left home when she was sixteen. Had a huge falling out with her family, ran away and moved clear across the country. She had no contact with them at all. When she tried to reach out to her parents after they moved to Flagler, she found out they were dead. So was her brother. She has a sister that apparently disappeared and can't be found. She won't talk about her family at all, though. Said there's too many secrets and she could get in trouble for sharing them. I think that's why she is the way she is, to be honest. She can't handle her past and has no closure."

California. A hippy life. A dead brother. A sister she can't find. Secrets she can't share.

Are you fucking kidding me?

"Why'd they move to Flagler?" Bodhi's voice breaks my concentration. "Out of all the places they could go, what brought them here?"

He knows. He made the impossible connection, too.

Ethan laughs. "My dad's cousins ended up here, but it was my mom actually that convinced him. Though she hates it here now. Apparently, she thought her brother would be here. She was hoping to find him. To reconcile. But he had died a while ago, here in Flagler. A motorcycle accident."

That's it. Too many coincidences. It's time to ask the big question now, the one that'll open this massive floodgate of past secrets. The one that will tie Ethan to Bodhi, the one that will tie Ethan to Porter.

My heart races as I ask, "Ethan, what's your mom's name?"

"CeCe," he answers right away.

"Is that a nickname?" Bodhi questions.

Ethan nods. "Funny, I spent almost my entire life thinking her name was CeCe. It wasn't until she was in the hospital last year that I heard a doctor call her by her actual name."

Bodhi grabs my hand under the counter. "What is it?"

The name rolls out of Ethan's mouth without a care in the world. It means nothing to him, his mom's name. He doesn't know who she really is, and how her life connects to Lenora's from years and years ago. He doesn't know that *his* life now connects to Porter's. He doesn't know that the sister his mom can't find could be found with one simple phone call. He doesn't know that the brother his mom lost was the entire reason Lenora moved to Flagler. He doesn't know any of this, and we don't tell him, because this is Ethan, the fourteen-year-old kid that calls *us* Mom and Dad. The fourteen-year-old kid that I find myself wanting to protect with everything I've got.

What *was* the name that slipped out of his mouth so carefree and untroubled, as we stood in his picture-perfect kitchen?

Isn't it obvious?

Ethan's mom is Declan Ryder's sister.

Ethan's mom is Porter's aunt.

Ethan's mom is Sienna Ryder.

chapter thirty-six

Bodhi – the next day

I think we should tell him," I say, buttoning up my shirt while Eva stands in my doorway.

She walks further into my room, her tight black dress causing me to break out in a cold sweat as she moves closer to me. She reaches for my shirt, buttoning up the last few buttons while I stare down at her. "We need to make sure it's really her first."

I hold her hands in mine. "How do we do that?"

"Go see Porter?" she cringes as she says it. "Bring some pictures? Talk to his mom?"

"That's really the best option we have here?"

Her red lips form a thin line. "What if Olivia dropped off the radar on purpose? What if she doesn't want to be found? What if she doesn't want her *sister* to find her?"

"Like Kenneth and Annie?"

"Exactly," she nods.

Her hair is so straight tonight, I can't help but run my fingers through the soft strands. "Then we go see Porter, and talk to his mom."

"Okay. But we don't need to talk about Porter tonight," she smirks, pinching my sides as she leans forward and places a quick kiss on my lips. "Or Ethan. Or Henry Channing. Or anything that doesn't solely involve you and me, okay?"

"I can do that." My fingers slip under her hair, and I press them against her neck. "We can't sleep at my house tonight, can we?"

She closes her eyes and shakes her head. "Here, or my house," she then says. "My dad ..." her eyes open, the bright green stares back at me as her pupils react to the sudden light. "He kindly asks that we put a stop to that. At least until Henry's in jail."

I kiss her forehead. "Understandable. Well, you decide then. Together or alone. Here, or your house."

"Together," she immediately answers, giving me a disapproving glance that I would even consider anything different. "Definitely together. And ... here."

"Yeah?" I look over at my bed. We haven't slept in my bed together at Calvin's since before the accident.

"Would Calvin be okay with that?"

"Would Calvin be okay with what?" his voice echoes as he comes down the hall. "Woah. Where the hell are you two heading tonight? Prom?"

Eva laughs. "Cocktail clam bake, at the Walker family house."

"Your doctor? Your nurse? The paramedic?"

"Yes," she answers. "Them."

"Well, you two look extremely dapper. Should I be taking pictures?" he suddenly asks. "Make you pose by a fireplace or something?"

"That's okay," I shake my head. "Hey, tonight, when it's over, is it okay if Eva stays here with me?"

Calvin's cheeks turn red for just a brief moment. "That okay with your folks?" he points to Eva.

She gives a quick nod.

"Then it's okay with me. I'll be upfront with you both though, I'll probably call Audrey when you leave and make sure you're not lying."

"I'm not lying, Calvin," Eva replies. "But feel free to call her."

"While you're both here, I've got a question."

My heart drops. I hate questions from Calvin. They usually involve Luke, Annie or Kenneth.

"Christmas break is coming up soon," he continues.

"Not really," I mumble.

"I already asked Ma and Pop, since they're technically your legal guardians," he goes on. "And I already talked to your parents, Eva. After Christmas, what do you two think about heading to see Annie and Kenneth with me for the rest of break?"

I *knew* it.

Eva slowly turns her head in my direction, her eyes slightly bigger than normal. I know she's not going to answer Calvin. She's going to leave this decision fully in my hands.

"Can we think about it?" I choose my words carefully.

"Of course. How about we talk more over breakfast in the morning? I'll invite your parents over, Eva. We can hash out all the details?"

I let out an uncomfortable snicker. "You want a decision by the morning?"

"Passports," Calvin simply responds. "You need one, Bodhi. An updated one. I need to get the ball rolling on that—"

"We'll talk about it," Eva interrupts, reassuring me with the way her small hand rests on my lower back. "Tonight, once we're home. We'll talk about it. Bodhi and me."

"Perfect," Calvin smiles. "Now get out here so I can get some pictures of you two in front of the fireplace I've never used."

"WHAT DO YOU think Calvin's going to do with the fifty pictures he just took of us?" I ask Eva, opening the passenger door.

"Bodhi, it's adorable," she declares, climbing into her seat. "He's enjoying this. Let him have his fun."

I close her door and walk over to my side. The unpredictable heat from the early October evening makes me yank at my collar to allow some air to get under my shirt. Eva's mindlessly staring out her window at Calvin's garage as I turn the jeep on. "You okay?" I ask her.

Her face spins my way and she gives me a fake smile. "Yeah, why wouldn't I be?"

Does she not realize by now I can read every emotion on her beautiful face? "You look lost in thought."

"I'm just ... tired?"

I turn the jeep off. "We don't have to go. We can stay here and do nothing. I'm sure Calvin could cook us something to eat ..."

She kisses my cheek, and then reaches over my arm and turns the jeep back on. "Not that kind of tired. Just tired of being worried. Drive, Bodhi. We're going to be late."

I turn the jeep around in Calvin's driveway and start making my way toward the Walker house. They live right outside of Flagler, in Ormond, and from looking at the GPS, they live on the beach. Eva's back to staring out the window. She's too quiet, which puts me in a weird panic mode. I reach down and take her hand into mine. She doesn't look toward me, but I see her smile in the reflection of the window. Her fingers wrap in between mine in a way that makes me understand what she needs right this moment, is for someone to comfort her.

"I know you said tonight we don't talk about anyone but us, but do you *want* to talk?" I ask, rubbing my fingers on her knuckles.

She turns. "About ...?"

"What has you worried."

I can feel her eyes on me, but these curvy roads keep me from turning to fully look at her. "I'm worried about Ethan," is the first thing she says. "And our friends, my family, your sister, you, us—"

I quickly look at her. "Us?"

"Not *us* in the way you're thinking," she immediately says. "Relax. Us in a way where I question when the moment will come where everything is solved, all the secrets are out, we're both safe ... and just happy."

"Oh," I look over at her and smile. "You want to know when life will finally be boring for us."

"Pretty much. I mean, Calvin, tonight ... asking us to go see Annie and Kenneth. On paper it looks like you and me, heading to a tropical destination to visit your grandparents to celebrate the holidays—"

"But in actuality," I cut in, "it's you and me, heading to a tropical destination, one I've been to numerous times but was never told about. To see the grandparents I thought were dead, with the grandpa I never knew existed, with my girlfriend who was forced to stay away from me for three years."

"Nailed it," she grins.

"You want to feel normal?"

"No. Normal is too boring. I just want to feel ... calm."

I bring her hand up to my mouth and give it a kiss. "Me too, babe."

I keep her hand in mine as we drive to the Walker house,

337

rubbing that soft spot in between her thumb and index finger. Touching her always brings *me* comfort, and I can only hope my fingers moving gently along her skin does the same for her. When GPS says we're less than a mile away, her fingers wiggle their way out of mine and she brings them up to the back of my head.

"We should go see Annie and Kenneth," she nonchalantly states.

I give her a quick glance. She's staring at me. God she's beautiful. I'd say yes to anything she'd ask right now because, yet again, her beauty has put me under a spell. "We should."

Her fingers twirl around my hair. "Bodhi?"

"Hmm?"

"You're my calm."

I purposely slow down so the green light ahead of us has a chance to turn red. When it does, I gradually hit the brake and then turn to her, bringing my hand up to the back of her head. I need to kiss her, and I do, long and sweet, right there in front of the traffic light. "You're my calm, too, baby." The light turns green and I inch us forward. The Walker house should be right up here on the left.

"Holy *shit*," Eva mumbles.

Holy shit is right. Their house, or better yet, their mansion, is massive. There are numerous different men standing around in tuxedos as I turn down their driveway, camped out next to a stone security station and gate. I roll down my window as one of them walks closer to us.

"Name?" he bluntly questions.

"Bodhi and Eva," I reply.

He scrolls along the screen of an iPad. "Ah, yes. Right here. Go ahead and drive down until you see the valet." He turns and the gate automatically rises.

"What'd we get ourselves into?" I mutter to Eva, slowly creeping past the security station.

"I suddenly feel underdressed?" she looks down at herself.

More men in tuxedos are standing in the middle of the long circular driveway. One puts his hand out to stop us, like I'd actually just run him down and keep driving. I roll down the window again, and he hands me a paper tag with a number on it. "Give this to the valet at the hors d'oeuvres table when you're ready to leave. Party is around the back, just follow the path," he points to a pebble-lined walkway that seems to wrap around the house.

I unbuckle my seatbelt and step out of the jeep, quickly walking over to Eva's side, but she's already being helped out. This punk, probably not too much older than us, has her hand in his, and he holds on to it even after her feet are firmly on the ground. She gives me a concerned look as he blatantly eyes her up and down.

Fucking asshole.

"I've got it from here," I loudly say, putting my arm around her waist and tugging her closer to me.

"Oh!" he jumps. "Yes, sorry! Have a good night!" he quickly walks away.

Eva clutches on to my hand as we start walking to the path. "I hate people like that," she whispers in annoyance.

I turn my head and see that he's watching us walk away. "I can take him," I jokingly say to her, trying to lighten the mood. "Want me to go kick his ass?"

She lets out a small laugh. "Maybe on the way out. Can you take my phone?" she hands it over to me. "I promised my parents I'd answer each and every text they throw my way tonight, and I don't have a place to put it."

I slip it in my back pocket. "Stay by me tonight, okay?" I request in the most non-overprotective way possible. "I think the wealthiest people in all of Florida are probably here—"

"Bodhi," Eva stops walking and plants a small kiss on my cheek. "Get used to it. Thirty million? This is your future."

We follow the path as it curves around the side of the house. I can hear light music playing, people talking, and the smell of something delicious as the backyard comes into view. The marble patio covers the entire length of the back of their house, stretching further than my eyes can focus. Their pool has its own island, with waterfalls and a lone palm tree that sits in the middle of what looks like a lazy river. Numerous tables are placed in rows under the covered portion of the patio, with twinkling lights hidden along the vines that wrap along the pillars. Tiki torches are lit and line a sand trail that takes you right down to the ocean. None of this looks real, almost like I'm staring at some photo spread in a beachfront living magazine I would find thrown around the side tables at my dentist office.

"This is the perfect time to run," I hear a familiar voice whisper behind me. We both turn to see Graham standing there, sipping casually on what looks like a very strong martini. "You two look great."

"Thanks," Eva replies, leaning in and giving him a careful hug. He holds his martini off to the side.

"You grow up in this house?" I ask in disbelief.

He looks around, like it's the first time he's been here. "Sure did. Wealth isn't all it's cracked up to be."

"You have siblings, right?" Eva questions. "Your mom, she talked about them—"

"Two. An older brother and an older sister. He's a surgeon in New York, she's a pediatrician in Texas. I'm the outcast who didn't follow in the family footsteps—"

"Bullshit," I hear Jackie declare. She walks up right behind Graham, throwing her arm around him and causing his martini to splash out from the sides. "Don't listen to him. If it wasn't for Graham's job, half the people who show up at our hospital would already be dead."

"Mom!" he cries out, nodding his head forcefully toward Eva.

"Shit," Jackie grumbles.

"It's fine," Eva reassures them both. "It's also true," she playfully pokes Graham in his chest. "I know I'm not the only one you've saved. You really should give yourself more credit."

Jackie taps him lightly on his head. "You two are by us tonight," she says to Eva and me. "Head of the table. Not going to feed you to the sheep. Dinner's in about an hour. Until then, hors d'oeuvres," she points to a table filled with tiny small plates, and an overflowing amount of finger food. "Drinks," she points to a bar. "Don't take anything from the waiters walking around, they will gladly get you all liquored up without even questioning your age. Dance," she swivels and nods to a free-floating dance floor over a large lagoon I hadn't even noticed. "The band will play any song you request." Yes, there's even a goddamn live band. "There are Hawaiian dancers down at the beach if you want to watch. Feel free to mingle, too, but keep it in the back of your mind that most of the guests here are on their third or fourth marriage, and are always looking for the next younger upgrade—"

Graham suddenly spits out his martini, spraying it all over Dr. Walker who has just approached.

Dr. Walker takes out a napkin from his chest pocket, and wipes at his face and arms, acting like this happens all the time. "Eva, Bodhi," he warmly greets. "Pleasure to have you join us tonight."

"Thank you for having us," Eva sincerely smiles. "Your house is stunning."

He waves it off like it's a shack in a trailer park. "How are you feeling?"

"Great," she responds. "Everything healed perfectly."

He tucks the napkin back into his pocket. "Wonderful to hear. Bodhi?" he then turns to me. "All is well with you, too?"

"Yes, sir."

He nods. "Enjoy yourselves tonight, stick together, though. These people are gold diggers and probably think you two are celebrities we paid to be here."

"These people are your *colleagues*," Graham points out. "People you've known for thirty plus years!"

"Which is why I know way too much about them," Dr. Walker chuckles. "And why Jackie and I have been to all of their second and third weddings. The night is young! Let me know if you need anything," he says to Eva and me. "Or if anyone attempts to wed you to their extremely successful twenty-five-year-old that still lives at home," he winks. "Let's go mingle, Jackie."

"Have fun!" she says to us as Dr. Walker leads her away. "We'll see you in an hour!"

Eva's whole body shifts to face me and her eyes find mine. She looks alarmed, nervous, questioning why the hell we agreed to come tonight. I slowly kiss her forehead, and then wrap my arm around her waist and turn to Graham. "We should have run when you told us to," I say to him.

He grins and raises his martini at us. "At least I can drink my way through the night."

"Will Holden be here?" I calmly ask.

"Yes. And he's been warned. What happened at dinner over the summer will not happen tonight. Speak of the devil," he looks down at his phone. "I'm going to go save him from the valet. You guys run into any problems, just let out a whistle ... or a bird caw. Something annoying and loud. I'll save you."

He walks away and Eva immediately turns her body into mine, throwing her arms around my neck. "Please. Please tell me this isn't a glimpse into your future?"

"*Our* future, and fuck no. I'm perfectly content with hiding our wealth from every single person in the world, besides the people who already know about it."

"Thank god."

I place my hand behind her ear, letting those few strands of silky hair slip between the tips of my fingers. "You thinking about our future right now?"

She places a kiss on my lips. "Maybe."

"Damn high school," I groan.

"Don't wish away any minute we get to spend together. Even if it's minutes of us in high school. They still matter, and they'll still count in fifty years."

"Yes, they will," I agree. I pull her closer to me, resting my forehead on the dip of her warm shoulder. She smells delicious, like a mix of vanilla and lavender. I would love to get lost in her right now, in the way she looks and smells. "I wish I could bottle up every single second spent with you, so that I never forget any of it. Like right now, and the way you look in this dress. How it clings perfectly to your body—"

I feel her lips quickly brush against my head, and then she pushes me up and away from her shoulder. "All you have to do is ask Calvin to make you a little photo album of all the pictures he took of us tonight. Then you can look at it whenever you want." Her eyes move past me, and I see her scanning our surroundings. "People are staring at us, and talking ... oh, and pointing now, too."

Doesn't surprise me. "Let them." I place a quick kiss on her lips, settling on the fact that I'll have to lose myself in her when we're back at Calvin's. "Where to, babe? Hors d'oeuvres? Take something down to the beach?"

"I could snack," she agrees, placing her hand in mine.

We walk over to the table, filling a couple plates with stuffed mushrooms and bacon wrapped chestnuts, then start walking toward the tiki torches. People watch us, but no one bothers to approach. One thing I'm absolutely sure of after walking past almost everyone at this dinner, is that Eva and I are definitely the youngest guests in attendance. We both laugh it off as we sit on strategically-placed tree stumps in the sand, watching the hula dancers and fire twirlers. Every once in a while, a group of adults walks down and joins us. A few nod their heads and smile our way, a few openly argue with each other as if they're the only ones on the beach, the rest completely ignore our presence. I prefer the latter.

A waiter suddenly saunters in front of us, carrying a tray of mouth-watering cocktails. "Mai Tai or Old Fashioned?" he asks.

"We'll take one of each," Eva smiles up at him.

"Good choice." He places them in her outreached hands. "Enjoy your evening." He then walks away, without even giving us a second thought.

"Eva, do you really think we should ..."

She takes a sip of the Mai Tia. "That's tasty." She then takes a sip of the Old Fashioned. She immediately turns up her nose, and hands it over to me. "This one is yours."

"Eva, do you really think we should be sneaking drinks? Plus, one of us needs to drive us back to Calvin's—"

"One drink, right now, is not going to prevent us from driving home in roughly two or three hours, right?" she questions me.

"No."

"Well then, cheers," she holds her glass up to mine. I clink it and we both take a sip. "Damn, I might need to get another one of these."

I swallow hard on my Old Fashioned. "Confession," I say, watching as she brings her glass back up to her mouth. "I definitely prefer beer and swim trunks, over Old Fashioneds and collared shirts."

She grins into her glass and slowly lowers it. "Confession. I'm really enjoying this drink right here, but I definitely prefer watching you drink beer in your swim trunks over sitting here in an uncomfortable dress, wishing we could sneak ten more of these and then disappear for twenty minutes."

I let out a groan, which only makes her laugh. "Legoland," I suddenly say. "That's coming up soon, right?"

She gives a quick nod. "Few weeks away."

"We're not going?"

She takes a big sip of her drink. It's already half gone. "Do you really want to spend an entire weekend with my family, in a Lego-themed hotel suite, riding kiddy rides with my little brothers?"

"No ..." I slyly respond. "What I really want to do is have an entire weekend with you, alone."

Her eyes light up. "I like that idea *much* better. Just one small problem. If Henry Channing is still around, I don't think my parents will let us stay together, alone. They'd want us to stay at Calvin's."

"Maybe Calvin will mysteriously leave on a fishing trip with Owen or something that weekend."

"I like that idea, too."

Graham and Holden suddenly appear from the path, looking as if they're searching for someone. I watch as they see us, and immediately start walking our way. "Finish your drink!" I hurriedly mumble, taking a huge sip of mine and then dumping the rest behind me. "We've got company." Eva drains hers, and we carefully place both glasses in the sand next to my tree stump.

"I thought you two took my advice and left!" we hear Graham call out at us.

"Just hanging out with the hula dancers!" Eva loudly responds. "I've got to admit here," she then says as they approach, "you never struck me as the type of guy who grew up in a family that would have fire blowers and dancers straight from Hawaii at their dinner parties."

Holden lets out a snicker as Graham turns red. "Graham grew up very privileged," Holden smiles. "Tell them the story you told me, about the African themed party when you were ten ... you know, the elephants and zebras—"

"I'd rather not," Graham frankly replies.

"Give him a few more drinks, and I'll get it out of him," Holden winks. "Eva, I saw your dad today—"

"I said no work talk!" Graham shouts out in annoyance.

344

"No work talk," Holden confirms. "I ran into him with your brothers, cute kids."

"Where?" she asks. "They were with Bodhi and me most of the day, surfing."

"Couple hours ago, fishing off High Bridge—"

"Rowan told me they were doing that this afternoon," I tell her. "He was actually really excited."

"Yeah? My dad has never taken my brothers anywhere by himself before."

"He looked like he had it under control," Holden laughs. "Bodhi, the leads on your little sister didn't pan out, unfortunately, but I won't stop, okay? I'm going in another direction."

"Yeah?" I raise my eyes.

He reaches into his pocket. "Just give me another week or so." His phone buzzes loudly in his hand. "Shit. I need to take this—"

Graham rolls his eyes. "Holden, you promised—"

"I'll be quick. I'm sorry." He turns and starts walking in the opposite direction.

Eva looks up at Graham. "I'm sure it was important."

"Yeah. He said one of his cases is close to wrapping up—"

"Dammit!" Eva suddenly exclaims. "Bodhi, *my* phone. I left it in the jeep." I reach for my back pocket, knowing good and well her phone is in it, but her eyes shoot a warning deep into my soul. "I promised my dad I'd answer all his texts tonight. If I don't respond, he'll freak. I hate to do this, but can you go grab it for me?"

"Sure ..." I slowly reply. She nods very slightly toward Holden. "Ah! Yes! I'll go grab it." I bend down and kiss her head, then I speed walk through the sand in the direction Holden disappeared.

It doesn't take me long to find him. He's sitting on a piece of driftwood, his back to me, right past the entrance to the path that will take us back up to the house. I quietly slip behind a row of palm trees, adjacent to where he is, but completely hidden out of his sight. Almost immediately, I pick up on his conversation.

"Olivia, that is not a good idea."

Olivia? Isn't that Porter's mom?

"I don't care what Porter has been asking," he continues. "Telling him that his dad is back in Flagler will not help the situation."

I wondered if Porter knew. I wondered if his dad had made any type of contact with him.

"We're close, Olivia. Close to putting him behind bars. I just need another week or so, then you can tell Porter." His fist suddenly hits the driftwood, causing me to jump in my spot. "You *have* to protect your child!" he shouts. "Isn't that what we've been trying to do from day one? Protect your child?" He pauses, his fingers picking at the layers of rotted wood. "As soon as he's behind bars," he then says. "You can see her then. We can't blow this now. We can't let him know your sister is here—"

What the fuck? Holden knows about Sienna?

"He'll try to use her. You know he will. He has no idea who she is. I can vouch for that, so can Brayden Calloway."

Eva's *dad* knows about Sienna, too?

"He's a typical teenager, he runs around with Bodhi and Eva."

Ethan. He's talking about Ethan now.

"No, he has no idea, and we need to keep it that way. We have a plan, and we're getting close. Then you can tell him all about her … everyone can meet. This kid has been through too much. He's had to grow up too fast. We can't spring this on him right now until we know everyone is safe. Telling him that he's forever linked to your family might just destroy him, which is why you *have* to stay quiet."

Why would Ethan care about being linked to Porter's family? Dare I say Porter might actually be a better role model to him than Frank and Hayes ever will?

Holden stands, looking back toward Eva and Graham, clearly trying to wrap up this phone call. "Soon. Very soon," he suddenly says. "No, Brayden doesn't know. I only told him about your sister because of Ethan. He's always with Bodhi and Eva. Brayden is too involved, too determined to mend his relationship with his daughter. I don't think he'd be able to keep this secret to himself."

Keep *what* secret to himself?!

"You too, Olivia. I'll be in touch soon." He throws his phone in his pocket and starts making his way back to where he left us.

I give myself a couple minutes, trying to comprehend everything I just overheard. I'm so confused, even more than I was before I walked over here. I need Eva. I pull her phone out of my pocket and walk back over to her. I'm waving it in the air as I get closer.

"Found it!" I loudly exclaim.

Holden is next to Graham, his arm wrapped around his shoulder. Graham gives me a puzzling look. "In ten minutes, you walked back up to the house, had the valet get your jeep, and then walked all the way back over here? Did you fly?"

"No," I start laughing. I hand Eva her phone, her eyes worriedly search mine. "I made it to the valet table, and then remembered I *had* Eva's phone. She gave it to me in the jeep."

Eva's face turns bright red. "Shit! That's right! I'm sorry!"

Graham looks between the two of us, and then his eyes focus on the empty glasses next to the tree stump. "You guys been drinking?"

I pull Eva up by her hands. "Hell no, Graham. We're responsible teenagers. Role models for the younger generation. Those were there when we walked down. Eva," I place a kiss on her cheek. "The dance floor is empty and I would love to work up an appetite before dinner. Shall we?"

"We shall," she smiles. "You two want to join us?"

"I need a few more drinks before you'll catch me out there," Holden replies. "Enjoy yourselves."

"We will," I nod. "See you at the table for dinner." I put my arm around Eva's waist and guide us back to the path.

"So?" she whispers. "What you'd hear?"

"Wait," I mutter. "Wait until we're out of their view. And damn, I almost didn't catch on to your quick secret spy plan. You're fast."

"I try."

We get to the dance floor just as the music changes tempo. The loud obnoxious sounds that were coming from the band are now soft and soothing.

"Last song before dinner!" the lead singer calls out.

I walk us right to the center, only a few other people are slowly moving along with the lyrics and guitar melody, making me feel as if Eva and I are put on display. She wraps her arms around my neck, while I bring my hands to her lower waist, quickly alert to the many faces of everyone watching us. We've never had a moment like this before, the two of us, dancing to a slow song while in the middle of a floating dance floor.

It's beautiful, and I suddenly don't give a shit about what I overheard Holden say to Olivia.

Eva's eyes are staring up at me, waiting to hear what I'm going to tell her. "I love you," is what finally rolls out of my mouth. Not what she was expecting, and not what I was planning on saying when I brought her out here. But in this very second, it's exactly what needs to be spoken.

She gives me a familiar grin. "And I love you."

"You're the most beautiful person here."

Her arms wrap tighter around my neck. "Yeah?"

"By far. No one even compares. No one will ever compare, actually." I bring one of my hands up to her blushing face, tucking the loose strands of hair behind her ear. "I'm going to tell you what I heard Holden say, but I just realized, standing here with you in front of me, that none of it matters." I take her hands off my neck, holding onto the one and giving her a twirl. Her dark hair fans out in the air, settling on her shoulders as gravity abruptly does its job. How does she have the ability to make my heart beat so fast? It doesn't matter how many days we've been together, how many weeks and months have passed, how many times I've held her in my arms. Every single second I have the privilege of simply looking at her, my heart reminds me of how madly in love I am. How she is the only person that will ever allow me to feel like this.

I pull her body back into mine. "It's you and me. Not any of them. The only thing that matters is us," I declare, my eyes looking directly at her red lips. "Say it. Say it back to me."

Her calm voice repeats, "The only thing that matters is us."

My eyes are still watching her mouth. I need to kiss her. I force myself to blink, to move my gaze. "Before I tell you what I heard, I'm going to kiss you, right in front of all of these people that are watching us. And trust me, we have an audience now." It's true, there's a crowd of people on the dance floor, watching the two of us move effortlessly in the middle. "My heart, it might stop if I don't kiss you right now. Can I?"

"You don't have to ask," she replies, and then her lips are on mine before I even have a chance to make the first move.

My hand cups her face, my thumb moving against her perfect jawline as our lips are together. I've kissed Eva hundreds of times now, but there's something about this kiss that makes the world stop spinning. Emotions mixed with desirable lust. The realization that love has no end. It can just keep going and going, forever, overflowing from our bodies as every day it grows more.

She pulls apart first, staring at me as her fingers brush her now wet lips. I know she felt it too, the way this kiss had the ability to bring us even closer together with its unspoken words. Her arms wrap around my neck again and her head settles on my chest, where my heart continues to madly beat.

The song is almost over, now's my chance to tell her what I heard before the band breaks for dinner and we have to sit with the Walker family and Holden. I lean my mouth to her ear, whispering everything I heard him speak out loud on that piece of driftwood. She doesn't move, just stays there and listens to it all, as we carefully spin around the dance floor, our audience watching every move.

The band stops playing, there's a soft round of applause, quite possibly for us. Everyone that was on the dance floor is now wandering off to go find their seats. Eva slowly lifts her head off my chest, her lower lip tucked firmly under the top of her teeth. She looks lost in thought, like she was earlier in my jeep.

I place a soft kiss on her forehead. "What do you want to do? Talk to your dad? Confront Holden? Go see Ethan? Call Porter?"

She looks around, watching as the dance floor empties, and we're the only ones left standing here. Her head suddenly goes back to my chest, and her arms hug my body in a way that screams out comfort. "I don't want to do anything."

Surprised, I question, "Nothing?"

"Nothing," she repeats.

"About any of it?"

"About any of it. I'm tired of taking on every little thing. I just want to be like this, you and me, together, perfect. Do you want to know why?" she lifts her head and asks.

"Why?"

She places a tender kiss on my lips before saying, "Because the only thing that matters to me right now is us."

chapter thirty-seven

Eva – the next day

Y ou're going to go?" Luna asks, pulling her sweater down to cover her hands. "Shit, when did it get cold?"

It's barely seventy degrees outside, and as the sun starts to go down this evening, the temperatures are dropping even more. Luna and Coop, and Beck and Kennedy, all showed up at my house after dinner tonight. The guys are down at my boat with my dad, helping him fix the speakers that have suddenly stopped working, while us girls are sitting around my firepit.

"When do you guys leave?" Kennedy asks, warming her hands in front of the flames.

"The day after Christmas. Owen's taking us, on his yacht."

"You're sailing to Turks and Caicos, on a yacht?!" Luna's eyes grow huge. "Shit, girl."

"That's dreamy," Kennedy declares. "Think of how romantic that will be. You and Bodhi, cuddled up as you sail the ocean on a yacht ... just pretend Calvin and Owen aren't there."

I smile over at her. "It does sound really nice, and I'm sure Bodhi will make sure it's just as romantic as you're dreaming up."

"Of course he will!" she exclaims. "He's probably already got a mental note going in his head of every little swoon-worthy moment he's planning."

"What about when you get there?" Luna questions. "Give us details."

"We actually had Annie and Kenneth on FaceTime this morning. I think they were both crying—"

"That's so sweet!" Kennedy emotionally says.

"We're staying with them. I guess they have a house right on the beach? They've already sent Bodhi pictures. They're just going to show us around and stuff. Visit. A typical holiday with the grandparents in the most nontypical way ever. Oh! Guess what we saw in the pictures? The ones they sent us of the inside of their house? *My* fucking pictures."

"Pictures *of* you?" Kennedy asks, confused.

Luna's eyes get big. "No! Your photographs? The ones you took? The ones Lenora sold?"

"Bingo. We saw three of them. I have a feeling the photographs that got shipped to the Bahamas and Turks and Caicos decorate their vacation rentals."

"No shit?!" Luna shakes her head.

"No shit. I guess we'll find out for sure after Christmas."

"Well, I'm excited for you guys," Luna says, inching closer to the fire. "I think this will be really good for Bodhi and you."

"Yeah," I agree. "It'll be nice to talk to them again, now that everything's out in the open. I mean, they left so suddenly after telling us all that shit ... now that we've had time to process it all, I guess this time we won't be so ...?"

"Pissed?" Kennedy throws out there.

"Yeah. Unless there are *more* secrets they plan on dropping."

"God, I hope not," Kennedy's face cringes. "Hey! You guys hear about the hurricane coming this way? My dad said we might actually have to evacuate this weekend."

"For real?" I swipe my phone on and pull up the weather. Sure enough, Tropical Storm Tammy is making her way through the Caribbean, projected to make landfall in Flagler on Saturday.

"She's just a Tropical Storm right now," Kennedy continues. "But they're expecting her to gain strength over the next few days."

"We haven't had a hurricane here in years," I place my phone back in the pocket of my hoodie. "I wonder if they'll cancel school?"

"Cancel school for what?" we hear Coop's voice coming from the direction of my dock.

"The hurricane heading this way," Kennedy responds.

"Funny," my dad appears. "We were just talking about that."

Bodhi walks out from behind him, looking down at the ground as he moves. Something's not right, and it actually humors me that I can so easily pick up on the fact he looks so horribly anxious. He lifts his head up, walking closer to me but avoiding my eyes at the same time. It's only once he's directly in front of me that he finally matches my stare. I immediately raise my eyes at him in question, and he awkwardly looks away. Usually, Bodhi would tug on my hands and stand me up, then throw himself in my chair and pull me down into his lap. But tonight, he goes and sits next to Beck, clear across the fire from me.

What the *hell* is going on?

"So, I was thinking," my dad announces, throwing another log onto the fire. "With the hurricane possibly heading this way, why don't you six get the hell out of Flagler for the weekend?"

Ah. Here we go. My eyes shoot to Bodhi as I ask, "And where will the six of us go?"

"Your Pop said you guys have a lake house?" Coop answers. "You've been holding out on us, Eva."

"The *lake* house?" I question in disbelief. "The one on Lake Seminole? I haven't been there in like five years. Is it still standing?"

"It is," my dad nods. "I was up there a few weeks ago. Took the old boat out of storage and brought it with me. Got the house all cleaned up. Was going to surprise everyone for the boys' birthday, but they conned me into Legoland instead. It's ready for some visitors if you all are up for it."

I lean back in my seat, shooting Bodhi a glare as I do. I then look back at my dad. "You want the six of us to drive four hours to the lake house, by ourselves, to hang out for the weekend, unsupervised?"

"Should I not trust you all?" my dad points around the fire.

"You can trust us!" Kennedy cries out, her eyes piercing at me.

"If this hurricane is coming like they say it is," my dad goes on, "you probably won't have school on Friday. Head out then, come home Sunday if Flagler's still standing."

"What about Mom and the boys?"

"They're leaving Thursday to go visit Gram and Grandpa."

"You don't want me to go with them?"

"Do you want to go with them?"

No. I'd rather be with Bodhi and my friends. "Not really. What about you?"

352

"Someone has to stay and make sure the house stays put."

"How heroic of you."

"Well, there you go," he grins. "I'll talk it over with everyone's parents and Dolly," he glances at my friends, "and make sure all the details get taken care of."

"This sounds amazing," Luna smiles. "Thank you."

"My pleasure." He points to the patio door. "I'm going to go help your mom get the boys in bed before I head out." He avoids my eyes as he turns and walks away.

Everyone starts talking about the weekend. What to bring, what to sneak, how the hell we can all squeeze into one car. I stay silent, though, and just stare down Bodhi, waiting for him to say something. He looks so uncomfortable. I almost feel bad for him, but my annoyance over the fact there's something he's not telling me buries those empathetic thoughts way down into the bottom pit of my soul.

When our friends leave, school tomorrow putting a damper on our late-night social lives, Bodhi follows me upstairs to my room. I was hoping he'd stay the night, but at this rate, I'm lucky he even came inside the house with me. My mom and brothers are already asleep, so I carefully close my door and place my back against it, watching as Bodhi silently takes a seat on the edge of my bed.

I wait for him to say something, but he doesn't. So I do. "You going to tell me what's going on?"

"Nothing's going on—"

"You haven't said *one* word to me since you came back from helping my dad on the boat," I angrily hiss. "Don't tell me nothing's going on."

He lets out a frustrated sigh. "Your dad asked me if we'd like to stay at your lake house this weekend—"

"You're lying to me. Why? Why are you lying for him?"

"I'm not."

"You are. My dad would *never* be fine with the six of us staying at our lake house for a weekend, alone. There's something he told you down at our boat, and you're not telling me."

"Why can't your dad just do something nice without you jumping to conclusions?"

"This is my fucking dad! Did you forget? And since when do you lie to me, for *him*?!"

He doesn't respond. He just throws himself back on my bed.

"Fine," I angrily mutter. I can literally feel the heat of rage searing off my face. "If this is how it's going to be tonight, then leave." I open my door as he flings himself back into a sitting position. I wave my hand in the open doorframe.

"Are you serious?" he asks, shocked. "You're kicking me out?"

"Yes, I am. Leave. I'm not going to let you sit here and lie to me. Just go."

His face, his beautiful face, looks so wounded that I have to turn away. I feel the cold air suddenly blow past me as he swiftly leaves my room. I can't breathe. I actually gasp with the absence of him. I quietly close my bedroom door, resting my forehead against it as my legs refuse to move. I can feel a panic attack coming on, not because of him, but because of what *I* just did.

Pain shoots throughout my palms and I look down. My hands are ghost white as my fists are clenched so tightly, I've cut off all blood flow. I unclench them, watching as my skin quickly turns pink in color. I flip them over, blood droplets form in perfect fingernail shaped patterns from unintentionally breaking through my own skin. I rub them on my jeans, streaks of light red line both sides now. I yank them off, kicking them across the room and searching for one of Bodhi's t-shirts that I know he's left behind. I find one in a pile of dirty clothes, and immediately strip out of my sweatshirt, replacing it with the familiar smell of him. I then crawl into my bed, where the tears immediately fall onto my pillow.

We've argued before. Hell, we've fought before, loud and hard. But we've never had a night end where we didn't make up. I've never gone to bed knowing that we're mad at each other. It's a horrible feeling, and all I want to do is rewind the night and be okay with the fact that I know he's hiding something from me. Bodhi never does anything without putting me first, why couldn't I see that as he silently sat in my room? He's protecting me by not telling me what my dad said, and instead of being grateful, I kicked him out.

An hour passes. My pillow is soaked with tears and I'm struggling to fall asleep. I reach for my phone. I have to call him. I can't let the night end like this. I swipe it on and go to push his number when I hear a light tap on my balcony doors. I jump out of bed, my phone falling loudly to the ground as I trip over my blankets that were cocooned around me. I shimmy them down and step out, reaching for the balcony doors at the same time.

Bodhi's standing behind them, looking just as distraught as I felt moments ago.

"What are you doing here?!" I quietly shout out, panic hitting me like a hard ocean wave. "You can't be walking between our houses at night when Henry—"

"I don't give a *fuck* about Henry Channing," he boldly responds. "I just spent an hour pacing around my room at Calvin's, convincing myself not to run back over here because *you* requested that I leave. I was trying to respect your goddamn request. But do you know what I realized roughly four minutes ago?"

"What?" I cautiously ask.

"That I *don't* respect your goddamn request." He pushes his way into my room, causing me to stumble backwards over the blankets on the ground. His hands grab at my body and he pulls me into his. "If I kiss you right now, are you going to throw me off your balcony?"

I bite down on my lip to keep myself from laughing. "No."

His mouth forcefully hits mine and he moves us over to my bed, lying me back as his body hovers above my chest. My arms wrap around his broad back, pulling him down. I *need* him this close. I need to forget that I ever made him leave.

"I'm sorry," I say into his mouth. "Bodhi, I'm so sorry."

His hands appear on either side of my face, and he abruptly pulls his lips away. I try to pull him back down, but he shakes his head. He takes a moment, staring down at me before he speaks.

"You were crying?"

"Yes."

"Because of me?"

"No. Because I made you leave."

The smallest smirk appears on his mouth. His thumbs press gently under my eyes. "I'm sorry, too, baby. I shouldn't have left."

"I didn't give you a choice."

"You're extremely frightening when you're pissed."

355

I reach for his hands and use his strength to pull myself up. "Why can't you tell me? Why are we going away this weekend?"

He doesn't answer me. Instead, he stands and walks over to my balcony, pulling the doors shut. He then firmly locks them before turning back. He looks over my shoulder, to my almost naked bed, and laughs under his breath as he reaches down and grabs all my blankets off the floor. He nods for me to stand, and then we silently make my bed together. When we're finished, neither one us moves. It's almost as if we're waiting to see what the other one does first. It's unnecessarily awkward, and I refuse to waste another second of this night not in his arms.

"Even if you can't tell me what my dad said," I quietly mumble, "will you stay with me tonight?"

He moves in front of me, his warm hand presses up against my cheek as he leans in and gives me a delicate kiss. I reach for the bottom of his t-shirt, pushing it up past his stomach, only breaking our kiss to pull it over his head. This isn't me telling him to do the same. This isn't me giving him the idea that we can fix this night with sex. This is me silently telling him I want to be in his arms, that I want to feel the comfort of his skin under me as I fall asleep. I need him to be my calm, and because this is Bodhi, he knows exactly what I'm saying without having to mutter a single word out loud.

His eyes are watching mine, so intensely, like he has the ability to read my thoughts this way. Most people would move their eyes, look in a different direction when someone is staring at them so powerfully. Not me. Bodhi's eyes on mine, locked in this embrace— if you could actually see love pouring from two souls, this is what it would look like.

He leans in, forcing my eyes to suddenly close, and then his lips tenderly kiss my eyelids. I feel his hand on my wrist, and he climbs into my bed, pulling me in with him. We settle under the covers, his arm draped protectively around my body as my head rests on the muscles of his chest. Every single ounce of anger I held against him a little bit ago has evaporated into the stillness of my room. I listen to his steady breathing, matching perfectly with mine. The way our hearts seem to sync in rhythm when we're together is beautiful.

"Eva?" my name is suddenly whispered.

I turn my head a little to look up at him. "Yeah?"

"Henry Channing's getting arrested this weekend. Your dad, he's somehow going to be involved in all of this. He doesn't want us home, you know, in case Henry finds out beforehand? He wants us out of Flagler, all of us, because he's afraid of what Henry might do if this plan doesn't work out the way he and Holden are hoping."

Jesus Christ. This is *not* what I was expecting.

"*Bodhi*," I say his name so emotionally, I can already feel the tears burning my eyes.

"This is what he told me tonight. This is why he's letting us all go to your lake house. He didn't want me to tell you because he's worried about you, and thought you'd try to get involved. I *told* him I don't keep secrets from you—"

I quickly place my lips on his. He doesn't need to tell me anything else. I just want to kiss him until he realizes how sorry I am, not just for how I behaved earlier, but also for letting my dad come between us yet again.

His hands push gently on my shoulders as he moves his lips off mine. "Eva, let me finish. After what happened to you this summer, I'll do anything to protect you, even if that means lying to you for your dad. You're going away with me this weekend, we're not staying here, okay?"

"Okay."

"You can't tell your dad that you know."

"I won't."

"You have to trust that he's doing what needs to be done."

"I will."

He pauses for a second before grinning, "You'll marry me after we graduate?"

I can't help but laugh at him.

"It was worth a shot. Just for the record," he says, his lips moving against my neck, making my entire body break out in chills. "You ever tell me to leave again, I'm not going to listen to you."

I smile into the familiar warmth of his skin. "I regretted it the second you walked out my door." He gives me one final kiss and then moves my body so I'm lying back on his chest. "Do we need to be worried?" I then quietly ask.

"I don't know. Your dad is worried enough that he wants your entire family, and our friends, out of Flagler ... so I think maybe we need to be a little worried?"

"But we'll be okay? All of us, and my mom and brothers?"

His hand slips under my t-shirt, and he trails his fingers up and down my bare back. "I think he's just being overly cautious. I don't think he trusts that we'd stay out of trouble, not after this summer. We'll be okay, because we'll be together, away from whatever is happening here."

Being together is the only way I want to be. "If you take away the fact that we're leaving Flagler because my dad's going to be involved in the arrest of Henry Channing, the weekend actually sounds fun."

"Oh, it'll be fun," he agrees. "I'll make sure of it. How many bedrooms does your lake house have?"

"If you include the master? Three."

"Perfect," he growls.

"Bodhi Bishop. I know what you're thinking."

"How can I *not* think about that?" he laughs. "An entire weekend with just you and our friends, no adults that we have to sneak around? The moment your dad brought it up all I could think about was how many times you and I can have—"

"Bodhi!" I quickly sit up and cover his mouth with my hand.

"I love it when I embarrass you," his lips move against my palm. I wince at the quick pain from his mouth against the small cuts left behind by my fingernails. He sees this, and his eyes look confused. He takes my hand off his mouth and flips it over, the moonlight shining directly onto what I'd rather he not see. "What is this?" he asks, grabbing my other hand and inspecting it. "What are these?"

"My fingernails. After you left—I didn't realize I had done it—"

"These are from your fingernails?"

I give a quick nod.

"You dug your fingernails into your skin?"

"Not on purpose—I didn't realize what I was doing until it was already done."

He closes my hands, and kisses the tops of both of them. "Don't do this, Eva. Don't hurt yourself over me."

358

"Bodhi, I already said ... I didn't realize I was doing .

"I know," he calmly responds. "I heard you, but yourself because you were mad at something that h̲ ̲.ed between you and me. You can't do that, and if I have to sit there and watch you after every single argument we have for the rest of our lives, so I can make sure you don't ever do this again, then that's exactly what I'm going to do."

"You would really do that?"

"Of course I would."

I sit fully up, staring down at this perfect person. "How do you see past all my faults so easily?"

"What faults?" he smoothly replies.

"I have faults."

"So do I."

"Mine are more difficult to look past."

He sits himself up. "It's simple. I love you."

"It's *that* simple?"

"To me it is. I love you. And when I think about those years without you, or that moment I thought you were gone forever, or any time you're standing there giving me that furious glare ... I realize every second I spend without you in my arms is a second I'm wasting in a life that doesn't guarantee us extra chances. It's why I came back tonight, because no matter how pissed you were at me, I couldn't let the night end without this," he tugs on my t-shirt so I fall onto his chest. "Without you in my arms."

I move my lips gracefully over his, as I run my hands along his stomach. "I was calling you when you knocked on my balcony."

"Oh yeah?" he grins.

"Yes," I push him down and he lifts his arm, waiting for me to snuggle into the spot I claim most nights. "Because I couldn't end the night without this, without you holding me."

His fingers start moving along my collarbone, slowly and deliberately. His own personal way of silently saying it's time for bed. He plants a soft kiss on my temple, and then trails smaller kisses down to that soft below my ear. "Always, babe," he then whispers. "Even when your hurricane winds blow me off track for a little while, I'll always come back and hold you, exactly like this."

chapter thirty-eight

Bodhi — Friday morning

I don't know about you," Beck says as he starts his truck, "but I'm really happy this hurricane isn't going to be as bad as they thought. Yesterday, Dolly and Gramps were talking about making me stay in Flagler to help board up the restaurant."

"Shit, bro," Coop pats his shoulder. "We would have taken Kennedy for you. No reason for her to stay behind."

"Thanks," Beck rolls his eyes, turning onto A1A. "Really feeling the love. *Damn*. Look at the surf," he points out the window. "Those waves are massive."

"Hurricane Tammy, making her appearance," Coop nods. "Downgraded to a category one or not, she looks like a bitch."

"I'm just glad they canceled school today," I chime in from the backseat. Beck's truck has the most space for us to squeeze in six bodies, so we're taking it to the lake house this weekend. Coop and I helped Beck out at Dolly's last night, so we crashed at his house. The girls stayed at Eva's and gave us prompt instructions on what time to pick them up this morning. We're surprisingly right on schedule

"I still can't believe we're doing this," Coops hits the dashboard. "I mean, Mr. Calloway might just be my favorite dude on the planet. To think we hated him for most of the summer, and now, he's sending us off for a weekend unsupervised at his lake house."

Beck turns to look at Coop. "You might question if maybe he has some sort of ulterior motive, sending his daughter away with her boyfriend and friends for the weekend?"

I start laughing. Beck has always been the smart one when it comes to the three of us. "You caught on to that?"

"Caught on to what?!" Coop shouts in a panic.

Beck looks at me through the rearview mirror. "I caught on to it the moment the two of you disappeared onto the dock, left us on the boat for ten minutes, then came back announcing we should go away for the weekend."

"Why didn't you say anything?" I ask.

He turns onto High Bridge Road. "Because I'm not stupid—"

"What the hell are you two ass-wipes talking about?!" Coop cries out.

The truck climbs over the drawbridge. "*Shit*. I've never seen it like that." The Halifax looks like rushing rapids of angry, murky sea water due to the storm surge. "We're definitely getting out of here at the right time. High Bridge will be flooded by tonight, for sure."

Coop throws his hands up. "Who cares about the goddamn water! What the hell were you two talking about?!"

"Henry Channing's getting arrested this weekend," I bluntly say. "We're going to the lake house so that in case shit goes down, we're not here to get ourselves in trouble."

Beck nods his head. "Figured it was something like that."

"What the goddamn hell?!" Coop whacks the window. "Why can't we ever be normal?!"

I lean forward, roughly rubbing my hand on his head. "Embrace it, Coop. This is our life."

"I am *not* embracing this shit," he hits my hand away. "I will take part in each and every festivity and chaotic moment you throw in front of me, but I'm not embracing this as *my* life."

I wrap my arms around his neck, pinning him to the headrest. "This. *Is*. Your. Life." Then I plant a fat kiss on his cheek.

"This is *your* life!" he squirms, trying to get out of my arms. "I'm just your sidekick!"

I release my hold on him. "I like that. My sidekick. You my sidekick too, Beck?"

"Can you have more than one?"

"Sure."

"Count me in."

Coop forms a triangle in the air. "Goddamn triangle, we meet again."

I roll my eyes. "Let's have fun this weekend, okay? I just want to forget about everything going on. I want Eva to forget about everything going on—"

"Just tell us, boss," Coop turns in his seat. "Tell us what you want to accomplish this weekend, and we'll make it happen."

"Top three?" I question.

"Top three," he nods.

"Lots of beer, lots of food, lots of sex."

"Ahh!" Coop cries out. "My ears! Goddamn, Bodhi! I assumed you'd be shacking up with Eva this weekend, but shit, did you have to give me a fucking visual?!"

Beck's laughing as he turns down Eva's street. "Remember when you wanted to talk about our sex lives while we were at Hayes' party? What happened to *that* Coop?"

"He's here," Coop shakes his head. "Praying Bodhi packed enough condoms ..."

"We don't use them," I stare out the window and announce.

Coop jerks his head in my direction. "You don't *use* them?!"

"Calm down, bro. I told you Eva's on birth control. She has an IUD. It's ninety-nine percent effective, which is higher in effectiveness than a condom, may I add."

Beck pulls down Eva's driveway. "What percent is a condom?"

"If used correctly? Ninety-eight."

"How do you know this shit?!" Coop loudly questions.

"I've done my research."

Coop's hand rests on Beck's shoulder. "You and Kennedy use them?" he quietly asks.

"Yeah man. Kennedy's on the pill, too. I think that makes us well over one hundred percent covered."

"You okay with your one percent chance of failure?" Coop turns to me and asks.

I shrug my shoulders. "I'd marry Eva today if she'd finally say yes, so if our one percent chance of failure ends up actually happening, no doubt in my goddamn mind it was meant to be."

Beck puts the truck in park. "How can you be so calm when you say that?"

The girls walk out from Eva's garage door. She leads the way, her hair hanging down past her shoulders, wavier than normal, which means she let it airdry after taking a shower. She has on tight ripped jean shorts, and a black halter top that shows off the skin of her flat stomach and tanned arms. The sun shines down on her as she walks out of the shadows, illuminating the streaks of red mixed in with the black of her hair.

She's a fucking goddess.

I point to her. "Because I'm one hundred percent certain part of my soul is in that body right there. I'm not scared of the unknown because I have *her*, forever." I open the door and step out, walking right over to where she is. Eva gives me a nervous smile as I get closer. My hands go to the bare skin of her lower back, and I breathe in the scent of her shampoo as I push her into me. "Everything okay?"

She nods into my shoulder and then looks up. Her eyes are glossy. I can tell she's been crying. "My dad stayed here last night, with us. He left really fast, early this morning. Woke me up, had coffee ready, sat at the counter with me, and hugged me when he left. Like, *really* hugged me. I just felt like he was saying goodbye, something didn't feel right—"

"We have to trust your dad."

"I know. I'm trying. I'm just worried."

I give her lips a gentle kiss. "Your mom and brothers left yesterday?"

"Yeah," she nods her head. "They're fine. She called me last night."

"The six of us are leaving right now?"

She looks over at our friends who are loading up Beck's truck with the girls' bags. "Yeah."

"We get to be like this, all weekend long?" I kiss her again, and tug on her shorts.

"Yes," she smiles up at me. "All weekend."

"Then let's trust your dad and get the hell out of Flagler, okay?"

"Okay," she agrees, weaving her fingers in between mine, and walking us over to the truck. "Thanks for driving us," she says to Beck.

"Thanks for having a lake house," he replies. "Coop, help me with the cover," he points to the bed of the truck. "We don't need all the shit back here getting soaked."

Eva suddenly reaches into her back pocket, pulling her phone out as it vibrates in her hand. "Ethan?" she says out loud, looking up at me, confused. "Why is Ethan calling me? He never calls me. He always calls you."

I shake my head and take her phone out of her hands. "No. We're not going to let Ethan's theatrical pleas of boredom put a bad start to this epic weekend." I turn her phone off, and then I pull out mine and do the same. "He asked me three times yesterday if he could go with us. Everyone, turn your phones off—"

"I sort of need mine for GPS?" Beck makes known.

"Yours can stay on," I declare. "Everyone else, turn your phones off for the next four hours. We'll turn them back on when we get there, got it?"

"Are you insane?" Coop's snide comment echoes around us.

"No. We don't need any shit keeping us here. Turn them off, or Eva and I go by ourselves."

"You suck," Coop declares, securing the cover. "And I'm going to sing the entire four hours, you know, because we're all going to be bored out of our frickin minds."

Eva gives me a concerned look. "What if something—"

"In the truck!" I exclaim. "Everyone!" I kiss the top of her head, and then hold open the door for her. "Everything is fine." I can tell she doesn't agree, but she reluctantly gets in, squeezing next to Luna as I climb in after her. "Do we have everything?" I call out.

Coop holds out his fingers and starts counting off. "Everyone's bags. Food. Smuggled beer and liquor. Fishing poles. Bait! We forgot the fucking bait."

I knew there was something we were supposed to do on our drive to Eva's this morning. "We'll stop at Tacklebox really quick," I announce. "Not completely out of our way. But we need gas first. I don't want to stop once we start—"

"God," Coop grumbles. "You're such an old shit."

I whack his head and throw my arm around Eva's back, pulling her into me while Beck turns out of her driveway. "The guys and I have a bet," I whisper into her ear. "Whichever couple catches the most fish this weekend gets the privilege of not having to be the designated drivers for any party we attend the rest of the school year."

Eva turns her mouth to me. "Do they not realize who they're up against? There's no competition."

The rain starts to slowly haze down on the windows while Beck pumps gas, not our typical Flagler weather. It's dreary, no sun, just full cloud coverage as the hurricane makes her way up the coast. She's apparently making landfall sometime tomorrow. They expect her to just be a tropical storm again at that point, but she sure is bringing some awful weather ahead of her. It only gets worse as we head to get bait, and the intracoastal along High Bridge Road already looks higher than it did twenty minutes ago. You'd have to be an idiot to be out on your boat today.

"Who's going to run into Tacklebox?" Beck asks, turning down the gravel road. "Are they even open?"

I can see the soft glow of a light inside, and a lone bike resting on the wall of the front of the shop, but there are no cars here, which is really unusual. "I'll go check," I announce.

"Me, too," Eva says. "I need snacks."

I duck my head against the cool mist as we quickly walk to the entrance. The rotted porch gives us slight cover as we shake off the rain from our feet. The main door isn't open behind the weathered screen, which is also really unusual.

Eva suddenly points up to the wooden beams. "The security camera. It's gone."

"That's definitely weird." I reach for the metal handle. "What are the odds they're actually closed for once?" I give it a tug, and the screen door creaks loudly as it moves toward me. I keep it open with my back and twist the handle to the actual door. It opens, but something feels off. The lights are dim, not fully on, and there's absolutely no noise at all. Usually the radio is blaring, mixed with the noise of Frank grumbling behind the register. My hand flails protectively behind me, grabbing Eva's as we walk further in.

"Hello?" she nervously calls out. "Frank?"

We both stop walking, standing in the middle of the soundless shop. The silence is piercing, eerie, and I have this obnoxious voice in my head telling me we need to get the hell out of here.

"I tried calling you," someone says from behind us.

We both jump, spinning around in the direction of the voice. Ethan steps out from what was a closed closet. His eyes are bloodshot, his face is red and blotchy. He leans up against the door and slowly falls to the ground, wrapping his arms around his legs.

"Ethan!" Eva cries out. She releases my hand and rushes over to him, throwing herself on the ground and carefully grabbing at his shoulders. "What's wrong?! Are you hurt?! Where's Frank?"

Ethan points to the counter. I turn to look, but there's no one there.

"What is it?" I ask him.

"He was behind the counter," is all he says, before burying his head into his knees.

"Frank was behind the counter?" Eva's worried voice asks. "Where is he?" She goes to stand, but I shake my head at her.

"*Stay there*," I demand. "Stay by him." She squats back down in slow motion, wrapping her arms around Ethan's trembling body. I walk over to the counter, resting my hands on the cool wood before I peer behind it.

I don't know which of these realizations enters my mind first, or maybe they all fly in so fast ... everything just hits me at once.

Frank Granger is lying dead on the floor behind the counter.

Frank Granger has been shot.

Frank Granger has not been dead long.

I close my eyes tight, hoping to get the image of him out of my head before I turn back to Eva and Ethan. She's watching me, her eyes filled with fear. I mouth his name, *Frank*, and make a gun motion with my fingers. Her face drops and she squeezes her arms tighter around Ethan, who's now hiding in her chest.

"Shh ..." she tries to reassure him with a quivering voice.

I try to get myself to stay calm. "How long have you been here?"

"Not long," he mumbles against Eva's body.

"Were you here?" I ask. "When it happened?"

His head nods.

"You were here?!" Eva cries out. "Ethan, *talk* to us!"

"I think they're coming back!" his panicked words make the room spin in front of me. "I heard them say they're getting a boat!

366

They're coming back, but he told me to hide—he shoved me in the closet—we need to hide! We can't let them see us!"

"Who, Ethan?! Who can't see us?!" I shout as I slide down onto the floor in front of him.

"Henry Channing, the guy with the red hair from the airport ... and your dad, Eva! Your dad shoved me in the closet!"

"My dad?!" she questions in disbelief. "My dad was here?! With Henry Channing?!"

"No! He was here with Frank! It was a setup—Frank knew about it! Your dad was here to make Henry think he was doing shit like this now—drugs, like he took over when Henry disappeared. I wasn't supposed to be here. I rode my bike from home. I was heading to the beach to see Callie—I don't know why I stopped to see Frank, but I knew he was here so I thought I'd just say hi or something ... your dad was in here with him. They both lost it when I walked in, but it was too late! The Suburban pulled up and I saw the two of them get out—your dad shoved me in the closet! Told me not to make a sound or to come out for anything—"

"Did you hear what happened?" I quickly ask.

"He wanted names, the guy with the red hair—"

"Holden?" I question.

"Yes! Him! He wanted names of people in the department that work for Henry! Henry was supposed to give him names—"

"Did he?" I ask.

"Yes! A shitload, in exchange for the drugs, for what Frank had! Henry was supposed to leave Flagler then, the airport—my dad. It was just a setup! Henry was supposed to leave!" he starts to cry and hits Eva's arm. "Your dad told me it was a setup—that Henry was supposed to leave thinking Holden and your dad were taking over, using the names to keep the drugs coming in and out of Flagler! That Henry would profit from this, that he would get a share of everything! Frank was supposed to come get me when they left! The police were waiting at the airport for Henry to arrest him! All the names! They were all getting arrested! But they started yelling, Henry was pissed your dad was here, said he wasn't loyal anymore—said he couldn't be trusted! Your dad, he asked Henry what he needed to do to prove he was on his side, that he was ready to take over ... and then I heard it! I heard the gunshot!" Ethan's hysterical at this point, rocking back and forth with his head in his knees. "I didn't see it. But I heard it. I heard the gunshot," his muffled voice whispers out.

Eva has her back up against the wall now, staring at the counter as she squeezes Ethan's hand. There's no emotion on her face whatsoever. I know what she's thinking. I know she thinks her dad shot Frank. I place my one hand on her leg, my other on Ethan's back, and then ask, "Ethan, do you know who pulled the trigger?"

He nods slowly, looking at Eva as he says, "It wasn't your dad."

Eva lets out a gasp and immediately starts crying. She buries her head into her hands as she loudly sobs. I don't know who I need to comfort more right now. I put my arms around both of their bodies and pull them closer to me.

"Who *was* it then?!" her voice wails out.

"Henry," he says. "It was Henry. Henry told your dad to clean up his mess, that would prove to him ... he doesn't know Owen's alive! He told your dad to clean up his mess like he did with Owen. He admitted to hiring Luke to get rid of your dad, he admitted to starting the fire at his house, to all the drugs and the blackmailing— he's blackmailed half of Flagler, but he shot Frank! He shot Frank for no fucking reason!"

"Did you call the police?" I hurriedly ask.

He shakes his head. "No! Eva's dad said the police would be at the airport—and Holden *is* the police! They have all these names, but what if the police are in on this, and they hurt my dad before Henry gets arrested? I *can't* lose my dad! I can't let Henry and Holden know I was here! They're coming back! With a boat! To get rid of Frank! We have to hide—"

"Fuck hiding! We have to get out of here!" I stand up, yanking them both off the ground. "We can't be here when they get back—"

Ethan pushes past me, to the window that looks out over the Halifax. His entire body starts shaking. "It's too late. Guys, they're already here!"

Eva grabs my arm. "The truck! Bodhi, the truck is out there! Our friends! We can make it to the truck before they see us!"

We don't have a second to spare. I run to the window with Eva, yanking Ethan by the collar of his shirt to the open door. The rain is heavier now, and my eyes shut as it pelts me in my face.

"Where are they?!" Eva's panicked voice calls out in front of me. "There's no one in the goddamn truck!"

My eyes pop open. The truck is empty, our friends are nowhere to be seen.

Ethan falls onto the wet ground. "They already got to them!"

Eva squeezes my shoulder. "Look!" she points to the dirt. Footprints. "There!" she cries out, pointing into the trees. I see Coop waving us into the jungle.

I hoist Ethan up by his arms, running past the truck and into the shelter of the thick palms. Eva throws herself into Luna and Kennedy, knocking them both to the ground.

"What the *fuck* is going on?!" Coop exclaims.

"Why are you guys in the trees?!" I shout back.

"Henry Channing!" Coop cries. "I got out to see what was taking you guys so long, and I saw him pull up in a goddamn boat with that piece of shit Holden and Eva's dad! We weren't gonna sit in the truck to see what the hell was about to go down!"

"You were just going to leave us in there?!" I loudly question.

"No, man!" he turns to the side, showing me his red cheek. "Beck punched me!"

"You punched him?" I shockingly ask.

"He tried to run back, after we got in the woods, to get you two!"

"So you *punched* him?!"

"He wouldn't listen! I figured you two had a better chance of hiding in there, than Coop did running in clear view like a fucking chicken missing its head! You've seen him run! It's like he's got fire ants up his ass!"

"True," I pat him on the shoulder.

Coop shoves my hand off. "You two mother—"

"What happened in there?" Beck asks. "Why is Ethan here and why does he look like that?"

"Frank," I immediately answer. "Frank was shot. He's in there, gone, behind the counter—"

"Oh my god!" Kennedy cries out. "We need to call the police!"

"No!" Ethan frantically yanks at her arm. "My dad is *with* the

369

police, at the airport. They'll kill him! Don't! Don't call them!"

"This was a setup," I quickly tell them. "Henry was supposed to get arrested at the airport after taking drugs from Frank. Obviously, the plan's not going very well."

Coop puts his arm around Ethan. "Who shot him, bro?"

"Henry."

"What do we do then?" Luna tearfully asks.

"We stay right here," I firmly respond. "We don't get seen and we wait until they leave."

I can feel Eva's eyes on me. "Then what?"

"I don't know, babe. I haven't thought that far—"

"Shit!" Beck hisses. "They're out of the boat! They're on the dock!"

We rush further behind the trees, completely hidden from the three men as they walk toward Tacklebox. Henry leads the way, but I can see Mr. Calloway as his eyes recognize Beck's truck. He almost falls backward. He knows we're here, somewhere. I have never seen so much panic on one person's face before.

"Who the hell is that?!" Coop suddenly cries out under his breath. We turn to see a truck pulling down the gravel road. It stops right next to Beck's.

"*No!*" Ethan groans next to me. "I think that's Hayes!"

Sure enough, Hayes steps down from the driver's side, swinging his keys in his hands, not a care in the world.

"What do we do?!" Kennedy frantically asks. "We can't let him walk in on whatever the hell this is! What if Henry shoots him, too?!"

Ethan lets out a loud growl. "I am *not* going to let that happen! I am *done* with this!" And before anyone can grab him, he walks right out of the woods and straight toward Hayes.

"Ethan!" Eva whispers loudly. "Bodhi, we can't let him do this!" she tugs on me. "Please! We have to do something! This is Ethan! We can't let anything happen to him! It will be our fault!"

She's right. We can't let Ethan be a sacrifice for Hayes, and we sure as hell can't let him be a sacrifice for *us*. I have to stop this, and there's only one person in Flagler who would stop Henry Channing dead in his tracks: me. I don't give myself a chance to back down. I don't give my conscience a chance to voice its opinion.

"I won't let anything happen to Ethan," I calmly state. Then I place my hand on her cheek, and I kiss her. I kiss her hard. I kiss her like there might not be another kiss. I kiss her like I need this kiss to mean *everything*, and when I pull my lips away from hers, I can see it in her face that she knows what I'm about to do.

My eyes find Coop and Beck. I quickly form a triangle with my fingers, then I shove her right at the two of them. Their panicked eyes grow large, but they understand. They know what I'm silently asking. They tightly wrap their arms around her, the only person who will ever own my heart, even though she's frantically thrashing against them.

"Bodhi! No!" she screams. "Don't do this!"

I lock my eyes on her beautiful face one last time. "I have to. Don't follow me, Eva." And then I turn and join Ethan.

chapter thirty-nine

Eva

Let me go!" I scream out. I claw my fingers into their arms and kick my feet at their legs, all while watching Bodhi disappear from my sight.

"No ma'am," Coop calmly responds. "You're going to stay with us, per request of Bodhi."

I try to bite his arm but he spins my body too fast.

"Eva ... Eva, just stop!" Luna starts to cry. "Please! Please just stop! Let me have her!" she desperately says to Coop and Beck. "Eva, come with me! Give her to me!"

"Is she going to run?" Beck's voice rings into my ear.

"No!" Luna stares at me as she shouts. "She's not going to run!" She reaches for my hand, and I feel Coop and Beck's arms loosen on my body. "I'm going to hold you, okay?" her eyes are pleading with me. "Like I used to at Hidden Treasure? When we were having bad days? I'm just going to hold you until Bodhi comes back, all right?"

I nod my head, placing my hand in hers. The guys let me go and Luna pulls me swiftly into her arms. Kennedy's body wraps around my back, and she and Luna enclose me. I silently sob as they try to hold me still. "I can't do this again! I can't lose him!" I hyperventilate. "We have to do something! Please! Please, we have to help him!"

"Think!" Coop paces. "Who can we call? Who do we trust?"

The answer is so simple, I don't know why I didn't think about it before. "Calvin!" I cry out, reaching for my phone as Luna and Kennedy release their hold on me. "We need to call Calvin!"

Beck grabs my hand. "Are you sure?"

"Yes!" I exclaim, yanking it out of his grasp while pressing the button to turn my phone back on. "He's the only person we can trust right now." I stare down, waiting for the screen to appear. "Five minutes?! I have a five-minute voicemail message from Ethan?!"

"He called you earlier?" Luna reminds me.

I swipe through my contacts, getting to Calvin and pressing his name. I don't wait for him to say hello when he picks up. "Calvin! We need you!"

"Eva? What's wrong?"

"We're in the woods, right next to Tacklebox! Henry shot Frank, he's dead—they're here! Henry and my dad, and Holden. I don't know what's going on—"

"*Goddammit*! Henry was supposed to be arrested today!"

"Yes! But something went wrong—"

"Owen, I told you this wasn't going to work—"

"Calvin! Listen to me! Ethan was here with us—he walked out of the woods, and Bodhi went after him! Bodhi's out there, and Henry's getting ready to see him! What do we do Calvin?! Tell me what to do!"

There's a pause, and I almost think he's hung up. "You stay right there, don't get seen," his strong voice comes through the phone. "Eight minutes. We'll be there in eight minutes." And then the phone goes dead.

"He's coming," I say to their worried faces. "He said *we*. I think Owen's with him."

"Well, well, well!" a familiar voice bellows into the misty air. Henry Channing. We run to the edge of the woods, peering through the palms as we crouch down and stay hidden. Henry has just walked off the dock. "Ethan Granger? Is that you?"

"Hi, Mr. Channing," he coolly says, shuffling his feet as he looks over at Hayes' surprised face. "Long time no see."

"Who do you have there with you?" he points to Hayes.

Ethan walks right next to him. "Maxwell Hayes. He's family, our dads are cousins ..."

"Where the hell is Bodhi?" Coop whispers next to me.

I point as my eyes immediately find him. He's right between the two trucks, hidden from everyone's view.

"You're Henry Channing?" Hayes questions. "Haven't you been missing? Since your house burned down and everything? I think we all assumed you were dead."

Henry ignores his question. "What are you doing here, Maxwell Hayes?"

Hayes points to Tacklebox. "Picking up something from Frank. I'm early. What are you doing here, Ethan?" he turns and asks.

"Goddamn stoner," Coop grunts. "Hayes was picking up weed."

"Frank's not here," Henry states.

"Uh, yeah he is," Hayes replies. "I called him an hour ago. Hey, aren't you Eva's dad?"

My dad and Holden appear from behind Henry. "I am," he nods, as calm as he possibly can be. "You know Eva?"

"I go to school with her and Bodhi."

"You let her switch schools?" Henry pushes my dad as he laughs. "Stupid move."

"Can I go see Frank now?" Hayes nods toward Tacklebox. "I've sort of got a busy day—"

"He's not there," Ethan shakes his head. "The door is locked. They must have closed early. Hey, can you take me home—"

"What the hell are you talking about?" Hayes pats his hand on Ethan's head. "I literally just talked to him."

"He's not here," Holden speaks up, walking closer to Ethan. "You guys should probably head out before the weather gets any worse."

Hayes looks curiously between everyone in front of him. "What's going on here?"

"Is one of those yours?" Henry points to the trucks. Bodhi's ducked down behind Beck's now.

"*Shit!*" Beck mutters. "He knows someone else is here!"

Hayes turns behind him. "Yeah, that one."

"Whose is that?"

"Must just be a boater," my dad shrugs.

Henry shakes his head and points to the Halifax. "No one is out on that today, except us."

"Don't do it, Bodhi," I whisper to myself. "Please don't do it."

It's like he hears me. His head turns slightly to the five of us, and he slowly shakes his head, putting his finger up to his lips.

Henry walks closer to the trucks. "If this one is Maxwell Hayes', and Ethan is too young to drive, then this one ...?"

Bodhi stands. "It's mine," he loudly announces, walking between the trucks toward everyone. My body instinctively wants to run to him, but I feel numerous hands digging into my back, keeping me from moving.

Henry starts hysterically laughing. "Bodhi? I'll be damned."

"Bodhi?" Hayes raises his eyes. "What the hell are *you* doing here?"

"That's your truck?" Henry points.

"My friend's," Bodhi answers. My dad starts looking around. I can tell he's waiting for the rest of us to appear. "I'm borrowing it for the weekend. Getting out of Flagler, stopped to get some bait, but Ethan's right," he throws his arm around Ethan. "The door is locked. I can take you home, I'm heading that way—"

"Hang on," Henry's deep voice demands. "What were you doing hiding behind it?"

Bodhi doesn't falter. "To be honest with you, Mr. Channing, I don't like you very much, and when I saw you get out of your boat, I figured my best move was for you not to see me."

"Honesty," Henry smirks. "Don't see that often. Where's Eva?"

My name seems to stop time. Everyone freezes and I quickly shut my eyes in dread of what he'll say next.

"At home," I hear Bodhi respond. "I'm heading there to pick her up right now."

"How about we let the kids leave," Holden suggests. "And we can finish—"

Henry lets out a loud grunt, turning to face Holden. This sudden movement allows Bodhi to make eye contact with my dad. He nods quickly toward the rest of us. My dad follows the nod, locking eyes directly onto me. He's panicked, looking between us and Henry, and then back to the boat.

"I'm not sure that's a good idea," Henry says to Holden.

"Uh, if you guys have some shit going on with Frank," Hayes uncomfortably says, "I can come back another time."

"Don't move!" Henry roars.

My dad's eyes find mine again. He quickly points behind him, to the boat, and then lifts his clenched fist, releasing the

375

shimmering key directly onto the dirt ground.

"The key!" I loudly whisper. "He dropped the boat key on the ground!"

"Henry!" my dad nervously starts walking over to him. He stops next to Bodhi. "These kids have nothing to do with our reason for being here. Don't make this issue an even bigger one. Let them go, and we'll finish what we came here to do."

"What the fuck did you guys come here to do?" I hear Hayes mutter.

"Still protecting this kid?" Henry points to Bodhi.

Luna grabs my hand, pointing further down the trees. The others have already started making their way toward the water. "We can get the key," she softly says. "We can get to the boat through the woods. They won't see us, we'll come at it from the other side—"

"What about Bodhi?" my eyes burn with tears. "We can't just leave him, and Ethan!"

She gives my hand a tug. "We'll get them," she promises. "But we have to get ourselves out of here first. He's going to find us. You know he will. Our footprints will lead him right to us."

I look back at Bodhi, standing so confidently next to Ethan. My dad moves directly in front of Henry, giving Bodhi a brief moment to look back at the woods.

"*Go*," he mouths to me, waving me down the trees. "*Go!*"

Luna pulls me up. "We are *not* leaving without them," I make clear.

"We won't. I promise."

My dad sees us moving, a relieved smile appears on his face. "I've never stopped protecting Bodhi," he then says to Henry.

I feel myself freeze, but Luna tugs my hand and keeps me going.

"Brayden," I hear Holden's nervous voice. "Now is not the time—"

"What the hell do you mean by that?" Henry heatedly asks.

"Come on, Henry," my dad sighs. "You've spent fifteen years trying to ruin this kid's life, and I don't even know why. Money? Greed? You felt threatened by a kid? But every single time you'd feel that control you had over Bodhi and his mom start to slip away, you'd run crying to me. You've spent fifteen years trying to ruin his life, I've spent fifteen years trying to keep that from happening."

We've stopped at the edge of the woods, where my dad dropped the key. I can see it, glistening in the wet dirt, maybe twenty feet in front of me. But one of us needs to step out of hiding in order to grab it, and although Henry's back is to us, we'll easily be seen by Holden and Hayes who have no idea we're here.

"I'll do it," Luna says. "I'm fast. I'll be quick." Before anyone can argue, she dashes out of the woods, straight to the key.

Everyone sees this but Henry Channing.

Hayes' eyes grow huge. "What in the—"

Ethan kicks him from behind, and Henry slowly starts to turn his head toward the Halifax. But Luna was right. She *is* fast, and she's quick, and she's back in the woods catching her breath before Henry sees anything.

"Goddamn Luna!" Coop is pulling her into his arms. "Don't ever do that to me again!"

She holds the key out, drops it in Coop's hand, and places a strong kiss on his lips. "At least I don't run like I have fire ants up my ass, right?"

Coop shoots Beck a pissed off look, and then buries his head into Luna's hair. I turn my attention back to everyone in front of Tacklebox. Now that he knows there are other people here, Holden has moved closer to Henry, while Hayes keeps staring at where we are in the woods.

"You can't tell me that you haven't profited greatly from Bodhi yourself," Henry says to my dad.

"No, I haven't," my dad shakes his head. "Unless you count the fact that my daughter actually smiles now. I definitely profit from that."

"Does Bodhi know all about the inheritance I've been sharing with you? The money his dad was after, the money his mom willingly gave up in order to get them away from that bastard?"

"I don't know, Bodhi," my dad turns to him and smiles. "Do you know about all of that?"

"I do," Bodhi replies. "And all of that money you gave him is sitting in my trust fund, waiting for the day I turn eighteen."

"*Eva!*" Kennedy's hushed voice calls out. "Let's go!" she points to the trail that will take us right to the dock where the boat is.

I follow after her, wondering what the hell we're going to do once we get on it.

"You're lying," I hear Henry angrily say. "You don't have a *job*, Brayden. How the hell were you living if you weren't using that money?!"

"I have a job," my dad responds. "Just not the job you thought."

"Are you hearing this, Holden?!" Henry yells out.

"I am," Holden's voice calmly replies.

"I *told* you not to trust Brayden Calloway. I told you there's no way he would be the one to step up and take over everything I was doing here."

The dock is right in front of us now. Quietly, we each step out of the trees, tiptoeing along the wood and right onto the boat. Thankfully, the palms and Florida overgrowth blocks the boat from view, but the angry water rocks it back and forth, thrashing us along with its movements and forcing us to brace ourselves against the seats. There's a heavy duffle bag in front of me, and every time the boat sways, the bag shifts, slamming into my legs. I grab it as it bruises me again, and sit down to unzip it.

"Jesus Christ!" I cry out, looking up at everyone. "Drugs. This bag is filled with drugs."

"Well, this one," Kennedy holds up another one, "is filled with stacks of money."

"Henry Channing's getaway," Beck declares.

"So, I'm gonna go now," we suddenly hear Hayes say. "I'm going to take Ethan with me too, because you guys are all fucking insane, and whatever is going on here, you can continue without us."

"Don't move!" Henry's voice shouts.

"Put the gun down, Henry!" I hear Holden demand.

I almost jump off the boat. Luna and Kennedy make a mad dash to grab me, tackling me into a seat. "We have to do something!" I cry out at them. "Be a distraction! Anything!"

"Already on it!" Beck announces. He's climbing into the captain's seat while Coop starts to untie us. "The water, it's moving that way. You see?" he points to High Bridge. "Those docks over there, we're going to get to those docks, or as close as we can. If

Bodhi can get himself and Ethan there, then we're golden."

"And if he can't?" I question.

"Then we think of a different plan."

Luna looks down the Halifax. "He's going to hear us, Henry Channing. He's going to hear the boat turn on."

Beck nods his head. "And hopefully the shock of that will be enough for someone to at least get the gun away from him."

"We're going to be seen," Kennedy throws herself into a seat. The boat starts to turn with the water and it hits the dock, lurching us all forward. "As soon as we get past the trees, we'll be seen."

"Then duck down and brace yourself," Coop suggests.

Henry's voice suddenly booms out. "I will not get caught because some shithead teenager goes and blabs who he saw today!"

"These kids aren't going to talk!" my dad cries out. "You're really going to do this? Think about Porter—"

"Leave my son out of this!" he roars.

"Do you honestly think we care about you?" I hear Bodhi ask. "Or whatever the hell you're doing here? Why did you come back anyway? You abandoned your son, had your perfect little planned escape using my dead dad's boat, and then you come back ... for what?"

"Turn it on, Beck!" I cry out.

He sticks the key in the ignition. "Here goes nothing." With a twist of his hand, the boat rumbles to life, the engine roaring loudly amidst the wind.

"Is that our boat?!" we hear Henry immediately shout.

Beck turns us toward High Bridge and we suddenly come into view. Henry's face goes from completely confused to absolutely furious, in a matter of seconds. He starts running toward us, the gun aimed at the boat.

"Freeze, Henry!" Holden shouts. He aims his own gun into the woods and lets off a warning shot. The sound echoes throughout my entire body and we all duck down, covering our ears.

Henry slowly turns back around, the gun now pointing between Bodhi and Ethan. "Would someone like to tell me what the *fuck* is going on?!"

Holden steps forward, keeping the gun aimed right at him.

"Henry, lower your gun. You will not hurt these kids."

"Who the hell do you think you are?!" Henry turns the gun on Holden.

"Just someone trying to do his job—"

"Your job?" he laughs. "You're just like him," he points to my dad. "Your job was to do what I say and to keep your mouth shut. I am not letting you two bastards and these children ruin my life!"

Beck has the boat right by the dock now. Bodhi gives Ethan a little shove and nods to us, then kicks the back of Hayes' leg to get his attention. The three slowly start to shuffle their way toward us.

"What are you going to do, Henry?" my dad asks. "Shoot everyone here?"

He looks between my dad and Holden. "You two," he then says. "You two are working together, aren't you?"

"Someone's got to bring you down," Holden replies. "I figured the one person who knows you better than anyone else in Flagler was the only person who could help."

Henry glares at my dad. "You think you're so innocent? All the shit you've done these last fifteen years?"

"I think you mean all the shit you *think* I've done these last fifteen years," my dad answers. "My one and only purpose since the day I met you was to protect Bodhi and his mom, and then it was to try to protect your son from *you*. All while trying to also protect my own family from you. I am done worrying about you and your fucking threats."

"You won't get away with this," Henry makes clear. "As soon as word gets out to everyone in this town who works for *me*—"

"Those days are over," my dad tells him. "You gave us that list in exchange for what's on that boat—"

Henry looks our way, and then starts laughing. "Do you honestly think *anyone* will believe you? You have no proof. It's your word against mine ... and if you're both *dead*, then it's nothing."

"That's not true," Ethan loudly states. Bodhi quickly grabs his arm, but Ethan shakes him off and boldly stares right at Henry. "There's proof. It's not just their word." He pulls out his phone and waves it in the air. "I was in the closet, when you told them everything, when you shot Frank—"

"He shot Frank?!" Hayes cries out.

"I was hiding," Ethan continues. "And I recorded every single thing you said. Every name you mentioned, every person you said you've blackmailed, including my dad ... and every crime you bragged about committing. It's all right here, on my phone. And I'm one tap away from sending that recording to every single person on my contact list—"

"You're all talk—"

"Want to see if that's true?"

Henry is fuming, but he slowly lowers the gun down to his side. "I *want* that phone," he demands.

"You can have it," Ethan nods his head. "But *only* if you let the five of us get on that boat, and *only* if you throw that gun in the Halifax."

"You think I'm going to listen to *you*?!" he shouts.

"Henry," Holden steps in front of Ethan. "You have a choice here." He yanks Hayes' keys from his hand and throws them at Henry.

"What the hell?!" Hayes cries out.

"Take the truck," Holden suggests. "Throw the gun in the Halifax, take Ethan's phone, and get as far as you can before anyone finds you."

"No one will find me—"

Holden shrugs his shoulders. "Then you have nothing to worry about. But if you try to hurt these kids, I *will* shoot you."

Henry glares at Holden. "I want what's on that fucking boat."

"It's all yours," Holden agrees. "Kids!" he shouts to us without even looking our way. "Throw the two duffel bags onto the dock!"

I scramble to pick up the one in front of me, passing it to Coop. He throws it on the dock, while Beck does the same with the other one.

"Brayden," Holden points behind him, never once taking his eyes or the gun off of Henry. "You want to grab those?"

My dad quickly rushes over and picks them up, placing them on the ground between Holden and Henry.

"Take them," Holden nods, walking backward toward the dock. "And get out of here."

"The phone," Henry barks.

"The gun," Ethan reminds him.

Henry walks a few feet closer to the Halifax and throws the gun into the rushing water. Ethan then steps onto the dock and tosses his phone over his head. It sinks right next to the boat.

"Are we done here now?" Holden then asks.

Henry picks up the duffle bags and throws them over his shoulders. Bodhi and Hayes are now on the dock with Ethan, inching their way toward the boat. We keep drifting though, the angry water pushing us farther away each time we manage to get close enough.

"You won't get away with this," Henry scowls. "One of you will go down for Frank's murder, I'll make sure of that. No one will believe you. Even if I'm not here, I'm *still* in control of this town."

"I don't think so," Ethan grins. "Everyone is going to know what really happened here. Everyone is going to know that you shot Frank, and everyone is going to find out each and every scummy person that works for you."

Holden looks toward Ethan, so alarmed, so worried. He starts to move his way toward him, just as Henry drops the duffle bags down to his sides.

"You have *nothing*," Henry declares, but you can tell he's unsure, and is panicking on the inside.

"*I* don't," Ethan agrees. "I never did. But that entire conversation I overheard inside Tacklebox is actually a voicemail on Eva's phone."

Holy shit. My heart literally stops in my chest.

"*Get down!*" we hear a familiar voice shout behind us. "He's got another gun!"

We fly onto the floor of the boat, bullets whizzing through the air as they come from Henry's direction. I look up just in time to see Holden dive in front of Ethan and Bodhi, all three falling into the rushing water. I try to get up, to jump off the boat, but there's too many hands keeping me down.

"Henry!" the familiar voice calls out. I squint, seeing High Bridge above us. Owen is standing on the edge of the railing with a hunting rifle in his hands. "Remember me, you sick bastard?! Think it's time to hunt some turkeys!"

Calvin appears right next to him. "Stay away from my family, you piece of shit!" And then Owen aims the gun, and I turn just in time to see him shoot out Henry's knee. "You move one inch," Calvin yells, "and he'll aim for your head next!"

I push myself up. We've drifted completely away from the dock now. "Where are they?!" I scream, searching over the sides for Bodhi, Ethan and Holden.

My dad is frantic, running along the edge of the water with Hayes as far as they can go before the trees block them. "That way!" he yells, pointing down the Halifax. "All three went that way!"

We don't have time to go back to the dock to pick them up. "Get us moving!" I push at Beck.

He jumps into the captain's seat. "I am! I am!" he cries out, trying to get us turned the right way. "Everyone look in different directions! Let me know if you see *anything*!"

I run to the front of the boat, scanning the murky water for any signs of them.

"There!" Kennedy shouts. "Someone's to the left!"

I see hair, lots of hair, and I know right away it's Ethan. He's struggling to stay above the water, and it only gets worse the closer the boat gets to him.

Coop hops over the railing, teetering on the edge. "I will not be putting tulips on your fucking grave!" he shouts out. "Get your ass as close to us as you can!"

Ethan starts to paddle his arms against the current.

"Hold my back!" Coop yells to anyone within reach. Luna and Kennedy cling to his shirt as he leans forward. He makes a grab for Ethan, catching him by the sleeve. "I got you!" he cries with relief. "I got him! Pull us in!"

We heave them over the railing, and they both collapse onto the floor. Ethan's gasping as he declares, "I'm more of a thorny rose type of guy."

"You son of a bitch," Coop hits him.

"I lost them!" Ethan then jumps up, rushing to the edge of the boat as he trips into the seat. "We got separated, and they drifted right past me! I lost them!"

"We'll find them!" I promise. "Right now! Bodhi's a good swimmer—"

"I know!" he nods his head. "I know Bodhi can swim, but Eva," his face drops. "There was blood in the water when we all surfaced." He starts frantically inspecting his own body. "It's not me! I'm fine! But I don't know whose it is!"

My vision starts to grow fuzzy, and I force myself to take a deep breath. "Ethan. What are you saying?"

He throws himself into my chest and clings to the back of my shirt. "Bodhi. Holden. One of them—maybe both of them ... someone got shot."

chapter forty

Bodhi

How the hell did I let Ethan slip away? One minute I had his arm, the next minute the current pulled us apart. "Where's Ethan?!" I shout to Holden. He's directly in front of me, looking way worse than I am, as we allow the water to drift us down the Halifax. There's no use in fighting it. I know we'll eventually be able to get to the shore, or at least find something to grab on to.

His body turns, and then he points behind me. "I think they got him! The boat is stopped over there—"

"Did they get hit?! My friends?! Eva?! Did you see?!"

"No. I think they're all okay. Someone was on the bridge—"

"Calvin, Owen, they shot Henry in his leg. I saw him fall."

He looks relieved, but suddenly disappears under the water.

I grab at his arm, yanking him up as he takes in a large gulp of air. "Don't tell me you can't swim!" I jokingly cry out.

He closes his eyes. "I can swim."

I don't let go though. Something doesn't feel right, *he* doesn't look right. I mean, I know we're being tossed down the Halifax after being shot at, but I'm not exactly panicking yet.

"Bodhi," his troubled eyes open and he stares right at me. "I knew your mom."

"What?!" I exclaim, squeezing tighter on to his arm.

"She hired me five, maybe six years ago, to get your little sister out of the Bahamas—"

"Are you fucking kidding me right now?!"

He shakes his head. "I'm not. I'm sorry I didn't tell you sooner. Please, just listen. I've been protecting her all this time, and I needed to make sure she was safe—"

"Safe from *who*?!"

"Your dad, Henry ... you."

"Me?! You're telling me my mom knew about her?! All that time she never—"

He suddenly slips under the water again. I forcefully pull him back up, but my arm aches from holding his weight, and I need my other arm to keep *myself* from going under.

"You need to use your goddamn arms!" I angrily cry out. "I can't keep us *both* from drowning!"

"Bodhi," his eyes close again. "I can't move my other hand."

"What do you mean you can't move it?"

"It's on my stomach. If I move it, I'm going to bleed out—"

"You've been shot?!"

He nods. "A couple times, maybe? Don't think about that right now. I need you to listen to me."

"Holden, I need to get you to the shore—"

"Jesus Christ, Bodhi! Just listen to me! Henry, he *cannot* find out who your sister is, do you understand me?"

"*I* don't even know who my sister is!"

"You will, soon, very soon—"

"You know where she is?!"

"Yes, I've known all along, but I couldn't tell you. You're going to figure it out, and when you do, don't let him know—"

"Why?! Why does Henry care?!"

"She's connected to you. He'd use her to get to you."

I see a thick tree branch up ahead, sticking out from the water like a spidery hand. I hoist Holden up as high as I can, and then I use my other arm to paddle over to it. The current is fierce and it keeps trying to pull me away, but I'm able to grab it with my fingertips.

"Throw your arm around my neck! I need my other hand!"

He winces, moving his arm, but he manages to wrap it around me. I use my free hand to securely grab the heaviest branch.

"Just hang on, okay?" I say, searching the Halifax for the boat. We've drifted far enough down, it's just a speck in my vision now. "They're coming," I lie to him. "And we're going to get you help."

He gives me a weak smile. "I should have told you earlier. I should have told you at dinner that night. I should have told you when I met you for the first time. But I couldn't let Henry find out. I needed to have him locked away before you realized ..." His face suddenly loses all color, and his teeth start to chatter.

"Hey!" I scream. "Don't you do this! Don't you give up like this! They're coming! Just keep talking, okay? Just keep talking to me! My mom, she hired you? How did she know I had a little sister, and why did she even care?"

"Skyla's mom, she asked your mom for help," his words come out raspy, but fast. "Your mom found me, here. I got her out, Skyla and her mom. But he found them—your dad. I've had to move them a couple times. She's happy though, Bodhi. And she's safe."

"How did Skyla's mom know how to find *my* mom?" He doesn't answer, just slowly closes his eyes. His breathing looks forced. I can feel his arm around my neck suddenly lose its strength. "Holden!"

His eyes pop open. They look different, calm almost. "I never thought the day would come that I didn't have to worry about her anymore. She's grown on me all this time. Sort of like my own kid. God, she looks like you, Bodhi—"

"That picture you showed us—"

"Your mom emailed me that picture, when she asked for my help. It was never in your dad's wallet. I just needed to know if you knew about her."

"I found the *actual* picture. On Luke's boat. Me and Eva, we found Luke's boat—that picture was on it, with an address to somewhere in Isle of Palms."

Holden's eyes grow large, but then he groans and bares down, his head hitting my chest. "You'll find her, just don't let Henry—"

"Henry's going to prison," I remind him.

He smiles with my words. "Where was the boat?"

"Ponce Inlet, Piddler Island—"

"Is it still there?"

I quickly nod.

"You need to go back. You need to look for a key—"

"We found a key! An old looking one? On a palm tree keychain?"

His grip tightens. "Don't let anyone have that key," he demands. "It wasn't his. Don't tell anyone about it. The Bahamas—"

We're suddenly being hit with rushing waves. The boat must be heading this way. My back is slammed against one of the tree branches and my hands slip down, disappearing under the water.

"Bodhi," Holden calmly says. "You can't support both of us."

"Yes I fucking can!" I groan, trying to bring my hands further back up the branch. "Do *not* let go of me!" His hold is growing weaker, but if I try to grab him, we'll be taken away by the current again, and I don't know if I have the strength to keep us both from drowning.

"He can't be the one to find me," his voice breaks through the sound of the angry water. "Graham, he can't—I'm not going to make it through this. It's okay, Bodhi. But if they pull me on that boat, he's going to be the one to find me. *Please.* Don't let him have that memory of me, of seeing me that way," he begs. "I can't come back from this. It's too much—"

"Goddammit Holden!" I cry out. "Don't do this!"

"Just tell him I love him, okay? And be there for him? You're like a brother to him. He told me that. Tell him he's the last person I was thinking of—"

"Holden! No!" I go to grab at him with one hand, but I lose my grip with the other and take in a mouthful of water.

"Think of Eva ... and your sister, and Ethan. They all need you, so *don't* let go." His arm comes down from my neck and his fingers loosely grab my shirt. "Bodhi?" he so peacefully says my name. "It was all worth it." And then he lets go, both hands raising above the surface as the water around him turns red.

I slam my eyes shut as I scream out in horror. I can't watch this. If I see him being carried away, I'll let go. I'll try to get him back.

Eva. Think of Eva. The way I could spend every second of my life holding her in my arms. The way my heart races every time she walks into the room. The way the world stops spinning when my lips are on hers.

Don't let go.

The waves are crashing against my body now, and I duck my head toward the branches, bracing for them to grow stronger. I know the boat is almost here.

"There he is!" I hear someone shout. "Son of a bitch, Bodhi! Don't let go!" *Coop.*

The wind overpowers me. I feel like I'm drowning with my head above water. And just when I find myself struggling to get air in my lungs, there are hands pulling at me from every direction.

"Let go, Bodhi! We've got you!" *Eva.*

My hands release the branch and my body is tugged back. It hits the boat hard, sending waves of pain over my suddenly chilled body. I can feel myself shaking as they try to pull me out of the water.

"Goddamn, he's like an elephant!" *Ethan.*

"Keep the boat still! He's slipping!" *Luna.*

"You try navigating this bastard against the wind!" *Beck.*

"Come on, Bodhi! Work with us!" *Kennedy.*

They're all here. They're all safe. I feel my body go limp with the realization none of them are hurt.

"Bodhi, *please*," I hear Eva's voice cry out. "You have to try, just help us! *Please!*"

I'd do anything for her. I spin myself around, throwing my arms on the edge with energy I didn't even know I still had. Then with one massive pull from all the hands clinging to me, I'm brought out of the water and fall directly onto Coop.

"You ever do that to me again, I'm gonna kill you," he threatens.

I roll off of him, trying to catch my breath. Eva's face suddenly comes into view. She looks so scared. "*Baby*," I mumble.

"Are you shot?" she asks with an uncertain voice, looking up and down my body.

"No."

"Are you hurt?"

"Not really."

She throws herself down on me, her head falling on that familiar place against my neck. Comfort. Her body intertwined with mine brings so much comfort. "You can't do that ever again!" she cries into my ear. "Don't ever leave me like that! Don't ever leave me behind! Do you hear me, Bodhi Bishop?!" she shakes my shoulders.

I can't help but smile. "Yeah, babe. I hear you." She kisses me repeatedly, all over my face, as I breathe in every second of her being in my arms. "I love you," I whisper. "More than anything."

She lets out a tiny sob. "I love *you*, Bodhi."

"Okay guys!" Beck shouts from the wheel. "I really want to get

389

the hell off this boat. Holden, everyone look out—"

"Wait!" Ethan's eyes grow large. "You're not shot?!"

I carefully sit up. Eva's wrapped around me like a koala, refusing to let go. I push her hair out of my face as I say, "I'm not."

"But Bodhi!" Ethan points to the water. "There was blood—"

"I know, Ethan."

Eva's arms come down. Her fingers rub protectively on my wrists. "Bodhi, where's Holden?"

I don't answer. I don't allow the words to leave my mouth, because then I'll be forced to live that entire moment over again.

"We have to find him!" Ethan cries out. "He jumped in front of us! This is my fault! Beck, take us down the Halifax—"

"Ethan," I shake my head.

"No, Bodhi! Don't! We have to find him!" He throws himself down in front of me, pushing my chest. "We can't leave him out here! Henry shot at us because of me! Because of what *I* said! Beck! He's got to be out there! Keep going! We have to keep looking!"

"Ethan, he's gone."

He punches me, over and over again in my arms, and I sit there and let him. "Don't say that! Don't you fucking say that!" he wails.

I glance up at Beck.

"Just tell me what to do," he quietly speaks.

"Take us back to the dock."

The boat quickly sputters to life.

"No!" Ethan screams. He tries to stand but I refuse to let him up. "Bodhi, we can't do this! We can find him! Please!"

We *could* find him, but that's not what Holden wanted, and I need to make sure we respect that. I grab at Ethan's hands, pulling him tightly to my chest. Eva's right behind him, wrapping her entire body around his back. And as Beck carefully guides the boat back to the dock in complete silence, Eva and I hold a hysterical Ethan between us, trying to shield him from this nightmare that he should've never been involved in.

Eva's the hurricane.

I'm the eye.

And now Ethan ... Ethan has become our devastation.

chapter forty-one

Eva – two weeks later

W e're getting ready to head out," my mom says, lingering by my bedroom door.

I pull my bracelets off and place them on my dresser. "Okay," I nod. "Have fun."

She walks further in and stands behind me, unclasping the necklace I was planning on taking off next. "There's no way I can convince you and Bodhi to come with us?"

I look at her through my mirror. "I don't think so. I think we both just need a really boring weekend with nothing going on."

Last weekend was Frank's funeral. Today was Holden's. His body was recovered by the coast guard, a mere five hours after Bodhi last saw him. I don't want to go to anymore funerals. I don't want to hear of anyone else getting arrested. I don't want to hear of another person that secretly worked for Henry Channing all this time. I just want to curl up on a couch with Bodhi for the next two days and try to forget everything.

My mom kisses the top of my head. "I know," she gently responds. "It just worries me, you guys being alone."

"We're safer now, than we've probably ever been," I point out.

Henry Channing is in jail, awaiting his trial. They're saying with all the evidence they have, the voicemail message that was on my phone, and numerous Flagler residents that took plea bargains in exchange for dirt on him, he'll get locked away for life.

"It's not easy to turn off the worry," my mom sighs.

I turn to face her and see my dad appear from the hallway. "I promise you both, the highlight of our weekend will probably be cold pizza and maybe a walk on the beach."

"No one's coming over?" my dad questions.

"Surprisingly, no," I answer. "It will just be us."

My parents exchange a look. I know what they're thinking. Sex. Alcohol. Drugs. Parties. Running away. Every possible thing a teenager can do while her parents are out of town.

"You guys can trust us," I remind them.

My dad sits on the edge of my bed. "Where do you plan on staying?"

"Bodhi's, but if you want us to stay here—"

"It's fine," my mom abruptly declares. "It's just two nights, your phone will stay on, Calvin will be here if you two need anything, and I trust that you guys won't go looking for trouble."

"I can assure you we will not go looking for trouble."

"All right," she kisses the top of my head again. "Boys are ready to go, Brayden."

He stands and also places a kiss on the top of my head. "I love you, kiddo," he says. "Try not to get too jealous when we send you pictures of all the fun we're having at Legoland."

I laugh under my breath. "I'm jealous already."

Once they both leave, I take off my black dress, putting leggings and a tank on in its place. I add an open sweater, as the air is definitely becoming chillier the closer we get to November. I remind myself of this as I carefully pack my bag for Bodhi's. We all rode together to the funeral, but he left after we got back, insisting he had some errands to run before I came over. Once I get to his house, I know I'll have no desire to leave for things I left behind at home.

The drive to Bodhi's has always been beautiful. I remember when I would ride my bike along this road, I always felt blessed to be able to see this type of natural beauty every day. But dare I say High Bridge Road almost feels tainted now? I search for the beauty each and every time I'm on it, but all I see is the spot where I crashed Luke's truck, the place where Frank died, the dock where Holden was shot. I need the beauty to come back. I need to be able to drive on this road without feeling like the world is caving in on me.

I pull my Volvo into Bodhi's driveway, parking right next to his jeep. The garage is already open, waiting for me to arrive, and I quickly pull my hands into my sweater sleeves as I walk over to it. The beach always feels ten degrees cooler than the Halifax. Mix that with the late October evening air, and I'm full-on shivering as I walk up the steps to the main floor.

Something smells delicious, and my eyes are drawn to the kitchen. The lights are low, the oven is definitely on and cooking something, the table is set, there's even a few candles lit along the counter.

"I wanted to make you dinner," I hear Bodhi say from behind me. I spin around and see that he's coming down the hall, carrying a bottle of red wine in his hands. "My mom, she had an entire case of red wine shoved discreetly in the back of her bathroom closet, underneath mounds of toilet paper. It's like she didn't trust me and the guys."

I wait until he places the wine on the table before I wrap my arms around his waist. "You did this, for me?"

He places a soft kiss on my lips. "For us. A small glimpse into our future. Every day, if this is what you want."

"This is definitely what I want," I assure him.

"I'm really looking forward to this weekend. We don't even have to leave the house if you don't want to."

I know my face grows red with everything that sentence could possibly mean.

"I embarrassed you?" he laughs, gently touching my cheeks. "I didn't mean it like that, unless you wanted it meant like that?"

I point to the wine. "Well, we do have an entire case to go through, right?" I joke.

"We don't need the wine to do *that* all weekend," he leans in and kisses me. "Take a seat," he points to the table. "I need to check on dinner."

I pull out a chair, watching him move around his kitchen, like he's been cooking dinner in here for years. "Can I ask ... did you just magically look up a recipe and whip this all up in the three hours since you dropped me off?"

He turns the light on for the oven, peering inside before walking back over to me. "No, but I did magically ask Calvin to go shopping with me, and to help as I put this all together."

My cheeks flame red again at the simple thought of Calvin helping Bodhi make dinner for the two of us. "Calvin was here? You planned this?"

"He left maybe ten minutes before you showed up. It was actually really fun. I think I might like cooking."

I stand up from my chair, my arms going around his neck before I bring my eager lips to his. "I think you're amazing, and I think I'm extremely lucky."

His hand gently cups my face. "We're both lucky, Eva, for so many different reasons." He brings my face closer to his. "Reason number one? I still get to do this, anytime I want." His lips brush against mine, very thoughtfully, almost as if he meticulously planned exactly how this kiss was going to play out. When his lips wander away, I feel them by my ear. "Confession. You will *always* be my reason number one, Eva."

"Confession. You will *always* be my number one, too. And your words will *always* make my entire body go weak."

His lips press hard against my forehead. "Dinner is just about done. Do you want some wine? Do you even like red wine? We don't have to drink tonight. I found it by mistake, searching the house for toilet paper—"

I place my finger over his lips. "I *do* like red wine. Is anyone coming over tonight? Are we really alone the entire night?"

He lowers my finger. "Beck and Kennedy left after the funeral to visit the University of Florida. Coop and Luna are babysitting her siblings. Ethan, his dad took him away for the weekend. He stopped by before they flew out. And I asked Graham earlier if he wanted to hang out with us tonight. He kindly declined. We are alone, the *whole* night."

"And we aren't going anywhere? Just staying in?"

"If that's what you want to do."

I look over at the wine. "Crack it open, Bodhi."

Dinner is delicious, and impressive. I figured this weekend would be nothing but grilled cheese sandwiches, ordering out, and eating leftovers from the fridge. I've never been a big eater, and I still struggle to remind myself to eat actual meals, but Bodhi seems determined to keep me well fed while I'm here.

He pours me another glass of wine when we finish, and pulls me out to the balcony. I'm starting to feel a little buzzed, as this is my third glass in less than an hour or so. I stand at the railing, watching the cars drive by on A1A, and the people going about their Friday night plans in our small beach town. The sun has just set, and no one dares to be in the ocean. She's all alone, showing off her talents each time a wave crashes effortlessly to the shore. The sand glistens in a sparkling array of colors as the water quickly appears on it, only to abruptly disappear as the salty ocean foam seeps through below the surface. It's a mysterious thing to watch, one I'll never grow tired of.

The cars. The people. The ocean. The noise. This house. Bodhi. I have *never* felt more certain that I want this to be my every day.

"Babe," Bodhi's voice breaks my train of thought, and his hand appears on my back. "What are you thinking about?"

I turn to face him. "How much I want this to be my life. How badly I want to be in this house with you, always."

His eyes light up and I know what he's going to ask. "You'll marry me now?"

I don't answer him. I'm afraid the wine would give me the liquid courage to say the one thing I've wanted to say each and every time he's asked this exact question. That yes, I'll marry him at seventeen. Screw high school, screw college, screw even worrying about any of that. I just want to be his, legally, and always, forever ... here.

He doesn't give me the chance to respond. I think he knows I'm on the verge of saying yes, and that this moment is not *our* moment. We're too young, and even with the entire world at our hands, that doesn't make us any older than seventeen. We need more life to pass us by before we make that type of commitment to one another. Instead, he kisses me, something we're both so familiar with, and good at. Something we can do every day until that moment comes when saying yes *is* the right answer.

"One day," he whispers against my lips, and then he takes my hand and pulls me over to a chair. I climb onto his lap, slowly so I don't spill the wine I still have in my glass. His lips find my temple. "Eva?" My name always sounds so elegant coming from his mouth.

"Hmm?"

"I need to find my little sister."

I sit up straighter. "I know," I agree.

The night Holden died, Bodhi told me everything he had said when they were in the water together. He then cried in my arms for hours, breaking us both yet again. How many times are we going to get broken? How many times are we going to have to fall apart?

"We need closure, Eva," he goes on. "We need definite closure, on everything, everyone does. I feel like we're stuck in limbo. Always waiting for the next big secret to get thrown at us. Always waiting for permission to spill what we already know. I mean, Ethan's family, your dad said he would personally tell Ethan's family about Olivia, but what is he waiting for?"

"He said Olivia doesn't want to talk to him, to my dad. I mean, he's the reason she lost Porter. He told me he was going to go see her next week, make sure this is what she wants before he tells Ethan's family about her."

"Okay, but my little sister? Holden knew where she was all this time. What was he waiting for? Henry to go to jail? Why? And then there's the goddamn key that means nothing ... we need to figure this shit out. Stop waiting for someone to tell us it's okay."

I take a sip from my glass, thinking about what our next step would be. I promised my parents we wouldn't go looking for trouble this weekend, but would they even have to know? "We do need definite closure. Luke's not coming back. Henry is in jail. Your grandparents, alive and ready to step up, but all this other stuff—"

"What do we do?" he groans.

I finish my wine and place the glass on the table. "Are you up for a small road trip?"

"That depends, where are we going?"

"Isle of Palms."

"*Eva ...*"

I sit up so we can see each other. "We need closure, this is where we start. The address that's on the back of your sister's picture. Let's go there tomorrow. It's what, a five-hour drive? We leave really early in the morning, get back before dinner—"

"What if it's a dead-end?"

"Then we check it off our list and dig deeper."

"You seriously want to make a ten-hour road trip tomorrow, knowing it could lead us absolutely nowhere?"

"You seriously want to stare at the back of that picture for god knows how long, not doing anything about the address staring back at you?"

Bodhi laughs, and his fingers tap against my own. "I think we should take a road trip tomorrow, then."

"I think that's a great idea."

His eyes suddenly look curious. "We don't tell anyone?"

I shake my head. "Nah. We'll tell them once we're home. Or we don't tell them at all."

"What if she's there, Eva? My little sister?" he leans back in the chair, taking a sip from his glass. "I looked up the address. Nothing comes up, not one single name is attached to that place."

"If she's there, then mission accomplished," I say.

"Do you think she's there?"

I bite down on my lip. "I don't know. We'll find out tomorrow though, right?"

"Yes," he nods, his hand suddenly wanders under my tank top. I feel his warm fingers on my bare back. "He told me I'd find her soon ... I don't know how he knew this—"

"Because he knew you wouldn't stop. That *we* wouldn't stop, because we do this together." His fingers press harder on my back, and my body naturally leans into his touches. I'd say it's the wine, but it's not. I *always* want Bodhi. I always crave him in this way, in how amazing it feels when he takes control over my body, claiming it for himself, but always putting me first in the process. I take his wine glass from his hand and drink what's left, placing the empty glass next to mine on the table. "I think we're done with the wine."

"Oh yeah?"

"Yes. We have a road trip in the morning that we need to be sober for, and right now, I really want you to take me upstairs."

His hand leaves my back, trailing up one of my arms and to the strap of my tank-top. He slowly lowers it off my shoulders, my sweater falling loosely down the length of my arm. He brings his lips to my neck and gently sucks against my skin. "Eva Calloway, what is it that you'd like for me to do with you upstairs?"

I run my fingers through his hair. "I can think of a few things."

"Tell me. I want to *hear* what you want me to do."

397

I look down at him, the liquid courage now raging through my blood like a floodgate has suddenly opened. Even without it, Bodhi always makes me feel so comfortable letting this side of me come to the surface. He's the only one who ever will. I can tell him exactly what I want, and he'd not only make it happen, but also never make me feel ashamed for having this wild, impulsive sexual side.

"I want you to carry me upstairs. I want you to take my clothes off. I want to feel your hands everywhere, and your mouth everywhere. And when you're done making *me* feel so epically incredible, I want you to lie me back on the bed, and then make *yourself* feel equally as incredible. I want to hear you. I want to hear you enjoying me. Can you do that?"

He stands and scoops me possessively into his arms. "Hell yes, I can."

chapter forty-two

Bodhi – the next day

One hour into our road trip, and my mind questions if we made the right decision.

Two hours into our road trip, Eva makes us stop for coffee, and I question if I should just turn us around.

Three hours into our road trip, her parents call and she lies, telling them we're heading out for breakfast. I question if her parents will ever trust us again if they find out where we really are.

Four hours into our road trip, and I question if I'll even be able to get out of the jeep when we get there.

"You need to calm down," Eva's reassuring voice blankets over me. Her hand appears on my leg, and she gives it a tight squeeze. "It's going to be okay. We've got less than an hour now, try to think about something else." Her hand leaves my leg, only to appear on my neck. Her soft fingers knead against my muscles. "Here's a thought ... think about last night."

I briefly glance over at her. Her legs are pulled up in her lap, the holes from her light jeans give a peek of the tanned skin underneath. She has on a very simple, tight black t-shirt. There's nothing remotely interesting about it, but snugged against her body, it's fucking captivating. Her hair is hanging in loose waves past her shoulders, resting on the hills of her breasts. I suddenly have visions of her last night, my mouth on those luscious hills, my name being repeatedly moaned.

Her laughter breaks my train of thought. "Did that help?"

"Little bit," I smirk. "Last night ..."

"Every muscle in my body is sore," she proclaims, stretching her arms over her head. "And I have a pretty insane bruise on my lower back—"

"Shit! You do?"

"I landed on that stack of books when we fell off the bed, remember? Pretty sure that's what it's from."

I stifle my laughter under my breath. We did indeed fall off the bed last night during the heat of our passion, and after throwing the books across the room, we finished on the floor. I pick up her hand, kissing her knuckles before weaving my fingers in between hers. "Tonight, you let me make you dinner again, and after, we do nothing but snuggle on the couch."

She smiles at me. "That sounds really nice." Then she scoots herself over in her seat, resting her head on my shoulder. "Wake me up when we're five minutes away."

I kiss her head. "Will do, babe."

The next fifty-some minutes go by too fast. I sit there, listening to Eva's deep breathing as she naps on my arm, feeling blessed even amongst all the chaos and heartache we've endured these last five months. She's definitely the rainbow after each and every storm, the only person who can remind me that there's still something in this world to keep fighting for. As long as I have her, no matter what has happened or happens, I'll always be able to find that rainbow.

"Babe," I kiss her warm forehead. "We're almost here."

She groans into my arm. "I'm so tired, and your arm is too cozy."

I would much rather she stay snuggled on my arm. "We've eventually got a five-hour drive back, and my arm is all yours."

She looks out the window at the passing scenery. We're driving over a massive bridge that should drop us off right in Isle of Palms. "We went through Charleston, right?" she asks. "We should kill two birds with one stone and go visit Porter's mom while we're here. Take over for my dad."

"One thing at a time," I request. "Besides, I'm not sure if I want to talk about Henry Channing today."

"I don't think Porter would want to talk about his dad. He called, you know ... after everything," she worriedly looks at me. "You were sleeping—"

"No I wasn't," I make known. "I know he called. I just didn't want to talk to him."

"You didn't miss much. He cried, *a lot*, kept apologizing like it was his fault. He's really happy he's in jail."

"I think we're all happy he's in jail."

She leans her head back on my shoulder. "Are you nervous? About what we might find at this house?"

"I feel like I'm going to piss myself," I honestly answer. "But I don't think she's here, so I just keep telling myself that."

We turn down Carolina Boulevard and are immediately met with a row of beautiful beach houses. They're huge, and definitely don't look like houses a single mother and her young daughter would live in.

"The yellow one," Eva points down the road as she watches the house numbers go by. "I think that's it."

I pull up in front of it, and sure enough, it's the address on the back of Skyla's picture. This house looks very similar to my own house. "Do you see the resemblance, or is it just me?"

"I see it," she nods. "But I'm assuming it's just a weird coincidence?"

"Eva," I almost laugh as I say her name. "Haven't we learned by now that nothing is ever a coincidence in our lives?"

"True. Let's get out, before we both change our minds."

Deep breaths. In and out. Don't piss yourself. We head up the driveway, my one hand clutching Eva's, my other firmly holding the picture of my sister.

"Ready?" Eva asks, her finger hovering over the doorbell.

"Do it now, before I bolt."

She pushes hard against it, and the musical notes can be heard even with the door closed in front of us. It abruptly stops mid-tune, and the sound of feet moving replace it. The door suddenly opens, revealing a middle-aged lady behind it. She looks friendly, and she's wiping her hands on a checkered apron as she smiles at us.

"What can I do for you?" she warmly asks.

I can't talk. I'm going to throw up, which might be worse than pissing my pants.

Eva catches on to my muteness and speaks for both of us. "I'm Eva, and this is Bodhi. We live in Flagler Beach, Florida, and drove all the way here because of this picture." She yanks it from my hand. "I'm sure this is going to sound really weird, but the little girl in this picture is his sister that he's never met, but your address was written on the back. You don't have a daughter, by any chance, do you? One that would be around eight years old?"

Her warm smile is replaced with sympathy. "Oh, honey, I don't. I have three sons, no daughters. Can I see the picture?"

Eva holds it out in front of her eyes, and immediately we see recognition on her face.

"You know her?" I find my voice and ask.

She shakes her head. "No, but I *have* seen her. I remember the curls, the hair ... you two have the same hair."

"When did you see her?" Eva quickly questions.

"When we bought the house, maybe four years ago?"

Holy shit. My heart is racing. "She lived here?"

She nods her head. "Yes, we bought the house from her mom. It was just the two of them, I think. I remember seeing them at the final inspection."

"Any chance you know where they moved to?" I ask.

"I'm sorry, I don't."

Eva turns to face me. "This is something, at least we know this."

"Wait!" I cry out. "If you bought the house from her mom, then you would have a record of who the previous owner was, right?"

Eva hits my arm. "You're a genius, Bodhi!"

The lady raises her eyebrow, "You don't know your own mom's name?"

"We didn't have the same mom," I clear up. "We had the same dad. I just found out about her, but my dad died in a car crash, and I can't ask him any questions—"

"Stay here," she says. "I've got a file with all the closing papers, and I'm sure her name is on there somewhere. I'll be right back."

She leaves us standing there, and I immediately rest my forehead on a thick white pillar. Eva's hand rubs up and down my back. "It's okay, Bodhi," her calm voice repeats over and over again.

Moments later, we see her walking back toward us. She flips through a stack of papers in a manilla folder as she leans against the doorframe. "She built this house," she looks up quickly and says. "Or she had it built, I should say. She was the only owner before us— ah! Here we go," she pulls out a long piece of paper, running her finger down the sheet, and then the name rolls out of her mouth in one rapid motion. "Lenora Bishop."

"Wait, wait, wait—*what*?!" I cry out.

"Lenora Bishop," she repeats, her eyes look confused. "You know her?"

"That's his mom," Eva quietly says.

"So you do have the same mom? *And* the same dad ...?" she tucks the paper back into the folder.

"No, we do *not*," I angrily respond. I turn to Eva, "I would have known if my mom was pregnant! She couldn't hide *that* from me!"

"No, she couldn't," Eva agrees. "Thank you," she turns to the lady and swiftly says. "Can I give you my phone number? If you remember anything ..."

I walk off the porch without even saying goodbye, taking shelter in my waiting jeep. I need to get the hell out of here. I need to think. I need to go back home. I need ... her.

Eva.

I see her walking across the street, the picture of my little sister still in her hand. She cautiously opens her door, watching my face as she gets in. I feel my emotions suddenly reach the surface, and I grab the steering wheel, shaking it as I let out a massive scream.

She doesn't say anything, just places the picture in the glovebox, and then immediately wraps her arms around me. "Don't shut me out, okay? I'm right here."

The thought never even crossed my mind. I breathe her in, burying my face in her silky hair. "I won't."

She kisses my neck, keeping her head tucked next to mine. "We're all that matters. We'll always have each other."

"We will."

"Your mom was *not* Skyla's mom," she confidentially declares over my shoulder.

"I know."

"But I think she owned this house, and I think she had it built for them."

"Yeah?"

She releases her arms from me, bringing her forehead to mine. "Yes. That's the only explanation. She paid for this house, and it was

403

in *her* name."

"What do we *do*, Eva? Where do we go from here?"

"We go home and search your house for anything we can find about *that* house," she points out the window. "She has to have something, somewhere, about this house."

I nod my head and start the jeep, not wanting to sit here any longer than we have to. I drive us back to the bridge that brought us over here. It's a little after eleven; we can definitely make it home before dinner. Screw looking for shit tonight. All I want to do is lie on my couch with Eva in my arms.

"Are you hungry?" she timidly asks, pointing to a sign outside the window with nearby restaurant options. "We can stop in Charleston and get some food. We need gas, anyway."

I'm not hungry, but all we've eaten today is a small pastry from the coffee shop we stopped at hours ago, and if Eva's hungry, I want her to eat. "Call Porter," I surprisingly suggest.

"What?! No, that's not what I meant—"

"Eva, we can't stop in Charleston and not let him know we were here. He's probably busy, anyway. Just call him, see what he says. Or at least ask him where we can get something good to eat."

She quickly kisses my cheek and says, "I'll put him on speaker."

His voice echoes through my jeep after the first couple rings. "Eva. Everything okay?"

"Hi Porter, everything's fine," she confirms. "I've got you on speaker, I'm with Bodhi ... we're actually really close to Charleston."

"What the hell are you two doing in Charleston?"

"We had a small errand to run," she answers.

"A small errand? Bodhi? What's she dragging you into now?"

I smirk at Eva's sudden pissed off face. "Just the typical shit, Porter. Are you around right now?"

"You want to see me?" Porter's shocked voice asks. "After my dad tried to shoot you all?"

"You aren't your dad, Porter," Eva bluntly reminds him.

You can hear him sigh into his phone. "I actually promised my brother and sister I'd take them to the park. I'm watching them this weekend. Where are you guys coming from?"

"Isle of Palms," she replies.

"What the hell are you doing there?"

"*Porter*," Eva's annoyed voice groans.

"Never mind," he laughs. "I don't want to know. You're going to go right past the park. It's under the Arthur Bridge, Mount Pleasant Memorial. I can meet you guys there in thirty minutes."

"Do you know where we can get something to eat?" I ask.

"Say no more," he replies. "I'll pick up some trash can nachos from Saltwater Cowboys. Thirty minutes, okay?" Then the phone goes silent.

"Well," Eva says with a hopeful voice. "That wasn't too bad."

"Yeah ... we haven't actually seen him yet, though," I point out.

Thirty minutes later, Eva and I are exhaustedly sitting on a park bench, a modern playground directly in our view. The air is colder here in Charleston than in Flagler, and it's completely shaded under the bridge. Eva's snuggled up against my chest, trying to stay warm. I keep rubbing my hands on her bare arms. She has no body fat, and probably feels much colder than I do.

"When we get home, how about we order in instead of you cooking for us?" she suggests.

"Yeah? My cooking was that bad?"

She kisses me right under my jaw. "No, it was delicious. But I just want to curl up on the couch with you and numerous blankets. I don't want you cooking. I want your warmth, Bodhi, all night."

"Funky Pelican?"

"*Yes*. Grilled cheese, onion strings—"

"You're making me drool."

She then laughs. "I wonder what the hell is in trash can nachos?"

I nod toward the street as a familiar Land Rover makes its way into a parking spot. "I think we're about to find out."

We watch as Porter steps down and opens the door behind him, pulling out a little boy that looks to be a couple years younger than Eva's brothers. He quickly picks him up and walks right in our direction, waving at us as he does. The little boy clings tightly to Porter's neck, yet he squirms his legs against his body.

"Hey you two!" Porter calls out, stepping into the playground. We stand to greet him. "This is my little brother, Ryder," he says to us, turning his body around so we can see him better. "And he *really* has to go to the bathroom, like getting ready to pee on me, that bad. He refuses to pee anywhere besides a toilet." He points to the line of restrooms in the distance. "I'll be right back. My sister," he nods to his Land Rover. "She's purposely being slow, but has the food. She knows who you guys are. Fair warning, she bites."

Eva lets out a muffled laugh as he quickly walks away. "He's cute," she then says. "Ryder? Doesn't look like Porter at all. His name, Ryder," she repeats. "Where have I heard that name before?"

My eyes suddenly see the other back door to Porter's Land Rover open. I watch as shiny black boots step down, followed by a sparkly pink skirt. The little girl leans into the car, her foot popping up behind her as the door shields the rest of her from view. She then quickly slams it closed with her body. She's carrying plastic bags of food in both of her hands that she looks down at as she walks.

Black shiny boots.

Sparkly pink skirt.

Her top is glittering in the sun from the uncovered parking lot.

And her hair, it bounces with each step because of the wild blonde curls that spring with her movements.

She looks up, directly at me, and I'm without a doubt, one hundred percent certain that I'm staring at my little sister.

"*Eva*," I gasp, hitting her arm repeatedly. She's looking the other way, watching Porter disappear into the bathroom. I grab her face and move it directly into the path of the little girl walking toward us.

It takes Eva one second, just one split second. Her eyes widen, she grabs my arm, squeezing so tight I know I'm going to have her fingerprint bruises there tomorrow. "Bodhi, it's *her*."

Holden is suddenly in my mind. The conversation I overheard him have with Olivia on the beach.

"You have to protect your child! Isn't that what we've been trying to do from day one? Protect your child?"

He wasn't talking about Porter.

She's suddenly less than ten feet away. Five feet. Three feet. Right in front of us. She holds out the bags of food and we hesitantly take them.

"You Eva and Bodhi?" her voice is raspy, like Luke's was. "I sure hope you are, or Porter's going to be pissed I gave the food to the wrong people. Shit! Don't tell him I said pissed, okay? He likes to rat me out to our mom."

I hear Eva chuckle under her breath. "I'm definitely Eva."

I'm too busy staring to say anything. I'm amazed at how much I see myself in her face.

"You're the one who broke up with my brother, right? For this guy?" she points to me, locking her dark brown eyes on mine. "I can see why, you're much cuter than my brother is."

"I'm Bodhi," I manage to spit out.

She tugs on her curls. "We have the same hair," she notices. "Can't even put a brush through the damn thing without looking like a poodle."

"This kid has been through too much. He's had to grow up too fast. We can't spring this on him right now until we know everyone is safe. Telling him that he's forever linked to your family might just destroy him, which is why you have to stay quiet."

He wasn't talking about Ethan. He was talking about *me.*

"Definitely don't brush it," I laugh at her. "Just have to let it do what it wants."

"Yeah," she gives me a smile. "Tell that to my mom and dad."

"Brayden is too involved, too determined to mend his relationship with his daughter. I don't think he'd be able to keep this secret to himself."

He was talking about *this.* This secret.

"How old are you?" Eva asks.

"Almost nine. Porter says I'm eight going on eighteen."

Eva smiles. "I can see that."

"You're very pretty," she suddenly says. "Your eyes, they look like my cat's eyes. Do they glow in the dark?"

Eva shakes her head. "That would be really cool, though."

"Shit," she murmurs, looking over our shoulders. "Here come my brothers. Just don't tell Porter I said pissed—"

"Your secret's safe with us," I wink at her.

"You guys are cool," she grins. "Much cooler than Porter."

Eva's chilled hand is suddenly in mine, her thumb presses tightly down, and I know what she's going to do. We need to know if what we're both thinking is really true. "Hey, Porter never told us your name," she says to this eccentric, curly haired, raspy voiced, brown eyed girl in front of us.

"Of course he didn't. Porter has shitty manners." She takes her hand, cups it, and places it right between mine and Eva's, ready for a handshake. Her chipped black nail polish suddenly sparkles, as a ray of sunlight shines down on her from the gaps in the bridge. Then she smiles, an instant dimple appearing on her chin, and she proudly announces, "The name's Skyla. Skyla Rose."

epilogue

D o you every wonder if your entire life is already planned out? Like there's a book somewhere with your name on it, and inside are all the details from the moment you come into this world, until the moment you leave it? Every single person that will play a part in your story, every single event that makes up your life, they're all in this book. Whether it's a fairytale, a mystery, a love story, a horror, or maybe a variety of all genres. Your book is written already, and all you have to do is live it.

My story has been written from the moment I was conceived. I'm sure of that. There were events in my life that were set in motion before I even knew the people who were involved. When I was little, I questioned why bad shit always happened to me. Why I didn't have a dad, why my mom got sick, why Eva left, why I spent three years of my life self-destructing. I understand it a little better now. I understand that sometimes bad shit has to happen in order to really appreciate the good shit.

Life is just a bunch of little hurricanes. One right after another. Sometimes they hit you and make landfall, sometimes their path changes and they just miss you, and sometimes you see them heading your way, yet they suddenly disappear. And just when you think you've got a moment to spare, a chance to catch your breath, another one forms and crashes right on you.

I should have known something was about to happen the moment Eva and I sat down on that park bench. I should have realized earlier that *she* was going to appear. All the clues were there, but I was blind to the fact that she was someone already connected in our lives. I should have known, because nothing in my life is ever a coincidence. Every little event has already been planned, and either I figure them out ahead of time, or I'm blown away by yet another hurricane that suddenly appears.

These hurricanes, some of them I claim, some of them will never leave. Eva, she's *my* hurricane, she will always be my hurricane. I can almost see it. The way she circles around my soul, a constant flow of energy, surprising me with her brutal strength every single day. I'm the eye, she's the hurricane, we're one storm, nothing will ever change that. But what about the devastation left behind from all the other little hurricanes?

Ethan. Graham. Porter. Kenneth and Annie.

These people, they're the devastation that gets forgotten from the hurricanes of life. They're not the hurricane or the eye, but the mess you find after the storm. The rubble you sort through as you search for memories that got lost over time. I was wrong when I thought I could break down a hurricane. There are too many parts, too many people, and I realize now that I missed one crucial piece earlier.

The aftermath.

You've got the hurricane, the eye, the devastation, and now the aftermath. After the storm passes, after the mess is evaluated, the aftermath is when everyone comes together to make life beautiful again. Everyone unites to ensure life will go on, the rainbow will eventually be found.

Eva's my hurricane, but she's also my aftermath. She's the beauty that follows each and every mess, the sun that shines after the dark clouds have disappeared. No matter what storm heads my way, or how often I find myself drowning in the surge of life, her radiant presence is my constant rescue boat.

Maybe one day life will calm down. Maybe one day I'll be sitting on the beach, old and gray, Eva right next to me, and we'll be reminiscing about how crazy those early years were. That day is not *today,* though. And as this part of my story comes to a close, I'm going to leave you with just one simple, final word, followed by the most foreshadowing sentence I've ever spoken.

Confession.

The hurricanes of my life have only *just* started to brew.

Do you need more Bodhi and Eva? Look for the third Confession book! Confession – The Antidote. Then follow Sarah Forester Davis on social media for her latest book news!

Made in the USA
Middletown, DE
24 December 2023